I0635497

The Dissection of Vertebrates

SHAWN MIHALIK

Asymmetrical Press

Library of Congress Cataloging-In-Publication Data
The dissection of vertebrates / Shawn Mihalik — 1st ed.
ISBN: 978-1-68287-024-2
eISBN: 978-1-68287-025-9
WC: 95,784
1. Polyamory. 2. Open Relationships. 3. Threesomes. 4. YouTube. 5. Wicca.

Cover design by Shawn Mihalik
Typeset in Garamond
Formatted in beautiful Central Oregon
Printed in the U.S.A.

Publisher info:
Website: www.asymmetrical.co
Twitter: @asympress

ASYM
METR
ICAL

For Katelyn

"The past two decades have witnessed a rediscovery among researchers of the value of comparative vertebrate anatomy. In large part this has been due to the establishment of phylogenetic systematics and the renewed awareness of the vast contribution that morphology can make to our understanding of the history of vertebrates. This is perhaps even more apparent now than just a few years ago."

—Gerardo De Iuliis, PhD,
and Dino Pulerà, MScBMC, CMI,
The Dissection of Vertebrates:
A Laboratory Manual,
preface to the 2nd edition

The Dissection
of Vertebrates

Rebekah Fleckman

I WANT TO TALK ABOUT Rebekah Fleckman.

Right now I'm lying on her couch in the house she shares with two roommates. Just a few minutes ago I asked her, "Where can I sleep?"

"Right there, probably," she said after a pause, "I guess. If you need to. I don't have any extra blankets or anything though."

"That's okay," I told her. "I can sleep anywhere, under any circumstances."

And then she left me here, fully clothed, and went to her room. I'm pretty sure I heard her lock the door.

Rebekah Fleckman knows my cousin, Jenna. They met I think freshman year. They were roommates that year, back when Jenna still went to school in Bozeman because she thought she wanted to major in sports medicine, although I'm not sure whether the house they lived in when they were roommates was this one. This one with the garage-sale couch, garage-sale coffee table, and posters with cartoons about condoms pilfered from the campus health clinic sticky-tacked to the walls. Jenna moved to Helena to study theater the next summer, but she and Rebekah are still friends, or at least acquaintances. That's how I met Rebekah, at like a birthday party or during a summer floating trip or something—I don't quite remember, except that it was through Jenna a few months ago.

I do know I flirted with Rebekah, and I got her number. I've always been good at getting numbers. I got her number and when the party or the floating trip was over and I'd gone back home to Ennis I texted her something like, *It was nice meeting you. You're pretty cool.*

Thanks, she texted back. *It was nice meeting you, too.*

I know what the texts said because I still have them. I'm looking at them right now.

So that was a while ago I met Rebekah Fleckman, at the beginning of the summer. It's the end of summer now. I didn't see or speak to Rebekah for a while after we first met, not until the other day. The other day when I called her and she answered and I said, "Hey!"

"Hey," she said.

For a moment I couldn't think of what to say next, so I just sat there with the phone to my ear, listening to her breathing. But then I said, "This is Jenna's cousin. We met at that thing."

"Oh, hi," she said. "Hi."

"Aaron," I said.

"Ohhhhh. Right. Hi, Aaron."

"So . . . I was wondering what maybe you were doing on Tuesday."

"This Tuesday?"

"Yeah, this Tuesday. I was just wondering if you have any plans."

"Well, I work most of the day, until 5:30, but then I plan on doing nothing."

I found out later she works at a gym. I go to the gym sometimes. Well, it's a room my buddy Vance set up in his basement, with a bench and a squat rack. I go there sometimes and work out with Vance. Rebekah isn't a trainer or anything, I don't think, but she works at a gym and she's in pretty good shape.

"Great!" I said. And then, after a few seconds, I realized the reason for my excitement wasn't obvious. "I'm going to be in Bozeman for a thing on Tuesday," I told her, "and I was wondering if I could take you to dinner." I didn't actually have a thing in Bozeman; I just wanted to drive up here to see Rebekah Fleckman.

She was quiet for moment. I could hear her thinking. "Well, like I said, I was planning on doing nothing Tuesday night. But, sure, dinner sounds nice. I could always eat dinner. I guess I could do nothing after, instead."

So I told her I would see her then. I'd pick her up at 6:15. Could she text me her address? I was excited. I hadn't had a date in a while. I'm good at getting numbers but I can't ever seem to translate those numbers into dates. I haven't been laid since high school.

But now I had a date with Rebekah Fleckman, and she'd even made a point of saying she didn't have any plans for after dinner, and I thought I knew what that meant.

The blinds above the couch in Rebekah's living room don't close all the way, so the moon is shining right on my eyes. Plus I'm like five or six drinks in, so I'm too full to sleep. I'm thinking about reading the textbook that's sitting on the table. It's a science textbook. I don't care much for science. I mean it's cool and all: animals and space and whatever. But I'm so good at understanding it. *Comprehending* it.

I thought dinner went well. I arrived in front of Rebekah's house at six o'clock. I was a little early, but I didn't think she'd mind. She doesn't seem like the kind of girl who minds things. I parked my truck by the curb in front of a sign that said PERMIT PARKING ONLY, 8 AM-6 PM, M-F. I let the truck idle in neutral. I texted her: *I'm here.* She didn't text back, but ten minutes later she came out the front door. She was wearing jeans and a tight black top and her hair was wet. There's something sexy about wet hair. Isn't there something sexy about wet hair? I was wearing khakis and a polo.

She waved and came over to the truck. I got out to hug her, but she didn't realize and she walked around to the other side to get in, so I got back in kind of quickly because I didn't want her to get in and realize she'd accidentally snubbed my hug. I didn't want her to be embarrassed.

Like I said, I don't go on dates much, so when I do, I'm never sure where to go. Usually I do Italian. Girls like Italian. Vance is Italian, and he's been to Bozeman, so I asked him what the best Italian restaurant in Bozeman is. We went to Cafe Fresco. It turned out that while Vance had been to Bozeman, he'd never been to any Italian restaurants here, but I looked on Yelp and it said Cafe Fresco was good. It said it had pasta and wine and creek-side dining, which sounded romantic. Creek-side dining. Rebekah would like that, I thought.

Dinner was good. The restaurant was nice. I got spaghetti and meatballs because it was pretty cheap, and she got something with salmon I can't remember the name of, which wasn't so cheap but that's okay because I did offer to buy her dinner and I was pretty sure we were going to have sex soon anyway. We each had a glass of wine. She ordered something white and I ordered what she had. It was sweet, which is good because I don't really like wine. When I'm hanging out with Vance we drink PBR.

We talked, me and Rebekah, over dinner. I didn't really learn anything about her, but I told her about the construction company where I work and about Ennis and about how I'm leaving for basic training in six weeks. "I'm going to miss Montana," I told her. "I'm going to miss my friends, my boys. They're my boys, you know. I'm going to miss them. I'm sure you have friends like that, who you'd miss if you were going away."

"Sure," she said, "but I do all right when I'm on my own."

Right now I'm texting Vance. He texted first and asked how the date went, so I'm telling him I slept over.

I wonder where Rebekah's roommates are—I haven't seen either of them.

After Cafe Fresco I started to drive her home. On the way, I had an idea. "Do you want to get some dessert?"

"I'm pretty full," she said.

"Right. Okay," I said.

I followed my phone's GPS back toward her house. We'd had a really good dinner, obviously, but I was starting to doubt my ability to perform when we got back. I was nervous. Like I said, it's been a while. "Hey, let's get some beer," I suggested. "We can talk some more. I like talking to you."

She seemed unopposed to the idea. I stopped at a convenience store and bought a six-pack of PBR. When we got back to her house I asked her where I could park so I wouldn't be towed.

She looked at me. She didn't understand what I meant, I guess. "It's after 6 PM. You won't get towed."

I just parked in front of the house. I could move my truck in the morning, or leave early. Although I didn't *want* to leave early —leaving early sounded like a dick thing to do. I like to imagine I'm not one of those guys who just up and takes off the morning after.

Rebekah drank only one of the PBRs. You'd think after five beers I might be a bit drunk or something right now, maybe extra sleepy, but I'm not. My tolerance is pretty high. One time I drank an entire six-pack and like four shots of Jose Cuervo because Vance didn't think I could. I started with the shots, one right after the other. Boom boom boom boom. I didn't even bother with a lime or anything. Then I drank the beers over the course of an hour and a half while Vance and I watched football. I was barely even tipsy.

Vance has just replied to my text. *Dude! Nice!* the reply says.

Rebekah and I played cards and board games. I've never really played board games with a girl before, but it was fun. We played Uno and Jenga. I joked that we could play strip Jenga. I told her one time Vance and his girlfriend took Jenga blocks and made it Dirty Jenga by writing things you had to do on them. Like sometimes you had to take a piece of clothing off, or run outside naked, or sometimes maybe you had to do something to the other person, like lick a body part. Rebekah laughed when I told her about this.

"I have Trivial Pursuit," she said.

One thing you might not guess about me is I like to write poetry. People don't really know that. Not even Vance knows I like to write poetry.

Not really *poetry*, I guess, mostly just haiku.

I tried to convince Vance to join the army with me. I told him it would be fun, a blast, an amazing adventure we could go on together, but he didn't buy it. I didn't honestly think he would. He has a girlfriend, and his mom lives with him in Ennis.

Everything is quiet. It's as if this house is empty, as if I'm the only one here. Maybe I should leave, drive home. Like I said, I don't feel drunk, so I could drive back to Ennis. Rebekah will wake in the morning and I'll be gone. I'm starting to think I'll never see her again. It's something I feel often: that I'm not going to see people again. It's like every person I ever meet, except Vance, I'm pretty sure is in my life for just that instance. Like either they'll walk away or I will.

Some Kind of Sex Magick

1

THE PLANE CAME IN FROM the South, banking left, tilting so sharply that there was a pain in John's shoulder as it pressed against the bulkhead just below the window out of which he looked. He could feel Beth next to him, leaning in, leaning against his body. Last time he'd looked at her she was asleep. Was she still asleep now? He didn't know, didn't want to check. He didn't want to see her for a while, which was why he was staring out the window. He'd spent almost the entire flight from Salt Lake, where they'd had their layover, staring out the window. It was how he spent the first flight, too: staring out the window. When the flight attendant had come by and offered beverages, he'd glanced at her politely, trying not to meet Beth's eyes, and ordered a club soda, extra lemon please. The flight attendant gave him the whole can; no one else on the flight wanted club soda, and if he didn't take the whole can it would go to waste. When the can of club soda, and the coffee he'd had in Salt Lake, caught up with him, pressing fiercely on his bladder, he'd held it. He regretted that now as the plane came in, pushing him against the seatbelt that a few minutes ago the kind voice had asked them to please put on, we'll be making our final descent into the Bozeman Yellowstone International Airport shortly, the time in

Bozeman Montana is 8:49 PM, the temperature in Bozeman Montana is 79 degrees.

In Salt Lake he'd pretended everything was normal. He'd pretended nothing had changed. He'd held Beth's hand as they walked through the concourse with their carryons; he'd agreed aloud while they ate that, yes, this burrito place did have superior vegetables to that other burrito place, even though he didn't think that was true; he'd sat by her side in the terminal while they waited to board, smiled when she looked at him before returning to the book she'd purchased at City Lights, by an author he wasn't familiar with. John was familiar with a lot of authors, like Beth was—books for them were a shared interest— but he wasn't familiar with this one, just as Beth wouldn't be familiar with many of the bloggers John read on the internet.

The situation hadn't actually changed, had it? They'd had an open relationship for a long time now, at least a year, in word if not in deed, because that was what Beth wanted. Jealously is a useless emotion, she liked to say. Sure is, he always agreed. But now. . . .

Polyamory was the word she used. Many loves. Who couldn't get behind that? Surely there was love enough in the world for everyone. Surely there was love enough in one person to embrace every soul.

2

JOHN AND BETH HEMPEL, NÉE Levitt (there'd been some confusion over whether she'd take his name—she hadn't been planning to, but at the last minute, the day before they applied for the marriage license, she'd changed her mind) had spent the last six days honeymooning in San Francisco.

They flew out of Bozeman, where they'd only just moved, hadn't even unpacked their few possessions into their new apartment, on a Boeing 737 to Oakland. It was in Oakland they'd rented an AirBnB. They hadn't seen the place yet, didn't understand what it meant to stay in Oakland, in the Fruitvale District, but they did when they arrived. John requested an Uber from his phone the minute they touched down and it was waiting for them just outside the baggage terminal, a black Mercedes, the only car available, 30 dollars extra because a ride in a black Mercedes with a cream leather interior and two complimentary half-size bottles of Aquafina was something you were supposed to be excited to pay extra for; and when they got inside the driver confirmed their destination and then said, Oh boy, what are you staying there for. And as he drove them up Hegenberger Road and then Foothill Boulevard where the AirBnB was, they understood. They saw the bars on the windows. They smelled the (not unfamiliar) scent of potsmoke and the ethnic food. They heard the blaring music. But surely everything would be okay. Surely they were being prejudiced, and surely this was unbecoming, especially for Beth, who loved all people, accepted all people (for why else was she with John?).

They'd never been to California before, alone or together.

And in the morning everything *was* okay. In the light of the sun they saw the colors, the murals that belied a rich culture. They met their host, who told them where they could get great empanadas, who told them that as long as they returned to the AirBnB before dark they'd be plenty safe.

They spent the first day there in Fruitvale, visited the empanada place and then an ethnic grocery, where they bought chorizo and eggs and sweet plantains, enough for several meals, for only 15 dollars, which was good because John and Beth didn't have a lot of money. John didn't have a job in Bozeman yet, and Beth hadn't started at the bakery, wouldn't start until they got back. They cooked the food in the AirBnB's kitchen. Only John ate the chorizo and eggs because Beth was trying the vegan thing again. They walked through the neighborhood, enjoying the warm and breezy air, and smiled at the children who stared at them, the children who were probably wondering *where did these white folks come from?*

John and Beth had sex three times that first day. She came every time. She came twice the second time. The third time John finally came too; they came together.

The next morning they woke early and made a pot—French press—of the coffee from a local shop their host had left for them in the freezer. Beth did her meditations, which were really more like kinds of prayers, in the bedroom while John sat in the kitchen and read articles on his iPad, scrolled through Twitter, but didn't update his status because being on your honeymoon was supposed to be about disconnecting from the online world and connecting more deeply with your wife.

Some days Beth could meditate for hours, but today she came out of the bedroom after 20 minutes, smiled and said, "Well, I'm ready to go if you are."

John turned off his tablet, looked up at her. She was beautiful, his wife. She had that sort of long black angelic hair that started as a solid thing, a piece of reality, and then became less concrete, became ethereal, the farther down it went. She almost never cut it. It framed her soft face and her soft shoulders and her soft breasts, framed her waist but stopped before her hips. She wore a black tank top, tight stonewashed jeans, and a wispy translucent vest that flowed to the floor. Everything about her was flowing all the time. He stood and kissed her. "I just need to finish my coffee," he said.

"You have almost a full cup. We'll get more in the city. It'll be even better."

Still, he took two more sips in quick succession, almost but not quite burning his throat, and then they walked the 15 minutes to Fruitvale station. They bought two BART passes, each with enough credit on them to last the entire honeymoon— they planned on taking the train across the Bay at least four more times . Probably they'd spend one day just at the AirBnB like the day before, having sex, relaxing.

They waited for the train while a white man with dreadlocks stood by the rails, shouting obscenities at no one. A black man played beautifully a weatherbeaten guitar. After a few minutes he stopped playing and told the first man to shut up, stop yelling. And that gave the first man someone to yell at. "Don't look at them," John said. "Don't make eye contact, just wait for the train." But Beth said she thought the whole thing was magical. "I can feel it here, the magic," she said.

Beth thought everything was magical. Said she could feel magic anywhere. But when she said magic she meant *magick*, with a *k*. Sometimes *magik*, remove the *c*, depending on who you asked. It was stronger in some places than others, she said, magick, stronger in some people than others, but it *was* everywhere. The earth by its very nature was made of it. The stars were made of it. The planets.

When she'd told him on their second date that she believed in these sort of things he'd thought *Oh boy* and said, I guess you want to know my sign now, don't you.

Of course not, she'd said, the Zodiac is flawed, a misinterpretation, but she *was* curious exactly what day he was born, and what year. He told her, ready to end the date, bid her goodbye, see her again never, but she took the date and typed it into her phone, said something about phase of the moon, and then told him they were going to be a power couple. That date ended with them cooking dinner at his place—red snapper, she was pescatarian at the time, not yet vegan—and making out for half an hour.

Indistinct sounds flowed from the platform speakers. The train rolled in. Stopped slowly. Then suddenly. They boarded.

As they rode John read an ebook on his phone; the book was about entrepreneurs. But Beth focused on the windows, on what lay beyond them, on the buildings and on the shipping crates and then the cranes, and finally, once the train went underground, even on the darkness rushing past.

They got off at 16th and Mission. John had read a review a few days ago of a hot dog shop in the Mission District; it was said to be one of the best in the city, if not the country, if not the world. The Flying Pig Bistro, it was called. First they ambled in the wrong direction for a block, and then they turned around. It had vegan dogs for her, every other sort of dog for him. They drank beer early in the day.

The plan was take the day slowly. Meander here and meander there. They had four days. But that first day in the city they did so much. After eating hot dogs, they started right there in the Mission, walking past the Armory, which they had tickets to tour in a few days, and toward Valencia, where they stopped for chocolates and cheeses and very small samples of ice cream. Even Beth nibbled on the cheeses and the ice cream. John found himself talking in amounts he often did, gushing about the technological history of the city. But Beth, she talked too, it was the literary side that interested her. She told him about McSweeney's, whose offices and pirate-themed storefront you could still find right over there, told him how the independent nature of the publishing company in a time when your options were either go with the big guys or work completely on your own, alone, with no support, was inspiring. "There's always another way," she said. "I'm always telling you that." It was true; she was. John was given to moments of panic, indecision, anxiety, and she would each time remind him there's always another way. They moved over to the Castro, stopped for tea at a little place on Sanchez Street with red decor, low tables, and pillows for sitting on. They lay in Delores park for a while, on the hill, and she told him about the days when those streets right there below them, when this entire district, will fill with people, shirtless, mirthful, some wielding sex toys or balloons in the shapes of sex toys, faces panted, carrying music in their tide, celebrating the rights of gays, transgender people, and bisexuals. "It happens all the time," she said. Of course John knew this, and he also knew that what Beth wished was that there was a pride parade going on right now. But there wasn't, although three women did lay topless on the grass behind them, black tape crossed over their nipples. Then John and Beth rode the Metro as close to Haight Street as it would take them. There she talked about Didion, about her essay on the place, about how when Beth first read *Marching Toward Bethlehem* as a teenager and knew she wanted inexplicably to live in this city, and how it was strange she didn't want to now, but she was so glad she was here, today, this week, with him, and how also Didion was very old and couldn't be long for the world, which made her sad.

They ate an early dinner at a place called Magnolia. Then they took an Uber to the nearest BART station and rode the train back to Oakland. They fucked slowly that night, sensuously, because they were tired.

The next day their legs were sore, especially John's, because he never exercised. Beth was a runner, was used to moving. John's feet he could barely stand on. But they took the train again, got off downtown, ate breakfast and drank coffee. They walked through Chinatown to City Lights. Beth had studied the Beats in college. They bought three books: two for her, one for him. They took a selfie in front of the sign for Jack Kerouac Alley. They took another selfie in the alley itself. They walked back through Chinatown. Beth bought some incense, even though she wasn't sure they'd let her take it on the plane. They lounged in the Yerba Buena gardens, reading their books, drinking more coffee and tea.

The next day was the one they spent inside, resting their legs, resting John's feet. Reading and fucking. Reading and fucking. John tried his best but didn't come that day.

The day after that they spent, again, in the Mission and the

Castro, exploring the Castro more deeply this time. The sex shops. More sex shops. They didn't buy anything, but they found a hidden little apothecary and Beth almost bought some crystals.

At four they toured the Armory.

They arrived for the tour early. The virtual ticket that had been emailed to them when they'd signed up (20 bucks a ticket) said to arrive at ten minutes before the start; Beth and John arrived at 3:40. John had a strong lack of respect for tardiness, especially in himself, and while this had the potential to clash with Beth's general attitude of *we'll get there when we get there, the universe will wait for us*, she always indulged him. Being late, or even on time, made him anxious, and anxiety when sparked could overwhelm him, had overwhelmed him in the past, and for a long while after he wouldn't show his face in public at all; so Beth, because she loved him, followed him no matter how early they might be. They were the first to arrive. The Armory's front doors were locked; a sign on white paper affixed with tape said they would open at 4 pm sharp.

"I told you," Beth couldn't help but say. She smiled.

John shrugged.

For a while it seemed theirs would be a private tour, but then another couple arrived—a bearded man and a stocky young woman—and then another, and then another, and then a group of three friends, maybe in their late twenties. None of the three friends seemed to John romantically involved. There was no third wheel. But Beth whispered, "That's a total triad right there."

"A triad?" John said.

"Yeah. Like the three of them are in a relationship. With each other."

"You mean all three of them?"

"Yep."

John contemplated the group.

"Don't stare," Beth said.

"I *wasn't* staring. I just don't see it." But she was probably right.

The doors opened. A woman said hello, gestured them in, introduced herself as Katie. Katie had a pierced septum and ample cleavage; she picked up an iPad and asked each tourist their name, checked the names off a list, told them all to wait in here, this is the lounge, this is where employees, including performers, eat, take breaks, play games, that sort of thing, we'll get started in a few minutes. Then she left the room.

The members of the tour group seemed to separate, dissipate throughout the room. One couple sat on a couch, held hands. The other examined together a piece of artwork, a painting hanging on the wall, realistic, explicit, a man with another man's penis inside him.

John looked at Beth. She smiled at him. He could tell the smile was humorous, displayed at the expense of his obvious nervousness. This was one of those situations where, were they alone, Beth would laugh and say, you're cute, I like you, and squeeze his hand.

John found himself in front of a glass display case—inside were items for sale: t-shirts, black riding crops branded with a red letter *K*, figurines, undetailed.

"They're hand-made," someone said. It was one of the two women from the group of three friends; she was standing next to John, staring also at the display case.

"The statues?" John asked.

"Yeah. The founder's mother is a sculptor. She makes them. Each one is original. That's why they're three-hundred bucks."

"How do you know that?" John said.

"I've taken the tour before. They told us."

"Oh. So you live in San Francisco?"

"No, no. We just like to visit. We're here at least once a year." She moved away to join one of her friends by a counter on which sat a clean coffee pot, a toaster, an empty bagel box.

Maybe Beth was right about the three. John looked around. Were these people like them, like he and Beth? They had to be, right? They were touring the world's most famous pornography studio, after all. What other couples tour porn studios besides the kind that watch porn together? And bondage porn to boot. Did that middle-aged guy with the glasses tie up his middle-aged wife with the dyed-blonde hair? Did she tie him? It seemed odd to think so. But anyone who looked at John wouldn't guess the same of him, would they? Hell, he'd never guessed it of himself, not until he'd met Beth, not until she'd convinced him to start exploring, together.

Katie came back in, clapped her hands, began to talk pleasantly about the history of the building. John rejoined Beth. She squeezed his hand. And together they toured the historic San Francisco Armory, headquarters and production studio—live sets and all—of the largest porn production company in the world.

The tour lasted 90 minutes, give or take—John took notice when he was being robbed of time, even if just a few promised minutes—and at the end they were given a coupon for 50 percent off a round of drinks at the Armory Bar, just across Mission, on the corner.

They were the only people from the tour group to go for drinks after, to take advantage of the coupons. "Lame," said the woman who had talked to John in the lounge. "Last time they gave us vouchers for one free download."

But surely discount drink coupons were more lucrative, and

that's why they'd switched. Because John and Beth went to the bar, ordered a drink each, John a whiskey, Beth a cosmopolitan, drank and talked and then ordered another at full price, and then another. It wasn't a cheap bar. The drinks were good, but not $80-for-six good, which is what they'd spent by the time they left, pleasantly tipsy, and decided they should probably catch the train, order a pizza when they got back to the AirBnB.

As they were walking Beth said, "I think we should do it here."

"What?" John said.

"The . . . opening," Beth said. "Would that be the word?"

"You mean our relationship."

"Yeah."

John stopped walking. "I don't know."

She stopped with him. "It's just, we've talked about it for so long. And we're in pretty much the most open city in the country."

"I don't know. You know I'm . . . apprehensive."

"Yes, well, and we're all apprehensive about growth before we make the decision to grow."

They resumed walking.

"I'm not saying we split up and go find other people," Beth said. "Baby steps. Let's just look online. Go on a date. Together. That's all."

Maybe that *was* all. Maybe John could do that. For her. And for him, too, if he were being honest. Of course he wanted it. What horny, heterosexual man didn't?

Two years ago, when John's mom found out that Beth, the woman he'd been dating the last three months, was bisexual (she'd dug up old Facebook photos of Beth with a freshman girlfriend), she'd called him asked him what the hell he was doing. He hadn't spoken to her or his father in years by then. "You can't date a homosexual," she'd said. "What if she cheats on you? She could cheat on you with another woman. If she likes both then she has twice as many chances to cheat on you." In the background John heard his father say, "Ask him what he's doing with a woman anyway. I thought he was a fag." John had hung up on his mother then, even though her question was one he'd once himself asked. It was officially the last time he would speak to her.

"I guess a date would be okay," John said as they descended into the subterranean yellow dimness of the BART station. "Okay, I guess let's try it."

So they took the train, walked from the station back to the apartment, ordered a pizza with marinara, mushrooms, olives— no cheese, no meat, and no fake soy-stuff either. Beth browsed OKCupid on her phone; John noticed she didn't have to download it—the app had been living on her phone, tucked away in a folder, ever since she'd used it to meet him. She said she found some matches, sent some messages. They went to bed early, but it took John over an hour to fall asleep.

"I found someone!" Beth said the next morning.

John was making coffee. He felt something in him stir. Was he getting hard, just a little? Were they actually going to do this? "Oh?"

"Yeah! His name is James. He lives in Stanford. He's free this afternoon."

Some of the coffee grounds John had been scooping into the French press missed their target, scattered across the counter. "Wait—*he?*"

"Well, yeah, I haven't heard from any women, so."

"Babe, I'm not ready for us to do our own thing yet. I thought this was going to be an *us* thing. Like together."

"Of course. It is. I'm not asking to go hang out alone with another guy on our honeymoon. This is just a date still, I promise. And it's both of us, together. It's just a first step."

And that's how they ended up spending the day in Stanford instead of San Francisco. That's how they ended up at a trendy bar, the patrons mostly students with wealthy parents or full-ride scholarships, hipster beards and faux-nerd glasses, some without lenses, John could have sworn, talking to a guy named James, with his own hipster beard, with his tight dark-gray t-shirt and solid pecs and flat stomach. Not ripped, not defined, but still tight and without the graspable inches of soft flab that John had.

And that's how they ended up in James's dorm room, high on James's pot. James's dick in Beth's mouth, John's in her pussy, and then vice versa. Beth said I want both of you in me, I want to be full, but John wasn't ready for that, and she said it was okay, she understood.

The truth is John wasn't ready for any of this. He probably never would be. Would it be different if it were him and Beth and another woman instead of him and Beth and another man? He liked to think it wouldn't. Besides, it *was* him and Beth and another man, and it was happening, and Beth was moaning and saying things about the energy in the room, the lovely energy, how she could feel it. And John loved her and was high and was married to her, and so he kissed her and focused, like she always told him to, on being in the moment, on being here, with her. And, evidently, with James.

It was too late to take the train back to Fruitvale Station. They slept at James's. James took the couch, gave them his bed. Even John slept well that night.

Between the BART passes, the expensive meals, the two unplanned trips to high-end bars, and everything else, they were almost out of money. They hadn't had much to begin with. But it was okay because they were leaving the next day, heading home to start their life. They had a new apartment waiting for them, their things delivered but not unpacked. Beth was starting her job at the bakery and would write her novel. John himself had plans; plans had formed.

Now the plane's wheels touched the tarmac. First the back wheels, solidly, and then the front wheel. A kiss, a tiny bounce, and then, again, contact.

Beth made a sound. John looked at her. She *had* been sleeping, but she was waking now. She stretched in that way she stretched without stretching, her chest expanding, her shoulders opening but her arms still by her sides, her hands still in her lap. She smiled with her eyes. John leaned in and kissed her and she kissed him back.

They debarked, carryons slung over shoulders, walked through the terminal and past the baggage claim, where they didn't stop because they had no other luggage. They travelled light, John and Beth. They had little and needed little. This shared value was one of the things that had brought them together. Simplicity. A sort of minimalism. Red wine. Alternative religious views (Wicca, atheism). Books, even if different genres. Food, even if different thoughts on whether eating meat was an acceptable human practice. Coffee. Film. Humanity. The way we, all of us, communicate, share, and grow.

Beth checked her phone. "Rebekah says she's almost here. She says she's running a couple minutes late."

"She's not late. Our plane was early."

They exited through the sliding automatic doors. John checked his own phone. It was 9:37 pm and the sun was still out in Big Sky Country; there was golden light as far as you could see. A silver Subaru approached the curb.

"There she is," Beth said, waving.

3

JOHN SAT IN THE BACK seat, Beth in the front.

The second half of a new Strumbellas song played on the radio and then transitioned to a single from the new album by Drake.

Rebekah Fleckman wasn't much into technology, John knew. She had a smartphone—who didn't?—and she was on Snapchat, but that was it. Mostly she just texted people, called her parents sometimes. He'd never seen her read an article on her phone, never seen her browse the web. He followed her on Twitter, but nothing had come from her account for like five years, well before he'd met her or Beth; she'd told him she'd created the account only because a communications elective she'd taken during her first year of college had had a unit on social media. Her profile photo showed her smiling at the camera in a youthful wall, her face framed by hair three or four inches shorter than it was now, giving her a boyish but still feminine appearance, drinking a Frappucino. John had memorized this photo. The account's last tweet was:

I think I enjoy being alone alot more than I should.

It had no retweets, no likes save one, from John.

Rebekah was on Facebook but she never used it. John visited her page sometimes just to look at pictures of her other people tagged her in.

Neither did she have access to a music streaming service. She didn't even use Pandora. The music playing now was on the radio, the actual radio, frequency modulation; most of it wasn't good, only popular. John never listened to live radio; this was the first time in three years, maybe four. Drake segued into Demi Lovato and for some reason Rebekah didn't change the station. John was certain she didn't like the music that was playing, but she didn't dislike it either, and this ambivalence intrigued him.

Rebekah asked whether Beth and John were hungry— airport food sucks, after all.

"I like airport food," John said, even though this honeymoon was the first plane trip he'd ever taken.

"We know you do," Beth said, rolling her eyes. "You like all food. But could you eat now?" She looked back at him, then at Rebekah. "I'm pretty hungry."

John already had his phone out, was logging in to their banking app. He and Beth had joint accounts since May. What was his was hers and what was hers was his. That's what being married was, according to some material for couples they'd read online when they were going through a rough patch. Here was the account summary. John quietly tipped his phone over the front seat, reached his arm around discretely so Rebekah wouldn't see that they were analyzing their pecuniary state (although he shouldn't have cared, should he, for Rebekah was his friend, and friendship meant trust and knowledge). Beth looked at the screen; the balance said $127. She shrugged, raised an eyebrow at John as if to say *Well?*

"I could go for a beer, I guess," John said. "And then you can get some food."

"Perfect," Rebekah said. "I want to hear all about the trip."

She drove downtown. "Open Range or somewhere else?" she asked.

"Open Range," John replied. Cost be damned. And something stronger than beer was suddenly appealing.

Beth requested they park a couple blocks away—her legs were stiff from sitting in airplanes half the day. It would feel good to walk.

John's still-sore feet cried out at the request, but he said nothing. It wasn't like they'd have their choice of parking downtown on a Friday anyway.

They parked; they walked; they were lucky and given a table immediately. A high-top with a lit candle in the center. Beth waved her hand over the candle and then stopped moving, held it there, brought it closer so that the flame was touching her skin. John and Rebekah watched. After several moments, Beth pulled away, unburned, her face neutral.

"Always amazing," Rebekah said. Beth waved her hand over the candle every time they came here, every time she had access to a candle. She burned candles in her own home and waved her hand over them, always pulling it away unscathed. She said it was just a matter of willpower, hardly even a magickal thing, if you knew how to focus. John thought it was just science, but a fear of pain kept him from trying it himself. John didn't like pain; he was not like his wife. Rebekah, too, he suspected, knew there was no pyromancy, but she loved Beth enough to pretend. You don't become a person's best friend without loving them enough to pretend.

They ordered drinks. John a whiskey, a good one. Rebekah

something called a Negroni; John had never heard of it; Rebekah said neither had she. Beth ordered a Moscow Mule—she loved the copper cups they were served in—and asked Rebekah if she wanted to share some truffle fries.

She looked at John. "What are you smiling at?"

"I'm not smiling."

"You're smiling."

He was smiling because he'd bought her a set of four of those copper mugs and she didn't know yet. They were waiting for her in the new apartment, in a box ready to be unpacked. "I'm smiling because I love you."

"You guys are gross," Rebekah said. John wondered how genuine her smile was. "Now tell me about your adventures."

"You first," Beth said.

"I don't have adventures."

"Sure you do. And if you don't you will now that we're going to be living here. What's been going on with you?"

Rebekah started talking and John looked at her, focused on her, was always delighted to focus on Rebekah Fleckman, but didn't hear her words. He was grateful for the direction Beth had steered the conversation. He didn't want to talk about the honeymoon right now. He still needed to discuss it with Beth, decompress. Debrief. They'd talked nothing of the threesome besides Beth this morning, as they took the train from Stanford back to Oakland to collect their things, asking John whether he was okay. He was, he'd said. Maybe it was a lie—he wasn't sure. Are *you* okay? he'd asked. Very, she'd replied. She said she'd had a lot of fun. The more John thought about it the more he had to admit he'd had fun too,—even if it was a sort of hazy, marijuana-clouded, lusty fun—but that didn't mean he was okay.

He was probably okay. He just needed to talk about it. But

with Beth, not Rebekah. But of course they'd talk about it with Rebekah, any minute now, because Rebekah was Beth's best friend and John had no friends and so by extension Rebekah was his best friend too. And Beth loved Rebekah and so, by extension, did John. Even not by extension did John love Rebekah. And John didn't want Beth to know he maybe wasn't okay so why, by extension, would he want Rebekah to know. He didn't. He *didn't*. But when they talked about it she might find out.

Maybe if it had been Rebekah instead of James he'd definitely be okay right now.

Maybe he was mad at her.

Maybe he wasn't jealous of Beth but mad at Rebekah. Or mad at Beth because instead of Rebekah the threesome had been with James.

The drinks came.

Rebekah was talking about how she was looking forward to going back to school. One more semester and then she could move on to graduate school. Four years of graduate school, she said, and then residency training—it felt like an eternity. But then she'd be a doctor. Maybe. Someday. If it was still what she wanted. Sometimes she wasn't sure it was what she wanted. Maybe she *wouldn't* be a doctor.

"And then you *will* be a doctor," Beth said, her hand on Rebekah's shoulder. "My best friend the doctor."

Rebekah and Beth didn't look like sisters. Sometimes best friends look like sisters but Beth and Rebekah didn't. Beth was prettier; Beth was beautiful. But Rebekah was pretty in her own way, in a way that, to John, was plainer, less engrossing. She didn't flow like Beth did. She wasn't ethereal. But she was stronger. She was more solid. She had a grounded core. That was it: a grounded core. It wasn't just her physical appearance but what Beth would call her aura. She knew where she was going in the world, even if she didn't realize she did. John knew she knew where she was going in the world. Anyone who met Rebekah would come away thinking, *that young lady doesn't know she knows it, but she knows where she's going in the world.*

She was talking about the semester she'd taken off. Saying she regretted it, felt lazy, realized now she should have stuck with it—she'd have finished sooner. John didn't think she was lazy. He wished they could have lived here in Bozeman then, when she was only working, not going to school. They could have seen her more. They could have spent more time with her. Maybe if they'd spent more time with her she would have said yes. Maybe it would have been Rebekah instead of James. A perpetual question was why did Rebekah care for Beth (for John?) when she so rarely saw her.

"You're not lazy," Beth was saying. "You needed the time off."

"Yeah," John said. "I think you did. I think it was good for you."

"Yeah, well."

The truffle fries came and John asked the waiter for another whiskey. He was feeling the first one, which he'd drunk quickly. Maybe if he had another he could talk about *it*.

"Oh," Rebekah said, dipping a fry in the restaurant's homemade ketchup, one of their specialties, "and I had a date last night." She popped the fry into her mouth, the whole thing, as if it were something smaller, like a cherry or an olive.

John didn't see the point of dipping truffle fries in ketchup —why pay more for truffle oil if you were just going to cover up the taste. But he couldn't summon enough umbrage to to distract himself from the pang of jealousy he felt whenever Rebekah talked about her love life. ("But I don't *have* a love life," she often insisted.)

"Really?" Beth said, taking a fry of her own, eating it plain, which was one of the reasons why John loved her. He loved Beth because she didn't eat her truffle fries with ketchup; he loved Rebekah in spite of the fact she did. "How did *that* go?"

"Not so good. I mean, it was fine, I guess, through dinner, but he was still there this morning."

Even though John had said he wasn't hungry, and even though he was feeling greasy from all the food he'd eaten in the last few days and knew he'd regret the starch immediately, he took a fry too. Then he changed his mind and took two fries at once. "And that's bad?" he asked casually. The jealousy didn't grow, exactly, but it was tighter. An urge to protect his wife's best friend was choking him like a moth-eaten scarf. Like who the fuck was this guy she'd spent the night with?

"He slept on the couch."

"And where did *you* sleep?" John asked.

"In my room. With the door locked."

"I see."

"Indeed," Beth said. "We see."

Rebekah shrugged. John considered ordering one more whiskey if the waiter returned soon.

"So you didn't want to sleep with him?" Beth said, sounding disappointed. Rebekah never wanted to sleep with anybody, and Beth often chided her for passing up opportunities, said if she relaxed a bit she'd open an undiscovered side of herself.

"I guess not. I mean, no, definitely not. I thought he'd just drop me off after dinner, but he pretty much invited himself in, so we played games and then I went to bed and when I woke up he was still there, and he'd even gone out and picked up coffee. He'd left, picked up coffee, and then come back. I came out of my room and he was sitting in the kitchen with the coffee."

"Oh dear," Beth said, for Rebekah hated coffee.

Rebekah shrugged again.

"What did you do?"

Yes, John wondered, what did she do? He caught the waiter's eye, raised his empty glass. The waiter nodded.

"You sure you want another one?" Beth asked him.

"Mmmhmm," he said. "Why not?"

"Well it's just . . . never mind. You just didn't drink this much our whole honeymoon."

"How *was* the honeymoon?" Rebekah said then.

"Uh uh," Beth said. "Not yet. You finish your story first. What did you do?"

"I just thanked him for the coffee. And then I went in the living room and vacuumed. Left him in the kitchen. I vacuumed for like half an hour, way longer than it takes to vacuum my living room. You've seen my living room. And—get this—when I came back into the kitchen? He was still there. And he was writing *haiku.*"

John's drink came and he immediately drank half of it and said, slurredly, "Haiku?"

"I know, right? He said he was leaving for the military soon, and he wanted to tell his friends goodbye, so he was writing them haiku."

"Is it haiku or haikus?" John asked, taking a good many truffle fries.

"I like haiku," Beth said. "Were they good haiku?"

"I guess. I didn't really read them. Then finally he left."

"What's his name?" John asked.

"Aaron."

"Nice. Are you going to see him again?" Beth said.

"No. *No.* He's texted me three times today and I just keep ignoring them. I only wanted dinner. That's the whole reason I went on the date. He called and asked if I had plans and I said I planned on doing nothing. I didn't mean I didn't have plans. I meant I'd actively planned to do nothing. But dinner . . ."

"Well, we had a date, too," Beth said, the words spilling from her mouth. And John realized Beth had been more than eager to tell Rebekah this whole time—because who else do you tell but your best friend after you've had sex with someone new?—but she'd been doing that thing for the last twenty minutes where she was a wonderful person and made sure to listen to others before talking about herself.

"Oh really?" Rebekah looked at John.

John reached for another fry, his hands craving a distraction. "We did," he said. "And we . . . slept with him."

Now Rebekah looked back at Beth. "You did?"

Beth smiled. "It was good. *Really* good."

And Rebekah gave Beth a high five, the way John would have high-fived his friends had the threesome been with another woman and had he had friends to talk about it with. "Congrats," she said to both of them. "I know you guys have wanted that for a while. And on your honeymoon . . ."

"Yeah," Beth said.

John shrugged and drank his whiskey.

And that was that. They moved to the topic of plans. They spoke a bit more about Rebekah's upcoming medical career, her uncertainty that it was going to happen, Beth's certainty that it would. "Because you're an amazing person," she said. "You're going to be a wonderful doctor."

Beth talked about how she was a little nervous, starting at Betty's Bakery. Also excited.

"Oh," she said, "and John is going to start a YouTube channel."

"Oh yeah?" Rebekah said, sipping her beer.

John nodded. He said it seemed like a natural extension of his journalism career, but independent, you know?

"Like what will your videos be about?"

John said he wasn't sure yet, but probably he'd make videos about technology, pop culture, movies and video game reviews, that sort of thing.

Beth took his hand and told Rebekah she thought it was a wonderful idea. John squeezed his wife's hand and fantasized that he knew Rebekah better than Beth did.

4

It was 2017 and it seemed like nobody had parents anymore.

Rebekah had parents, sure, she visited them in Helena like every other weekend, or sometimes they came to visit her, and Beth liked Rebekah's parents, thought they were nice, liked her mother's haircut that never seemed to change and her father's anchor tattoo. The anchor tattoo that had made him congenial to the fact that Beth had convinced Rebekah to get a tattoo in high school, at the beginning of senior year, when she wasn't yet eighteen and thus the tattoo artist had been legally obligated to get a signed form of parental consent but hadn't, hadn't even asked for ID, and when Rebekah's mother found out she'd been furious, not at Rebekah for getting the tattoo and not so much at Beth for convincing her, but at the artist for not getting the signed form of parental consent, but Rebekah's father had calmed her and said did it really make a difference—Rebekah would be eighteen in four months anyway and if she'd waited until then to get the tattoo she wouldn't have needed consent and her mother couldn't get mad at the guy, so why bother being mad at him now, and besides, look at the tattoo, it's harmless, just a star inside a heart on the inside of her right wrist, like a pentagram of love, which shouldn't upset your Christian sensibilities because it's *love*.

As for Beth, she had an actual pentagram tattooed on her body, at the base of her boney spine. She had also, in various places, including the tip of each hipbone, the sigils of Taurus, Aquarius, Leo, and Scorpio, representing each magical element: Earth, Air, Fire, and Water. The sigils weren't in wide use anymore amongst Wiccans—most modern magicians used the simpler symbols, a yellow square for Earth, a red equilateral triangle for Fire, apex upward, etc.—but Beth was a purist. Although she did also have two of the symbols—the triangle for Fire and the silver crescent that meant Water—tattooed elsewhere on her body. Because these, Fire and Water, were what she felt inside her, what she could best control, and having the sigils and the symbols was a way of doubling down, of connecting deeper with the power with which the Universe had blessed her. Beth had these seven tattoos. Plus an eighth—a dolphin, leaping, on the inside of her left ankle—just for fun.

Beth had these seven tattoos, but she didn't have her parents. Almost nobody had their parents anymore. John didn't, not in any way that mattered.

Beth's parents had died when she was twelve years old. They'd been struck by a drunk driver while they were on their way to a hotel after dinner. The dinner and hotel reservation hadn't been for anything special, not a birthday or an anniversary, but Beth's parents had made a point of spending at least one night alone together each month. Beth had been at home with the babysitter, her grandmother. She hadn't been in the car. She hadn't died. The police said her father had been driving. Both her parents had been wearing their seatbelts. The guy who hit them survived; he'd been very very drunk.

Beth's grandmother raised her. For a long time associating it with the manner of her parent's death, Beth didn't touch alcohol until she was twenty-one years old. Her grandmother died a year ago, peacefully, in her sleep.

The need to communicate with her dead parents is what led Beth to the study of magick, to spells and crystals and the moon. She never was able to contact them, though. It turned out that what's dead is dead. The demons she'd heard about, the ghosts she thought might be the souls of those who'd once walked the earth, rarely came to our world. If they did, it was because they were cursed, damned. They existed in their own realm, were born there, died there themselves, and they preferred it that way. Demons were as lonely as humans. If they existed, that is. Beth believed they existed. She believed she met one once, and she believed he'd been very very lonely.

But loneliness wasn't a bad thing. We could all be alone together, embracing one another in our solitude and allowing ourselves to be embraced by it. There were moments in which human aloneness was a magnificent, subsumable thing.

Moments like unpacking boxes in your new apartment with your new husband, who is also alone but was alone right there with you. Unpacking boxes and realizing you need a whole new set of dining plates because here are the ones you used to have, broken, shattered into big and small pieces, because maybe someone did not handle with care. Oh well. You're ordering pizza tonight anyway; you'll just be eating off paper towels. Unpacking boxes and finding the one with your bed linens, saying to John I guess we'd better put the bed together so we have somewhere to put these bed linens. John saying well can't we unpack some more boxes first, what's the rush? You giving him that look. *That* look, with the squint and sparkle.

Making love on the bed. Making love, as far as the phrase

goes, not a thing you usually do, but something that is possible and happens.

It was one of the compatibility questions on the dating app:

The phrase "making love" is:

A. Beautiful
B. Hokey and overly sentimental
C. Referring to a very specific kind of sex

And John had always thought the answer was B, but you convinced him it was C, and you remind him of it every once in a while.

It isn't John's fault, by the way, that it always takes him a long time to come. He doesn't need to be embarrassed about it, you tell him.

Getting tattoos on the tips of your hipbones had really hurt. Getting tattoos on the tips of your hipbones had been excruciating.

5

THE FOLLOWING IS HOW REBEKAH Fleckman met Beth Hempel.

They were fourteen. Both in their final year of middle school. Some districts call it junior high and some call it middle school, and in some the two terms are interchangeable, but in Helena it was just middle school. That final year of middle school, just before high school, is a time ripe for making new friends; and if you're lucky, new friends made in your final year of middle school are friends made for life.

It was New Year's Eve. Rebekah's friend Katie Wallace had invited her to a New Year's Eve party. Katie Wallace was not Rebekah's best friend; when she was fourteen Rebekah didn't have any best friends, just regular friends, and friendship in these cases was just another word for acquaintanceship, for *we go to the same school* or *we go to the same church* or *you're on the track team too so I guess I'd better get along with you*. Fourteen-year-old Rebekah wasn't antisocial; she was on the aforementioned track team and she'd played lacrosse for an ill-fated season before the district banned it after a girl broke her leg in a particularly gruesome way (it was the first time in her life Rebekah saw an exposed tibia, but it would not be the last), plus no other Montana districts had lacrosse teams, so always it was just

Helena Middle School vs. itself, and after the girl's injury the school board was like, *okay, if we're not even playing against other schools, which is to say there's no chance for pride or glory, why are we letting our students take the risk?* Rebekah also played timpani in the school orchestra, although she was never very good at it; but you had to play *something* in the school orchestra—it was required. Rebekah wasn't antisocial, but she wasn't social either. She was a good student. She didn't know who she was.

Katie Wallace's New Year's Eve party was held in Katie Wallace's garage. Rebekah's father dropped her off. He told her he'd pick her up just after midnight. The invitation had included a sleepover option, but even at fourteen Rebekah did not do sleepovers. She liked her own bed, and she saw no reason to sleep in a bag on Katie Wallace's floor.

Katie Wallace's garage door was closed but bright light was visible through its windows and Rebekah could hear "Single Ladies (Put a Ring on It)" playing loudly behind them. She could see people inside, through the windows, other girls, dancing. Yet instead of entering through the obvious side door, Rebekah approached the house's front. She knocked confidently, as if she was here to spend time with Katie Wallace's parents. As if she was more suited to spending time with adults than with her immature peers. But no one answered her knocks. Through the living room windows Rebekah could see the main part of the house was dark. She acquiesced and entered through the side door, joined the other teenage girls in the garage, because she had no choice.

"Heyyy!" Katie Wallace exclaimed. "Rebekaaaah!" She hugged Rebekah and planted kisses in the air inches away from each of Rebekah's cheeks. She called Rebekah "Dahling" and evoked a bad posh accent. It was a trend among the girls in Rebekah's grade at the time—bad posh accents—for they were all suddenly old enough to have seen *Mean Girls* but not old enough to have learned from it (in time it would become apparent *no one* had learned from *Mean Girls*, ever). Rebekah for her part never did have any interest in seeing the film, and never would.

The music kept on playing but the girls in the garage stopped dancing. There were maybe a half dozen girls, not counting Rebekah or Katie Wallace. Rebekah would never remember exactly how many other girls, because she didn't care. All the girls save one went to Helena Middle School, and Rebekah knew or had at least seen them around. Still, Katie Wallace was playing the delighted host, and she felt it necessary to introduce Rebekah to the girls one by one. "You know _____, don't you?" "_____ of course is in our English class." "_____ here is in seventh grade, so you may not have met her, but she's just *so mature,* so I thought she deserved to come to an eighth-grade party." Then Katie came to the final girl in the line-up: toothpick-thin, raven haired, unmistakably goth or goth-aspiring. "This is Beth. Beth goes to CR Anderson."

"Hi," Beth said. She extended an awkward hand but immediately retracted it, as if realizing handshakes weren't how fourteen-year-old girls greeted one another. She offered no other form of salutation, just stood there in the loud and cold garage.

"Soooo, anywayyy . . ." Katie Wallace said, putting her hands together. "Let's keep the party going, yeah?" Katie turned the music up (she'd never turned it down, so now it was the sort of loud only teenage girls can stand) and the partiers resumed their spastic dancing. Even Beth danced, although she didn't talk to anyone. Rebekah danced and made conversation with some of the others, never initiating but giving the impression of interest with her responses.

Katie Wallace brought her a drink. "It's something called tequila. I took it from my parents. But we have to make sure we put it away by midnight, because they'll be getting back like at 12:30."

"Thanks," Rebekah said. This would be her first clandestine taste of alcohol, but not her last.

"Listen," Katie said, lowering her voice even though she would have had to have been yelling for any of the garage's other occupants to hear her over the Red Hot Chili Peppers. "That girl, Beth, is a little weird, okay? Her parents just died. I only invited her because my mom made me. My mom knows her grandma or something. I'm pretty sure she's a dyke?"

"Your mom's a dyke?" Rebekah said.

"What? *No.* Fuck you," Katie Wallace said. And then she laughed. "You're funny. I think that's why you're popular."

"I'm popular?" Rebekah asked, raising an eyebrow in manner beyond her years.

"Yeah. You're, like, at least a little popular."

Teenage girls, it turns out, can dance for over four hours without stopping, and that's what the half-dozen or so in Katie Wallace's garage did that New Year's Eve: they danced. The dancing was awful, Tourettic, and Rebekah didn't at any point feel a true part of it, but she danced. Katie Wallace bragged about the playlist she'd put together on "my very own MacBook my mom got me for my birthday." Sara Bareilles. Usher. Chris Brown. More Chris Brown. Coldplay. Rihanna. More Rihanna. Flo Rida (featuring T-Pain). Chris Brown again (also featuring T-Pain). When Katy Perry started playing some hours into the party, Rebekah noticed Beth, who all night had been withdrawn, dancing but worse than of the other girls, containing herself to a six-inch by six-inch imaginary box on the cement floor, perk up.

Katie Wallace, obviously drunk except none of the girls knew what drunk was, noticed too. She said, "Hey girls, it looks like Beth here *really* likes this song. Maybe *she* kissed a girl. And maybe *she* liked it."

The other girls laughed, but their laughs were uncertain. Beth let out a couple good-natured *HA*s.

"Beth is a dyke," Katie said. Then she sang it. "Beth is a dyyyyy-yyyyyke."

One of the other girls—Rebekah had no memory of who— said, "Katie, whoa, stop it, okay?"

But Katie Wallace was singing louder. To the tune of the Katie Perry song she was singing, "Beth Levitt. Is. A. Dyke. She kissed a girl and she . . ." and the rest of the lyric disintegrated into first mumbles and then unsteady humming. Katie continued to hum the Katie Perry tune for some time, even after the music had transitioned to Metro Station and then Jordan Sparks. (Soon would come a future where no one remembered 50 percent of the artists on that night's playlist.)

The time was 12:07 before any of the girls had the wherewithal to look at a clock, and when they realized they'd glossed without ceremony over the purpose of the evening— ringing in the New Year—the party died a quick death. Katie Wallace fell asleep or passed out in the garage's corner, on what Rebekah was pretty sure was a large dog bed. One of the other girls sat beside her and also lost consciousness. Someone turned off the music and then everyone was unfolding sleeping bags. Headlights penetrated the garage windows, and Rebekah knew her father was waiting for her.

Rebekah saw Beth, holding a sleeping bag of her own, but she hadn't unrolled it. She appeared frozen. Her eyes were closed. A backpack sat at her feet.

Rebekah approached her. "Hey," she offered.

The pale, thin, black-haired girl opened her eyes. "Hi."

"I'm not staying the night. Are you staying the night?"

Beth nodded.

"Well, if you want, you can stay the night at my house instead. My parents are really nice."

Beth looked around the garage. "Okay," she said. "That would be nice."

As they walked down the driveway in the dark toward her father's car, Rebekah said, "I don't really like those girls either."

"Oh—I *like* them," Beth said. "I like *everybody*. But sometimes I just get a little nervous. I don't really have any friends."

At school the next week there was a rumor going around that Katie Wallace had gotten alcohol poisoning at her own New Year's Eve party, that she'd almost died. Katie Wallace swore it wasn't true.

6

NINE DAYS AFTER MOVING IN to the new apartment Beth spotted one more box sitting underneath the coffee table. How had she missed that one? How had John missed it? Beth opened it, shook her head and laughed. It had the knives she'd been searching for, the three that were missing from the knife block and that she was afraid they'd somehow left behind in the old place. It also had a tablecloth that they probably didn't need, could probably get rid of, two Christmas ornaments she kept because they'd been her grandmother's, and a Fiona Apple CD.

Why the fuck did she still have a Fiona Apple CD? Fiona Apple, sure—but a CD?

She put the CD and the table cloth in the "donate" bin by the front door, took the cardboard box into the kitchen and broke it down and set it next to the garbage can where she'd see it and remember it needed recycling. She depressed the plunger on the French press, slowly, slowly. Poured herself a cup. It was okay coffee. She got it free from the bakery, one free pound a week, which was more than enough, even for her and John's copious habit. But the bakery was a bakery, not a coffee shop, so.

Beth sat at the kitchen table, sipped the coffee, read the news on her phone. There was a lot going on in the world, and much of it made her angry. Like that another black man had been killed by a white police officer. Or like that another black man had killed a white police officer, a different one in a different city. Or that Texas was trying to pass another anti-abortion law. Or that the President was a mysogynist, a bigot, and was not fixing the world, and it was a shame because Bernie would have fixed the world. Beth had voted for Bernie, even volunteered for his campaign, passing out stickers and sometimes free hats. And when he'd lost she'd voted for Hillary. And when Hillary lost Beth had marched on the state capitol with 10,000 other humans. There was a lot to get angry at, for everyone on every side. The dodecahedron of politics, culture, was not a fun one to roll. Beth tried mostly to ignore it. She didn't like being angry. Except for occasional bouts of activism, she tried to keep the politics far away.

What was also far away was the subject of each and every picture she scrolled through and double-tapped on Instagram. But at least there was beauty there. Fellow sisters of the world, sunsets from last night, yogis on the mountain or by the ocean or in front of vast windows, whatever city behind them, welcoming the day. Beth had already done her yoga this morning. Her yoga wasn't usually physical, but it didn't have to be. Maybe a few sun salutations, but the core of it was spiritual. She'd opened her chakras. She'd said her prayers. And now she sipped her coffee. It was 5:30 AM and the bakery opened at six and that's when she had to be there. The apartment wasn't far from downtown. The apartment wasn't far from the food co-op. The apartment wasn't far from the cheap grocery store above the brewery. The apartment wasn't far from anything, which was good because they didn't have a car, not anymore; three days ago they'd sold it (they'd purchased it when they first moved in together, after they'd gotten back together, because in Helena they'd needed one), and so now they had some money. A few thousand. Enough to last until she got paid and until John started making money in whatever way he ended up making money. And he'd find a way, Beth knew. She believed in him. She lit incense for him. He did not believe in setting intentions but she set intentions enough for both of them.

The apartment's kitchen was sparse. None of their furniture was new. Some of it had been John's when he'd lived with roommates in Missoula. Some of it had been Beth's when *she'd* lived with roommates in Missoula. Roommates—how were they? They'd be wondering how the honeymoon went, if they wondered about her at all.

There was the kitchen table, which sat four people, five if they brought out the folding chair. The French press. The toaster. In the living room, the old couch, found at a garage sale when Beth first got to Missoula for college. The coffee table, wood, scratched and scuffed but classy. The single bookshelf. The books on the bookshelf, and then the overflow, stacked upon the floor. Books on Wicca and spells, literature, fantasy, physics and metaphysics. The small altar, candles, gemstones (amethyst, emerald, agate, in a box a piece of bloodstone for when Beth needed to manipulate her, well, blood); the bowl, a statue of the Buddha, a statue of Ganesh, a statue of Christ. A red cushion in front of it all. How good of John to tolerate all this, maybe even to love it.

In a corner of the bedroom John had his own space. A white sheet hung against the wall, a camera on a tripod, a large studio light the technical name for which Beth didn't know (John probably didn't either—he told her it had many four- and five-star reviews, which is why he'd bought it). He had a couple vlogs recorded. He'd upload them as soon as they had internet. The guy from the company was supposed to come this week.

Beth put the coffee mug in the sink. John would wash it for her. She went into the bedroom, kissed John on the cheek. He stirred, rolled over. Mumbled that he was getting up soon. Mumbled for her to have a good day, be safe, my love.

"*You* be safe," she told him.

She listened to RadioLab through headphones as she walked to work.

Beth knew John was in love with her best friend, but it was okay, she didn't mind. Beth was in love with Rebekah too.

Beth had been in love with Rebekah since they first met at that New Year's Eve party in Katie Wallace's garage. And even though they formed that night an immediate bond in their conspiratorial ditching of the other girls and retreat to Rebekah's house—Beth's first sleepover—they saw each other only sporadically until high school, nearly nine months later, when finally they went to the same building, where they could begin to eat lunch together every day, to study together, to try out for the soccer team together, talk about that mysterious thing that is dating as a teenager together.

Beth did not kiss Rebekah that night they first met (although Beth had kissed one girl by then)—she did not kiss Rebekah until the final year of high school. It happened, of course, drunkenly (Rebekah drunk, not Beth, who didn't drink yet), like it always did: with each of her roommates; with her lab partner, Veronica Brown; with Penny Grossman, the librarian's daughter. When they find out you're bisexual, all your women friends want to try kissing you, once they get drunk enough to admit it. You become an object of their experimentation. The difference between Rebekah and the other drunk girls in Beth's life was by the time they kissed Beth loved Rebekah more than anyone she ever had.

The summer sun was out, low, as Beth walked to Betty's Bakery. The summer sun had one more month of life in it, maybe a month and a half. Beth could check her moon book for the exact date it would cease to rise before the time she left the house each morning. Some witches memorized these things. Beth didn't. She just checked her moon book. Or the MoonBook app on her iPhone. "A MoonBook app," John said. "Wish I would have developed that. Sell it for a buck ninety-nine, make a decent chunk of money."

There was almost no one else walking this early in the morning. There were cars on the road, but almost no one walking. An old man across the street was led by his dog; the man wore thick sunglasses; he may have been blind. A block away a woman pushed a stroller. Beth could feel the life on this street, these blocks. She could feel the old man's life. The woman's life, resplendent with a sort of maternal energy Beth wondered whether she herself would ever be possessed by, would ever want to be possessed by. Beth could feel the energy of the child on the stroller, could tell the child was a male even though the front of the stroller was covered by a morning-chill-reducing blanket.

All around Beth was energy, and it cloaked her, warmed her skin in a way the sun could not. Life was something Beth appreciated more than most people did. There were many things she was sure she didn't appreciate enough, but life wasn't one of them. Because she'd known death. Death had its own energy. She could feel death, too.

Downtown more people were walking. Beth took her

earphones from her ears and rolled them up and put them in her dark jeans pocket. Outside the door of Betty's Bakery she paused. She looked at the door. She imagined her arm outstretched but did not actually raise it. A limb of pure energy. She drew with it on the door an inverted V, starting at her left thigh, then her head, and then her right thigh. And then she drew another one: Left shoulder, right shoulder, back to left thigh. The star she'd conjured glowed before her, lines of pure energy, pure spirituality, pure thought—which were three ways of saying one thing, she firmly believed, or chose to believe, or liked to believe (which were three ways of saying the same thing). She opened the door and let the lines wash over her she as crossed the bakery's threshold.

"Good morning," Karen Davenport said. Karen Davenport was the owner of Betty's Bakery. She was in her late fifties, a divorcee, had graying hair and still-smooth skin, dressed as might a schoolteacher who'd been raised in the seventeenth century: frilled hems, sometimes large feathers in her hair.

"Good morning, Karen," Beth replied. Smiling her Beth smile. If you smiled, others smiled.

There was no Betty at Betty's Bakery; there never had been. Only Karen, twenty years of recipe perfection, and too much love of alliteration. "I've never even known a Betty," Karen said when, during her interview before the honeymoon, Beth had asked about the name. "I had an aunt named Beatrice, but that's the closest, and I never actually met her."

"Well, and it's a lovely name, though," Beth had replied. "Betty's Bakery, I mean." And maybe she didn't believe it, but just by saying it she did. She found reality was only a matter of invoking your own will—such too was the nature of magick.

Karen and another baker were filling the display case with

muffins and scones and croissants. Beth helped them. She helped them put on the shelves various fresh loaves. At six she turned the sign in the window from CLOSED to OPEN. She brewed fresh coffee, filled the large carafes at the coffee station. At 6:11 the first customer walked in, and Beth helped him, took his order at the register, put his muffin in a bag and handed him a paper cup. She helped Karen and the other baker—she did not know the other baker's name; the other baker was there every morning but never talked—clean the back of the bakery, where the baking was done. When a customer came in a bell would ring. Beth would take care of them. With every customer she was more than cordial—she was genuine. She let the spirit in them reflect the spirit in her, and in this way she made the world better. At 7:05 Karen and the other baker left, Karen first thanking Beth, telling her she was doing a great job, help yourself to a pastry, don't forget, and kissing her on both cheeks. At 7:10 Beth ate a *pain au chocolat*. At 7:17 another customer came in, and behind them another. And then another. And soon there was a line to the door and Beth stopped noting the time, just interacting. The line for a long time did not shrink.

In this way passed the morning and Beth was happy. Beth was very happy. Beth was newly married and had a new home in a great city and had two best friends and a job two of the benefits of which were talking to kind people and smelling fresh bread all day.

But when the bread sold out and then the pastries sold out and the coffee in the carafe was three hours old because nobody had ordered any for a while and so she hadn't had to make more, and she turned the sign in the window from OPEN to CLOSED and then cleaned the carafe and brushed the crumbs from the display case and mopped the floor and shut down the tablet-based register and took the cash drawer back to Karen's office so Karen could pick it up in the morning, something failed her.

Something failed her because when she left the bakery at one o'clock she felt good. She felt amazing.

The sun was still out and as she walked back home, headphones in, finishing the episode of RadioLab and starting another (she'd fallen behind on her podcast listening during the honeymoon), she ate another *pain au chocolat*, which she'd set aside some time around eleven. She'd eaten at least one pastry every day for the last week, since the first time Karen told her to help herself. Most days she ate two. Sometimes she ate *pain au chocolats*. Sometimes she ate plain croissants. She didn't much like muffins but she ate one once. She loved the lemon-ginger scones.

Today she saved half the second *pain au chocolat* for John and when she entered the apartment she called to him.

Something failed her because there was no answer. "John?" she said, and poked her head into the bedroom.

"John?" she said again.

Something failed her because she was still feeling good. She didn't sense it until she saw it.

She left the bedroom and walked through the narrow hall back to the living room. She heard a sound. She stopped, turned back. Walked back to the bathroom door, which she'd passed and which was open.

There was John.

John was on the floor, the back of his head against the toilet. There was vomit on his shirt, vomit on the toilet seat, vomit on the floor next to him. His eyelids were open and then they closed. Open and then closed. When they were open she could barely see his green irises.

"Fuck," she said.

She dropped the waxed bag with the pain au chocolate in it. Down she went to her knees. She felt John's head. His head was fire. "Fuck fuck fuck. *Fuck.*"

And then she saw the bottle, the little white bottle with the cap off. The empty bottle. The bottle that had once held . . . she picked it up . . . ibuprofen. Fifty capsules—a hundred? She wondered when they'd bought this bottle, how much of its contents they'd used since.

She slapped John's face. She screamed, "FUCK!"

She found her phone. Her back pocket. She dialed 911.

The operator said an ambulance was on its way. The operator asked for more details—can you tell me more about your husband's condition, is he breathing—but Beth threw the phone into the wall.

While she waited, she smacked John again. She smacked his face as hard as she could. She slammed two fists into his chest. "Fuck you," she said. "Fuck you fuck you fuck you." John mumbled sounds. Something dripped from the corner of his mouth. Maybe vomit. Maybe blood. Something dark but chalky. "You promised you'd never do this again," Beth cried. "When you proposed you said you wouldn't ever do this. I hate you I hate you I hate you."

Hokey and Overly Sentimental

1

TWO YEARS THREE MONTHS AND maybe one week earlier, Beth decided she was going to try dating men, for a change, and what better way to find a man eager to date a woman than with an online dating app.

She had friends who'd had or were having success with online dating. Her roommate Jessica spent the night with a new guy she found on Tinder at least once a week. And her other roommate, Melanie, had a stable boyfriend she'd met on Plenty of Fish, and nobody was even using Plenty of Fish anymore, which was a testament to how long that relationship had been going on.

Beth set her profile up on OkCupid. She wasn't looking to meet the man of her dreams, doubted it was even a man her dreams were made of, but she was hoping for something casual, maybe several somethings, something shorter than long-term but longer than a one-night stand. She wanted to experience sex with a man, but she also wanted to connect with one on a spiritual-type level, to feel within her and around her the potential of masculinity. All her life thus far had been infused with the feminine.

She didn't date in high school, but she did kiss three girls. And then at the beginning of her freshman year of college she met Raylene and lost her virginity and tripped on mushrooms with her three times (the third time was boring, nearly ineffective, the potency of the psilocybin having been dulled by the two earlier experiences) before Raylene decided she wasn't going to cut it as an artist after all, at least not "within this system and its affluent-dominated patriarchal oppression" and dropped out of the university, moved back home to Alabama . . . or it might have been Rhode Island—she told Beth where she was from but that was while they were tripping on the mushrooms.

After Raylene came Marla, who had blue hair. After Marla, Evelyne. After Evelyne, Marla again, with fiery orange hair this time, up above and down below. Then Portia, who wasn't born with that name and who was the first person to make Beth come.

Her sophomore year Beth joined a coven. She'd been practicing Wicca solo until then, learning by reading the internet and books she'd found in Helena and Missoula's few esoteric bookstores. The internet she found unreliable, the websites about witchcraft too colorful or garishly designed or too fantastic—but books, she realized, had never failed her (this realization would, in time, prove faulty). She visited the student union and asked one of the councilors there about any Wicca groups on campus. The councilor, a tired-looking woman with whom Beth could not yet empathize but nonetheless tried, gaped for a moment and then said she was sure they had nothing like that here. Beth smiled and asked whether she could please just check. The woman smiled back and did indeed check and wouldn't you know, there *was* a sort of Wicca group here, I . . . I never would have thought so. So Beth joined the group. And in that group she met the women who for the rest of college would be her Sisters.

And also Kyle, who she fell in love with at a distance, but Kyle was all feminine energy, and after kissing her one Midwinter he admitted that he was gay, but that he'd liked kissing her, in a way, could they do it again? And so they did it again. And then one more time. But that was all, just three kisses, all in the same night, while nearby the Sisters drank grog and danced around a fire and sacrificed, in a most sacred ceremony, the head of a stag one of their uncles had killed during a recent hunting trip. The antlers represented fertility. The coven members would never have killed just for the sake of a ritual, but since the uncle was already a hunter. . . . When the head was only skull and antlers, they roasted venison and feasted. Even Beth partook, as a way of saying thank you to this being for giving its life.

But then Kyle started getting weird. He got his septum pierced and his ears gauged, which wasn't the problem. The problem was he started crafting his own spells involving small animals, rodents and snakes and even, according to his book of shadows, which one of the Sisters found, a house cat and a dog. He was trapping the animals but not killing them. He was stealing the pets from his neighbors. He was dissecting them alive. Removing organs, pineal glands. The Sisters cast him out of the coven in a unanimous vote and reported him to a campus councilor. Somehow the story got out and there was an op-ed in the paper: "Wicca in Missoula: What Should We Do About It?" But no one cared. The op-ed prompted not even one letter to the editor.

After Kyle Beth dated three more women: Shawna, Jessie, Marla again, with silver hair above, no hair below. That third time they dated, Marla became the second person to make Beth come.

How Beth had found so many partners organically she'd never know, but doing so *had* taken a lot of her time, so she figured she'd go the simple route now.

She had Melanie take a few new pictures of her, but mostly she used ones she already had on Facebook.

BETH'S OKCUPID PROFILE

Username: spiritgirlMT
Bisexual, Woman, Single, 5' 6", Thin
White, Speaks English, Some Latin, Other (but it's not important),
Attends college
Never smokes, Drinks socially, Sometimes does drugs, Vegetarian,
Doesn't have kids but might want them, Gemini

My self-summary

Hi! I'm not really sure what to put here. I'm a fun, outgoing person, up for trying new things. (After reading some other profiles on here, I guess I'm also unoriginal. Also, self-deprecating.) I'm looking for a sort of casual relationship/friendship. I want to meet new people and through those people grow. I'm a Wiccan, which means I practice magick, but I'm not particularly concerned with finding other Wiccans (there aren't many in Missoula anyway). And don't worry, I don't talk about spells or goddesses or whatever all the time; but if my religion does weird you out, move along I guess. Feminist, which the above applies to as well: if you don't like it, move along.

What I'm doing with my life

I'm currently in my third year of college. Majoring in literature and creative writing. Minoring in Latin Studies. Sometime's I work at a coffee shop, but not often. Yay, scholarships!

I'm really good at
Love spells? Kissing? Definitely giving massages. Playing the pan flute. Math (even though I don't enjoy it). Making great French press or pourover coffee.

Favorite books, movies, shows, music, and food
Bell Witch, Mother Mother, Hedwig and the Angry Inch, Amanda Palmer, Kendrick Lamar, Bob Dylan, EDM, Deadmau5, Nirvana, Lana Del Rey, Glitch Mob, The Breakfast Club soundtrack (I've never seen the movie, though), Pulp Fiction, Shakespeare in Love, (I don't know. I don't watch a lot of movies.), Orange is the New Black (I don't watch a lot of TV, either, but I watch this one with my roommates and it's great), Neil Gaiman, any of the Beats, Joseph Conrad, Allison Bechdel, Joan Didion, Ernest Hemingway, Allison Monroe, Mary Karr, Jean M. Auel, just about anything you can think of really, my favorite novel is Song of Solomon but my favorite genre is urban fantasy, coffee, pizza, chocolate (but not chocolate ice cream, which sucks, although other ice cream flavors are pretty much all great, seriously, all of them but chocolate)

The six things I could never do without
Besides the obvious, I don't have an answer to this. I strive for minimalism, and a sort of non-attachment I guess. But there are definitely things that greatly enrich my life: dancing, sex, friendship, reading, coffee, that new canned wine (although you should know I don't drink like *a ton*, and I only just started drinking, like I never once drank underage).

I spend a lot of time thinking about
What happens after death. Are my parents at peace? Where do wishes go? The Beats. Whether Burroughs killed Vollmer on purpose, and if it was an accident, what kind of person does that make him?

On a typical Friday night I am
Drinking with my roommates or reading a book or dancing in the woods.

You should message me if
You're awesome. I guess I have high standards. ;)

After a day she changed her sexual orientation (on the profile, not in real life) from bisexual to straight. It turned out when men saw *bisexual* they thought they'd found their threesome's illusive unicorn. Beth wasn't Opposed to threesomes—in fact she fantasized about them often—but it wasn't what she was looking for *right now*.

She answered the various profile questions, was baffled by some of the multiple-choice ones: Are you more horny or more lonely? (Weren't those often the same thing?) How often would you and your significant other have sex? (Well that was fifty percent up to them.) If you don't do anything at all for an entire day, how does that make you feel? (Um, if you didn't do anything for an entire day, didn't that make you dead?) On average, which best describes how often you GET WICKED DRUNK? (What was with the all-caps there? At the very least GET should be lowercase, yes?) Which word describes you better: carefree or intense? (Could a person not be both?) Are you a cat person or a dog person? (Either one of those sounded scary in a literal sense.) Would the idea of a quiet evening reading books ever appeal to you? (Did people exist for whom that *didn't* appeal—if so, Beth didn't want to know them.)

But supposedly there was an algorithm at work. Supposedly, if you answered the questions, answered them *honestly*, a piece of software on a server would find you your perfect match.

And find a match it did—*fast*.

His name was Ric. No *K*. They were an 86-percent match, according to the algorithm. She did not "like" him within the application; he found her profile first. He sent the initial message. It said: *Hi*.

Melanie told Beth you weren't to engage with guys who opened a message thread with "Hi", and Jessica concurred, said she'd never met anyone that way but fuckboys, certainly not real men, but in developing her own policy Beth decided she *would* respond to those messages. To not respond seemed unfair: "Hi" was how people greeted each other in real life—at bars, for example. Pickup lines were oft maligned. How else was a man to approach a woman if not "Hi"?

So she responded. She responded with: *Hi*.

Because here was the method to Beth's madness: she'd decided that if the man said only "Hi", she she would say only "Hi", placing back on him the onus of continuing the conversation, of being interesting.

For several hours Ric did not respond. Beth forgot about him. She put her phone on silent and retreated to her bedroom, opened her laptop and continued working on a paper about Emerson's journals which she'd started yesterday and which counted for one-third of her grade in American Classics. Emerson had said a weed was a plant whose virtues had not yet been discovered, and Beth liked that, and she used that in her paper to talk about dandelions and dandelion salad and dandelion root tea. And then dandelion wine, which brought her to Bradbury, and then her paper was coming together, and she knew she had the grade locked in.

She finished the paper's first draft, saved it, backed it up to Dropbox, which she'd never heard of until a professor in his syllabus required its use, said never again would he hear from a student the excuse of hard drive failure, never again, dammit. Beth checked her phone and there was another message. Received just now.

It said: *I'm Ric.*

At this point Beth tapped Ric's username and scanned his profile. It was bare. There was nothing in the **My self-summary** or the **I'm really good at** or any of the other sections. But he'd answered questions and their match percentage was high. And he had three photos, two close-ups of his face—sharp cheeks, shaved head, one ear gauged, the other unblemished—and one mid-distance shot—tank top, tight arms, tattoos.

What the hell. She'd bounce the ball in his direction one more time.

I'm Beth.

Would he catch that? Would he throw it back, or would he step up for a proper conversation?

Three minutes later: *Hi Beth. Who's your favorite Beat writer.*

Beth: *Burroughs. Naked Lunch fascinates me.*

Ric: *No doubt. I like the way its structured. You know Burroughs said it could be read in any order. You ever tried that?*

Beth: *No, have you?*

Ric: *Yeah. I've read it three times. Forwards, backwards, and then I bought a second copy and tore the pages out and threw them, picked them up and read them in the order they'd fallen.*

Beth: *Huh. Wow. That's hardcore.*

Ric: *It's not hardcore. But it was cool. You ever read Edgar Rice Burroughs?*

Beth had to Google the name. Then she typed into the messenger: *Tarzan guy? No. Is it similar to William S. Burroughs?*

Ric: *Haha. Not at all. It's actually pretty racist.*

Beth: *Oh. Haha.*

Ric: *So do you want to come over?*

Beth didn't answer right away. She set her phone down and stared at the screen. Come over? She'd been lead to believe a customary online first-date was coffee. Although in the three days she'd been using the app no one had asked her for coffee. She'd had several conversations that had fizzled. She'd been sent two dick pics, one tiny, one grotesquely bent. But no invitation for coffee. And no invitations to come over. She thought about asking Melanie and Jessica what *they* would do. They were downstairs watching *Supernatural* reruns on TBS. She could go down and ask them.

 Instead she asked Ric: *Isn't coffee more appropriate?*

Five minutes later he responded: *I don't do coffee dates. I'm a busy man. I don't have time for coffee dates. If you don't want to come over, I understand. But that's my offer. Accept it or don't.*

Beth put the phone aside. She retrieved a textbook from her bag and lay down on her bed. She fell asleep instantly.

When she woke, the book was on her chest, unopened. She looked at her clock. It was early evening. She'd been asleep maybe fifteen minutes.

She retrieved her phone from her desk, started to type: *N—*

She deleted the letter. She wondered whether the girls downstairs could feel her hesitation, whether it permeated the walls of the house.

She typed again: *Now?*

She hit send.

No answer.

No answer.

No answer.

And then: *Now works.*

He sent her his address. She almost typed *I'll see you soon* but didn't; she wanted the last message to be his. Because when you texted the opposite sex, unlike when you talked to them in person, you wanted the last word to be theirs. You wanted to leave a thread unpulled.

So instead she dressed. She'd been wearing the same sweat pants and Public Enemy t-shirt for two days, hadn't left the house. Now she put on black jeans. Black eyeliner. She didn't change the t-shirt, just put on deodorant. Her legs were a week unshaved, her armpits two weeks, but these weren't things that concerned Beth, even if deep down she wondered about them a little now: lesbians after all didn't tend to care about body hair, but would a man? The Montana autumn was chilly, so she put on her black longcoat. It was a man's longcoat; she'd found it at a thriftshop. She crept down the stairs—she could hear Sam and Dean arguing on the television in the living room—slipped on her sandals, and shut self-consciously the front door behind her.

The address Ric gave her wasn't far. She could walk it in twenty minutes, fifteen if she hurried. But should she hurry? That was a question.

Would she appear desperate if she hurried? Would she appear desperate if she made the walk from her brick house in the university district to Ric's downtown apartment (for it couldn't be anything but an apartment if it were downtown, and it *was* downtown, on Higgins) in fifteen minutes? In ten minutes? Oh, but how silly this line of thought was. Beth smiled despite herself. She'd spent at least ten minutes getting ready, and Ric had no idea where she lived. For all he knew she too lived downtown. For all he knew she had a car. It didn't matter how fast she got there. Hell, part of her—call it her sense of self-preservation, misinformed or not—was still saying she shouldn't go there at all.

But here she was, walking. Her feet were moving. One black sandal in front of the other. The large losoe metal buckles on the sandals clinking with each step. *Clink clink. Clink clink.* She should have worn different sandals.

Past the Roxy Theater. Past the smoke shop. Past everyone's favorite ice cream stand (voted one of the top ten in the country). Past the Asian restaurant and the Italian restaurant and the breakfast place. Past the bookstore on the corner. Past the bakery. Over the Higgins bridge, over the Clark Fork, the eponymous river of *A River Runs Through It* (Beth hadn't read the book or seen the film). Past the Wilma theater (*two* indie theaters in Missoula!). Past the stationary store, the candy store, the rug merchant. And then this, here, is where the apartment was supposed to be.

Beth opened the app on her phone, double-checked the address. Checked the address of the rug merchant, the address of the Mexican restaurant next to it. Yes, this was where she was supposed to be. Between the two establishments was a door she'd never noticed in all her years of walking up and down this street. Above it in white block letters was the number from Ric's message. Beth turned the knob, expecting for some unvoicable reason the door to be locked; it wasn't. Inside, to the left, was a set of mailboxes. Next to each mailbox was an intercom button. She found the one for apartment six, depressed it. The speaker at the end of the row of mailboxes didn't make a sound at first, not even a crinkle of static or an I'm-listening-to-you hum. But then, a deep voice, clearer than a voice on an intercom had any right to be, clearer than a voice on a cell phone, clearer, maybe, than the voice of a person standing in your very presence, said, "Yes?"

"Um . . . it's . . . me," Beth said. "It's Beth. Levitt."

"Come up."

Beth winced. She'd given her last name. You weren't supposed to give your last name.

He'd said come up, and for a second she was confused. She spun and there behind her were two sets of stairs, one going up, one going down. She hadn't, somehow, noticed them when she'd come in. The stairs going down dissolved into basement darkness, their end unknowable. Beth took the ones going up, like he'd said to; they were lit, not bright, but not dim either, and the source was unapparent.

Up top, a hallway. Past one door— number four. Past another—number five. Finally—how long *was* this hallway— number six. Beth knocked.

The door opened. "Ric, I presume," Beth said, for lack of any better words. The man before her was wearing the same shirt as in his profile photo, the black tank-top that showed his round tattooed shoulders, his strong tattooed arms, each somehow rounder and larger and stronger and more firm than in the photo on her phone's three-and-a-half-inch screen. The shirt was tight. His chest was powerful. And despite it all one couldn't say he was anything but lean.

"You got here fast," he said. "Come in."

There was little conversation. He offered her a drink. She said sure. He went into the kitchen and she remembered the warnings she'd read in the campus safety handbook (which had grown considerably larger in a revised edition this semester after last year a bestselling tell-all book was published, naming the city the college rape capital of America). Oh, goddess, what was Beth doing here?

She followed him into the kitchen, determined not to drink anything he gave her unless. . . . But no, it was all right. Look, he was uncorking the wine bottle himself. He twisted the corkscrew and then set it aside. The cork gave a satisfying *pop* as he pulled. He poured two glasses of the red. They clinked them together wordlessly, a silent toast.

Beth followed him back into the living room. He gestured for her to sit on the livid microfiber couch. She did, at one end. He sat at the other.

"So . . ." Beth said.

He took a sip of his wine. He smacked his lips in a not-impolite way. He smiled in a manner that was not unkind. His eyes were not unkind. His eyes were the bluest she'd ever seen. Or were they black?

"This is a nice place," Beth said. "I didn't realize there were apartments up here."

"Thank you," he replied. "I bought this place . . . some time ago."

"You mean you don't rent?"

"No."

"So what do you do?"

"Entrepreneur," he said. "I help people. Personal growth sort of thing."

"That's cool," she said. "There . . . must be a lot of money in it."

"There isn't. But I derive a great deal of satisfaction from my work."

Beth took a sip of her wine, nodding. Surely this had been a bad idea. Surely this would be Beth's last night alive—in the morning they'd find her body in the river or in an alley. Or they wouldn't find her at all. There'd be no body left. Who knows what this stranger in front of her might do with it.

But these thoughts—these perfectly rational fears—did not make Beth want to leave. On the contrary, they kept her rooted, kept her strong, like a tree that had been planted just now in this surprisingly clean, bright, well-appointed apartment, a young tree, a limber tree. "Are those books in Latin?" Beth asked, noticing the titles on the shelf against the wall.

"Indeed they are," he said. "I studied Latin long ago. I read them from time to time."

"I have some books in Latin too. I studied Latin too. Still study it, I mean. It's my minor."

"I'm unsurprised," he said.

"Oh." She didn't gulp, not exactly. "Why?"

"It said so on your profile."

Beth laughed. Any tension she'd been holding dropped away. "*Oh*. Oh, yeah. I guess it did. Haha. Haha."

Ric kissed her then. When had he gotten close enough? One second he'd been on the far side of the couch and the next . . . . Beth melted into the kiss, kissed him back. He tasted like the wine. Smelled like something she'd never been this close to before.

They made out on the couch for a while, their half-full glasses of wine on the sparse low coffee table. After some time—impossible to say how long, for the kissing had been more intoxicating than the wine—he put his hand inside her shirt from below, ran it up her stomach. His hand was strong, but not rough. Not the way she'd always imagined a man's hands would be. It was like a woman's hand, but tougher, more sinewy. He

74

"Good morning," he said, when he saw her eyes were open.

"Do you want to go again?" she said.

He laughed. "I'm afraid I have a very busy day. Let's make you some breakfast."

He made her waffles. She hadn't noticed the waffle iron on the kitchen counter the night before, but it was there now. She ate them. He sat with her, a plate in front of himself—only a long time later would it occur to her, in a random memory, that he hadn't eaten anything. After breakfast he saw her to the door. He kissed her lightly on her lips.

"Thank you," she said. "Really."

"You're welcome, Beth," he said.

"No, but I really mean it this time. After last night, I don't think I'm ever going to be satisfied again."

"I know," he said. "I'm sorry." He laughed, but there was something . . . sad? . . . there.

Beth knew she was never going to see Ric again. She wasn't *naive*. She knew this hadn't been a more-than-one-night thing. She spent the next few days at the house, rewriting the Emerson paper, leaving only to attend class. When her roommates asked her where she'd gone that night, she said she'd had a date. They knew what that meant. They asked for details but for some reason Beth didn't want to give them, told them only that it was "really really good." A couple nights later she opened OkCupid to reread her conversation with Ric—for nostalgia's sake—but it was gone. In its place, a message that said *This user has deleted their account.*

When, the next weekend, Beth finally ventured downtown again, she found she couldn't remember where the door to his apartment had been. She thought it was between the Mexican restaurant and the rug merchant, but there was nothing there.

Only a brick wall. No door, no blocky white numbers. Had it been the next block over, by the coffee shop and the yoga studio?

Or the optician's office?

Or the other yoga studio?

Or somewhere on the other side of the street?

2

THREE WEEKS PASSED, MAYBE FOUR, before Beth went on another OkCupid date. She got drinks with a guy whose name she soon forgot but whose long red hair and untamed red beard and pungent personal odor she likely never would. He was nice enough. The date lasted an hour—two polite drinks—and she never saw him again. She received many pings from men— sometimes a dozen a day. Most were from men with whom she hadn't matched—and their match percentage was below 80 percent, sometimes far below, and Melanie had told her at the beginning that as a general rule, even if you're looking only for hookups, you shouldn't engage with people below 80 percent— and their salutary messages were variations of *Hi* or *You're cute*. And even though this was how Ric had messaged her, she felt uncompelled to answer these other men. One guy did say *What are you up to?*, and she responded with *Studying. You?*, and then he sent her a picture of his underwhelming penis, semi-flaccid, leaking semen. Two other men sent her dick pics as well. "Only five dick pics so far?" Jessica said after Beth had been on the site for a month and a half. "Consider yourself lucky." Then Jessica showed her how to set the application to filter messages from users below a certain match percentage, or users whose message or profiles contained certain words, or—and yes, Beth did use this feature—certain attractiveness levels, although this one wasn't so effective, since even very large men, even obese men, tended to label themselves as having just "a little extra". And when she used these filters the amount of messages she received dwindled drastically.

Too drastically. Beth decided, if she was going to keep using this thing—and honestly, her enthusiasm for it was dwindling, she should just start going to bars like people used to, start picking up women again—she'd need to be the one to take action.

So, with a certain half-hearted energy, she messaged a not-unattractive young man with the username Tech_Lover_1992.

Tech_Lover_1992 responded almost immediately. He and Beth chatted for a few hours, revealing little about themselves but relating to each other via the coincidence of a few shared interests, and at 1 AM, just as Beth's need to go to bed was becoming more urgent than her desire to talk with this semi-interesting stranger on the internet, he suggested they meet in person. *Coffee?*

Coffee would be perfect, Beth typed. *Tomorrow?*

Tomorrow's no good. I have a thing. Friday?

Friday works for me.

Awesome. Here's my number. My name's John.

Hi, John. I'm Beth. Here's mine.

And so in the way strangers on the internet sometimes do, they met for coffee on Friday. Beth walked down Higgins dressed in her usual sort of attire—although with a gray scarf pulling the look together—past the ice cream place and the candy shop and the rug merchant (still no door—where *had* that fucking apartment been?)—and saw John outside the coffee shop, reading on his cell phone (sci-fi, he'd tell her, nothing particularly good, but fun, diverting). When she said "John?" he looked up at her and stood and put his phone away. He was dressed in flannel and denim, like most Montana men. He had a beard that wasn't present in his profile photos; it was either new and not fully in yet or just grew that way. He was . . . shorter than she expected. But just a little. He hugged her and she was surprised but hugged him back. "Let me buy you a coffee," he said.

Already this date was more human than any she'd been on in her entire life.

They talked books. They talked philosophy. They talked school. They *talked*, and it was interesting. He was a student at the university, a senior, a year above her. He was majoring in new media journalism. He wrote for the student paper. He'd also had articles published in the Missoulian. Tech reviews. A couple movie reviews (*Transformers: Age of Extinction, G.I. Joe: Retaliation*). He'd been circulated as far as Billings and Coeur d'Alene. "I guess you could call me a regular contributor."

Look, Beth thought, here was *another writer*! His predilections weren't the same as hers, his aspirations not literary, but aspirations they were.

He told her how he'd come to Montana. How he'd left the Republican Midwest in a moment of unfettered frustration with a broken system. "I guess it wasn't really a *moment*," he said. "It had been building in me for a long time. All through high school I was enraged by bigotry and religiosity. You know that transgender bathroom stuff? One of those was us, my school. It was ridiculous. I didn't know the kid but I'd seen him—her— and I never would have known she was a man. Or . . . you know what I mean."

Sure. She knew what he meant.

"So, yeah, after graduation I surprised my parents by telling them I was coming to school here. They were surprised, a little upset—my dad thought I'd be around to keep helping with his towing business—but Montana, right? A red state. That couldn't be so bad. But then they learned more about Missoula. And, oh no, it's a liberal place. How awful! I told them it was the way the whole world was going, evolving, and they'd have to get used to it. Still tell them that, when I talk to them."

So he didn't talk to them often?

"No, not really. I guess you could say the relationship is strained. I posted pictures on Instagram of myself at the pride rally here a couple years ago, and ever since my mom has been convinced I might be gay, that I'm just not telling her. Says I could tell her if I was—I'm not, by the way—but yeah, like that wouldn't destroy anything that was left between us." Beth never would learn that the story John told her on that first date was far from the whole truth of his parental relations, that some of it was only a warped version of truth, that some of it was pure fiction.

Beth told him she didn't have a relationship with her parents either, only it was because hers were dead.

"Oh. Oh, shit. I'm sorry."

"It's okay. I'm just saying I guess I kind of know how you feel. Kind of."

"No. No no no. I'm an idiot. I'm just whining and you don't even *have* parents."

She put a hand on his arm. She was liking him. "Really, it's okay."

They talked for a few more minutes. They drank their coffees. Then, his beverage still a third full, he told her he had to go. He said he had a friend's birthday party to go to, could he call her later?

"You don't have my phone number," she said.

He reminded her they'd exchanged numbers the night before.

"Oh, yeah," she said, embarrassed.

Months later, he'd reveal to her that, while there had indeed been a birthday party that night, it wasn't for a friend. John didn't have many friends, not in this city, hadn't been able to grow close to anybody these last few years, because the cut he'd made by leaving his hometown had never quite been cauterized —should have made it with a lightsaber, he'd joke. The birthday party was just for someone he kind of knew, someone from a class. He'd had been lucky to have even been invited. And it had started hours later, that birthday party; there was no need for him to leave the coffee date so abruptly. He'd ended the date, he would later tell her, because he sensed there was a chance it was going well, and he didn't want to stay because every minute the date continued was another minute he might fuck it up. He would also tell her, months later, that he'd received a blowjob at the birthday party, from a girl whose name he didn't know but who he'd seen around campus. When he would tell her this, the confession would be laced with extreme guilt, profound shame. But it's okay, really it's okay, Beth would tell him. You can't cheat on someone after just one date. That's impossible. And as long as you're honest, you can never cheat at all.

Beth stood when John stood. He hugged her again, but this hug felt more appropriate than the one at the beginning of the date, more welcome, more earned, more warm; the hug felt the way Beth, as someone whose religion encouraged her to be deeply in tune with all living things, craved for hugs to feel.

John left, placing his coffee mug in a bus tray on his way out. Beth too still had coffee. She sat again, continued drinking. Played on her phone.

She didn't hear from him that weekend. She spent the weekend at home, with the roommates. The roommates asked about the date, and she told she thought it went well. "Do you think it went well?" she asked them. Well they weren't there, were they? So she gave them details, really just a play-by-play of the conversation, and maybe it was just her but they seemed ambivalent. On Sunday the three of them binged the first season of *The X-Files*, which had just been added to Netflix. They watched all 24 episodes.

On Monday afternoon, while she was on campus after a class struggling to open her rusted bike lock, Beth received a text. From John: *You said on Friday you like Shirley Jackson, didn't you?*

I did, she replied, letting the lock, which maybe she'd been making progress on, fall against the bike rack with a clang.

The New Yorker *just published a new story by her. Previously unreleased, I mean. Not "new" new, obviously.*

Oh? That's cool!

Five minutes later they'd agreed to a second date. *Drinks? Tomorrow?*

Drinks. Tomorrow!

Twenty more minutes Beth fiddled with the bike lock. In the end, a campus janitor had to cut it off. A new one would cost her twenty bucks. Better that than having your bike stolen.

The only thing people ever seemed to steal in Missoula were bikes. You could leave your laptop on a table in a coffee shop, but if you didn't lock up your bike you were asking for trouble.

3

THE SECOND DATE STARTED AWKWARDLY, as all second dates do. More awkward than the first because now they were past step one, now there was a concrete chance this might go somewhere, if they didn't screw it up. They met at a distillery, ordered a mango-something and a martini. John had shaved his scruff, giving his face a babyish appearance. By the end of drink one they were talking like they had been at the end of the first date: as familiars, not yet friends. By the end of drink two—Bloody Marys—they were more than friends: they were people who wanted to make out with each other.

They *couldn't* make out with each other, not just yet, and they couldn't vocalize their desires, but they could keep the date going. Not here—two ounces of alcohol served inside a distillery was the limit under Montana law—but somewhere. Turns out sometimes two ounces is a lot: the next few hours were a blur, a memory inside a dream.

Was Beth hungry? Of course she was. Well then let's get food. Let's get dinner. What was she in the mood for? Why didn't he decide? Hesitation. Stuttering. This restaurant, that restaurant. Or, if you don't think this is weird, we could cook at my place. My roommates are out of town, all of them. We don't have a dorm but like an apartment thing over on Orange.

Okay!

What would they cook, though? No food at the apartment. A stove and various pans and an oven, and a variety of seasonings, but no food. A mildly drunken jaunt down to the grocery store, also on Orange. What's on sale? Fish is on sale. And arugula. And let's get some goat cheese for the arugula—it'll be a salad. Olive oil at the house. Balsamic vinegar. All we need for dressing. What kind of fish? Salmon? Tilapia? Red snapper? Tuna steaks? Salmon's always a good choice. Salmon *is* always a good choice, let's get salmon. By the way, can you cook? Me, no, not so much, I mean I can make cereal. Pasta, sometimes. It's okay, we'll look up a recipe. It's salmon, how hard can salmon be? Should we get like some wine? Do *you* want wine? I think so— do *you*? A bottle of red wine. I'll pay for all this. Oh, let me get it. Let's split it? Okay.

Then they were at the apartment. It was dark, lived-in, musky. Four young men lived here. Three of the young men somehow not home. I have my own room. Greg has his own room. Carl has his own room. Ivan sleeps on the couch, which folds out, but I guess really he's at his girlfriend's most nights anyway; still pays rent, though. Do you have incense? *Incense?* Never mind, let's just open a window. Open the bottle of wine— a screw top, thank God—we don't have a corkscrew. I didn't even think about that—we're more like beer guys here, I guess.

But then the giddiness induced by the mango-something and the Bloody Mary started to wear off. Beth asked if she might use his restroom.

"Of course," he said. "It's down that hallway."

There were five doors in the hallway. The three bedrooms? A

closet? But the bathroom door was the only one that was open; she didn't have to play *What's Behind Door Number X* despite John's vague directions. Beth sat on the toilet. Here she was again. A second apartment, a second man, and she wasn't sure why she'd come. This wasn't like Ric's. Yes, she'd felt uncertainty there, too, but it had been a different kind of uncertainty: at Ric's she hadn't been sure why she'd *wanted* to come, but the wanting was never in doubt. Here, at John's, she wasn't sure there was a wanting. At the distillery her desire to press her lips to his had been undeniable. Was it still present now? She didn't think so. But she *was* here. She stood. She flushed. She looked at herself in the mirror. The mirror was flecked with spots of water and dried toothpaste. Closely Beth stared into her own eyes. Who was she? All her life she'd known who she was. Even if at different times—before her parents died, after they died, after moving to Missoula and starting college—she'd been different people, she always knew who that person was, could identify that person. But now? Now, here, in this this nice young man's bathroom . . . . Could this really be the moment she was going to lose herself? It didn't make sense.

"Who are you?" she whispered.

The figure in the mirror almost whispered back, but turned on the faucet.

Of course she wanted to be here with John. Of course she did. He was lovely. How could she even have doubted it?

She turned to rejoin him.

He was waiting for her with two glasses of wine. He handed her one.

"Thank you," she said. She took a sip.

"Is it any good?"

"I have no idea."

And together they laughed. Another sip. Another. The gradual return of the evening's earlier tipsiness. Once again a dream within a memory.

Frying pan on the stove. Season the tilapia. Oh shit, I thought we bought salmon. Oh, shit, me too. Ooops. I guess we can just find another recipe. Laugh about the mishap for several minutes, together. Find another recipe—almost identical to the salmon one. Fish, it seems, is fish. Oil in the pan. Seasoning on the tilapia. Already did that. It'll just be a little over-seasoned, a little salty. High heat? Low heat? Medium heat. Make the salad, which means just put feta on the salad. Oil, vinegar, toss it a bit. Salmon—*tilapia!*—not quite ready. More wine? Please. How's school going? Good. Really good. You? Good, I guess. Good. Oh, look, I think it's finished. Hmmm, sure, let's call that ready. Plates? Paper okay? Definitely. Sit at table. Cheers. Cheers.

After dinner they made out. John asked if he could kiss her, which was the opposite of what anyone who had ever kissed her seriously had done—most people just leaned in, went for it, maybe grabbed the nape of her hair—but she said yes, and so he kissed her. First just in the middle of the kitchen. Then against the kitchen counter. Then he realized he'd left the stove on and they had to pause for a second while he turned it off. And then he asked if she wanted to go to his bedroom.

"Um, actually—" she said. "Actually—let's take this slow. Can we take this slow?"

She'd surprised him, she could tell. Hurt him maybe. "Of course," he said. "No, yeah—of course."

"I'm sorry. I didn't mean to lead you on or—"

"No, no. It's okay. Really. I understand."

"Okay. You're sure?"

"Totally."

"Okay." Now what? "So maybe I should get going . . ."

"Yeah, okay."

"Do you want help with the dishes?"

"Hey, no, no—I got it."

"Okay."

"Okay."

Beth retrieved her purse, which she'd slung over the back of a chair when she'd arrived. At the front door she paused. "Hey," she said, "I enjoyed this. I really enjoyed this. Text me again, okay? Or call me."

"Okay," he said.

She moved to hug him, realized that was ridiculous, kissed him on the cheek instead. "See you soon," she said.

"See you soon."

"Dinner was lovely."

Beth walked home, stone-cold sober.

After last night, I don't think I'm ever going to be satisfied again.

I know. I'm sorry.

4

POOR JOHN. HE'D PROBABLY NEVER call her. She'd spurned him, wounded him, and she didn't even know why.

The next day Beth decided to send him a text. To preemptively schedule date number three before he could decide they had no future. But instead of typing her message on the screen she called him instead.

She listened to the phone ring against her ear. Once. Twice. Three times.

"Hello?"

"Hi, John?"

"Yeah. Yeah!"

"Hi. I just wanted to say thanks again for cooking me dinner."

"I mean, you did most of the cooking."

"Well, we cooked together, didn't we?"

"Yeah, I guess we did."

"So, hey, listen. Do you want to see a movie on Friday?"

"A movie? With you? Yes, of course!"

"Okay. Great."

"What movie?"

She hadn't considered that. "Um, any movie."

"Yeah, okay."

"Cool."

"Cool."

"Great!"

"So I'll . . . uh . . . I'll see what's playing, and then I'll text you. And we'll go to the movies."

"Perfect. See you then."

"See you then."

At a movie you didn't have to talk, weren't *allowed* to talk, lest you disturb your neighbors. But you could, if you put your coat over his lap and were sure to keep your movements contained, discreet, give your date a handjob. Beth began to give John a handjob underneath her trench coat once it became clear the movie wasn't very good. She hadn't planned to, although she had decided she'd be doing something for John tonight, something to make up for the way she'd inexplicably treated him at the end of the last date. After all, she did want him. She'd decided it: she wanted John. She liked him. He was a good person, had made sacrifices for certain of his ideals, was making things, putting things together, had set his life on a path, a path that was more clearly defined than the one she was one, even if by his own admission he didn't know what direction the path was going. His path had borders. Edges. John had edges. She could see that now. After meditating on it she could see it. Somehow she'd missed it at first, but the edges were there, and they were dark and she could appreciate their darkness.

As she gave him the handjob under the trench coat in the dark theater, she marveled that this was only the second penis with which she'd interacted. She wished suddenly that she could see it, but of course she couldn't, not here in the theater with a bad action movie threatening to cast explosive light on them without notice. But she did see his face, or most of it, and when it began to contort she stopped her stroking and removed her hand from beneath the trench coat and patted him playfully on the knee. No reason to make a mess in the theater.

After the movie they went back to her place. John mumbled a shy "Hello" to Melanie, who frowned inexplicably at Beth as they went up the stairs. In her room Beth picked up where they'd left off three days ago at his apartment. She kissed him, ran her hands through his hair, massaged his scalp. She removed his pants, used her mouth, emulating what she'd seen in online porn, using only the techniques that had looked like they would feel good but would also be fun to administer. And, in time, he came into her mouth, and for a fleeting moment, just before she swallowed, she felt the thrill of doing something dirty. But then it was gone. John insisted on returning the favor, said it was one of his favorite things to do, but after twenty minutes she smiled down at him and said it felt great but she was getting tired.

Okay, he said, wiping his chin. They fell asleep in her twin bed. Beth was the little spoon.

5

LOOKING BACK, SHE'D NEVER BE able to remember the date of the first time they had actual penetrative sex. The weeks after that first one melted together into their own indefinable history. Beth and John. John and Beth. It happened in the middle of the night: she woke from a dream, a nightmare the details of which she could not remember, only that it involved, maybe, her parents, their car, and a demon that was haunting them, or haunting her, or both, or there were two demons and the demons were her parents and they were following her through life, tormenting her, telling her again and again that her wants and needs and desires could never be fulfilled, they were debauched immoral, or, worse, amoral—we were Christians, Beth, we loved you and we were Christians and now you're some kind of Satan worshiper, some kind of Harlot, some kind of Babylonian courtesan, fucking women and incubi and who knows what else, we're so disappointed, we're dead and we're so disappointed. That might have been the dream—it was one she had often. Or in the dream that night there might have been just one demon, and that demon was her, Beth Levitt, there was no incubus, for there was only Beth, and she preyed on . . . who? . . . her parents, her dead parents, everyone. *That* might have been the dream; *that* was one she had often too. If only she could master lucidity, control the dream, manifest it under her own power, destroy that which haunted her. . . . She'd tried to learn. There were spells, her coven's High Priest said. There were herbs. So that night she'd had a dream, and she'd woken from it, and her heart racing or her breath was racing, and deep inside her, forcing its way to the surface, through her skin, through her skin's pores, was a creature called Ignominy. Oh, but there was John, sleeping. And what Beth could do, wanted more than anything to do just then, was to climb on top of him. So she climbed on top of him, started kissing him, his mouth, his hairless chest, its subtle concavity (pectus excavatum, it was called—his was a mild case), his stomach, his stomach where the hair did start. Back to his lips, and he woke then, stirred. Is this okay? she asked him. First he said nothing and then he said yes, hell yes. So she summited him. She slid into herself the length of him. How long she stayed there who knows? Five minutes. Ten. One. He mumbled something about a condom, shouldn't they use a condom. *Of course*, she said. How stupid of her, she thought. When he'd girded himself she let him take control, if you could call it control. And then, when he was finished, she was asleep again.

But *when* had that happened? She could never remember. That first night they'd slept in her bed? A week later? Surely no more than a week later. One day, a few months before they were to marry, when their sex life had begun to include things like light bondage, occasional choking and slapping, she asked him, "Do you remember when we first fucked?"

"Of course I remember. I'd never come so hard before. I didn't say it then, but I mean I'm pretty sure that's when I knew I wanted to be with you forever."

"Yeah, but when was it? Like how many days . . . how long had we been dating."

"I don't—" John looked up from his phone. "I guess I don't know."

"Yeah," she said. "Me either."

"But I love you. I know that."

"I love you too."

And Beth did love John. But how odd that they could not remember.

6

THEY NEVER HAD "THE TALK", the one where a new but not brand new couple discusses where is this heading, what are we, what does this mean. What do you want. What do I want. A month after their first date Beth and John were walking on a Saturday night across the Orange Street Bridge, having just met members of her Capstone Project for drinks at the Golden Rose Bar, a place always washed in either too much light or not enough, viscid floors and glutinous tabletops, cheap liquor, dirty ice, one-dollar PBRs between the hours of 8 PM and midnight. As they walked, John took Beth's hand. "Are you dating anyone else?" she asked suddenly.

They stopped walking. Who stopped first? "Of course not," he said. "No—why would you think that?"

"Oh, no. No no no I didn't think that. I was just asking."

"Well I'm not." He paused, hesitated. "I love you, Beth."

That was the first time he said it. Those three words. When had this happened? she wondered. Somewhere she'd lost control. She missed the tenderness of a woman's lips.

And after that they were together, boyfriend and girlfriend, college sweethearts, you could say (although no one did), if such a phrase didn't make you want to throw up in your mouth a little, like a couple years ago it might have made Beth.

Beth had held a man's hand only once, and that man had been a boy: Richard Dickinson, in high school, who had asked her to prom and to whom she had said yes because he was sweet and kind and his parents hadn't been able to afford braces so his top front teeth stuck out over the bottom ones, which were slanted inward and the bottom of the top ones pressed against the part where the bottom ones met the gums, giving his smile a dorky, embarrassed flavor, forcing his chin to jut forward with its three or five wiry hairs . . . . No else would go out with Richard Dickinson if she said no, would they? Maybe they would but she couldn't take the chance, couldn't be the one to leave a nice young man behind, and his *name*—his parents had named him Dick Dickinson and hadn't even bought him braces—so she went to prom with him, let him pick her up at her grandma's house in his father's Subaru, her grandma taking pictures with a polaroid she miraculously still had ("Grandma, let's get you a digital camera—they don't even make *film* for these things any more—this company went out of business like three years ago."); she let him drive her to the high school, dance with her in the gymnasium under epileptic lights and a papier mache disco ball, hold her hand as they walked back to the car a few hours later, lean in and press his lips to hers in front of her grandma's front door . . . except she'd turned and given him her cheek instead.

But now she was halfway through her junior year of college, had kissed five boys (two of them, at two separate parties, whose names she never learned), had had her brains fucked out by Ric, who'd maybe never existed, and was now in the habit of holding John Hempel's hand on the regular, like every day, because every day she was seeing him, meeting him for lunch or watching TV with him in the living room of the house she lived in but wasn't really hers, or watching TV with him in the living room of his own apartment.

For months she seemed to live at his place, even though it was an extra twenty minutes walk to campus, an extra ten minutes via bicycle. It was just that John's roommates were home far less than hers; they had privacy at his apartment; at his apartment they had space. At his apartment they could fuck on the couch; John could bend her over the back of the couch and take her from behind in a way she discovered felt better, far better, than any other way he fucked her—was he going deeper? was she more open, more accessible? did his confidence benefit from not having to see her face? Oh, goddess, was it that last one? But, no, because even when she wasn't bent over the back of the couch, when his roommates *were* home and they had to quietly make love in John's room—not fuck—it was always only getting better. More satisfying every time, it was. Like with each thrust their compatibility was growing. And when John's roommates *were* home, they welcomed her, shared their beer and their weed, were quiet if she needed to study or—and she'd been doing this less lately—meditate, pray. Not like *her* roommates, who when John was around seemed chilly, resentful, or if Beth didn't know better, jealous. "They don't like me," John said. And Beth replied, "Oh, of course they do. Don't be silly," but honestly she wasn't sure. Honestly she didn't think they did. Honestly she wondered if it was her they no longer liked. But then John's roommate with the TV—and as kind as he was, as generous with his things and his alcohol and even his weed—moved out, so if they wanted to watch television they had to do it at her place, so they gradually stopped watching television. In the whole of the rest of their relationship they would never own one.

I hear you've been hiding someone from me, Beth received via text one day in sub-zero February. The text was from her best friend, Rebekah Fleckman. Rebekah Fleckman, her best friend who she barely kept in touch with anymore. Her best friend who in high school she'd secretly loved, whose naked body she'd always wanted to see, but Rebekah was too self-conscious to reveal her body, even to other women, especially to other women ("It's different with a guy. They're not going to judge as long as they get to fuck me"). Her best friend who she saw maybe once a semester now that they went to different schools, 200 miles apart.

I haven't been *hiding* anyone, Beth typed. *I just forgot to tell you.*

Yeah. I think you forgot to text me altogether.

Hey! You could always text me, you know.

I know. I am. Right now.

Good point.

So what's his name? Rebekah asked. *And what's he look like?*

His name's John, Beth replied. *He's cute. I really like him.*

Well am I going to have to fight him?

Fight him for what?

Space in your bed. My spring break plans got cancelled, and I know you're never doing anything fancy, so I figured I'd come spend a few days in Missoula with my best friend.

Yeah, girl! That sounds great.

Sweet!

And yes, you will have to fight John for space in my bed. He's a little territorial. Like a lion.

I'll bring an air mattress. ;)

Like a lion? What? What sort of thing was that to say.

John was going to love Rebekah, Beth told him. "She's like pretty much the only family I have, besides my grandma."

"I'm excited," John said. "Sounds great!"

But spring break wasn't until April, and it was now only the end of February. So uneventfully the weeks went on. Beth went to class. John went to class. Beth's grades remained high. John's grades remained high. In early March John went to Butte for a weekend to profile for the *Missoulian* the new Chief Executive of Silver Bow County (such a profile wouldn't normally have been written for a county chair, but this guy was notable in that he'd been elected after the previous Chief Executive had died in a well publicized skiing accident just a few miles from Missoula), and while he was gone Beth decided to do some writing of her own, finally putting to paper (or, rather, laptop screen) the first two chapters of a dark urban fantasy novel that had been germinating inside her since the day, at sixteen, she'd finally made peace with her parents' deaths. In mid-March they celebrated John's birthday. He admitted it was the first he'd celebrated since he'd moved across the country. He as a rule didn't tell people when it was, but he couldn't very well keep such vital information from the woman he might some day marry, now could he?

Marry? Did he just say marry?

They were eating carrot cake. Beth had made it. With buttercream frosting (margarine instead of butter—she was trying veganism again). A marble-sized bite of it fell from John's fork when the fork found itself frozen just below his chin, above the fork, above the chin, Beth's own panicked look reflected in and then transferred to John's eyes. "Oh, shit," John said. "Oh, shit, oh fuck—"

"Did you—?" Beth started to ask, unsure whether she should be embarrassed, whether *he* should. Unsure whether she should be terrified.

"Yeah—I said marry. *Fuck*. I didn't mean that. I mean—"

"You didn't mean it?" Beth said, her voice trailing off.

"I mean, I meant it. I meant that maybe someday, y'know, maybe. Like maybe someday, in the future—did you want me to mean it?"

"John, we've been going out for like four months. We're still students."

"No, right. Right, I know. I just meant—like in the future —" John's face was noticeably red. He'd put the fork down on the paper plate. He'd moved the plate from his lap to the floor of his apartment. They were sitting on the floor. The marble-sized piece of carrot cake that had fallen was still stuck to the bottom of his plain one-size-too-big dark-blue henley. "I just meant, like, in the future, maybe."

Was his lip shaking? His bottom lip? Was he going to cry? Was Beth dating a crier and was she okay with that? Of course she was—there was nothing wrong with a man opening himself to his femininity. But if he did actually cry in front of her—if he took it from concept to reality: that might right now be more than Beth could handle.

"It's okay," she said, trying to smile, trying to laugh. "I get it. I totally get it."

"You do?"

"Of course," she said. And then she said, not insincerely, "It *is* there, the possibility. In the future."

John laughed. "Okay," he said. "Okay. Whew. Oh boy." He picked up his cake. "I guess I just shook myself up a little."

Beth laughed with him. "You shook *me* up, you . . . goofball," she said. *Goofball?*

"I just—well I love you, you know?"

"I do," Beth said. "I love you too."

And she knew then that she meant it. Just as she knew then

that nothing in this world is controlled by anything. Nothing is designed or part of a system or makes any sense.

7

WITH APRIL CAME MIDTERMS AND then spring break. And with spring break came Rebekah Fleckman to Missoula for three leisurely days. And it didn't even occur to Beth, during those three days, that there should be anything odd about the fact that John was always present with them. She didn't spend time with her best friend alone, except for at night, when John went back to his apartment; even then Beth encouraged him to stay, felt bad kicking him out, as it were, but he said, "No, really, it's fine. You need your girl time." Girl time being between 1 and 8 am. At 8 am he would join them once again, holding up a paper bag: "I brought bagels!" And Rebekah, spreading cream cheese (with chives) across an everything would say, "Oh, I like *him*. You should keep *him*."

For three days they drank beer. They floated the river. They saw two movies. They wandered the city in a perpetual haze of mild intoxication. Somewhere in there a trinity formed: perhaps it was simply by virtue of the fact that John loved Beth, and Beth loved Rebekah, and thus Beth should love John; and Rebekah loved Beth, and Beth loved John or had at least at this point admired him for John, and thus Rebekah should admire John too. Simple math: the transitive property. The evening of the third day they sat in Beth's house's living room, sharing a joint, Rebekah regaling them with a story about taking too much molly during last year's spring break in Vegas. Beth fell into a soft cannabis-induced sleep for nearly an hour. When she woke, John and Rebekah were still talking; they both looked tired, if not melancholy, and when they saw she was awake she couldn't help but detect a sense of conspiracy between them, but a positive sort of conspiracy, the sort of conspiracy that says we've been talking and now we're friends, we've shared things and now we're friends. Beth insisted John stay at the house that night—it was far too late to walk home.

"I kissed her once," Beth said in the early morning of the next day, after waving goodbye to Rebekah from the porch and watching her car vanish around the bend toward Brooks Street, toward Highway 12, toward Bozeman.

"You *what?*" John said.

"Well, yeah. I mean, it was in high school. You know—she knew I was gay but it wasn't something we'd ever really talked about, me being gay, but then one day we did, and then a few days later she was a little tipsy and kind of curious . . . it didn't really do anything, though. She just giggled and giggled and giggled."

"Wait," John said. "Hold the phone . . ."—that was one of the things John did that Beth was beginning to love: used phrases like *hold the phone*—". . . you being *gay?*"

Oh. Had she not told him? "Did I not tell you that?"

"You most fucking certainly did not."

"Huh."

Oh, right: her online dating profile had said she was straight. She'd changed that because of . . . well, because of men.

"I'm hungry," she said, turning and retreating into the house, which was empty—Melanie was in Cancun and Jessica was visiting her family in Portland.

John followed her. "What the hell, Beth?" she heard him say.

She searched the kitchen cupboards for a coffee mug; for some reason she couldn't find one; they'd all disappeared.

"No, but really . . ." John was still saying. "What the fuck?"

"I mean—I'm not *gay*, obviously. I'm . . . bisexual." *There* was a mug, on the table, the mug she'd been drinking from just a little while ago, before Rebekah had left, when they'd all been sitting, eating bagels, Rebekah an everything, John a cheddar, toasted, Beth a . . . the mug was empty.

"Yeah, well *obviously*. Obviously! I mean, did you just *kiss* women. Did you just *think* you were gay, like in high school—?"

Beth picked up the french press; there was still some coffee in it. She poured it into her mug. "No. No, I've dated women."

"How *many* women?"

Glorious coffee, not hot, but still warm. Warm enough.

"How many, Beth—?"

"Hold on. I'm counting . . ."

"You're count— Oh for fuck's sake. For fuck's sake!"

"John, what—?"

"Do you still like women?"

"What kind of question— Of course I do."

"Great. Just great. So you could just cheat on me with a woman at any time."

"I thought you were all for gay rights. You said you went to Pride, and—"

"I did. I am. But this is different. You're my . . ."

"What?"

"My—"

"I'm your what, John?"

John's voice softened. "My girlfriend."

And inexplicably, Beth was the angry one now. "I'm not *your* anything, John. I don't belong to you."

"Of . . . of course not. You know that's not what I meant—"

"Isn't it? Newsflash, John: even if I weren't gay I could cheat on you whenever I wanted. With a man."

"No, I get that. I'm not saying— Wait, are you saying you want to cheat on me?"

The mug was empty again, and the French press would be no help. She could only lie, say of course that wasn't what she was saying, but Beth could never lie; she could only tell some sort of truth. "I don't know what I want right now."

"You don't?"

"No. Okay?"

"Um . . . yeah, okay. No, okay. I get it."

"I think you should leave, I guess."

"What?"

"Get out of here, John."

And he did. He left her standing in the kitchen with her empty mug.

Later that day she felt stupid.

For much of the day she seethed, even brooded (and brooding had never been a thing Beth Levitt was wont to do). Made another pot of coffee and lay on the couch with a book and tried to read it, tried tried tried to read it but her thoughts wouldn't stay there; she'd will them to anchor themselves to the page and they'd laugh at her, taunt her—did she really expect to stop thinking about John? What an asshole he was. Her whole life Beth had experienced little (no?) persecution for her sexuality, even as a teenager growing up in the conservative, mostly Catholic state capital. But suddenly with her boyfriend it was an issue . . . .

Her *first* boyfriend. She'd never had another. She'd never had a girlfriend either, not in a way that meant a *relationship*. Not in a way that had ever provided the opportunity for the occurrence of a *first fight*.

This is when she began to feel stupid. Maybe she'd been insensitive.

She closed the book, filled a large glass with water from the tap, and retreated to her room upstairs, where for an hour she tried to write another chapter of the urban fantasy novel—she wrote a page, maybe two, didn't like what she'd written—before laying on her bed, able to think only of Ric's words. Not John's, Ric's. Suddenly she felt exhausted.

After last night, I don't think I'm ever going to be satisfied again.
  I know. I'm sorry.

Beth was woken by a strip of moonlight glinting across her eyelids. Or Beth was woken by a loud noise echoing from somewhere in the city, reaching her ears impossibly. Or Beth was woken by the tiniest reverberations of the legs of an ant or a termite or a spider along the baseboard of her student-sized room in the house she shared with two roommates, right now empty, the house, right now dark, right now intimidating and eery and a ghostly presence unto itself, with its own life, its own death. Or Beth was woken by the highest form of sexual climax, vibrating throughout her whole body. One of *those* dreams.

She'd been dreaming of Ric, whose last name she didn't know.

She felt guilty for dreaming of Ric. She felt guilty for the lack of empathy she'd shown toward John and his concerns. When had that been—this morning? yesterday? What time was it and how long had she slept?

She didn't feel stupid anymore, just guilty.

Her phone told her it was just past 11 pm. She could barely see the numbers. She'd fallen asleep with her contacts in. The screen was bright, blurry. Her eyes ached. Her eyes were painfully dry. She dictated to her phone: "Send a message to John Hempel: Hey, I'm really sorry about earlier. I guess I should have told you. Can we talk? Can I come over?"

In Beth's phone's contacts app everyone was listed under their real name. She knew lots of people who used nicknames in their contact list, but she didn't. She wanted to remember everyone's real name. She wanted that connection with people, loved seeing that look in their eye when you've met them only once before but here you are meeting them again and you've remembered their name—that look flattered look, a little guilty because they haven't remembered yours. So everyone was listed in her phone under their real name. Except for Rebekah Fleckman, who in Beth's phone was called "You Go Girl". Because there are some people whose name you'll never forget.

Beth stood in front of the bathroom mirror and peeled laboriously her contacts from her corneas—she peeled first the left eye, then the right. The peeling was almost audible. It was certainly tactile. She squeezed rewetting drops into her eyes before putting her glasses on. She rarely wore these glasses: tortoiseshell, thin frames, small lenses, something a writer might wear or something Daniel Craig might wear in one of his dark, non-James Bond thriller-type movies, where he played the journalist or the detective. Beth liked *The Girl with the Dragon Tattoo*. She recalled now—such a weird time for a recollection—that she hadn't listed that on her online dating profile, under favorite books and movies. Beth liked Lisbeth Salander. She liked Rooney Mara as Lisbeth Salander. She liked her clothes and her hair.

Back in the bedroom her phone's vibrational motor buzzed. Beth knew it had a vibrational motor because John had told her so. He told her that one of the benefits if she were to upgrade her phone to the latest model from her years-old one would be a more efficient, more discreet yet just as perceptible, vibration motor. The new message said: *I guess. When?*

Tonight? Beth typed. The screen was no longer blurry. *In the morning?*

Tonight is fine, John replied almost immediately. *I'd like to talk. I'm sorry too. I shouldn't have reacted the way I did.*

It's okay, Beth sent back. *I understand.*

I guess it's kind of hot, actually...

LOL. Yeah. Maybe we can have a threesome sometime. Typing that was a risk—technically they were still fighting, they hadn't made up yet—but she thought he'd like it.

Haha. Okay. How about with . . . Rebekah?

If only, Beth responded. *She'd get too giggly.*

Haha. Okay.

I'll see you soon.

See you soon. I love you.

Beth put on a black hoodie. This was no longer trench coat weather. The weather hadn't been trench coat weather since early March. But even in a hoodie Beth Levitt was graceful. Even with dry red eyes she was graceful. She stepped out into the night, not having to sneak past anyone in the living room watching *Supernatural* marathons.

Beth walked through the Missoula night. The Missoula

night was not the Montana night. How strange it was to realize this: in the Montana night you could see the stars above you, millions of them lighting your way, uncountable, bighorn sheep in the distance, blue water, hundreds of square acres of natural beauty; but the Missoula night, despite it being a subentity of the Montana night, was beautiful in a wholly different way, a human beauty rather than an earthly one. How disconnected from one another the two had grown: humanity and earth. How strongly connected to them both Beth aspired to be.

She felt good about the fact that her first fight had lasted less than twenty-four hours.

She would have cycled to John's place, saving time, but her bike's reflectors had been stolen a few weeks ago. She'd locked up the bike itself but someone had stolen the reflectors; she'd left her purse hanging accidentally over the handlebars while she stopped into Bernice's for a pastry, but the thief had taken nothing from it; the thief had taken only the reflectors.

Tonight as Beth walked she could hear cars a few blocks over, on Brooks Street. She could see the light pollution from downtown bordering the part of the skyline where dark cloudy atmosphere met the tops of houses. But was it really pollution if it came from so wonderful a place: downtown? Sometimes Beth used to walk these streets on weeknights with fellow members of her coven, nights she didn't have an early class the next morning; they'd share a couple psychedelic mushrooms, small doses, and walk together so that the colors changed around them, so that the lights stretched and grew and warped and enveloped them in a psilocybic mystical experience. Only in the woods though would they take stronger doses and commune with astral spirits. Here now as she walked it was as if Beth had taken a dose of something. She hadn't taken a dose of anything but as she walked the lights around her changed, grew, ascended and descended. It had been months since she'd gone into the woods. Weeks at least since she'd performed morning prayers and meditations. Or evening prayers and meditations. It was difficult when someone else was in bed beside you falling asleep to slip away and perform your evening prayers and meditations, especially if you didn't really *want* to slip away. Could she even remember how to perform the lesser banishing ritual of the pentagram? Invoke a circle of protection? Invoke the greater gods?

She did not go the straightforward way to John's apartment, the way that was mostly a straight line. She took a detour (funny: people always think of *detour* as meaning *faster*, but really it just means *detour*) down Higgins to Third Street, past that same bakery where her reflectors had been stollen.

She didn't know why she walked that way, but if she hadn't, her path would have taken her straight to John's apartment, at Orange and Sixth; it wouldn't have taken her past the Orange Street Bridge. But here it *did* take her past the Orange Street Bridge. First it took her to the Higgins Bridge, the edge of the river, but did not ask her to cross it. It took her left from there, past Bernice's Bakery, which was owned by the first husband of the woman who wrote the best-selling memoir *Wild*, the movie adaptation starring Reese Witherspoon, fun fact, and past the salon Boomswagger, where you better have made an appointment weeks in advance if you wanted them to cut your hair. Past a bar whose parking-lot signs made it very clear parking was for their customers only. Past not one but two acupuncturist studios. Past the Missoula food bank. To the start of the Orange Street Bridge, again at the edge of the river.

There were cars on the bridge tonight.

There were always cars on the bridge but tonight they

weren't moving. Traffic had stalled. And amongst the cars were people, at least dozens of people. And amongst the people, coming from some of the cars, from at least a few of the cars, were flashing lights, red and blue. Most of the people were trying to peer over the bridge's railing. Men who came from the cars with the flashing lights were urging the people to back off, stand back, but with voices that belied authority.

From here the path should take Beth left, and just three blocks away would be John's apartment. But she approached the bridge and asked a woman, about her age (sometimes it seemed everyone living in Missoula was about her age), with dreadlocks, what was going on.

"Someone fell in the river, I think," the woman said. "Someone fell off the bridge."

"No, that wasn't it," a tall man said, turning from the edge. "He didn't fall—he jumped! Guy just *jumped*. I saw him."

"Cops said he fell," the woman said.

"Well I saw him jump."

"Well," the woman said, "they're down there with a boat, pulling him out of the water."

"Is he okay?" Beth asked. "I mean—is he okay?"

The tall man snorted. When he snorted his chin flesh wiggled and Beth could make out a tattoo on his neck. "'Course he's not okay. Probably dead, jumping into the river. Probably wanted to die."

"God, I hope not," the woman with the dreadlocks said.

Beth squeezed next to the tall guy and peered over the railing. She could discern shapes in the water, nothing else. Then someone shined a flashlight . . . .

"They got him!" someone near the other end of the bridge called. "They got him on the boat. I think he's moving!"

8

BETH DID NOT VISIT JOHN in the hospital. She thought about visiting John in the hospital—he texted her, asking her to come, and she called and got his room number from a receptionist—but ultimately she did not visit him, nor did she respond to his texts. More than once she started to type a text message to Rebekah, to let her know what had happened, to confide in a friend, but each time she deleted the message unsent; she didn't know how to describe the situation. Then Melanie and Jessica returned home from their respective vacations, so she told them what happened instead. They sat with her in the living room. Melanie handed her a beer.

"I knew something was wrong with that guy," Jessica said.

Beth looked at her.

"Jessica," Melanie said. She made a phlegmy sound.

"What?" Jessica said. "It's true. You thought he was weird too. You said so."

Melanie looked at Beth and then averted her eyes. "It's true —he is a little weird."

Beth drank her beer even though she didn't like beer.

She didn't visit John in the hospital because she knew that if she visited him she'd have to talk to him, have to ask what happened or listen to him tell her what happened even if she didn't ask, and if they talked about what happened he'd have to clarify whether he fell from the bridge or whether he jumped, and Beth didn't want to know the answer. She already knew the answer.

The person she did visit in the hospital that week was her grandmother. Beth's grandmother called her one afternoon and in a hoarse voice told her she was at St. Peter's Hospital in Helena, had been there for the better part of a day, would be there for a while, they didn't know how long, a week, maybe two, maybe just a few days. Oh, it was no big deal, she assured her granddaughter, no big deal at all. She'd fallen, you see, that's all, she'd just been taking out the garbage that morning—she should have taken it out the night before; she always took it out the night before but she'd been having memory lapses lately, part of getting old, you know, and well so she forgot it was the day before garbage day and remembered only the morning of, at like 5 am, and the garbage man always came before six, and she just didn't want to let the bag sit there until next week, so she took it out then, the sun having not yet risen—and oh well she just missed the first step, the top step, of the front porch and went tumbling down the porch, how silly, and her hip had hit the concrete walkway and cracked something painful was all. She didn't want Beth to worry, just thought Beth should know; they were taking good care of her, giving her great food—yogurt and stuff like that, chocolate milk in a little carton with a straw sticking out so she could drink it easier.

Beth asked Melanie and Jessica for a ride to Helena and Melanie didn't have to be back to her campus job until break was over the following week, so she said she'd take her, no problem. So together they went to Helena.

In the hospital room Beth's grandmother was sleeping, a plastic tube protruding from her nose, an IV in her arm. "For nutrients," the doctor said, "that's all. And the breathing tube is just because . . . well your grandmother isn't getting any younger."

"How long is she going to be here, in the hospital?" Beth asked, her voice almost a whisper, either because she didn't want to wake her grandmother or because she didn't want to wake herself.

"Hard to say. Hip's broken, and I'm sure you know that can be a real bad thing, real bad. It'll either heal or it won't, you know? Often times we see this sort of thing turn into pneumonia."

"How often?"

The doctor shrugged, looked the tablet he was carrying as if he had the answer pulled up on there. "Thirty percent of the time. Sixty percent?"

"I see," Beth said.

"And honestly, even if it heals, it'll be prone to break again. Take less than a fall down three stairs onto concrete next time."

Beth nodded.

"Can I be honest?" the doctor asked.

Even though the doctor had already been qualifying his statements with *honestly*, Beth nodded again. "Of course."

"I think I'd—I think you may want to consider putting her in a, a place where they can take care of her."

"A nursing home."

"Not a nursing home . . . assisted living. Better, I think."

The doctor showed her some x-rays on his tablet and Beth thanked him and then he left the room.

Melanie put her arms around Beth in a sideways hug. A few

strands of her shoulder-length blonde hair and Beth's hip-length raven hair clung to each other statically. "Oh, Beth, she's going to be okay," she said.

An hour later Beth's grandmother woke. She smiled groggily when she saw Beth sitting next to her bed.

"Hi, grandma," Beth said.

"Oh, my dear," her grandma said throatily. "Oh my sweet Beth, I've missed you. You never visit anymore."

"I've missed you too, Grandma. I'm going to move back to Helena for a while. I'm going to help take care of you." Beth hadn't planned on saying this. In fact, this was the first manifestation of the idea at all.

Her grandma protested but Beth insisted, knowing that, despite the idea's irrationality, it was what she needed to do. Melanie protested too. But after an argument in the hospital corridor, and then in the hospital waiting room, and then back at Beth's grandma's house where Beth and Melanie spent the night, Melanie agreed to drive her back to Missoula, help her pack her things, save for the few furnishings Beth had purchased for the house, affix her bicycle to the back of Melanie's Subaru, and then drive her one more time to Helena. Beth would take an incomplete on all her classes. It was just for the semester. Just for a little while. She'd help her grandma settle back in, recover, grow stronger, and then when her hip had healed Beth would come back to the university. It couldn't take more than the rest of the spring and summer. Everything would be great again by fall.

"We'll leave your room empty for you," Melanie said, hugging her one last time. "We're not gonna rent it out."

One would be forgiven for thinking the summer that followed was the summer Beth Levitt found herself, but no one ever really finds oneself, especially not during summer, when the sun beats hot and school is out and magpies block your path on every sidewalk. At best, one only ever returns to a more grounded state.

Beth's bedroom in her grandma's house was exactly as she'd left it: the double bed with the dark grey comforter and black knit blanket folded neatly laying across the bottom, dream catcher hanging above the pillow; the closet, still half-full with clothes Beth hadn't had room for when she'd left for college, seasonal clothes she'd intended to swap out whenever she visited, but she'd rarely visited, leading her to buy new clothes in Missoula, new sweaters, new hoodies, the famous trench coat, some of these clothes in the closet brightly colored, gifts from her grandmother who at first in high school had had a hard time accepting Beth's love of gothic-styled things as more than *just a phase*; the pewter writing desk, smaller even than the one in her Missoula bedroom but far prettier, on it only a half-pint-sized Buddha, a stack of personalized stationary, and a fountain pen ("I want my own stationary," fifteen-year-old Beth had said when she'd seen her grandmother writing a letter on hers, and her grandmother had bought if for her for that year's birthday; but Beth had never used it, for it turned out to write letters one must have someone one wants to write letters to—now she could write to Melanie and Jessica . . .); the altar on the north wall, empty right now because Beth hadn't yet unpacked her things. Beth lay on the bed and fell swiftly, dreamlessly, to sleep.

Beth had the house to herself for a few weeks. Then in mid-May her grandma returned home. "You kept the place so clean," she said as Beth wheeled her through the door (Beth had built a makeshift ramp over the front porch stairs, and it seemed to be holding steady—the doctor said her grandma wouldn't need the chair for long). "You always were a very tidy girl."

Every day Beth made breakfast, vacuumed, retrieved the mail, watched television with her grandmother or sat in what used to be her favorite chair—so comfy, so soft—reading books. She'd offer to look over the bills, write checks, but her grandma wouldn't have it. "I'm not an invalid, dear. My mind works fine, you know. I can write my own checks in my own checkbook. I can balance my accounts thank you very much."

Whenever Beth brought up getting a job—just something part time, like at a coffee shop or a bookstore or the gym—her grandmother instead gave her money. "You're not going to be here very long, you know. You're going back to school at the end of the summer. Enjoy yourself."

One evening in early June while they were sitting at the kitchen table, eating a large, colorful salad with seitan-based "chicken" Beth had made, watching the news, mostly election controversy, on the 20-inch TV Beth's grandmother kept on the kitchen counter, Beth's grandmother said, "You know, I think I'm going to vote for Hillary. I think I like that Hillary."

"I'm glad, grandma," Beth said.

Beth had intended to rejoin Helena's local Wiccan coven, but, never large to begin with, it had effectively dissolved while she'd been away at school. The High Priestess had been offered some finance job in New York and had moved away.

But still Beth found the time, the motivation, to reconnect with her spirituality, to recover what she'd inexplicably lost these last several months. Now each morning after rising and using the restroom and putting her contacts in she returned to her room and said a prayer. She spent hours sometimes in the morning meditating, after breakfast. She unpacked her Book of Shadows and recommitted to writing in it every day: what was the phase of the moon? what rituals had she performed? how did it all make her feel?

In late June her grandmother, who was sometimes using a walker but mostly still used the wheelchair, said, "You know, I think I'm going to vote for Donald Trump. He says what he means, and that's rare." And Beth shrugged, because you never did know with old people.

Beth spent time reconnecting with old friends on the astral plane, friends she hadn't visited since high school. More and more her nighttime dreams were lucid. John texted her once— *Hey*—but she did not respond.

She did not do any drugs that summer. Her grandmother kept no alcohol in the house, and so Beth drank no alcohol. She stuck to her vegan diet and a few days a week went for five- or even ten-mile runs. Some days she supplemented the runs with intense hikes of Mt. Helena. Some days she felt she had more energy than she'd ever had in her entire life. Some days she was very tired and read books in bed.

In early July Beth's grandmother started to . . . well, Beth starting thinking of them as glitches.

The first day it was a little thing: Beth's grandmother forgot where she put her glasses, the glasses she'd kept as long as Beth had known her on a beaded chain around her thin, frail-seeming neck, and sure enough there they were, looking as if they could pull Beth's grandmother's whole head to the floor, and Beth had to tell her. "Grandma, they're around your neck, on your chain right there.

The second thing was actually a few somewhat larger things strung together: First Beth's grandmother asked how email worked, how does that thing work you're always typing on, Beth dear? And Beth had to remind her that, grandma, you worked as a telecom salesman for like a decade—grandma, you used to write software for the State. And then Beth's grandmother said, oh that's right, and then she sat for a few minutes, quietly, present not there with Beth but in another time, before shaking her head and saying, "Oh but I *am* enjoying this vacation. I don't want to go back to work."

"Grandma," Beth said, "You've been retired since I was seventeen."

And her grandma smiled at her and said, as if annoyed, "I know that, dear."

Weeks went by. Beth's grandmother repeatedly forgot where she'd put her glasses. A half-d0zen times she forgot. A dozen times. Always they were around her neck, except for once when they were on top of her head. And the TV remote, where had that gone—what's it doing in the refrigerator dear, why'd you put the remote in the refrigerator? And will you get the mail? I'm expecting a letter from Todd, any day now I'm expecting a letter from him. It's so hard sending mail when you're overseas.

And Beth did not remind her grandmother that grandpa Todd died over those very same seas, when the plane carrying him back from Vietnam went down due to engine failure (or enemy fire, or even friendly fire, as the conspiracy theories went). Beth had never met him.

Beth wondered whether she should call the doctor. Or *a* doctor. Which doctor should she call? Surely not the same doctor who'd fixed her grandma's leg—right? Surely he didn't fix brains, too. Beth held off on making any calls. Probably weird things like this were just what old people did. And Beth's grandmother *was* old. It occurred to Beth she didn't know what year her grandmother had been born.

One evening they sat at the kitchen table eating a brothy miso soup Beth had made from a recipe she'd found on Pinterest, served with fresh bread from a local bakery. Beth's grandmother ate butter on her bread; Beth ate her own bread with huckleberry jam. Together while eating they watched *Jeopardy!* "Alex Trebek sure is handsome," Beth's grandmother said.

Beth smiled. "I guess he is. But I like him best when he doesn't have his mustache."

"Mustache or no mustache, I'd sit on that face. Indeed," Beth's grandmother said.

"*Grandma!*" Beth nearly choked on her miso soup.

"I'm still young where it counts, dear," her grandmother said.

Shaking her head, trying not to laugh, Beth stood and deposited her bowl in the kitchen sink. The bowl wasn't empty—there were still a few spoonfuls of soup—but Beth had recently read an article that said you should stop eating before you're full, that by leaving a little food on your plate, you were challenging yourself to not indulge. She poured the remaining soup down the drain, feeling a pang of guilt as she did so (but the article had been on *Motherjones*, so surely this was the right thing to do!), rinsed the bowl, and put it in the dishwasher. She checked the oven and inside it the huckleberry muffins she was baking were nearly done.

"I think I'm finished too, dear," her grandmother said.

Beth took her bowl—which was almost completely empty—and repeated the process. "Why don't you go sit in the living room," she said. "I'll make us some tea and bring the muffins out."

"That sounds lovely. That sounds lovely. You're such a lovely girl." Her grandma stood creakily from the table and, leaning on her walker, shimmied out of the kitchen. She paused as she walked by to kiss Beth on the cheek.

Beth put the kettle on, scrolled through Pinterest on her

phone while she waited for the kettle to whistle. While the tea steeped she checked Snapchat, watching a video Melanie had shared of firedancers at the Missoula BrewFest. Should she share a response? Beth never Snapchatted anymore. There was so little about her time in Helena worth sharing. Which was not to say that Beth was discontented. She was not unhappy.

The oven timer went off and Beth backed up and bumped her elbow against the kitchen counter. In a fraction of a second the tingly pain rippled through her funny bone and down her arm and caused her fingers to relax and she dropped her phone. The phone clattered on the tile floor.

"*Fuck*," she muttered.

"Is everything okay?" her grandmother said from the living room.

"Just fine, grandma," Beth said. She rarely swore, and never around her grandmother. "I just bumped my arm. I'm okay. Almost ready."

She picked up the phone. A crack had spiderwebbed through the screen, but it still turned on, still appeared to respond to her touch. "Dammit."

Tucking the phone in her pocket with one hand Beth opened the oven with the other and after putting on a mitt pulled out the muffins. She unloaded them onto a plate. Prepared a side of butter, a side of jam. She did not oversteep the tea and added cream and honey to her grandmother's cup, preferring her own black. On a silver tray her grandmother had owned for decades she carried everything into the living room. For a while they nibbled and sipped in familiar silence.

After a time Beth's grandmother said, "You really are lovely, Beth. You're such a lovely girl."

Beth was taken aback by the sincerity in her grandma's voice.

Sure, she'd called her lovely before, called her lovely *often*, but that was just a thing you said to people you care about. It was a thing grandmothers said to granddaughters. It was a thing said by old people who had raised young people to the young people they had raised. They meant it every time they said it, of course, but that didn't mean it didn't feel strange to hear it said with such gravity. Beth put her hand on her grandmother's. How much contrast there was between the two hands. How different was their skin. It was the same skin, but so different. "Thank you," Beth said.

"I don't— I don't think I ever told you this, but you're so much like your mother."

"Really?" Beth *had* been told this by her grandmother before. Many times.

"Oh yes. She loved you so much. She would love the woman you've become. She would be so proud of you."

"Maybe she *is* proud of me."

"Maybe," her grandmother said.

Beth squeezed her grandmother's hand and then leaned back in her chair. She began to spread jam on another muffin.

"You know your mom also believed in an afterlife, like you do."

"Really?" Beth said. This she had *not* been told before.

Her grandmother nodded. "Spirits, souls, angels, all of it. But not in a Christian way. I never raised her to be like that, either. She was a lot like you."

"I didn't know that," Beth said.

"When your mother was very little—maybe five years old— we had a dog, a puppy. Your grandfather was about to go away, to join the war. He was a conscientious objector, you know. At least in his head he was. What a man, your grandfather—he didn't like war, and he certainly didn't like the *Vietnam* war, thought we had no business being over there, bothering people, but he was also such a loyal man. To me, to his daughter, to his country. So of course being drafted was conflicting for him. He was conflicted. He didn't sleep for three nights, I remember. If he joined the war, he'd have to leave us, and he'd have to fight people he didn't believe in fighting. But if he objected, well he'd maybe go to jail, and so he'd still have to leave us, and he'd be abandoning his country—he was so torn. It really hurt him. But in the end he went. And your mother—when she found out she cried and cried and cried. She didn't understand what it meant that her daddy was fighting a war, but she knew what it meant that he was leaving. She begged him not to go, but he knew if he didn't, he'd probably have to leave us anyway. But the day before he's scheduled to leave he wakes up while we're still asleep and takes the car, and he comes back with a puppy. A golden retriever puppy. Let your mom name it. And do you know what she named it?"

Beth shook her head. She'd never heard this story. She never knew her mother had had a dog.

"Button. Can you believe that—Button! I told her, I said, 'he's going to grow up to be so big, golden retrievers get so big, and when he's big he's not going to look like a Button.' But your mother, she didn't care. And she and Button were inseparable. Button got big fast and your mother would ride him like a horse around the house. Or they'd lay by the fireplace—unlit, because I never did learn how to make a fire without your grandfather's help—your mother reading a book and using Button as pillow."

"Huh," Beth said. "I didn't know this."

Her grandmother nodded. "Your mother loved that dog. And they became inseparable after Todd—. Well, one day I'm in

124

the kitchen and I get the call . . . you know . . . *that* call. You never get used to that call . . . . Todd's plane . . . and normally they'd come to your door and tell you, you know, but they couldn't that day, for some reason, probably because so many people were dying, they had so many people to tell . . . and so I thank them and I hang up the phone and I look down and there's Button, staring up at me. And he licks my knee as if to say 'I'll handle this,' and he walks off into the other room. So I compose myself, and I find your mother by the fireplace, and she's lying there with her head in Button's lap and she's sad, but she's not crying. And she says, 'It's okay, mom, I already know. Button told me.'"

Beth's grandmother was crying now, telling this story. "Oh, grandma . . ." Beth said, looking for the box of tissues that were usually here in the living room.

"Please—it's okay." Her grandmother wiped her eyes on the sleeve of her sweater. "Just . . . memories. You know?"

"Of course," Beth said. After a pause she asked, "What happened to Button?"

"Button? He lived for—how long was it?—twelve more years? He was a good dog."

"I never knew mom had a dog," Beth said.

Her grandmother nodded. "She loved that dog."

They returned to the familiar silence. Beth felt she should say something more, should tell a story of her own. But about what? College? High school? There were no other stories for her to tell. She'd not yet had any other experiences. Nothing of her own to share. And for having nothing to share, she felt guilty. For several minutes they sat there quietly in the living room.

"Whatever happened to her?" Beth's grandmother said suddenly.

"Who, Grandma?" Beth asked.

"That . . . that girl. The one we were just talking about."

Beth tilted her head. "You mean my mother?

Her grandmother nodded again. "Yes, her. Whatever happened to her?"

By early September Beth's grandmother was dead. The memory problems got worse, and in August Beth called the doctor. Alzheimer's, of course—what else would it have been? "And I'm afraid she's going fast," the doctor said. They put her in an assisted living facility, and Beth called the University and informed them she wouldn't be returning for the fall semester after all; she needed to be with her grandmother; but next spring, definitely next spring she'd be back. And on a gelid September morning a nurse found Beth's grandmother in her bed, not asleep, but not awake either. There's nothing we could have done, the doctor said.

It turned out Beth's grandmother had been drowning in debt. Her retirement savings had long run out, and there were hospital fees, and a couple years ago medications Beth hadn't known about, from a battle with left-sided colitis Beth also hadn't known about, fought by her grandmother during Beth's senior high school year. And credit card debt, too, tens of thousands of dollars worth. On what her grandmother had spent tens of thousands of dollars of credit Beth couldn't imagine at first, and then after convincing the company that she was most definitely the next of kin, dammit, that these debts were hers now, and reviewing the reports, she knew: her college education. Beth had her own student loans but her grandmother had paid half her tuition. Had insisted on paying half. Said it was Beth's mother's plan. Said she had the money saved for exactly that purpose. She'd been lying. But why? Why had she done that? If she'd let Beth pay for it, then yes Beth would have had twice the student loans, but the interest . . . the interest . . . .

In total the debt Beth's grandmother left behind was nearly $200,000. Beth's only option was sell the house.

What she wanted to do was burn the house down, collect the insurance money—how cathartic would have been a fire, and around it she could dance like she used to, in the woods, with her coven, with the people she realized only now she'd for a long time been missing deeply—but her grandmother hadn't had insurance. Not health, not homeowners', not life.

So instead Beth held a burning bowl ceremony in the backyard, writing all her sorrows on a piece of the personalized stationery her grandmother had bought her for her sixteenth birthday, the stationary seeing its first use, and throwing those sorrows into the fire; then she sold the house in which she'd spent her teenage years and these last few comfortable months for $210,000, and she paid off all her grandmother's debts, and the rest she kept in her savings account, hoping it would get her by for a while.

Because what would she do next?

She told Melanie she was coming back to Missoula, was ready to return to her room in the house in the university district. Awkwardly, via text, Melanie told her they'd rented it. They'd filled the space. Beth could come get her furniture, if she wanted, but it was just, they needed the money, and it didn't seem like Beth was coming back, surely Beth understood. Of course she did, Beth said, don't worry about it.

Two days before she had to leave her grandmother's house, two days before the new owners were scheduled to move in, Beth sat on her bed in her teenage bedroom. The rest of the house was empty, the rest of the furniture sold or disposed of. Sometime around midnight, unable to sleep, Beth kneeled before her altar and whispered an incantation, beseeching multiple goddesses to lend her wisdom and courage. Then she scrolled across her phone's cracked screen and found John Hempel's name and pressed the little phone symbol next to it.

It rang three times before he picked up. "Hello? Beth?" John said.

"Hi—" Beth said. "Um—how are you?"

He was quiet at first. "I've been worse," he finally said. And she could hear his wry grin making its way to her through the airwaves. "Hey—it's good to hear your voice."

Comparative Skull Structures

1

"Fun fact about the creature that lies before you," the bulky professor said, adjusting his circular brown eyeglasses with one hand, gesticulating with the size-11 scalpel he held in the other: this professor seemed to favor sharp cutting implements over the standard devices teachers used for pointing: long sticks, laser pointers, index fingers. "The luna moth lives for just seven days —or one week, if you prefer—because in their adult forms they do not have mouths. And thus, without mouths, they cannot eat. So, students, what do you suppose they do instead?"

The class was quiet. A few students muttered possibilities to one another, but no one ventured a formal answer.

"Anyone?" the professor said.

Rebekah's academic schedule said the teacher of this class was supposed to be Doctor Linda Epstein, but obviously the man at the front of the room wasn't a Linda. Rebekah at first had feared she was in the wrong class (it had happened to her before), and honestly she was still thinking that might be the case, but the presence of a dead insect and various cutting implements on the table before her seemed to indicate that she was, indeed, in some sort of anatomy class, although it may or may not have been the intermediate anatomy and physiology class in which she was supposed to be present at this time, 10:05 AM on the first Tuesday of the semester.

"This is not a trick question," the professor said.

The class had begun only moments ago. Students had trickled in, and as they did the professor, standing at the front of the room, said "Welcome welcome" and told them to each pick a tray, if you please, whichever specimen looks most appealing to you, and stand behind it. His first formal words to the students had been "Fun fact about the creature that lies before you . . ."

There were coughs. Then one young man—Rebekah, having picked a station near the front of the room, couldn't see who— offered: "Proboscis?"

"Indeed," said the professor, raising an eyebrow, ". . . not. Indeed not. Like I said, this is not a trick question. The adult luna moth has no mouth. It has no proboscis. No way to take in food of any kind. It does not eat. Oh—it eats in its larval and pupal stages, of course, or else it could never grow big and strong"—the professor flexed a muscle, and there was a smattering of chuckles—"but as an adult it does. Not. Eat. This we have established. And as you know, or should know, or I hope you know, having made it this far in life, living creatures have two basic functions. What are they?"

Still no one offered an answer. Rebekah was confident she knew where the professor was going with this, but despite her propensity for choosing seats near the front of the class (the better to absorb and learn), she'd never been one to win participation points.

The professor sighed. "Listen, kids—yes, *kids*—I'm empathetic toward first-day jitters, but for most of you this is your fourth year. Your seventh or eighth first day. And if you count the first session of each class as an individual first day . . .

well then you've had *dozens*. And to that I am *not* empathetic. You want to be doctors you're going to have to talk to people. Also, side note, you're not all going to be doctors. Most of you will fail. You will have many many opportunities to fail and most of you will embrace spectacularly those opportunities. Don't say I didn't warn you. Now, last chance: what does the adult luna moth do with all its time? If living creatures aren't eating then they are—? And if you make me tell you the answer well then shame on each and every one of you."

Someone said, "Mating?"

The professor pumped a fist. "Fucking! Yes! Living creatures exist to either eat or fuck. There is nothing else."

Most of the students laughed now. Rebekah was one of them —she'd been correct in her personal guess of what answer the professor was looking for, and now she was mildly annoyed, as she often was, that she hadn't answered.

"Yes, you," the professor said, pointing to a student who had his hand up. "What is it?"

"Well," the young man said. Rebekah turned to look at him. He had a thick, oiled beard, thick, black-framed glasses, well-coifed hair. "But what about humans?"

"What about them?"

"Aren't we the exception? I mean we make art, we write books, that sort of thing."

The professor pursed his lips together before speaking. "I see," he said. "You're an artist, I take it?"

"A poet . . ."

"Of course, of course. Ladies and gentleman, a poet in an anatomy class. How cute. How clever . . ."

There were laughs again. Rebekah's wasn't among them but she *was* amused.

"Masturbation!" the professor shouted. "Just another form of fucking."

"But—" the poet muttered, but his protest was drowned by the laughter, which grew louder.

"A doctor-poet," the professor said, shaking his head. "But anyway . . . . Class, this *is* Intermediate Anatomy and Physiology. I *am* Doctor Reginald Martin. I'm afraid Doctor Epstein, a dear friend and colleague of mine, decided late into the summer to take a sabbatical so she could assist on a fascinating research project in Brussels. In this class we will, indeed, work quite deeply, quiet graphically, with bodies, but first we're going to cover some basics from a new perspective. I know you weren't expecting to do any dissection on the first day of class, and thus I doubt any of you have brought lab coats, but worry not: the *Actias lunae* before you are all quite preserved and drained of bodily fluids. And plus they're just bugs. Now pick up your number-11 scalpels and make a sagittal cut down the thorax if you please thank you very much."

2

JOHN HEMPEL HAD ONCE CONFIDED in Rebekah that he thought his life should have come with a disclaimer against bad things. Something like:

WARNING! DO NOT READ AHEAD IF YOU ARE TRIGGERED BY: DEPRESSION, SUICIDE, UNEMPLOYMENT, THE OCCULT, DEPICTIONS OF ROUGH SEX, QUESTIONABLE CONSENT, WHITE PRIVILEGE, MALE PRIVILEGE, ETC., ETC., ETC. . . .

But it was too late for all that.

Was it too late for John? was the question.

No, was the answer, Rebekah thought as she watched him.

It couldn't be too late for John Hempel because once again despite his best efforts here he was, alive, awake, drinking orange juice from a straw and eating a mealy porridge that, unlike some food Rebekah had seen served in hospitals, didn't look vile, just bland. It had been served with a packet of honey, but John's fingers didn't seem to want to work, not completely. Rebekah watched him steady the straw as he leaned forward to put his lips around it, and he grasped the handle of the plastic spoon and brought it trembling to his tongue to deposit the porridge, but it appeared he could find neither the precision nor the strength to open the honey packet, which looked like a fast food ketchup packet, and which even if he could get it open probably had only a stingy amount of honey anyway, and when Rebekah offered to open it for him, he hardly acknowledged her presence. He ate the porridge plain. Then, when the bowl was empty and Rebekah could imagine it sticking to the inside of his belly, he sucked down the rest of the orange juice and then pushed the food tray. It swung away on a hinge, a mechanical arm, like a robot's arm. Rebekah observed him as he fell asleep.

A few hours later he woke, when the nurse came in to check on him. She took his blood pressure. "Getting stronger," she said.

"Can I, I wonder, get something else to eat," John said, looking at her. "Like maybe can I get a hamburger? Some fries?"

She shook her head. "Not yet. You maybe did a number on your stomach lining."

"Really?" John said, incredulous. "I destroyed my stomach lining by ingesting some ibuprofen?"

"Maybe you did, maybe you didn't," the nurse said. "It was a lot of ibuprofen."

Rebekah chimed in then: "Any NSAID can cause damage to your stomach lining if you're particularly sensitive or if you take too much. In rare cases just one or two can cause bleeding, in certain people."

John jumped. Rebekah watched him jump, satisfied that the sound of her voice had had the intended startling effect. The nurse clicked her tongue and grabbed John's arm and made sure his IV was still in place. John's head turned left and right, his eyes seeming to come into a sort of unknown focus as they found Rebekah and, next to her, Beth, who was sleeping.

"The hell?" John said. "How long have you guys been here."

"All day."

"Everything looks good," the nurse said. "I'm going to go now. I'll come back later."

"All *day*? But I've been awake. I didn't see you."

"You woke up once. Beth was in the cafeteria, getting food. I said hello as soon as you woke, said it like a dozen times, but you didn't seem to hear me. You just saw the food in front of you and dug in. It was like nothing else existed for you but the food."

"But . . . no. I was awake for like forever, eating that stuff. It took forever."

"Three minutes. You scarfed the whole thing down in three minutes and then you were out again. I don't think you were even awake, not really."

John sat back in the hospital bed. "Well I remember the food."

An uncomfortable lull settled over the hospital room. Rebekah didn't know what else to say. John looked tired. Either he too didn't know what else to say or didn't have the energy to say it. Or maybe he'd already forgotten Rebekah was there. Rebekah's eyes settled on the room's other bed, which was empty. She wondered whether she should wake Beth. Beth had fallen asleep only maybe twenty minutes ago—and she'd been so tired. All day she'd been awake, all the previous night and evening. The whole time she'd been with John, or at least as close to John as the doctors would let her be. She'd sat with him on the bathroom floor. She told Rebekah she'd tried to induce vomiting, like the dispatcher on the phone said, while she waited for the ambulance, but she couldn't bring herself to put a finger down her husband's throat. She'd cried as she told Rebekah this, as if not triggering her husband's gag reflex somehow made her a failure. Rebekah hadn't known what to say—Rebekah was bad at comforting people. She was ineffective. She was bad at pathos, and she knew she was bad at pathos. It's why her friendship with Beth, who was so good at pathos and compassion, was so unlikely, such a miraculous thing. It's okay, she'd told Beth. It sounds like bad advice anyway, sticking your hand down an unconscious person's throat. I don't know why the dispatcher even told you to do that. Then the ambulance had come and Beth had ridden in it with John and watched as the paramedics checked his vitals. At the hospital she'd watched them pump his stomach until a nurse realized she was there and made her retreat to the waiting room, where for a long time she'd waited. Sometime during the waiting is when she'd called Rebekah, but even though at that point it was only early evening Rebekah was asleep. She'd fallen asleep watching Netflix on her laptop on the sofa in the living room she shared with her bitchy roommates and her phone was in the kitchen. She'd woken up when one of her roommates had come home and she'd talked to her for a while and then she'd gone to bed in her own room, at no point interacting with her phone. It wasn't until early this morning she saw the message, listened to voicemail, but when she did listen to it she called Beth immediately and Beth was here, in John's room, where John was sleeping, where the nurse said she could stay because she was close family, but she might have to leave if they ended up needing the room's other bed, at least until visiting hours or until John woke up. "I haven't been able to sleep all night," Beth said. "I've just been sitting here." And Rebekah had driven to the hospital and here with Beth all day she'd been sitting. She didn't know how else to help her friend but sit with her. And now Beth was asleep and Rebekah didn't know whether she should wake her: the poor, exhausted thing.

John said, "What's NSA . . . NSAI . . ."

"NSAID," Rebekah said. "Non-steroidal anti-inflammatory drug. Aspirin, naproxen. Ibuprofen."

"Oh," John said. He stirred in the bed. "Listen, Rebekah . . . I don't know how much Beth told you about why—why I'm here —"

"She told me," Beth said, not meaning to sound ungentle.

"Oh. Well, I'm sorry. I mean, I realize how much this hurts other people. I do. I don't know why I did it. I've done it before —I don't know if she told you—"

"*You* told me."

"I did? I guess I did. Well, I've done it before and I don't know why I did it then, either."

He looked at Rebekah as if she might be able to tell him the reason. She couldn't. Never in her life had she been close to this sort of situation. Even now she did not feel close to it (although she never felt close to anything). She could never care enough to attempt to take her own life. She shrugged. "Hey. Maybe you should tell *her* that. Maybe you should talk to her."

John nodded. Sighed.

Beth stirred in the chair next to Rebekah's. They were not comfortable chairs. How stiff Beth's neck must be. "Hey there, beautiful sleepyhead," Rebekah said. She stroked Beth's long hair.

Beth made a sound and blinked as she sat upright. "What's . . .?"

"Look who else is awake. Look who actually sees us now."

Beth blinked again. "John?" she said. And then, "Oh, John." She stood and rushed over to him, to his bedside. She hugged him. Rebekah thought of warning them to watch out for the IV, but she knew it didn't matter. The IV was just for sustenance, nutrients, and she'd watched John eat that porridge, drink that juice. He was fine. Probably for dinner they'd give him that hamburger. "I love you. I love you," Beth was saying, crying.

John was crying too. "I'm so sorry. I'm so sorry, my love."

Rebekah stood. "I'm going to go," she said. "Give you guys some time alone."

Beth turned to her, sniffled. She smiled. "Of course. Thank you. *Thank* you for staying with me. I'll text you soon. I know you missed a lab for this, I'm sorry."

Rebekah made a dismissive gesture. "It was a silly lab anyway. I'll make it up."

"Thank you," Beth said again. She hugged Rebekah, kissed her cheek. Rebekah returned the hug as best she could return hugs. Usually she bristled at physical contact, but nearly a decade of friendship had instilled an appreciation in her for the warmth of Beth's hugs.

Before leaving Rebekah said, "I love you both. Feel better, John."

In the corridor she returned the smile of a young male doctor, an intern, most likely, possibly a resident. Soon, five more years, maybe three, Rebekah would be an intern. After this semester she planned to volunteer in this very hospital, the Bozeman Medical Center (which had a much more logical name than any hospital called St. Something), get some hands-on experience as she finished her undergrad degree.

In the waiting room she stopped at a vending machine and bought a root beer. She opened it in the elevator. She was hungry, but she'd had only the single dollar bill on her. She had to work this evening, but first she stopped at Hardee's and bought a large fry. She ate the fries in the fitness center parking lot before going in—it seemed wrong to bring fast food into a gym.

She walked in a minute later than her shift was supposed to start, but that was okay, that happened all the time, they were lax about such things here. It was a decent job, working at this gym. The gym itself was small, locally owned, and as such its facilities appeared, to most people, sparse. There were only three treadmills, three elliptical machines, one stair-stepper. There was a Concept2 Rower, but it sat mostly unused in a corner. And because the gym had so little cardio equipment (and because it didn't offer contradictory incentives like Free-Pizza Tuesdays or Donut Wednesdays) most people who came in and inquired about a membership walked out disappointed, membership unpurchased, heading instead for the fitness center down the street. "They're cheaper anyway," was a common refrain, often said snidely to Rebekah, who was grateful to have not signed up an undoubtedly high-maintenance customer. "You know, you really would get more business if you had things like free pizza. Or a tanning salon." But the gym did have plenty of business, plenty of people who wanted to use the numerous sets of free weights they offered, people who wanted to spend their mornings or afternoons or evenings or lunch breaks in the squat rack, lifting heavy things, in silent unbothered solidarity with the other patrons doing the same thing; these were the people who made the job easy, these people who wiped down the equipment after use, these people who put their weights away in the correct place, these people whose only complaint was that the gym didn't have enough pull-up bars, which the owners were finally correcting. Rebekah liked this job well enough. Three days a week, sometimes four, she came in, stood or sat at the administration desk, and smiled at members as they walked in and scanned their key cards. And now that she'd started school again she would use the time to study. It would be so easy to read her textbooks, uninterrupted, unneeded—so rarely here were the employees needed.

Which was why Evelyn, the co-owner's, reaction to Rebekah's arrival today was so surprising. "Where the fuck have you been?" she said when Rebekah approached the desk and began to remove her jacket.

Rebekah looked at the digital clock on the counter. "What do you mean? I'm right on time. Pretty much."

"But I've been trying to reach you for an hour. I texted you. I even called."

"Oh. I don't check my phone much."

"Yeah, well. Anyway, Gingerlynn called and said she had an emergency, and so she can't lead her Hip Hop Fit class at 4:15."

"What sort of emergency."

"I don't know. It doesn't matter. Something about her dog throwing up, maybe?"

Rebekah considered revealing that she, too, had had an emergency. That one of her friends had attempted suicide. That that's why she was, technically, late. Rebekah didn't normally reveal such intimate details to others, often not even to her friends, her few friends, and certainly not to her employers, but she wanted to do it to spite Gingerlynn, who was insufferably pale and bouncy and air-headed, and whose name for God's sake was Gingerlynn and who for God's sake taught a class called Hip Hop Fit. But she didn't. Instead she said, "That sucks about the dog."

"Sure, I guess," said Evelyn, typing at the keyboard of the check-in computer. She hadn't detached her gaze from it since Rebekah walked in. "So, yeah, I need you to teach the class."

"I don't teach classes. I've never taught a class."

"You just plug your iPod into the speakers and dance. Yell a bit, like encouragingly, pump them up. Maybe have them punch the air with some little weights."

"Punch the air . . ."

"Yeah, whatever."

"Okay, so but why don't *you* teach the class?"

Evelyn looked up, raised an eyebrow. "I'm gonna watch the desk. I don't dance. Which of us do you think is the better dancer?"

It was a fair point. For someone who owned a gym with her husband, Evelyn was far from fit. Although it was worth noting that her husband, who unbeknownst to Evelyn Rebekah had slept with twice a couple years ago, just because, and who could be seen here using his own equipment on a daily basis, was. Quite so, in fact. Rebekah had only had sex with him the two times though, both behind this desk after hours, and that was fine with her because he'd been kind of selfish, honestly, had finished fast, and she'd only done it because why not, she'd been bored, she only really ever slept with guys because she was bored and they were there, not ever because it was something she had a strong desire to do; she tended to have sex only a few times a year.

"Okay, good point," Rebekah said. Although she wasn't the fittest herself. She looked it, but that was just luck. She tended to eat whatever was available (which often, in her apartment, was Twizzlers, or nothing) and rarely took advantage of the free gym membership her employment offered. "One thing though. I don't have any music on my phone."

"Just use Pandora or something."

"I don't even have that."

Evelyn finally looked at her. "Are you serious?"

Rebekah shrugged.

"Here—use mine. I have a Jay-Z station on there you can use."

Rebekah walked over to the gym's sole class studio. She told herself she would rather be using this time reading her biology textbook, but the truth was she hadn't even brought it with her.

There was no one in the studio yet. Students tended to arrive for these sorts of classes at or near the scheduled start time. How disappointed they'd be when they walked in to find Rebekah Fleckman, not Gingerlynn, teaching them. Gingerlynn taught all the classes here: yoga, pilates, Hip Hop Fit, Tae Kwon Do for Seniors. Everyone but Rebeka loved Gingerlynn.

Rebekah plugged Evelyn's phone into the studio's speaker system and waited.

She waited for ten minutes before an elderly woman walked sheepishly into the class, dressed in men's basketball shorts and a baggy t-shirt and carrying a water bottle. Rebekah struggled to remember the woman's name, and then she did. "Hello, Mrs. Cook," she said.

The woman looked at her. "What are you doing here?"

"Gingerlynn is . . . sick today. I'm teaching for her."

"Oh, that's a shame."

"Yes, well. A few more minutes then and we'll get started."

Mrs. Cook took a spot near the back of the studio. She unscrewed the lid from her water bottle and sipped.

Rebekah looked at her own phone. There was a clock at the back of the room, above the wall-sized mirror, but she checked her phone instead because looking at the clock at the back of the wall would have meant continuing to face Mrs. Cook. The time was 4:17. All signs pointed to this being a one-student class. Usually these classes filled the studio. There was a whole subset of the gym's members who'd joined just to take these classes; they didn't use the equipment, they just took Gingerlynn's classes; sometimes members told their friends about Gingerlynn and her classes and those friends signed up so they could take the classes. Women and men took these classes—Gingerlynn often wore yoga pants and a sports bra, and she had large breasts. But today it looked like would be just Rebekah and Mrs. Cook.

Mrs. Cook stood quietly, arms at her sides. She smiled at Rebekah. Rebekah returned the smile, glanced at the clock.

Rebekah and Mrs. Cook.

But then at 4:19 another member walked in, a woman Rebekah saw working out here sometimes. And behind her was a woman Rebekah didn't know. And then a young man. And then several more women and a couple more men, middle-aged. Quickly the room became half-full. Everyone was talking, saying hello, then they quieted, took their places, looked forward.

"Um, hi," Rebekah said. "Gingerlynn is out today, but I've got a great playlist queued up here, so lets get started. Let's start with something slow." She pressed *play* on her phone, hoping the first song of the algorithmically generated playlist would, indeed, be something slow. When it wasn't, she smiled and said, "Got ya. When we're exercising, it's important we're kept on our toes."

Everyone laughed and Rebekah decided to roll with it: many of her dance instructions over the next hour involved quite literally staying on one's toes. Three people came in late. One person laughed, looked at Rebekah and mouthed "thank you" as she walked out, seemingly embarrassed. Rebekah nodded at her and smiled and continued dancing. "Great work, everyone!" she said over the music. "Let's, um, shake that moneymaker now."

When the class was over and the studio empty, Rebekah mopped the hardwood floor, soaking up the sweat that had pooled on it in multiple locations. As she used a towel to wipe away her own she realized she didn't have a change of clothes. Surely she didn't smell so great. Oh well.

Evelyn left—after failing to thank Rebekah for covering the class—and Rebekah was on her own. At 5:30 the gym began to fill with patrons, squeezing their workouts in after their nine-to-fives. By seven it began to empty. By 7:30 there were just two men, jock-looking types, but too old to be student athletes, which was the only kind of athlete you could be in Montana. Probably businessmen, then. Rebekah combed the gym while the men were finishing their workout, taking turns lifting and spotting each other on the bench press. Rebekah wiped down equipment with a sanitizing solution. Vacuumed the couple small carpeted sections. Swept the main floor.

"Did you know the Earth is flat?" one of the men said to the other while Rebekah re-racked a few stray plates.

"No it isn't," the other man said.

"No, yes it is, totally."

"Dude, are you stupid? What the hell are you talking about?"

"No, man, it's true. Neil DeGrass Tyson was talking about it on Twitter. Like apparently it's a big conspiracy. Like we've never even been to space, that's all a lie. Cuz space doesn't even really exist, not really."

"Neil DeGrass Tyson . . . ?"

"Yeah, totally. I'll show you the the tweets when we're done."

"Dude. That's crazy if it's true."

"I know, right? Crazy."

Yes, this was an okay job. It was solid, as far as jobs go. It wasn't Rebekah's first job, or even her favorite, but it was the one she'd held the longest. A few days after turning sixteen she'd applied for her first job, as hostess at an Applebee's in Helena. They called her back the day after she submitted the application, interviewed her the day after that, and hired her on the spot. Since then she'd never had a problem getting any job she wanted. She could probably get a better job than this one, no problem, but she didn't desire to. She didn't even *need* this job. She hadn't even needed that first job at Applebee's. Her parents were supportive, had always been supportive, both of Rebekah and of her older brother, who lived in New York City and was some sort of analyst, dating a single mother of a two-year-old son. Rebekah's parents had even told her not to get that first job; focus on your studies, they told her, focus on school, focus on sports. If you learn to work hard for things you care about, then you'll always be a hard worker, but, honey, there's no way you're going to care about working at Applebee's. Easy for them to say —Rebekah's dad had founded a popular Montana pizza chain, and her mother made and sold natural beauty care products on the internet (she started with Etsy but then the business grew and now she had her own website and the products themselves were manufactured off-site by probably migrant workers at a factory in Arizona). In a way, Rebekah was an heiress—if her brother didn't want the pizza chain for himself, that is (was that how things still worked? no matter—Rebekah didn't want the pizza chain either). But Rebekah believed—not exactly in hard work for hard work's sake—but in autonomy. She liked doing things for herself. So she got the job at Applebee's and still played soccer and still made the high school honor roll. Her senior year she quit the restaurant and worked for six months at Macy's. Upon moving to Bozeman for college she transferred to the local Macy's, quit after two months and started working a bookstore. She liked the bookstores because she got a discount on books and really could just bring any book home if she wanted to as long as she brought it back; but in the end it wasn't worth it; Rebekah wasn't a big reader, although she could read quickly if she wanted to, was capable of focusing for long periods of time when truly interested; she read a couple books a month, mostly mystery novels, not counting textbooks. She got a job on campus that offered only five or so hours a week, so at the same time she started working at the gym. When the school year was over she no longer worked the campus job, but the gym stuck, and she'd worked here ever since. Last year, her "gap year" as she liked to think of it, her hours at the gym were pretty much full time; now that she was back in school Evelyn had kindly scaled back Rebekah's hours and hired one more staff member, a young man Rebekah had met but didn't normally cross paths with since they worked opposing shifts. It was an okay job. Once or twice a month Rebekah's mom stealthily dropped a few hundred dollars into her checking account.

The flat-earthers had left by 7:50. The gym closed at eight but of course no one was going to be coming in to work out for less than ten minutes, so Rebekah locked the doors. She finished cleaning up. She logged out of and shut down the front desk computer. She went home and ate pizza one of her housemates had ordered. She hoped Gingerlynn's dog was okay—she did not want to have to cover another fitness class tomorrow.

3

A COUPLE WEEKS LATER ON a Saturday while they ate lunch at the bakery where Beth worked, which had just begun to offer sandwiches and soups, Rebekah told Beth about the flat-earthers.

"Oh, wow," Beth said. "That's crazy."

"Right?" said Rebekah.

"Yeah. I mean, the world *could* be flat, you know? There's really no way to tell."

"Oh," Rebekah said. "Um . . ."

"I mean people can tell us that it's round. Like astronauts can tell us, people that have been to space, but subjectively, within the confines of our own experience, there just really is no way to be sure unless we go to space and see it for ourselves."

"Oh."

Beth looked up from her sandwich (no lunchmeat, just vegetables—avocado, tomatoes, sprouts—and dijon mustard), saw the look on Rebekah's face, and laughed. "Oh goddess," she said, "you must think I'm crazy. I'm just talking, like, *hypothetically*. Like *theoretically*. Philosophy, you know?"

"Oh," Rebkeha said. "Ohhhhh." She laughed, too, feeling something approaching but not quite gratefulness. She'd feared for a moment she'd have to sever ties with her best friend. (She still wasn't sure.)

"We could all be living in a simulation, for all we know. John likes to talk about that a lot, that we might be living in a computer simulation."

Rebekah was eating a bowl of cream of mushroom soup and she slurped a spoonful. She didn't know who made the soups, whether Beth had a role in it, but she did know the serving of them had been Beth's idea—so she didn't mention that it was awfully watery for a cream soup, and that the mushrooms had been too finely chopped, so finely that they tended to dissolve before she could taste them. But she had a French baguette and she dipped it in the soup and that was good; it was all better than the food she normally ate. "How *is* John?"

"He's . . . good. John's good," Beth said.

"That's good."

"Yeah."

"How's he . . . feeling?"

"Good. He's feeling good."

"Good."

"Yeah. It is good. He went to Best Buy last week, bought some camera equipment. Like a camera and a tripod for it. And a tripod for his phone."

"Didn't he already have all that? I thought he bought that stuff after the honeymoon."

"Well, and he did, but he thought it could be better, and after what he's been through . . ."

"Of course."

"Yeah. And he's already filmed a couple videos. First I guess he did one on his old camera and uploaded it as a test, and it got a handful of views, which he says is good. But then he deleted it."

"Why'd he delete it?"

"He said it was just a test. This was before he bought the new camera. He said the old camera was good in a pinch but he needed better equipment if he was going to take it seriously."

"Is he? Going to take it seriously?"

"What do you mean?"

"Well, you know guys. They get excited about stuff, like video games or technology. Or art. Remember that guy I dated freshman year who wanted to be a lawyer and then switched his major to art, but then a few months later, a couple months after we broke up, I ran into him and he was majoring in law again? So they get excited is all, but it doesn't always last."

Beth frowned. "Yeah. No—yeah—I know what you mean. But John has been thinking about this since the honeymoon, so he's pretty excited."

Rebekah did not mention that the honeymoon had hardly been more than a month ago. Instead she nodded. She said, trying to sound supportive rather than sympathetic, "That's true. If anyone can make something like that, it's John. He's the smartest guy I know."

"He is," Beth said. "He's the smartest guy I know, too."

John *was* the smartest guy Rebekah knew. Almost two years ago she'd realized how smart he was, as she sat with him in Beth's living room, Beth asleep on the couch next to him, Rebekah on the other couch. They'd been talking about television shows, Netflix, and then the talk had turned to what Rebekah was studying, medical stuff, anatomy, some of the physics she was taking at the time, and John had kept up with her, had followed what she said. In some cases he'd been able even to steer the conversation; he'd asked questions, inserted opinions. He'd gently removed Beth's head from his lap and placed a throw pillow under it and joined Rebekah on the other couch and she'd realized that this journalism major her friend was dating knew as much, if not more, about her chosen field as she did.

"So has he posted any other videos? What's his channel's name? How do I find it?" Rebekah was taking her phone from her purse as she asked these questions.

"It's . . . I'm not sure," Beth said. "Search for his name, I guess? It might just be his name."

It was just his name. Rebekah found it easily. She subscribed. There were no videos so far.

"Yeah. He's filmed a few, but he says he doesn't want to upload any until he has a backlog. But he's filming every day. Several a day." She laughed. "He changes his shirt like three times a day so he's not wearing the same one in all the videos."

Rebekah laughed too.

Beth looked suddenly wistful. Her gaze went first to her sandwich. She took a bite and then looked to the bakery's ceiling lights. After chewing a moment, she said, "I think he's taking this pretty seriously. He's incorporating and everything. He started an LLC. He has his own credit card for it. He had to put the purchases on the credit card, of course. No way we could afford a good camera, not right now. But soon, I think."

"That's good," Rebekah said. "That's all good."

"Yeah," her friend replied. "It is. He wants to get a new computer too. For editing."

And then Beth asked Rebekah how school was going. How did it feel to be back, after taking a year off?

Rebekah sighed. It wasn't conscious. If she could have decided she would have decided not to sigh, but she did sigh. "It's fine."

Beth frowned. "Just fine?"

Rebekah sighed again, unaware she was doing so. "It's school. I guess just as I sit there in labs I remember why I skipped a year."

"No—I get it," Beth said. "I didn't even finish, remember? Neither did John?"

Rebekah didn't comment that, yes, speaking of that, she'd never approved of her friend's decision to not return to college. That was a key difference between the two of them: Rebekah had returned to school—she was going to make something of herself, no matter how long it took—while Beth, it seemed, was not. And the revelation at the beginning of this lunch that Beth was being promoted to assistant manager of Betty's Bakery after such a short amount of time (ostensibly because the soups and sandwiches were a hit) did not count. "Isn't it great?" Beth had said just half an hour ago. "Karen, the manager, is trusting me with so much responsibility." But to Rebekah it was clear *trust* meant *you do this work so I don't have to*. It was, after all, what happened to Rebekah herself at the gym all the time. It was also a cycle Rebekah was determined to step out of—some day.

"Sure, sure," Rebekah said. "I guess you do know how I feel."

Beth hesitated. "Actually . . ." She paused. "I . . . don't. I'm a pretty empathic person. I've learned how to read people. Their . . . energies. Auras, you know? It's not hard if you study it. But I can never read yours."

"No?" Rebekah asked.

Beth shook her head, sadly. "No."

"Well," Rebekah said.

And then Beth laughed. "Of course, I know you don't believe in that stuff anyway."

Rebekah shrugged. "I'm more of a scientist."

"I know you are. That's okay. Maybe that's why I can't see your aura."

"Maybe," Rebekah said, trying to smile.

"But that doesn't mean it's not true. It really helps, my faith. The goddess. She helps me through things. For a while I sort of lost my practice, but I'm practicing again, stronger than ever. And it helps. It helps with . . . John and . . . everything."

Everything? What else was there for Beth than John? If there was something, Rebekah hadn't seen it, not for a long time.

"Can I tell you a secret, Rebekah? If it wasn't for Wicca I'm not sure I could ever be happy."

Rebekah had no response. Her soup was lukewarm now. She couldn't finish it.

"But I *am* happy. I'm a very happy person." Beth straightened, emanating confidence.

"I'm glad," Rebekah said. "You deserve happiness."

4

DOCTOR REGINALD MARTIN PACED UP and down the aisles between the lab tables, examining the students' work. "Nice cut," he'd say quietly to one student. "A little rough around the edges there," he'd say to another. "Remember to hold the scalpel like *this*." Mostly he'd just making *tsking* noises, or little clicks of his tongue, or extrospective *hmm*s. This is what he did, all the time. It was a comprehensive summary of the Reginald Martin class experience. In the first class session he'd been funny, if not intimidating; now he was, at best, just intimidating.

Rebekah looked down at the creatures before her. There were two of them. One of the two, the lamprey, lay on its back, its three fins (anterior dorsal, posterior dorsal, caudal) removed so it could lay flat, so it wouldn't role sideways, which would have made the dissection process difficult. A long cut had been made from just beneath the head to just above the tail along the creature's median plane. It was not a fresh cut. It had been made last week. Rebekah had made it herself with a size-ten scalpel. Next to the lamprey in the dissection pan lay a worm-like leathery structure. The structure wanted to curl upon itself, but two pins, one at either end, kept it stretched, affixed to the pan's blue rubber bottom. This structure was an intestine. Like the lamprey's main body, its intestine also bore a slice down its median plane, and this cut had also been made last week. When you pulled the two sides apart with your probes, you could see inside the intestine: its longitudinal ridges and its typhlosoles. Rebekah couldn't tell the difference between a longitudinal ridge and typhlosole. She'd spent the entire last class trying to tell the difference.

If she couldn't tell the difference between a longitudinal ridge and typhlosole inside a lamprey's intestine, Doctor Martin had said to her, how would she ever make it as a physician who worked on humans?

Everyone else in the class had gotten to poke around the kidneys, the ovaries; Rebekah had been stuck on the intestines.

They were supposed to spend an entire week (three classes) on the lamprey, but Doctor Martin had gotten sick and had cancelled last week's second and third classes, and today he said they didn't have time, they needed to move on if they were going to get to the good stuff.

And so Rebekah picked up the size-ten scalpel and looked at the second creature on the lab table in front of her: *Squalus acanthias*. Spiny dogfish, or mud shark.

Shark.

Of course the thing was dead, preserved in a formalin solution before being moved to a different mix of chemicals, and plus the creature was only two feet long. This was no Jaws on the table. But that didn't stop some students from emitting shrieks when they first pulled theirs from the specimen bags. Rebekah had not shrieked. She'd just placed her shark on the table—not gently, but not carelessly. She was grateful for the first time today that her lab partner, a short young woman with close-cropped pink hair and thick plastic-framed glasses with equally plastic-looking lenses who should probably have been a women's studies major rather than a med student, was not here today. Why she wasn't here today Rebekah did not know. Three minutes into class when the girl (Rebekah didn't know her name; she'd been told it but hadn't cared enough to commit it to memory; in her phone the girl was just called "PinkHair LabPartner") hadn't shown up Rebekah texted her. Ten minutes later now and Rebekah had received no reply. But that was a good thing: PinkHair LabPartner might have run screaming from the classroom at the sight of the dead shark on the table. Hell, something about the creature made Rebekah herself want to leave: not its rows of teeth, not its sandpapery skin, not even its deadness, but its eyes, which seemed far from dead and one at a time bore into you as if they knew a secret about yourself you didn't know and they weren't telling, or worse, might tell.

Every student had his or her own lamprey—lamprey's were inexpensive—but the sharks were assigned one to a two-person team. Since Rebekah's partner wasn't here, Rebekah had her own shark. The downside of that was that, like last week, she'd probably fall behind. The plus side was who hasn't wished they could have their own shark?

Rebekah was already trailing. Doctor Martin paced the room criticizing or complimenting each student's dissective cut, but when he approached her lab table he could only note (aloud) that she'd yet to make a cut at all.

"I'm sorry," Rebekah said, not knowing what else to say.

Doctor Martin shook his head. "Here," he offered kindly. He stood behind Rebekah—she could feel his front on her back; they were roughly the same height—and put his right hand over hers, taking control of the scalpel while she still held it. "The hardest part is often knowing where to start. It can feel . . . I believe *squicky* is the word I've heard students use. Let me help you." Guiding her hand, he made a cut across what on a mammal one might think of as the creature's throat. Then, starting from the center of that cut, he moved the blade up. His instructions to the class had been to begin by cutting open the shark's abdomen, just like they'd done with the lamprey, but that was not what he was doing here. He sliced from throat to a millimeter below the mouth. Still holding Rebekah's right hand with his, he used his left to pick up a probe. With the probe and the blade he pulled apart the two flaps he'd created with his cut. Exposing the mud shark's jaw. "Now look here," he said, pointing to the bone with the probe. When he talked Rebekah could feel his breath on the nape of her neck; she could smell it, too, and it was not unpleasant, vaguely cilantro-like.

Rebekah was aware of, and thought about now, a small subset of the human population to whom cilantro tasted like soap. For something like four to fourteen percent of people it tasted like soap. Something to do with OR6A2 genes and aldehyde.

"And now look at this one." Doctor Martin guided her to the lamprey. He made the same cut on it, again pulled apart the created flaps. "The lamprey technically has no jaw, and yet you might say that the lamprey and the mud shark still have comparative skull structures." He looked at her.

Rebekah glanced around the lab. Every other student was focused on their own cutting.

"Now what do you think about that?" Doctor Martin asked.

"Um, yes, you might say," Rebekah said. She took the probe from him, shook him off. "Thank you, Doctor Martin."

"Call me Reginald," he said, smiling. He resumed his pacing and Rebekah, choosing to be unfazed, picked up a larger, rounder scalpel, a size twenty-three, and proceeded to cut along the the shark's abdomen. She made the cut quickly but cleanly. She pushed aside the musculature and searched for the intestines. A few minutes later Reginald Martin was back at her table. "Very nice," he said. "Much better."

"Thanks," Rebekah said.

"Please see me after class, if you don't mind."

"I . . . um . . . have another class eight minutes after this one, at Johnson Hall."

"Of course," he said. "Office hours then. This week. This afternoon if you can manage it."

Rebekah didn't say anything and Doctor Martin walked on. He did not return to her. In the next 90 minutes Rebekah was able to remove the stomach, the heart, the large intestine. Even in the larger intestine of the mud shark did she have trouble picking the typhlosoles from the longitudinal ridges, but after repeatedly consulting the textbook, and then the shark intestine, and then the lamprey intestine, again and again and again, she began to get the hang of it. In fact, since both were essentially just folds in the internal surface of the organ, she found if she pulled the flaps tightly enough and pinned them that way, she could make the longitudinal ridges and the typhlosoles disappear, and then there was nothing to identify, and she could move on to other, more interesting organs.

Rebekah did not go to Reginald Martin's office that afternoon. She went to her computational biology class, and then she went home and ate Oreos that were beginning to go stale and tried to read the most recent Cormoran Strike novel. The next day she worked at the gym—Gingerlynn hadn't had any more problems with her dog (who, she'd insisted when Rebekah made a comment to her about having to cover her class, was "really really sick that day, like he was throwing up and shitting at the same time, projectiley, I've never *seen* so much brown and green") so Rebekah's shifts had returned to normal, and she spent them at the desk, greeting gym members, reading textbooks, watching YouTube videos on the staff computer, and because it was a morning shift she didn't have to do any cleanup or closing down of the facility, and she even had thirty free minutes after the shift she was able to use to squeeze in her own workout, the first in weeks—before attending her Myth-Lit class, the sole non-medicine-related class she had this semester (due to an oversight her junior year she needed the easy credit). MSU was not a liberal arts college, and the Myth-Lit class was uninsightful, but the coffee cart outside it sold good large muffins, muffins made at Betty's Bakery.

She had another lab with Doctor Martin on Wednesday, which she attended. They were continuing to dissect the mud shark. Beth's lab partner still had not returned and thus she still had the shark to herself. She'd removed its intestines, its colon, its stomach (there was nothing unusual inside the tiny stomach, no license plates, no oil cans, no human appendages), its heart, its kidney. Its uterus ("Interesting," Doctor Martin said, "These are all supposed to be male specimens."). Doctor Martin said nothing to Rebekah about the office meeting he'd requested. He said nothing about the fact that she hadn't gone to seen him on Monday, or that, according to the parameters of his request, she had just two days left to do so. He said nothing to her at all besides acknowledging the peculiarity of her shark's gender. He just paced the aisles like he always did. In fact, the only other vocal remark he made during that Wednesday class was to tell another student that "Sharks and other cartilaginous fish don't have swim bladders, Mr. Yoo, and you'd know that if you'd taken the time to study your textbook." Doctor Martin seemed to have memorized all his students' names; he was the only instructor Rebekah had this semester who'd done that. Did that mean he invested more time? Or did he just have a better memory? Rebekah made notes in a spiral-ring notebook while dissecting. The organs of the mud shark would have a place on the final exam, Doctor Martin had hinted.

Rebekah did not visit Doctor Martin's office after class on Wednesday. When she thought about why he might want to see her she felt dread, also excitement. When she didn't think about why he wanted to see her she felt nothing. Most of the time she didn't think about it.

Her mother called her Thursday evening while she was sitting in her room, not doing anything important. Through the wall she could hear one of her roommates fighting with her boyfriend, telling him in a loud voice something about how he never did what she wanted him to do, but also how he never stood up for himself. The argument was happening over the phone so Rebekah couldn't hear the boyfriend. The poor boyfriend, she thought. Rebekah didn't like her roommates. Her own phone rang and she looked down and saw her mother's picture on the screen. She answered the phone.

"Hey, Mom," she said, placing it to her ear. Rebekah didn't like holding her phone to her ear so even as she said hello she was looking around the room for her headphones.

"Hey, Bek," her mother said. Except it wasn't Rebekah's mother. Her mother didn't call her Bek. Her mother called her Rebekah. Only one person called her Bek, because he didn't care that she didn't like it, and in a way she *did* like it when it was coming from him.

"Oh, hi . . . Dad," she corrected. "What are you doing on . . . Mom's . . . phone?" She paused repeatedly, distracted—she couldn't find the headphones.

Immediately she began looking for the other pair of headphones she owned, the ones that had come with the phone (the first pair she'd been looking for had been a birthday gift last year, from John), the ones that didn't sound as good, not that she cared (she rarely listened to music). She couldn't find those either; she hadn't used them in months.

"I dropped mine, I guess," her dad was saying.

"You dropped your headphones?"

"What? My headphones? No—my phone."

"Oh—right. You *guess* you dropped it?"

"The screen cracked."

"That sucks."

"Yeah. It still works, but I don't like using it."

"Okay." Rebekah couldn't find the other headphones either. She gave up. She fell backwards onto her bed and set the phone to speaker and placed it on her breasts. From this position she was staring into the phone's speaker grill. Somewhere in there was a microphone, she knew, a tiny hidden microphone.

"How are you, honey?" her father said.

"I'm good. Why? How are you? How's Mom?"

"Mom's good. I'm good. I had the day off, because of the holiday, so that was nice."

"Cool. That's cool." Today was a holiday? What holiday? A holiday on a Thursday? What Thursday holiday besides Christmas or Thanksgiving would shut down a pizza chain?

"Hey, Bek, your mom and I haven't heard from you in a while. We just wanted to see how you're doing?"

"Is Mom there with you?"

"No . . . your mother didn't have the day off. She's at one of the restaurants going over some stuff."

"O-kay," Rebekah said slowly.

"Anyway."

"I'm good," Rebekah said. "Just going to school. Studying. Working. Nothing new."

"That's great!"

"Yeah."

"Meet any guys?"

"What?"

"At school. Or other places I guess. Anyone special? Have you been on any dates?"

Sometimes her parents took an obscene interest in this area of Rebekah's life. It was awkward enough for her whenever her mother asked about it; she hated discussing it with her father. Sometimes, when she was back home, visiting, or they were in Bozeman visiting her, they'd both sit her down and ask about it; they'd try to do it casually, over dinner or while they all sat in the stands of a Bobcat game, waiting for the first play, but always it was obviously a preplanned topic of discussion on their part. How's your life honey? How's work? How are the roommates? And also boys, what about boys? That's sort of how it sounded, too: never did she get the impression her parents wanted to know about the *men* in her life, but instead the *boys*, because their daughter, it was assumed, if she'd found someone to spend her time with, couldn't have done so with anyone mature enough to be labeled a *man*. Rebekah Fleckman was twenty-three and that this seemed to be all anyone ever thought about annoyed her.

"No, Dad. No one right now."

"What about that guy with the haiku? Did you ever hear back from him?"

Aaron. Of course she'd heard back from him. He'd texted her a half-dozen times in the week after their sole date at the end of the summer. She never responded. Then he stopped. "No," she said.

"That's a shame."

"Dad, you just said it yourself. He wrote *haiku*!"

"I like poetry. Your mother likes poetry."

"Well."

"You used to like poetry, when you were little."

She doubted it. She said so.

"Anyway, didn't you say he was joining the army?"

Rebekah yawned. "Something like that."

Her father was silent for a moment. She could almost hear him shrugging, as if he didn't know what to say next. She sat up abruptly. She'd remembered where the headphones were, the good ones. She took the phone off speaker mode and placed it to her ear. "What else is new with you and mom?" she said, leaving the bedroom.

Her father took a moment to answer. "Nothing," he whispered.

"Oh, okay. Well—"

"We're proud of you, though, you know, Bek."

"Thanks, Dad." She was in the kitchen now, rummaging through the junk drawer that had been designated hers. Each roommate had her own junk drawer.

"No, but I mean it. We're proud of you."

"Thanks," she said again. "I mean it too."

"Going back to school. Finishing what you started. It's great."

She pushed aside a screwdriver, a container of screws, a protractor, three AA batteries, two AAA batteries, a small handblown glass pipe she'd never used (she'd never touched anything more mind-altering than alcohol when in her own home) but that had been a gift from Beth, several sheets of folded paper the contents of which she'd have to go back and check sometime because they might be important, a D battery, a finger-sized flashlight meant to hang on a keychain, a keychain with three unidentified keys on it, a plastic container of inch-long nails, a hammer, several cheap plastic click-top pens accidentally taken from her bank after making deposits (the owners of the gym had apparently never heard of direct credit). No headphones.

"I hear you, Dad. Thanks." She said it not entirely congenially this time. She didn't mean it. Her father had no right to be proud of her accomplishments, even if she had some. No one did. Her accomplishments, if they existed, would be hers and hers alone. She did not say this.

"Okay. I just wanted to make sure you know that. I love you, Bek."

"I love you, Dad." She'd been certain the headphones were in this drawer. Last week she'd been listening to something—she couldn't remember what—while boiling water for ramen.

"Well, talk to you later." The call ended. Had her father been crying there, at the end? It sounded like he'd been crying, maybe. Rebekah hadn't been paying enough attention to tell.

Somewhere behind her a door creaked open. Rebekah turned her head and her roommate was in the kitchen with her. "Hey," Rebekah said.

Her roommate looked at her. Rebekah stood, phone in one hand, junk drawer open. "Hey," her roommate said.

"Have you seen my headphones?" Rebekah asked. "They're pink, with kind of a lime-green accent."

"Yeah. I borrowed them the other day."

"From my *room*?"

"They were on your desk."

"Where are they now?"

"Not sure."

"Do you know what holiday today is?"

"What?"

"Never mind."

Dr. Reginald Martin's office was sparse and smelled of cigar smoke and black pepper. Rebekah knew it was cigar smoke and not cigarette smoke or pipe tobacco because, while she'd never tobacco herself, she could recall her father lighting a cigar on three occasions: 1.) when she was six years old and the family opened their third restaurant (and their first outside of Montana, in Post Falls, Idaho, never mind that the location closed less than two years later); 2.) when she was nine and results of a complicated test came back from the doctor and confirmed that Rebekah's mother, at thirty-nine, was indeed *not* pregnant, thank God; and 3.) at Rebekah's high school graduation party, where her father had tried to get her to smoke one with him, saying it wasn't himself he was lighting up for, but her, come on, let's celebrate, and when she repeatedly declined he broke down and cried "But I just haven't had a reason to smoke one of these in so long, everything has gone to shit in my life" and she couldn't tell whether he was serious, and she went to find some friends and when she saw her father again fifteen minutes later he was completely normal.

Rebekah made a comment about the scent to Dr. Martin.

"Actually," Dr. Martin replied, "I don't smoke cigars. It's just a candle." And as if he thought she might not believe him he produced said candle from a drawer in his desk and lit it.

If the office smelled of cigar smoke and black pepper, then it also looked as if it smelled of cigar smoke and black pepper. Which was to say the chair behind the mahogany desk was large and leather-upholstered, most of the books on the shelf against the left wall had cracked leather spines, probably even gilded pages, and a globe colored various shades of sepia sat on the window sill. By the door stood a person-sized coatrack, and on the coatrack hung a newsboy cap and Rebekah's winter coat. It was still autumn but that morning the sky had cracked open and unleashed the season's first heavy snow. Dr. Martin's wool coat hung not on the rack but over the arm of his leather chair. Rebekah was sitting in a smaller, cheaper chair on the opposite side, unsure what else to say. She wouldn't have taken her coat off —she didn't plan on staying long—but Dr. Martin had insisted.

Dr. Martin said, "I'm glad you stopped by, Rebekah. I've been wanting to talk to you."

"Is this about my work?" Rebekah said. "Because I know I'm slow with the dissecting, but—"

"Not at all," he interrupted. "In fact, as we learned today, I think your slowness was a deception." For this morning she'd been the only student to have finished removing and labeling every organ and structure of her mud shark specimen (her lab partner still had not returned to class, and somehow Rebekah divined she never would) and to have put them back in the proper place. If you were able to magically fuse each structure back together and somehow imbue life back into a dead mud shark, Rebekah's shark would have operated perfectly. It so happened that this morning's lab was the last they'd have with the mud shark ("Next week, we move on to a human brain! And yes, that did escalate quickly."). This was unfortunate for everyone who hadn't completed their work with the creature, because, Dr. Martin announced at the end of the class, the anatomy of the mud shark would be on the final exam in its entirety.

"About that," Rebekah said now, "don't you think it's ridiculous to make the final about a fish? We're medical students, not veterinary students, we're going to be saving *human* lives some day."

Dr. Martin smiled. "Do you know how many medical students drop out of med school? Not fail, but drop out? In the their fourth year?"

"No?"

"Ninety-six percent. Ninety-six."

"Is that true?"

"It doesn't matter if it's true. The point is most of the students in that lab are going to end up being veterinarians, I shit you not. Or dentists, in which case I can't help them."

"What does any of this have to do with—"

"I've been reviewing your academic record," he said, and from the drawer in which he kept the cigar-scented candle he produced a tablet computer.

"Are you allowed to do that?"

"And your grades are good. Really good. They could be great, although I understand why you might not put the energy into that—what's the point, right, when really good is good enough."

"Yeah, I mean I've thought about it that way, I guess."

"So then but you took a year off, I see, last year." He stood from the desk and walked around it, knelt next to her chair, handed her the tablet. "Two whole semesters."

"Yes," she said, taking the tablet. She was put off by his telling her things she already knew about herself. What was the point in him handing her proof? Did he think she didn't believe in the reality of her own past?

He didn't say anything for several moments. He looked into her eyes as if challenging her, and she, in a decision she would later sometimes regret, met the stare, issuing a challenge back. Then he asked, pointedly, "Why?"

What the fuck was this? Rebekah wondered. And then, moments later, when Reginald Martin's tongue was in her mouth she knew he'd been lying about not smoking cigars. She could taste it on him, could smell it on his breath and on his tacky tweed clothes. She wondered what the point of the candle was then—was it some kind of misdirection? Sure, you weren't allowed to smoke on campus, and that extended to faculty offices, but he could just blame it on the candle.

Later that afternoon, at his apartment, after they'd fucked, while they lay in his bed, he rolled over and like a character in a bad movie lit a cigarette. He offered her one. "I don't smoke," she said.

"No," he said, "of course not."

Rebekah hadn't orgasmed, but she was breathing heavily. Martin was not. As she caught her breath and her heart rate slowed she had time to wonder how old he was.

"Fifty-three," he said, even though she hadn't asked the question out loud.

She pondered this before saying, "It doesn't matter."

When she woke it was dark outside Reginald Martin's bedroom window, and he was no longer in the bed beside her. She lingered there for some time, warm beneath the sheets. When finally she stood she took the sheet with her, pulled its edge with a tug from beneath the mattress, wrapped it around herself. There was a mirror against the wall but she did not look at herself as she passed it. She found her purse on the floor where she'd left it and from it she retrieved her phone. She checked the time. It was just after seven in the evening and she wasn't hungry. She left the bedroom and found Reginald Martin sitting, wearing only a pair of striped boxers, at his kitchen table. An amount of belly fat spilled over the waistband but did not force the waistband to fold over itself. An empty plate was in front of him. He was reading a magazine. He looked up as she entered the room. "Hello," he said. "Can I get you anything? A cup of coffee."

She adjusted the sheet, which was slipping, threatening to reveal a nipple. "I don't drink coffee."

For a few moments he looked at her, as if answering discerning the answer to a riddle. "No," he said finally. "I don't suppose you do."

The rest of the semester passed in a contrapuntal haze. Classes, the gym, labs, mystery novels partially read and Netflix series started but abandoned. Homework. Infrequent lunches with Beth. Reginald Martin's apartment whenever she was bored.

The first time she left his place he asked for her number. She gave it to him. And hardly had she left his driveway than he had texted *I hope you had fun. :)*

I did. Thanks, she replied.

Each time he texted her some variant of this. Why? she asked him, the morning after their sixth, maybe seventh, liaison.

"So I have a record," he replied. "So you don't try to falsely accuse me of rape or something. I have evidence it was consensual."

"Why would I accuse you of rape?"

He said nothing.

"Well, anyway, you don't have to keep texting me. It's fine. I consent to this and all future sexual intercourse."

The Monday before Thanksgiving she had dinner at Beth and John's house. "Friendsgiving," Beth called it. Attendees included and were limited to John, Beth, Rebekah, and a young woman named Darlene, who worked with Beth at Betty's bakery. Beth made a ham, green beans, and new potatoes; and rectangular pieces of soy for herself, because she wasn't eating the ham. Rebekah brought wine. Darlene brought wine. Beth, John, and Darlene drank one bottle between themselves. Rebekah before she knew it had polished off the other.

On actual Thanksgiving she drove to Helena and celebrated with her parents, an aunt and uncle, three annoying cousins, and another aunt—a serial monogamist, currently single, cloying. Rebekah brought homework with her and, between helping to prepare the meal and playing touch football in the backyard with her father and two of the young cousins, she studied. "How studious, that daughter of yours," she heard the cloying aunt say. "She's a good kid," she heard her mother reply. Rebekah made only a small note of the fact that between Wednesday and Friday when she returned to Bozeman, the only exchange she observed between her parents was "Pass the gravy."

Rebekah studied. She studied studied studied. At work she studied. At home she studied. Exam time came in early December and she passed each one. Physics, cell biology, inorganic chemistry. She'd taken a workload that had hovered somewhere between heavy and unheavy, noncommittal in its lack of ease or difficulty, finishing all but two pre-med course requirements so that she could spend her final semester as an undergrad volunteering at the hospital. In Dr. Martin's class they progressed through the textbook; after the mud shark was the human brain, briefly, a detour, then the perch, then the mudpuppy; "I know you're all sick of fish," Dr. Martin said, so then they dissected a frog; everyone in the class had dissected a frog before, some of them multiple times, in high school, in other labs, and so the students were restless and the frog unit lasted just two days; after the frog, a cat; after the cat, a short return to the human brain ("I apologize that we did not work as deeply with mammals as I promised we would—it's just that you all move too slow."). When the final exam came and it was indeed focused on the mud shark, Rebekah had the highest score. She barely passed the Myth-lit class, but she did pass. Her GPA hovered steady at 3.2.

In Dr. Martin's class, when she needed him, he was "Dr. Martin". In his bedroom she never said his name. Once, he made her come, surprising them both. He used two fingers inside her and motioned until her core shook. It wasn't earth-shattering, but it happened. Despite trying he was never able to reproduce the effect.

And then the semester was over and she wasn't in his class anymore and as she dressed in his bedroom one frosty December morning ("My radiator's on the fritz, the landlord keeps telling me he's going to fix it."), pulling on her stockings, she said aloud what until that point had been unspoken but understood: now their entanglement was over.

"Of course," he said. "I understand. It's been a privilege having you in my bed."

A privilege? Never had she heard that before. A pleasure, a good time, a nice lay—never a privilege. She hesitated to believe it. In the end she chose not to. It was just a thing he was saying. Flattery. Ending on good terms. She rolled a striped wool stocking over her knee.

"Can I make you one last breakfast?" he asked, sitting there in the bed, contemplating an unlit cigarette.

"I've never eaten breakfast here," she pointed out. She could count on three fingers the number of times she'd stayed the night.

"Can I make you *a* breakfast, then? No last about it. Although technically it would be the last, wouldn't it . . ." He trailed off, as if to suggest that maybe it wouldn't be the last, just the first, that maybe she'd someday find herself here again.

And while she knew that would never happen, she *was* hungry. At home she had only bagels and possibly spoiled cream cheese, and she should eat something real before meeting her parents at the airport.

"Excellent!" he said, after she affirmed he could make her something, if he wanted. He clapped his hands together and it was the most cheerful she'd ever seen him. He put on a worn black AC/DC t-shirt and together they walked to the kitchen. He gave her a cup of coffee even though she didn't drink coffee. She added two spoonfuls of sugar, then a third, and sipped it uncertainly while checking her phone. No messages. Marketing emails. Your Macy's credit card payment is due. John's latest YouTube video had 20,000 views—a new high, as far as Rebekah could recall. She started to watch it with the volume low as bacon began to sizzle on the stove. John's intelligence impressed her as much as his weakness, his neediness, alienated her from him. It was like as much as she cared for him (and why shouldn't she? he was her best friend's best friend) she could do so only through this glass screen.

"So, Ms. Fleckman," Reginald Martin said ten minutes later, putting a plate in front of her and joining her at the table. "Since this is the last time I'm probably going to see you, who are you?"

"I'm sorry?" she said. Eggs, bacon, toast.

"What are your plans, Rebekah?"

Her plans. She did *have* plans. She was going to go to medical school.

"Are you excited about it?" he asked around a mouthful of toast.

"Of course," she said. She wouldn't be doing it if she wasn't excited about it.

He nodded. "Good." He piled a forkful of eggs onto his own toast and took another bite. He chewed for a moment. Then he said, "You see, I'm just not sure I believe that, though. I think it's a crock of shit."

Rebekah had not yet partaken of her food. She'd only applied salt and pepper to the eggs. Her coffee mug was still almost entirely full. "Excuse me?" she said now.

"I think you're full of shit, is what I'm saying, and I think you know it."

"What the fuck?" Rebekah said. "What the actual fuck are you talking about?"

He took another bite. "Now, no need to get defensive. I'm just telling you what you need to hear. I think you're sort of dead inside is all. You have no ambition, no real goals. There isn't anything that defines you as a person."

Confused, but not exactly angry, she stood from the table. Where was her jacket? Her purse?

"Now now, it's nothing to be ashamed of. Most women are. Dead inside, that is. Unfeeling, uncaring. Passionless. I've seen it dozens of times. Hundreds. Over and over again."

Rebekah was by the door, clumsily trying to put one foot inside a shoe.

Doctor Martin was standing from the table now. He wiped

his face with a paper napkin and picked up Rebekah's purse from the floor. Handed it to her. "You have potential, if it's any consolation. Lots of potential. You could be anything if you wanted to be, really *wanted* to be. I can see."

She took the purse, reached for the doorknob.

"I wouldn't be telling you this if I couldn't see the potential. Usually I just let the women go, say nothing, because they're hopeless."

Rebekah's brain wasn't entirely processing the situation. She was working on instinct. It was telling her: get out of here, this isn't a safe place, behind you lies danger. The warnings were flashing through her head, blinding her. She wasn't spinning, the world wasn't spinning, but she was dizzy. Before she could walk out the door Reginald Martin's hand was on her shoulder. She flinched, but he was just handing her her coat, which she'd nearly left behind.

"I'm telling you because I like you. I think you're a good person. Most women aren't good people."

"You're an asshole," she said to his face. She said it far more calmly than she would have expected. Although she must been displaying *some* passion, because he wiped away spittle with the paper napkin she hadn't realized he was still holding.

5

THEY WERE SPENDING CHRISTMAS IN New York City with her brother and his girlfriend. Rebekah's brother's name was Bret and Rebekah couldn't remember the girlfriend's name. She'd been told it before but she couldn't remember it. She knew the girlfriend had a two-year-old son and while she couldn't remember his name either she knew it was something like Zacharius or Archibald or Cain, some name she'd heard before in the Bible or literature but never attached to a real person. Rebekah hadn't seen her brother in six years. He never came home for the holidays, which was why finally they were going to visit him. As children they'd gotten along just fine. He didn't post on Facebook much (neither did Rebekah), but she knew at some point he'd posted there he was voting for Donald Trump. Her father may have liked that post, now that she thought about it—she couldn't remember. Not a day went by that Rebekah didn't feel at least in some small way disconnected from the people around her.

Did this make her lonely? Was everyone alone? Wouldn't that mean no one was?

She was quiet during most of the six-hour plane ride (by some miracle her parents had scored non-stop tickets), pretending to read *The Name of the Rose*, which she'd almost forgotten to bring. "The greatest mystery novel of all time," the librarian had said when Rebekah was there last week, and while Rebekah had doubted the claim the librarian added, "Shame that he died, not so long ago," and so Rebekah had felt compelled to the check out the book out of a sense of maudlin respect. Was she really dead inside? she wondered. Certainly not, if she was capable of feeling respect—*maudlin* respect—for an author she'd never met, or for anyone at all. And yet . . . did she love people? She found herself thinking for some time of Beth and John . . . .

"You okay, Bek?" her father asked, and though she hadn't been sleeping, his question jolted her awake?

"How's that, Dad?" she said.

Her parents had driven over that morning from Helena, and they'd all three of them be flying together out of Bozeman-Yellowstone. "We'll pick you up at your place," her mother said over the phone, when they were making the arrangements, "and then we can all go to the airport together."

And while it didn't matter either way Rebekah told them that, no, it was okay, she could meet them at the airport. She didn't know why she didn't want them picking her up. They'd been to her apartment many times. But Thanksgiving seemed like not so very long ago, and suddenly she'd do anything to prolong, even for just twenty minutes, seeing her parents again.

"But then we both have to pay for parking, and that doesn't make any sense."

"It's okay," Rebekah said. "I get free airport parking—through the university." And it was just the sort of nonsensical lie her mother was in the habit of believing.

Now, on the plane, her father from the seat next to her was

saying, "You've been staring at that book for at least an hour, the same page, you haven't changed it once."

"Oh," she said, caught. "I guess I'm just tired."

"Late night?" her father asked. He winked.

"Ew," she said. "Dad, *ew*. Don't."

He shrugged. "I just want you to be happy."

She didn't see how that was relevant.

"Anyway, I haven't touched a paper book myself in years. Not since your mother got me that Kindle for my birthday."

"I got you what?" her mother said from one seat over, pulling an earbud from one ear.

"Nothing," her father said. He sounded annoyed.

"Whatever," her mother replied. Was that a sneer? She replaced the earbud and went back to watching whatever movie was playing on her iPad.

"You haven't said anything about . . . well—notice anything different about me, Bek?" Her father's snide smile indicated he'd been waiting for her to comment on his new mustache this entire time. Frankly, she thought it looked ridiculous.

"Your hair's thinning faster, isn't it?" she said.

Her father frowned.

"Anyway, like I said, I'm tired." She asked a passing flight attendant for a pillow and when it came she closed her eyes, leaving her father to do whatever it was he did on long flights.

She'd slept long and well the night before, so she did not sleep now. She couldn't stop repeating in her mind the words *dead inside*. She wondered how she'd come to yell the word *asshole* at a fifty-something-year-old man who took perverse pleasure in licking hers (certainly he took far more pleasure from it than she received); she did not laugh at this question, as objectively humorous as it was.

Dead inside.

Dead inside.

Dead inside.

She must have fallen asleep eventually because she repeated those two words like a mantra and no time passed before they were touching down at LaGuardia.

Before today Rebekah had never left Montana, save for a trip to Idaho when she was seven to visit the ill-fated Post Falls restaurant, followed by a trip to Silverwood Theme Park, the only amusement park worth visiting in the American Northwest. Thus, New York, as her first real non-Montana destination (because weren't Idaho and Montana really the same place, with their big skies and and craggy fields and rocky mountain ranges?) was a culture shock to her. Or at least it would be, if would have the opportunity to see any of it. As it was her family seemed interested in spending the week only in the Brooklyn neighborhood in which her brother lived.

"This is nice," Rebekah's father said as they exited the cab and met Bret, who was standing on the sidewalk outside his building, waiting for them. Rebekah had tried to convince them to take an Uber, but her parents had only a vague conception of what an Uber was, even though the ride-sharing company had been operating in all major Montana cities for at least a year. Rebekah had the app on her phone, she told them, she could just summon a car and her parents could pay her back, or not, if they didn't want to, she could get this one, it was coming out of the money they insisted on dropping into her bank account each month anyway (although, come to think of it, no payment had dropped this month—and for that maybe she was, in a way, grateful). But by the time she had her phone out of her back pocket her father had already been standing in the middle of the pickup lane outside the terminal, his kneecaps coming *this close* to being cracked by a screeching honking yellow taxi. "Be careful!" Rebekah's mother yelled. And her father had replied, "Don't be such a pussy, this is how you have to do things in New York"

Bret took his mother's black suitcase (too big to carry on—they'd spent fifteen minutes waiting for it at the luggage conveyor). "The neighborhood's okay," he said. "It used to be better, but now it's nothing but hipsters. Artists and social justice warriors. Feminism."

He said *artist* and *feminism* with the same intonation, not exactly disdainful but suggesting he didn't believe such concepts existed in any concrete way.

He looked at Rebekah. "Hey kid," he said. He hugged her with the suitcase-free hand. He didn't offer to take her bag, which was just a small backpack. They followed him inside, up a narrow flight of stairs, and then another flight. Rebekah's dad grunted as he pulled his bag up the stairs; it was smaller than her mother's but just barely—technically within the airline's carryon guidelines but stuffed to the seams and as heavy as, if not heavier than, her mother's.

"Now this—*this* is nice." Rebekah's mother appeared comically awestruck as they entered the third-floor apartment. It *was* nice, Rebekah had to admit, if smaller than the place she shared with her two bitchy roommates in Montana. It was, though, slightly bigger than Beth and John's apartment. Two bedrooms, a modern kitchen, room for a dining table seating six (eight, it looked like, if you inserted a leaf), lots of stucco molding with ornate-but-to-Rebekah's-eye-generic designs, a living room separated from the kitchen in no particular way, bookshelves with books on them. This last detail was a surprise: Rebekah had always assumed her brother didn't read books. She couldn't remember him ever looking at one as a kid. But now, while she admittedly wasn't a prolific reader herself, it seemed Bret might be better read than her.

Bret shrugged. "Yeah, the apartment is okay too. Someday— soon, I hope—I plan to get a place in Manhattan. Closer to work. Closer to . . . well . . . parties and stuff."

"What's the rent like?" Rebekah's mother asked.

"$1900, but I can afford more than that."

"$1900? A *month?*"

"Jesus, dear," Rebekah's father said. "It really is like you have no idea how big cities work, do you? And this is *the* Big City. Nineteen-hundred is a steal, isn't it, Bret?"

"Dad. Don't be mean," Rebekah said, surprising herself

There was a silence, and then her father, chastised, placed his suitcase on the floor.

"And Evelyn lives here with you?" her mother asked. "And her kid, Enoch?"

Evelyn! Enoch! Those were their names. How could Rebekah have forgotten? Most women in the periphery of her life were named Evelyn.

Enoch, though?—how stupid.

"Um, they did. They don't anymore," Bret said

"Oh?" her mother said. "Why not? Is everything okay?"

"Everything's fine. They're fine, I'm sure. We broke up is all. A while ago."

"How long is a while ago?"

Bret shrugged. "Five months?"

Her mother slapped Bret's shoulder. "And you didn't *tell* us?"

"When should I have told you, Mom?"

"Any time, you think? We talk on the phone every week!"

This was was news to Rebekah, who talked to her brother on the phone not at all.

"It's not a big deal. She's fine. I still . . . see her."

"I don't even remember seeing you change your relationship status online."

"I didn't. I don't ever use Facebook, Mom. You know that. I never updated my status to say we were dating in the first place."

"And well I wish you'd use Facebook more. Then maybe we'd know what's going on with you."

He shrugged again. "I'm on Twitter . . ."

"Fuck Twitter. I tried Twitter—it's garbage."

Rebekah gaped. Both her parents, she was beginning to notice, were swearing more than she'd ever heard them swear before.

"Dear," her father said.

"Shut up," her mother said, inappropriately angry. She turned back to Bret. "Why did you break up with her? She was a nice woman. She was good for you. I thought you were going to settle down. Isn't that what you want?"

Rebekah, uncomfortable, examined the bookshelves. Her father retreated to the bathroom.

"It used to be, I guess," Bret said. "But not anymore. Not for a while. I couldn't be spending all my time taking care of a kid. I have work to do."

"Your work is fine. You have plenty of money, you said. What more work do you need to do?"

"Mom, I don't want to be an analyst forever. I want to change the world."

"Oh, big boy, big dreams. And how do you plan on doing that?"

"What? I don't know . . . I guess I'm going to— I've already started, okay?"

"Started. You've started. Are you even still working at the . . . I don't what the fuck you call it? The analyst . . . shop?"

"I haven't quit my job, Mom, if that's what you're asking. I'm working forty hours a week, sometimes sixty. I work my ass off."

"And you couldn't spend some of the money you make from that taking care of a nice young lady and her nice young son?"

"*God*, Mom, he wasn't *my* kid. I'm not spending all my resources on some *other guy's* kid. Sure, a year ago the guy I was would have been happy to do that, but I'm no cuck anymore."

"*Cuck?* What the hell does that mean?"

Rebekah knew the answer to that one. Anyone who spent any amount of time on the internet during the last election— and granted she'd spent only some—would have come across the word. The conversation was interlocking with the books on the shelf, like pieces of an out-of-focus puzzle, and she was beginning to get a semi-clear picture of what might be going on in her brother's life.

The bathroom door opened. Apparently her father could only pretend to urinate for so long. "Hey, so," he said, clapping his hands together. "Let's go check out the neighborhood, yeah?"

Rebekah's mother capitulated. Her behavior was surprising to Rebekah: in twenty-three years Rebekah had never known her mother to be confrontational, but now, after a day of hardly saying a word to anyone, she seemed to crave argument.

Rebekah hadn't yet taken off her coat. She waited for everyone else to put theirs back on, and then they all followed a quiet, almost stoic Bret back into the Brooklyn street. Again Rebekah's father began to call for a cab, but Bret told him don't be ridiculous—you walked in Brooklyn, and they weren't going far. Indeed, he led them to the end of the next block. A brewery on the corner.

"They brew beer here?" her dad asked as they slid into a booth. He glanced around the small establishment, incredulous.

"This *is* a taproom," Bret replied. "They do the brewing in the back. It's a small operation."

"I don't see any beers on the menu but domestics," Rebekah observed.

Rebekah's mother, who wasn't a beer drinker and probably couldn't tell you what the difference between craft and domestic was, said nothing. She was brooding. Her fractiousness was making the group uncomfortable.

Bret winced. "So . . . technically the operation is illegal." He said *technically* in a way that made it sound smaller than the other words.

"This place is illegal?" Rebekah said. She wasn't concerned, just interested.

"Not the restaurant, just the brewing part. It's a small business. Kind of secret. Most people who come here don't even know about the beer."

Rebekah's father was nodding his head approvingly.

A waitress came by. "Hey, Lori," Bret said to her with familiarity. "Four MGDs and a large basket of cheddar fries." She didn't say anything, but she smiled and nodded and disappeared.

Rebekah knew beer. She knew what MGD usually was. "Some kind of code?" she observed.

Bret pointed to the restaurant's back wall. "See those signs there? The Budweiser and the Miller Genuine Draft signs? They have a whole bunch of them they hang up. Coors. Busch." He pretended to shudder. "Keystone Light. And not just domestics. Heineken. Guinness. Modelo. Et cetera. Each time you come in here, they'll have two or three hanging up. They mean different things. Each one refers to a different *kind* of beer."

"So MGD is . . ."

"IPA. Now you never know much about it, but you can ask Lori once she brings it. If it's the same IPA they had last week, then it's really good."

"I don't like IPAs," Rebekah's mother said.

"You'll like this one," Bret told her. "Trust me. And if you don't, no biggie. Budweiser is a stand-in for cream ale. And they have cocktails. They have a regular liquor license; just not a brewing license. Get whatever you want. I'm buying."

Rebekah's mother did like the IPA, it turned out. And also the cream ale. And a second cream ale. A second IPA. Before she knew it Rebekah was sitting at a booth in a dark illegal brewery in a strange city with her drunk mother, drunk father, and only slightly drunk brother. Rebekah herself was drunk too. It was a peculiar family moment in that it was just that: a family moment. How long since there had been one of these. When had the family last been together like this, all of them? Three years ago? Five? Shit—even longer? Bret had gone to school in Bozeman for two semesters before telling his family he'd changed his mind, he was leaving, he'd applied to the NYC School of Visual Arts and by some miracle had gotten in (he'd never been a model student—if Rebekah's grades were mediocre, Bret's were embarrassing). He was going to be an artist. A graphic artist, maybe, or maybe comic books. Somewhere along the way he'd become an analyst instead. An analyst of what, Rebekah didn't know. She'd never heard the story. "Analyst" was just a term to her, some sliver of New York jargon. There were no analysts in Montana. She didn't even know whether her brother had graduated. Had he switched schools again, once he got here?

He'd returned to Montana for the holidays only twice that she could remember. Or had there been a third time, but she'd had to stay in Bozeman for work that winter? That sounded right, like a thing that had happened. In any case here they all were together, drinking craft beer. Craft beer—Montana and New York weren't so different in that respect, although at this point maybe it was a predilection shared by all of America . . . except maybe the South. Rebekah shrugged; she didn't know much about the South. Bret asked her what she was shrugging about and she said she didn't know. They ordered another basket of cheddar fries. Chicken fingers. Still hungry, the group moved up one more block. You have to try New York pizza. From time to time Bret received a text message. Often he was checking Twitter; he'd open his phone, open Twitter, shake his head as he scrolled. Rebekah sitting next to him saw some of the posts in his feed; she shook her head too, in response to her brother shaking his head. Her parents at some point became wrapped up in each other's presence. Her father was saying something, something obnoxious or inappropriate, and her mother was laughing. That might have been joy on her face—joy, or alcohol. Her father made a pun and they all groaned. In response he made two more puns, playing off the first. As the group stumbled back to Bret's apartment in the dark—snow was falling now, sticky puffy flakes —Bret made a quip about how maybe they *did* need a cab at this point, even though the trip was only two blocks.

When they arrived back at the apartment Rebekah took the couch. Her parents retreated to the guest room. In the middle of the night she woke and she could hear them, either arguing or having sex. She didn't know which and both discomfited her.

* * *

Late morning sunlight woke her. Her mouth was dry. Her head hurt. The apartment was empty. There was coffee in a Coffeemate coffee pot on the counter. And a note that said:

Sis,

I'm off to work. Mom and dad are still asleep as I write this. I imagine you'll wake up before them? I'm not sure—are you a late sleeper? Anyway, take one of these, they'll help.

Bret

Next to the note was a small aquamarine packet. Like a condom wrapper or an Alka-Seltzer pouch. It said "Snowglobe, for Hangovers" in white letters. Rebekah had never heard of it before. Had New York discovered the cure for the common hangover?

She opened the packet, dissolved the pale blue tablets she found within in a large glass of water. Chugged the effervescent concoction. She'd never liked drinks like that—chalky, bubbly. She ignored the coffee.

Her brother's bedroom door was closed. The guest room door was ajar. She knocked on it. "Mom? Dad?" she called softly.

At her touch, the door opened further. The room was void of human life. The bed was made. Oddly, not even her parent's suitcases were visible.

She couldn't tell whether the Snowglobe tablets were working. She returned to the kitchen, filled the glass with plain water this time, returned to the couch and slowly sipped it while checking her phone.

A text from Beth, received the night before, asked: *Did you make it?*

Rebekah smiled. Her friend, always concerned. *The flight was good*, Rebekah replied. *In New York. Safe.*

Rebekah started a group message with her parents. *Where are you guys?*

For a while she sat and drank the water. Realizing suddenly how full her bladder was, she went to the bathroom. She took her phone with her. Some people, she'd been told, mostly coffee drinkers, took massive dumps in the morning. Not Rebekah— she just peed a lot, for a long time.

She decided to shower. When she was done she put back on the sweatpants in which she'd slept. In her bag she found a fresh t-shirt with a faded Batman logo on the front. She supposed the Snowglobe was working. She found some bread in her brother's freezer. She toasted it, applied peanut butter. She ate. Then she took *The Name of the Rose* from her bag and read for a while before falling asleep again.

She mustn't have slept long. It was just past noon when she woke again. She was feeling close to normal now. Her stomach churned only a little bit. The apartment was still empty. She changed into jeans and thought about going out. Rebekah wasn't an explorer, but what else was there to do?

By the time her parent's returned, neither speaking to the other, she'd finished *The Name of the Rose* and had moved on to one of the books from her brother's shelf. She did not ask them where they'd been, and they did not say.

"What time does Bret get home?" her father asked just after 7 pm.

"I don't know," her mother replied. "He didn't tell me." She looked at Rebekah. "Did he say anything to you?"

Rebekah shook her head. "Nope."

So they ordered pizza, had it delivered to the apartment. It was then that Rebekah realized she'd be eating a lot of pizza during this trip. She wouldn't be surprised if the only non-pizza meal she'd have would be Christmas dinner, four days from now. She was hungry. She ate four slices. They turned on Bret's television, discovered he had a Netflix account (big surprise—who doesn't?) and watched two and a half hours of some HGTV faux-home-improvement show called *House Hitlers*. It was the sort of show where you got the impression that two attractive twin brothers remodeled a place by themselves but what the producers didn't show you was the dozen-person contractor team that did the real work between shots. Rebekah wanted to watch a movie but her mother wanted to watch *House Hitlers* and her father said he didn't care, so Rebekah said she didn't care either, and they watched *House Hitlers*.

After her parents went to bed Rebekah snuck into the kitchen and retrieved a fifth slice from the refrigerator, then a sixth. There was one slice left and she thought she should probably save it for her brother; although she didn't think he'd care—anyone staying out this late had doubtlessly eaten by now. She gave some thought to increasing the frequency of her workouts when she returned to Bozeman. She'd need it, after all the pizza, although seeing as how the pizza was the first thing she'd eaten all day, she was doing fine, calorie-wise, not that she cared about calories. At no point did she worry about her brother. Staying out late was what people did in big cities. With everything there was to do here, one could be forgiven for forgetting one had family in town.

When Bret finally came home Rebekah was not asleep. She was lying on the couch with headphones in, intending to watch a movie on her phone but instead having been caught up in a cascade of memes and reposted late-night talk show clips; this

189

had never happened to her before; she'd never spent this long at a stretch on the internet. "Hey," Bret said, removing his own headphones. "Mom and Dad asleep?"

"Yeah."

"Sorry I'm late. I was going to hang out with you guys, but work went late, and then I got invited to dinner and, well, I was already in Manhattan, so why not? And then the train was slow."

Rebekah noticed Bret's bloodshot eyes, wrinkles around them that had not been there yesterday. "Doesn't matter to me," she said

"Good day?"

"It was fine."

"New York's pretty sweet, isn't it?"

"Yeah. Hey, there's pizza for you in the fridge."

"Cool. Thanks." And to her surprise he retrieved the slice, put it on a plate, and took it with him into his bedroom.

Rebekah put her phone on its charger and promptly fell asleep.

And in this manner the rest of the trip proceeded until Christmas Eve: Rebekah's parents seemed to stay in the apartment 90 percent of the time, content to watch all day every day their son's large television during their visit to supposedly the Greatest City in World. Where they went that first full day Rebekah never learned, but clearly it underwhelmed them. As for her, Bret promised every day to take her out when he got home, but always did he end up working late; he never again came home red-eyed though, or under any apparent influence; he was just tired, his mind fatigued after a full day of analyzing. Even on Saturday—Christmas Eve eve—he had to work. He left late that day, making breakfast for his family (eggs, bacon, waffles in his waffle iron—her recent experiences with home-cooked breakfasts

190

left a bad taste in Rebekah's mouth that this meal did not quite wash out), and then went to work; before he left he said, "Hey do you guys mind if we do Christmas Eve dinner at my friend Darius's place? He said he'd love to have us," and then he was gone for the day. And so Bret did not take Rebekah out. And she did not go out with her parents. She could not read with the television on so she went out herself. Each day she went out, one of her brother's books in a messenger bag she borrowed from him slung over her shoulder. She'd take the train, was the plan. She'd explore New York City. She'd go to the Met. She'd go to the Strand. She'd ascend the Empire State Building ("Better not," said Bret. "It's expensive and not worth it."). She'd read on a bench in Central Park, like you saw in the movies. But she never made it farther than the restaurant-*cum*-illegal brewery at the end of the next block over, where she drank enough to maintain a pleasant buzz while she read her brother's books and got to chatting with the waitress from the first night, Lori, who often worked double shifts and who was more than a little acquainted with her brother.

"Yeah, I know him. I mean, he's in here a lot. It's one of those neighborhood hangout sort of things, you know? He says he has this place"—she made air quotes—"'on lock.'"

"What does that mean?" Rebekah asked.

"Something like that he owns the place, without really owning it, you know?"

"Sure," Rebekah said. She didn't know. She thought the phrase sounded like bullshit. But she was willing to acknowledge that having things "on lock" sounded like something legitimate one did in New York City. She noticed Lori was smiling, and the smile was wistful. "But you know him even better than that, don't you," Rebekah observed.

"Well," Lori said. "I mean . . ."

Rebekah held up a hand. "It's okay. I don't need to know."

"If it helps," Lori offered, still smiling affectionately, "he's also, like, a total asshole."

"Well," Rebekah said.

"But what about you?" Lori said.

"What do you mean?"

"What do you do?"

"I'm in school," Rebekah said.

Lori was nodding. "Yeah, cool. I did that too. Well, then I dropped out."

"That seems to happen a lot. Why did *you* drop out?"

The waitress shrugged. "Lots of reasons."

"Oh, yeah?"

"Yeah. A bad thing happened. Then I followed a guy. Not a bad guy—just a guy. And I liked him and he seemed to know what he was doing, so I followed him. Went out west with him. California. We didn't like it there like we thought we would. Came here instead."

"Oh. That's a long journey."

"Yeah, well. And we did the whole thing on a motorcycle."

Rebekah said that sounded cool, adding, "I guess."

"Not really," LoriLoriLori said. "And then after a while together here we broke up. He cheated on me. Again. He's still in New York, I think. We're still Facebook friends, but I'm like, never on there."

Rebekah shrugged in a not unkind way. She didn't feel like talking any more.

"I don't think anybody uses Facebook anymore, do they? I mean, not like our age. I mean, I guess you're a few years younger than me, but you know what I mean. Like our generation. My parents still use it. My parents don't like me. I used to be *very* religious, but I'm not anymore. That was hard for them to accept. So anyway, after we broke up I got kind of empty. I missed him a lot. It made me sad."

"Sad and empty aren't the same thing," Rebekah said.

"So why are you sad? Some guy screw you over too? Like I said, I know how that feels."

"What? No—I'm not sad."

"Oh. I'm sorry."

For a moment Rebekah didn't respond. "It's whatever," she finally offered.

"Well, anyway. I really like your brother!"

This was the day before Christmas Eve and Rebekah decided she didn't want to come to this brewery anymore, but she couldn't anyway because the place was closed on Christmas Eve and the family had dinner plans.

Darius was five years older than Bret and lived in Tribeca, in a twelfth-floor apartment with white walls, white furniture, and mostly white art: ceramic sculptures, three-dimensional collage, paintings that were mostly texture with certain flecks of black. Darius's apartment had a spacious kitchen that opened onto the living room. The living room's glass windows stretched from floor to ceiling. One of the windows was a disguised sliding glass door. The door led to a small balcony. The balcony had a potted plant whose pot was as high as an adult's knees and whose green leaves reached the bottom of the balcony above. The balcony above was also Darius's; it was attached to his bedroom. Darius's apartment was two stories and to get to the bedroom or the master bath you ascended a spiral stLoriaircase that had probably been salvaged from an old fire station.

"Darius is a senior analyst," Bret had told them on the Uber ride over. "He makes a lot of money. I mean a *lot*. Also, I know his name is Darius but he's not black. Darius is from Pakistan. Just thought you should know that before—just so you're not surprised."

"Why would I be surprised?" Rebekah's father had said. "I'm not racist."

"It's a just a black-sounding name, is all," Bret said.

"'Black-sounding.' Now that's a racist thing to say."

Also during the ride over Rebekah's father had marveled at the miracle of Uber. He'd made Bret show him how to install the app on his own phone. "Just like that?" he said. "You just hit the button? Wow. Hey," he said to the driver, "I bet you make some money doing this."

"It's okay," the driver said.

Rebekah's dad had spent the rest of the ride chatting with the Uber driver.

Rebekah's dad when they arrived at Darius's apartment said, loudly, "Huh." When Rebekah's mother elbowed him and glared at him he said, "Excuse me, *dear*. I just thought he'd be *darker*."

Darius shook her father's hand. He hugged Bret, Rebekah, and her mother. He kissed Rebekah and her mother's cheeks. "It's a pleasure to meet Bret's family," he said. "I've heard wonderful things."

Darius offered them all champagne. "Nothing like good champagne during a celebration. We'll switch to wine for dinner." He went to check the oven, where he was cooking both a turkey and a ham. He explained that actually his girlfriend was cooking them, but she'd forgotten an ingredient and had run out to a corner market, which should still be open, and he'd of course agreed to keep an eye on them for her.

"You're all going to love Darius's girlfriend," Bret said. "She's from the Philippines."

Darius's family arrived, and a few more of his and Bret's friends. While Darius spoke with no trace of an accent his parents' were heavily Pakistani. His mother's English wasn't strong. Rebekah's mother and Darius's mother nonetheless got along. Darius's father and Rebekah's father were discussing the nuances of small-business ownership; Darius's father ran a deli on Long Island, where they'd lived "ever since we came forty years ago to America." Rebekah drank her champagne in gulps.

She found Bret and Darius on the balcony. Darius had just handed Bret something small and white and Bret had washed it down his throat with his own champagne.

"What's that?" Rebekah said.

They turned to her, startled.

"Is it Ecstasy?" she asked. "Something like that?"

Bret laughed. "It's Xanax," he said.

"But really," Rebekah said, "what is it?"

Bret stared at her. "Sis, we're about to have Christmas dinner with our families. I haven't seen mine in years and Darius's still haven't assimilated to American culture. And his girlfriend's friends, who even though she's a Filipina are BWBs, are coming by too after whatever party they're at right now. We each just took a Xanax."

"What's BWB?" Rebekah asked. She vaguely recalled seeing the term in one of her brother's books.

Darius laughed.

Bret said, embarrassed, "Basic white bitch."

Rebekah held out a hand. "I'll take a Xanax."

Darius looked at Bret. Bret shrugged. Darius produced an orange prescription bottle and gave her one of the pills.

"Thanks," she said. She put it in her mouth, washed it down with her final swig of champagne, and went back into the apartment to get a refill. She saw her brother make a gesture, maybe to stop her, but she ignored him.

She didn't honestly believe that what Darius had given her was really Xanax, even if the prescription bottle had had the name of the drug typed in a sans serif font so large she could see it if only briefly, but she also didn't care. If her brother was taking it, it couldn't be that bad. And already she was feeling more mellow, more relaxed, not that she'd been particularly anxious to begin with—or ever in her life. Anxiety was not an emotion with which Rebekah Fleckman was familiar. Apathy, disappointment, occasional worthlessness or hopelessness (not about herself, but about whatever she was doing): but never anxiety.

Which was why it was odd now that she could recognize the opposite of anxiety; she couldn't put a word to it, but she knew it was there, bubbling at her surface.

She sipped her champagne and gazed at a piece of minimalist art on Darius's wall. It was mostly white, the art, like the wall around it. Square. Or not square, maybe, not quite. Not even quite a rectangle. Large, maybe six by six or six by five-and-a-half, but with one side slanted, slightly, so that one vertex was maybe 92 degrees, another 88. You could see the skewing only if you stared at the piece for a long time, like Rebekah was. And who had the time for that? Darius probably didn't even realize the piece was skewed. Probably he thought it was perfect, balanced, like everything else in his apartment. But Rebekah knew. She had the time to stare at it and see. What was there to do in New York but gaze for a long time at things?

There was no Christmas tree in Darius's apartment.

Rebekah's father was standing beside her. She didn't know whether he'd been there for minutes or had just arrived. He said, "I don't really like it. It's too much red."

Rebekah hadn't even noticed the painting's colors. Whatever Darius and Bret had given her had washed everything out. Did Xanax do that? Did Xanax wash everything out? Also the piece was mostly white, like the wall. There was color but most of it was white. The color was two colors: purple and red. The purple and red were streaked across the canvas. Cris-crossing. Rebekah could hear the paintbrush (or had the artist used a palate-knife? these were violent strokes): *shkikt, shkikt, shkikt.*

But mostly the painting was white. The canvas was white and it had been painted over with white paint before the color had been applied. And then the streaks of red and purple. Purple was a mix of blue and red. So it was blue, red, and red, the painting. But mostly white.

"It think the red's just fine," Rebekah said. "I think there's too much white."

"Huh. I hadn't really noticed the white."

"I'm happy, Dad," Rebekah said in response.

"Oh? Well that's . . . great, Bek. Honey."

"It is great."

"Listen, I've been wanting to talk to you for a while about something. Well, your mother and I both. Your brother, he's doing really well out here, you know? He's doing well. And someday he'll probably be a *senior* analyst—whatever that is— and live in a place like this. And maybe he'll find a girl and settle down. Here. I don't think he's ever going to leave New York."

"No, I don't think he will," Rebekah agreed

"And, well, so. Someone's going to have to run the pizza business. And I was just thinking—you could come back to Helena . . ."

She looked at him. Suddenly she was seeing more than the painting. Suddenly she could feel the glass in her hand: it was cold. It should have been warm by now because she was holding it but it was cold. "Back to Helena?"

"Yeah. Either now—or after you graduate. Whatever you prefer. But you could come back and I could show you the ropes. And then someday—soon—I could give you the company."

"What would *you* do?"

"I'd like to retire soon. Travel. Maybe live on an island for a while?"

"You and Mom want to live on an island?

"Or you know, a different country. Just—somewhere else. Things are pretty bad here. In this country, I mean."

"I think things are okay. And you both grew up in Montana. I can't picture Mom living on an island. She likes the cold. She *loves* the cold."

"An island's just an option. So what do you think? And you could even have the house. If we end up traveling, that is."

"I think this painting has just the right amount of red. I really do."

Darius approached and said dinner was almost ready and would they like red wine, or white?

Dinner was delicious, what they were able to enjoy of it. Darius's girlfriend had baked both a turkey and a ham, and the ham had been skewered, crusted in pineapple rings, fresh, not canned. Darius was adamant that only fresh unprocessed food be consumed in his home. ("And pussy!" Bret said, and they and some of the other guys snickered and fist-bumped.) The potatoes came from a rooftop garden in Brooklyn and had no trouble growing in winter if you knew what you were doing. Everything else had been shipped in from various parts of the world, by necessity, but the market Darius insisted his girlfriend do their shopping at did their best to procure their goods from locales as close as seasonably possible. On the table were mashed potatoes and new. Sweet potatoes with a sugared pecan topping. Green salad, green green salad. Asparagus, baked, brought by Darius's mother. "She also baked a pie, a rhubarb pie, didn't you, Mother? My mother makes the very best rhubarb pies."

Darius's mother blushed. She was such a small woman, quiet and proud. "To our parents, our families," Darius said, raising his glass. He looked joyfully at his mother and father. Bret raised his glass and smiled at his mother and father, and then at Rebekah. Everyone else raised their glasses and said "To family!"

("And to pussy," Rebekah heard Bret mutter to one of the guys, and there was more snickering.)

"That was lovely," Rebekah's mother offered when the toast was over.

"And the bread," Darius continued, "is homemade. I made it. I used a breadmaker, but still."

His girlfriend said, "Darius has been making homemade bread lately."

Rebekah hadn't learned the girlfriend's name and never would make an effort to, but the girl seemed sweet, younger than Rebekah.

Darius had just handed the boat of gravy to his mother, who was passing it to Rebekah's mother on its way to Rebekah's father when the boom sounded. It was a loud boom, deep, but distant. Dishes on the table maybe shook or maybe didn't, it was hard to tell whether such things were real or imagined, just the mind filling in cracks in one's situational awareness. But the boom was real.

"Shit," Bret said.

"I think that came from the east," Darius said.

"How can you tell?" Rebekah asked, genuinely curious, for she had a shitty sense of directional perception.

"What was it?" her father said. "Darius, can you turn on a TV?"

"My son does *not* own a television," Darius father said. It may have been the first time all evening Rebekah had heard his voice and it oozed scorn.

Darius was already standing, moving toward the stairs. "I'm getting my laptop."

Bret had his phone out. "Nothing in the news yet. But Twitter . . . yep. It was explosion."

"Where?" Darius's father asked.

"Oh my," Rebekah's mother said.

"Hoboken," Bret said.

"Where's that?" Rebekah's mother said. "Is it close?"

"New *Jersey*," her father said, emphasizing the second half of the name. "Across the *river*."

"So not close?"

"It's on CNN now," Bret said. "But there aren't really any details."

"Fuck CNN." Darius was coming down the stairs, a MacBook open in the crook of his arm. "Breitbart already has the story. And Scott Adams is tweeting about it."

"Doesn't Adams live in California?" Bret asked.

"Who's Scott Adams?" Rebekah's mother said.

By pure coincidence Rebekah knew who he was. Bret had had several Dilbert anthologies on his bookshelf. Rebekah had breezed through them all.

"He's in New York for Christmas, though," Darius said. "Anyway—yeah, it looks like the explosion was in Hoboken, but there's also a shooting happening near Yankee Stadium."

"My God," Rebekah's mother said.

"Are people hurt?" Darius's girlfriend asked.

Darius was nodding. He sat back down, placing the laptop on the table. His girlfriend had pulled his plate to the side, clearing a space. His eyes were still on the screen. "It's still happening, but hundreds of shots. Maybe dozens dead. Maybe more."

"And the explosion happened in a restaurant," Bret said. He was still looking at his phone. "Took out most of the block, though."

"How big was the block?" Rebekah wasn't sure who asked this. She was pretty drunk by now, and whatever Darius had given her (it probably *was* Xanax, she'd decided, after googling the affects of Xanax) had mixed with the alcohol to make her think she was more hyperaware than she really was. But she was aware she wasn't as aware as she felt she was, which negated the condition.

"Fucking Muslims," Darius said. Then he hit his fist on the table, and now the plates and glasses did definitely shake. "Fucking *Muslims!*"

For an undoubtedly shorter time than if felt like to Rebekah there was silence, then her father said, "I'm . . . surprised to hear you say that?"

"Why?" Darius said. He'd already calmed down, was breathing even, deliberate breaths.

"Well . . . because you're . . ."

"Muslim?"

Bret put a hand to his own head. "Oh, Dad . . ."

"Well, yeah," Rebekah's father said.

"Mr. Fleckman, how very racist of you," Darius said, mirroring his father's scorn. "I'm Pakistani—that does not mean I'm a Muslim."

"I just thought . . ."

"I am a Christian, sir. Like yourself."

"Well, I'm technically an atheist, but I don't give it a lot of thought . . . My wife is really the Christian."

"An atheist—that explains much," Darius's father muttered into his glass. Everyone seemed to have forgotten that people were probably dying, but Rebekah was still hyperaware of it. Of course, she was also hyperaware of the fact that people were probably *always* dying, at any given moment, and that everyone always seemed to be forgetting about that.

Her phone buzzed in her pocket. A message from Beth said: *Oh my goddess I just heard about the terrorist attack!!! Are you okay?!!!*

We're okay, Rebekah typed. *It's happening on the other side of town.*

"I'm just saying you can't just go and blame Muslims," her father was saying. "We have no idea what the motive here is."

"Is it ever anything else, Mr. Fleckman?"

"Fuck—" Her father said. "This what happens when Donald Trump is president. Racism. Bigotry. Bret, how are you friends with this guy? Don't tell me you're like him?"

"Hey—" Rebekah's mother said.

"Shut up," her father said. "Bret?"

Bret wasn't saying anything.

"I did vote for Donald Trump," Darius offered. "And I'm guessing *you* voted for Clinton."

"Damn right I did. And for good reason. Look at the mess we're in now. The war—"

"And you voted Bernie before that, am I right?"

"Damn r—" Her father paused. "Yes."

Please be careful. Let me know you're still okay when it's all over.

I will. You guys okay?

Yeah. John's getting online. He's going to do a live stream.

"I voted for Trump, too, Dad," Bret said.

"You did?" Rebekah's mother said. "You told me you voted for Hillary."

"No I didn't. I always said I voted Trump. You both liked my post on Facebook."

Darius's mother spoke up then. Again she was blushing. Humble. Even as she said, "A lot of people secretly voted for Trump," she wasn't argumentative.

"But it wasn't a secret—" Bret started.

"Even though he said he'd deport people like you?" Rebekah's father asked Darius's mother.

Darius scoffed. "People like us," he echoed. He turned to Bret. "Did you hear that? 'People like us' your father just said."

"Dad—" Bret started.

"I didn't mean—" her father said.

"And you wonder why we voted for Trump," Darius said.

"I don't know what you mean . . ." her father said.

"Well it's almost as if you spend years calling people racists and bigots, they're going to turn against you. How about that, Mr. Fleckman?"

"Hey," Rebekah said. Then she asked if they could pull YouTube up on the laptop. She told them her friend was broadcasting and she wanted to watch.

Three hours later Rebekah and her parents and Bret were in a hotel room four blocks away. Between the shooting and the bombing the death toll stood at 121. It was rising as medics failed to save members of the critically injured, but the shooter had been apprehended. He'd been shot by police but was still alive. His name had not been released, but undoubtedly it would be by tomorrow, and the media would run wild with it. For a several tense hours everyone remained in Darius's apartment. Eventually they moved from the dinner table to the living room, where the environment seemed more conducive to following the evening's developments. Darius removed a white ceramic lamp from a side table and set his laptop in its place. For ten minutes they all watched John's live stream, then they switched to Periscope, where an alt-right pundit Rebekah had never heard of was reporting from the scene of the bombing in Hoboken. More wine was poured and eventually the bottles were empty. Everyone but Rebekah's parents partook of the rhubarb pie. Darius's girlfriend's friends texted to say they wouldn't be coming, for obvious reasons, better to return to their homes. When the attacks were finally over and the mood in the apartment had grown less tense, Darius said that undoubtedly the subways were closed right now and even though it was unlikely there were going to be more attacks tonight, it was best if the Fleckmans didn't make the commute to Brooklyn. He offered to let them stay the night. He had air mattresses. He had a couch.

Rebekah's father said thank you (insincerely) but they would just get a hotel room, if you don't mind.

Of course, Darius had said. Stay safe, he'd said, as he he walked the family to the building's foyer. Bret, he'd said, call me tomorrow.

And so now they were in a hotel room, four blocks away. The walk to the hotel had been fraught with the looming possibility of peril. Heavy with fear. Rebekah herself did not feel these things, but to her parents it was if they had been pilloried personally by the night's events. "I'm not coming to New York ever again," her mother said.

The emaciated old front desk clerk told them they were

lucky there were any rooms available, let alone one with two queen beds. Renting a room without a reservation on Christmas Eve: *ridiculous!*

But the clerk had been hyperbolizing, probably venting frustration at having to work on Christmas Eve—ridiculous!— for a room had been available and that room was lovely. Two queen beds. And a toaster. And a Nespresso coffeemaker. And a balcony.

Rebekah's parents and brother were sleeping and she was standing on the balcony, leaning on the railing. She was not ready for sleep. She did not want to wake hungover again, so better if she didn't have to wake at all. Just let the drunkenness fade fade fade.

She heard the sliding door open behind her and Bret was there. He was lighting something, and then smoking it. "Joint?" he said.

"I guess one puff," Rebekah said. "Thanks."

After she handed it back to him he said, "I guess that didn't go so well."

"What didn't?" Rebekah said.

"The . . . the whole evening. Christmas Eve."

"Oh. I thought it was all right."

For a few minutes neither spoke. Snow was falling, but most of the flakes dissipated before they ever touched a surface. The balcony faced west and you could see smoke meeting the clouds way out there.

"Sometimes I regret voting for Trump," Bret said. "Sometimes I regret it a lot and sometimes I'm glad I did."

"When did you become . . . would the alt-right call them activists?" Rebekah asked.

"You could tell?"

"I saw your bookshelf. Plus you used the word *cuck*."

"Oh, well—when does someone become anything? It never became, like, official."

"Do you have a blog?"

"I did, at first. But I'm not a writer. I couldn't keep a schedule. Mostly I just tweet."

"Really? You tweet?"

"Well . . . retweet. Darius is the active one. Says he's going to run for congress some day. Says the swamp's still full, and he's the one to drain it."

Rebekah nodded.

"You know—can I tell you a secret? I was in love with Evelyn. *Really* in love with her. And that kid of hers . . . . Aw man, that kid was great. So *smart*."

"So why did you dump her?"

"Darius. Convinced me I shouldn't be spending my resources on someone else's kid. And he said Evelyn's blue hair and piercings meant she was damaged. He was probably right."

"Was he?"

"I mean—I was going to marry her, Rebekah. I was gonna propose."

"Well, if it helps, I didn't vote at all in the last election."

"Doesn't matter," Bret said.

And it probably didn't. It didn't matter who anyone had voted for: the world would always be the same. "I think our parents are getting divorced," Rebekah said.

Bret nodded. "They are. Mom told me a couple weeks ago."

"Typical. Fuck them, I guess."

"They didn't tell you?"

"No."

Several more minutes of silence. Bret smoked his joint.

When it was halfway finished he put it out with his fingertips and returned it to a small bag he produced from his pocket. "Well, good night, sis."

"Hey," she said, before he could walk away.

"Yeah?"

"Do you think I'm . . . dead inside?"

He was unfazed by the question. He considered it for the briefest of seconds. "Sis, I hardly even know you."

"Good point," she said. "Anyway, yeah, good night."

"Good night, sis."

He left. Rebekah turned back toward the city, watching the lights, the snow, and the smoke.

6

DURING THE FLIGHT BACK FROM LaGuardia to Bozeman Yellowstone, which unlike the flight to New York was not a straight trip but required a layover at Minneapolis-St. Paul, Rebekah's parents told her about their pending divorce. At Minneapolis-St. Paul they had nearly three hours to kill so they ate lunch at an upscale airport restaurant. Rebekah had pork chops. Her parents did not tell her during the meal but waited until they were back on the plane. At 40,000 feet they told her. Probably they told her at 40,000 feet because they anticipated an averse reaction, and there was only so much an angry person could do in a metal tube above the earth. Always deliver bad news to a captive audience. Probably they anticipated an averse reaction but what she gave them was indifference. False surprise and then indifference. While she too had *them* captive she told them she didn't want the pizza business, sorry Dad, either sell it, shut it down, or no island life for you. You made this country, you can live in it.

Back in Bozeman she slept for two days. At first she had horrible dreams. She couldn't remember them but they were horrible, even gory. Then her body calmed, her mind calmed, and she settled into a rectitude of slumber. Everything was right while she was sleeping. As she slept her body purged the alcohol, the marijuana, the Xanax—had she put anything else inside herself? But maybe the Xanax was still there, a sliver of it, maybe a sliver of it would be flowing through her blood for the rest of her life, like a raft on a lazy river. She'd been in a lazy river once, at the Silverwood Amusement Park.

She worked a shift at the gym. She thought about quitting the gym but she did not want to find another job. She wanted to work at the hospital but she couldn't start working at the hospital yet, not for pay, only volunteering. She was going to start volunteering on Monday, a week before classes started again. She had only two classes this semester, only two needed to graduate, and so she'd committed to spending most of her time at the hospital. Maybe they'd start paying her. Before her shift at the gym was over Evelyn, the co-owner, said, "Hey, did you hear they're putting in a Planet Fitness?"

"They are?" Rebekah said.

"Yeah. So I guess we're like, totally fucked."

"My brother's girlfriend is named Evelyn," Rebekah said.

"Oh yeah?"

"Well—they broke up."

"Oh. So, yeah, Planet Fitness. We're totally fucked."

Mrs. Cook came in for Hip Hop Fit and when she saw Rebekah at the desk asked how her Christmas was.

"It was good," Rebekah told her.

"Oh good," Mrs. Cook said. "I regretted asking the question as soon as I asked it."

"Why?"

Mrs. Cook pointed to Rebekah's name tag. "I saw your name and thought maybe you were Jewish. I didn't want to offend."

Monday came and Rebekah went to the hospital and was

given a brief orientation along with two other female volunteers and then she was assigned tasks. She set about the tasks. She delivered lab samples and lab results and x-rays. She brought fresh towels to patients in private rooms who asked for fresh towels. She changed the handsoap in a bathroom. She saw in the emergency room a woman come in with a metal dowel piercing her right arm. She was told as long as she was committed to learning she'd see a lot of things like that here. A nurse told her a patient had requested a bowl of sherbet and could Rebekah get that from the cafeteria and bring it to his room in the rehabilitation ward?

Rebekah retrieved the sherbet from the cafeteria. She stepped into the elevator and pushed the button and the doors closed and only then did she see that Doctor Reginald Martin was in there with her. "Hello," he said.

Rebekah looked at him; then she looked away. "I forgot you were a doctor. I only ever thought of you as a teacher."

He thumped his chest. "Best cardiothoracic surgeon in the state."

"Which probably isn't saying much, in Montana," she offered.

He nodded. "Which probably isn't saying much."

The elevator doors opened and Doctor Reginald Martin stepped out.

"Wait—" Rebekah said. She put her arm out to stop the doors from closing.

He turned back to her. "Yes?"

"I think you were right. About me. I think I am dead . . . inside."

Doctor Martin smiled. He shook his head. "No, Rebekah Fleckman, he said. You're not."

"Room 302?" Rebekah asked a nurse at the desk in the rehabilitation ward.

The nurse pointed and Rebekah followed the signs on the hallway walls. You'd think room 302 would be near the front of the ward, but the numbers ran backwards here. "I have your sherbet," Rebekah said as she entered the room.

The patient was writing in a notebook. He looked up. "Oh, hi!" Aaron, her ex-roommate's cousin, who she'd gone on a date with last summer, who'd slept her couch while she'd slept in her room with her door locked, who'd sat in her kitchen all morning writing haiku, said.

"What are you doing here?" Rebekah asked.

He pointed to the cast that ran from foot to mid-thigh. "Injured my leg in the Middle East," he said. "There was an . . . explosion. What are *you* doing here?"

And that *was* the question, wasn't it?

Wasn't *that* the question?

Like, Subscribe

1

WHAT HE DIDN'T UNDERSTAND WAS why they'd got the fucking cat.

Of course at the time it made sense: would they ever have children? Maybe. Maybe not. Certainly not right now. But they were together and responsibility was something people who were together were supposed to share, and cats bestowed responsibility. Less than a child, yes. Less even than a dog. But that was okay when you had important things to do, when you were working hard and your YouTube channel was taking off and your wife was maybe going to make some progress on that urban fantasy novel but even if she didn't she was managing the bakery now. And managing bakeries and filming and producing well-informed and informative YouTube videos were responsibility, but they weren't the kind you could share. A cat was sharable. John could empty the litterbox every day. Beth could make sure the cat had food and water.

Plus John at home all day was sometimes lonely. A cat wasn't just responsibility but also love.

It was a known fact that John was sometimes lonely. It was a known fact that in the past John's loneliness or fear of loneliness had caused him to do terrible things. Terrible things to himself but also, when you thought about it, terrible things to others. The same terrible things he did to himself were the same terrible things he was doing to others. That's what his therapist told him. He'd gotten a therapist but not a psychiatrist. Sometimes Beth told him maybe he should visit a psychiatrist, just once or twice, so that he could get a prescription. "There's no shame in taking medication. You could be doing real good, John, taking medication. Not just for yourself but for others. Fight the stigma. Burn the stigma down." But he didn't like the idea of taking medication. Sometimes in the past he'd done drugs, but not daily. Sometimes he wanted to dull everything, but not daily. He hadn't told Beth that his therapist said he was hurting other people, because then Beth would point out that didn't sound like a thing a good therapist was supposed to say, and she would be right. John didn't want to find a replacement therapist. Finding a replacement therapist would take time, time better spent working on the YouTube channel, making videos. So he just kept going to the one who said that by attempting suicide he was doing real damage to the ones he loved. Which was probably right. Also ironic: if there were people around to hurt, then clearly John wasn't lonely, was he? Clearly you're not lonely, John, just selfish.

This last admonition came not from the therapist, but from deep within John's own self.

And one cat had been fine, really. John loved Bernard; in fact, in addition to cleaning the litterbox, John had become the one who did most of the feeding. He played with Bernard during the day, let Bernard sit on his desk while he worked, next to the iMac he'd bought on a credit card (Beth had great credit; John had none), put a little cat bed there, moved his Webby award (two months into YouTubing, with only a few thousand subscribers, he'd been given a Webby Award; the entry fee had been only $150). Bernard would sleep and purr. John would edit videos, respond to comments, tweet. At first he was locking Bernard out of the bedroom only when he was filming, but then he stopped doing even that after once forgetting: after sitting down to edit he noticed Bernard in the background, staring unmoving at something on the wall, an unseen fly or spider, for the entirety of the video's thirteen minutes. Even between jump cuts the cat didn't move. And because a thirteen-minute video took far longer to actually film—this one had taken three hours because it was full of complicated words about global economics and John kept stuttering over them—there was no fucking way he was going to film it again. So he posted it. Title: THE BREXIT VOTE MORE THAN ONE YEAR LATER AND WHAT IT MEANS FOR YOU (PLUS BERNARD STARING AT A SPIDER). Bernard had been a fucking hit. Commenters had gone wild for Bernard. For a week there were Bernard memes in subreddits. Bernard the cat had his own Instagram account now. John remembered to update it sometimes. John no longer locked the door, so sometimes Bernard wandered in. *Spot Bernard* became a thing in the comments section of John's videos. John loved Bernard.

And then a month ago Beth had found a stray. An orange something, foot badly injured, undernourished, capable of walking but with a limp and a heartbreaking low-pitched moan. John let her take it in. It recovered within a week. She took it to the vet; it had had its shots. It was their cat now.

And like Bernard, Jean-Luc Picat was a good cat. But two cats on the desk was more than one. Jean-Luc Picat started sitting in the cat bed, so Bernard relocated himself to the surface of John's iPad, put too much pressure on the screen, caused liquid-crystal bubbles of blues and greens.

And then there was the hair. The hair was the real problem. John and Beth's apartment was small and hair was everywhere. Now John fed two cats. Cleaned the litterbox for two cats (two cats seemed to produce not twice the shit of one but three times, maybe four). Vacuumed every day when he used to vacuum once a week and still there was hair on all his fucking clothes. Hair on his sweaters. Hair on his coat. Hair on his jeans. He applied a lint-roller and the next second Jean-Luc Picat was rubbing himself on John's leg. Fucking orange.

Right now John was dressing to meet a reporter from the *Bozeman Daily Chronicle*. He put on a black t-shirt. Over the t-shirt, he buttoned a beige cardigan. The beige cardigan, it seemed, was covered in orange cat hair. Orange blended well with beige, but it didn't blend with black, and upon donning the cardigan, the black t-shirt became covered in the cardigan's transferred orange hairs. Bernard meowed then, moved to climb John's leg; and though it wasn't his blue-grey hairs on the black t-shirt, John kicked, not violently, but not without frustration, and shouted, "Fuck off!"

Bernard, unshaken, wandered into a corner, licked himself. Jean-Luc Picat joined him, helped him clean the hard-t0-reach places.

On his way out the door John texted the reporter. Could they meet not at Betty's Bakery but at the brewery a block away from it?

John didn't want to see Beth right now. For her sake. He was protecting her. He knew his frustration with the cat hair would stick with him all afternoon. He knew if he saw her he'd blame her. He would try not to blame her, but he would blame her. Then he would probably say something to her about it. Probably something nasty, something mean. She didn't deserve that.

The real problem was the interview. John was petrified about the interview.

Beth texted him then: *Are you nervous about the interview?*

He replied: *I'm nervous as hell about the interview.*

You're going to do great.

Then a text from the reporter: *Sure. No problem!*

John told Beth: *We're going to do it at the brewery, not the bakery. Figure a beer might calm me down.*

For a minute she didn't reply. Probably she was working, pulling an espresso or talking with a customer. Or probably she was hurt John had changed the location. Then: *That sounds like a great idea! Good luck!*

John anxiously wondered whether he should change the black t-shirt to a button down shirt, put on a tie under the cardigan. Was one supposed to dress up when meeting reporters? But he didn't even own a tie. Maybe, since he was getting more subscribers, he should buy a tie.

This was his first real interview. It was local but it felt substantial. Buzzfeed had interviewed him last month, but the final article had consisted of only a series of GIFs from his videos, and it turned out that series was just part of a larger series of GIFs from other "up and coming" YouTuber's videos. And only like a thousand people had seen it, the "article."

According to one common theory there was no such thing as an "up and coming" YouTuber anymore. Just as no one now could make it as a blogger. The heyday had passed. If you were trying, good luck.

There was a loud thud from the living room. Bernard and Jean-Luc Picat were wrestling, had bumped into Beth's altar. Some crystals and a book by Alister Crowley had tumbled to the floor.

2

THREE TIMES NOW JOHN HEMPEL had woken in a hospital bed. Four if you counted the appendectomy when he was nine, which he didn't. There was nothing substantial about an appendectomy. You don't have an appendix, so what? Neither do I—but I *did* try to kill myself. Three times I tried to kill myself.

That's what made John special. There was nothing special about having lost a vestigial organ. But pills, icy water, makeshift noose: *those* were special.

Three times John had woken in a hospital bed. The first time he hadn't known Beth, and so he hadn't thought about her. The second time when he woke she was all he thought about: did she love him? did she hate him? why wasn't she there, waiting for him when he woke up? had she even heard? had she even heard he'd jumped from the Orange Street Bridge? had anybody? had the paper even covered it? did he still work for that paper?

(He didn't still work for that paper. They fired him *in absentia*. They'd reported the news, that someone had jumped from the bridge, but they hadn't published his name, his association with the paper. They'd said sources said the jumper had sustained major injuries, even though all he'd received was a concussion and a mild case of hypothermia. From the hospital bed he'd called his editor, Corvus. Corvus told him he'd been terminated. John replied with a laugh that yes, well, he'd *tried* that, hadn't he, but he was just fine. No, terminated from the paper, Corvus said. And John, who never expressed anger, had expressed anger. And Corvus had only said: "John, you were never a very good reporter anyway.")

The third time John woke in a hospital bed (not counting the appendectomy), he'd been prepared to see Beth next to him. Before he'd taken the pills he'd been prepared. He'd looked at the dosage, done some research on the internet, and figured as he took the pills with a little luck he'd be just fine. Beth would find him just a few minutes after the overdose and she'd call for an ambulance and he'd wake a couple hours later with her beside him, loving him. The only danger was that she wouldn't come home, or she'd come home late. Technically they had an open relationship now—it was official, after the honeymoon threesome—and so what if she met someone while working at the bakery and went home with him (or her) instead? It was in the rules they'd "agreed" on. She had only to text him if she was going home with someone else. Communication. It hadn't happened yet, but it *could* happen. So if that happened then he'd either sleep off the massive dose of ibuprofen or die. Or maybe he'd vomit, his body's way of telling him he'd done a dumb thing and hey man I'm going to try to get this out of you, okay? And if he vomited while lying on his back he could choke on the vomit and die. And if he died . . . well wasn't that the point?

Wasn't it?

But he hadn't died. The first time he hadn't died. The second time he hadn't died. The third time with the pills he hadn't died. The third time he'd woken up, knowing finally his wife would be there by his side, and he'd turned and and seen . . . Rebekah Fleckman.

And oh god this wasn't a possibility he'd foreseen. How stupid, John. She's your friend. She's Beth's *best* friend. She says she cares about you and you have no reason to think it isn't true. How couldn't she be there with you, in the hospital, when you woke up after taking a whole bottle of ibuprofen, her face a mix of exhaustion, beauty (a different sort of beauty from your wife's, a harder, less easeful beauty), and concern. You have friends, John; you are not alone.

So far he hadn't told his therapist about his feelings for Rebekah. But she, the therapist, was getting closer. Soon she might pry it out of him.

But Beth had been there too, sleeping near Rebekah's shoulder, her long long hair ever gossamer, diffusing all light that met its edges, her soft lips pouting, her tongue moving between her teeth in a sucking motion as it always did when she slept, giving her the faintest of overbites. Only momentarily had John been confronted with Rebekah, because Beth had been there too. Beth was there. Beth was there.

And Beth was not angry. She cried when Rebekah left the room. "Oh John," she said. "Oh my husband, my sweet sweet husband, what are we going to do?"

Now wasn't the time for wry words, for epigrammatic jokes. He'd taken her hand and joined her in crying, for the first time in his life ashamed.

The first time John had attempted suicide there had been no shame. Just boredom. Boredom at the beginning, when he first decided to undertake the task, boredom in the middle, while he undertook it, and boredom at the end, when he realized he'd failed. Well and spite. Boredom and spite.

It wasn't John's fault that in his late teens he was something of a miscreant. Not a criminal or a bad person, but a teenager, an adolescent mess of hormonal soup, interested in violent video games and chasing girls. Easily susceptible to cultural influence: engaging in illegal street racing immediately after leaving the theater after seeing the latest in a series of Hollywood blockbusters about illegal street racing; playing a video game in which your digital avatar can enter a strip club and pay for a lapdance, and thereafter trying IRL to sneak into a strip club so that the fleshy more real avatar that is your body can get a lapdance, even though you don't have any money and are underage; reading *Catcher in the Rye* and embodying all the world's adolescent angst because you've realized that is your duty, that is what you were made for. Enough money to get into the strip club, not enough to pay for a dance. But no worries about figuring things out from there because the bouncer doesn't even let you in. Your fake ID is shit. But then a week later a different bouncer does let you in, but the asshole manager, fearing for his own skin, calls the cops when you try to order a drink, a Michelob Ultra—what your dad drinks.

Dad. Dad dad dad.

When the cop brought John home and told his parents where he'd been picked up, what he'd been trying to get away with, there were words. "He's certainly *your* son, isn't he, Franklin?"

"*My* son? Just what do you mean by *that*?"

"Alls I'm saying is I don't go out and try to screw whores, so he doesn't get that from me."

"Strippers are *not* whores, Carmela! Some strippers are good people. And anyway the boy's sixteen—he just wants some action."

John reminding his father that he was seventeen, not sixteen.

And then John taking all that angst he'd decided to embody and shouting, "You know what? I'm neither of yours son!" as he slammed the front door and took off into the Midwestern night, hearing behind him his mother shout, "Now you've really screwed him up, Franklin!"

The cop was only half a mile away. John was an idiot. The cop picked him up again five minutes later, said, "You do this again Imma hafta take you to the station, don't matter what your parents want me to do."

John snuck out the next night. Didn't try to go to the strip club again, just met up with some local boys, some other miscreants to whom the term more readily applied. Smoked some dope. They called it "dope" in the Midwest. Broke into a JCPenny and stole a pair of women's shoes, rearranged a few pairs of mannequins into explicit sexual positions.

Went out with the same group multiple times. For weeks he went out with them. His grades slipped but not drastically, for they hadn't been spectacular to begin with. Slightly less than average did not make one an outlier. The group never did anything truly bad. After the shoes they didn't steal again. In fact the group's leader-by-default, a flamboyantly quiet kid named Jake Metzinger who'd dropped out of high school and smoked Kiss Superslims and looked like a cross between James Deen (the porn star) and Bill Nye, declared one night that he felt guilty and led the group in returning the shoes to the JCPenny, along with a note of apology (they left the shoes, in the original box, in front of the disabled automatic doors, wary that were they to try to enter the department store they might face beefed-up security). The note explained that the shoes had been worn only once.

John was inside a Gamestop at 1am playing XBOX with Jake and two other boys when a passerby noticed the light and decided it was suspicious. Neither of the two cops to respond to the call were the one who'd picked John up before, but still he had to spend the night in a cell.

When the next day his parents brought him home he shouted "I hate you both!" and retreated violently to his room.

"We don't know what to do with you," his mother told him some hours later, sitting on his bed, having brought him his dinner: a bland sausage-and-potato soup, two store-bought rolls. His poor mother—never much of a cook. "Your father and I. We should let them keep you, the police, I have half a mind. Other half thinks you should be in Willingdon Oaks." Then she left the room, left him to eat his dinner. For the next month neither of his parents hardly spoke to him. He left each morning for school, returned each evening. His grades returned to normal. When his father looked at him all John saw was disgust; when his mother looked at him he saw pity, as if she didn't know what pity was or how to correctly apply it, as if she couldn't understand that within John, a normal hormonal teenager, there was nothing to feel sorry for.

All the boys who'd been caught at the Gamestop had to appear in court. It was a formality. The judge, a tired old man who'd probably once had teenage boys of his own, yawned and dismissed the case and said you didn't hurt anyone, just don't do it again.

But on the ride home from the downtown courthouse John's father demanded, "Was that a faggot you've been hanging out with?"

"Who?" John asked, genuinely taken aback by the question.

"The kid with the bowtie. And the curly hair."

"Jake?" John said. "He's just a guy. I don't know if he's gay. Does it matter?"

"Carmela! Carmela!" his father called when they returned home. John's mother had refused to attend the hearing. "Carmela!" he said again, shorter this time.

John's mother appeared at the top of the stairs.

"Your son's been fucking faggots."

"*What?*"

"No—I haven't. I— What the hell, Dad?"

"I knew it," his mother said. "Oh God oh God. I knew something else was wrong with you." Abruptly she gave way to tears. Tears John couldn't discern the authenticity of.

Thus John found himself in Willingdon Oaks, the "best children's behavioral health hospital and residential treatment center in the state."

"Is there anything wrong with him?" the administrative assistant asked when his parents, together, suddenly a team, dragged him in.

"He's gay," his father told her.

"I'm not gay," John said.

"And he's a criminal. He's a deviant and he needs help."

"Do you have like a chart?" the woman asked. "Something from a doctor?"

His mother, whose voice ever since the day of the hearing had been growing progressively shrill, said, "We're his parents and we're admitting him—got it?"

The administrative assistant yawned, typed something into her computer. "We have the room. Look—I can keep him for up to two weeks without a reason if the parents admit him, but then you have to take him home."

"'S'better than nothing," his mother said. "Right?"

After a pause his father nodded. "Yeah, better than nothing." To the administrative assistant he said, in the sort of whisper that everyone in the room can hear, "Listen, he's probably not actually gay. But he's been hanging 'round with gay kids. Can you make him stop that?"

As if only to get John's parents out of there, because she had better things to do, the administrative assistant feigned consideration. "Sure, why not, I guess. Fill this out, and this, and do you have insurance?"

As a male nurse or orderly or whatever the proper term was (when John asked the guy just shrugged and said, "Whatever") led him through a heavy off-white-painted steel door with a small grid-like window and ancient keypad on the ancient knob, John wondered where the doctors were in this place. Thus far he hadn't seen one. He wondered whether he'd even seen a medical professional—the administrative assistant certainly hadn't had any sort of license, and the longer John walked alongside this nurse or orderly or "whatever" the more he could smell the guy's body odor, a pungent mix of onion, marijuana, cleaning supplies, and cured saliva, and the more he suspected the guy was a patient who'd stolen the green-blue scrubs he was wearing from some Lysol-saturated supply closet.

His father's conspiratorial line to the admin assistant had confirmed what John already suspected: his parents didn't think he was gay, they just didn't want to have to deal with him for a while. Which wasn't to say they weren't homophobic—they were, and doubtless the sound of Jake's braying voice, not to mention his form-fitting leather jacket and rococo bow tie, had genuinely disgusted John's father. It wasn't like John's parents were even particularly religious, not in a practicing way; they never went to church, not even on holidays (which as a family they hardly celebrated); sometimes his father prayed; sometimes when John was very young he told John John had better pray to God he didn't find the wooden paddle John had hidden, lest he hit him with it extra hard. No, not particularly religious, just weirded out by homosexuality. In all honesty, John had inherited that propensity for being weirded out by gayness, but what manifested in his father as hate morphed within John to something more akin to fascination, and then rebellion. In the florescent halls of Willingdon Oaks Youth Behavioral Hospital seventeen-year-old John missed Jake and the other guys. He wouldn't exactly call them friends, but they were people, and he was surprised to find himself craving their admiration.

When the heavy steel door closed behind him it cut off the sound of his parents' arguing about the forms' intricacies. John was glad for the cutting off. For a moment he savored it, before the whatever told him to move it along, kid. The whatever couldn't have been older than twenty-two.

John carried over his shoulder a backpack, the same one he used for school. His jeans threatened to fall around his thighs and with one hand he held them up. The administrative assistant had looked in John's bag and asked his parents whether he was suicidal (planting a seed?). Shock on their faces—were they realizing finally the nature of where they'd brought their son?—they said of course not. Satisfied, the nurse said John could keep his books, his notebook and pen, his toothbrush, even his handheld gaming system, but he'd have to remove his belt, his shoelaces. Policy.

The whatever showed John to a room (cell?). It had a comfortable-enough bed with wooden posts, a two-by-two window with metal bars, a toilet and sink in a small-but-private alcove. "This is yours," he said. "You're in Ward A, which means you're not at risk. Someone will get you at six o'clock for dinner."

* * *

228

One shan't be faulted for wondering how John's parents had gotten him to Willingdon Oaks. Surely he put up a fight. Surely he refused to be ferried to what at school was the fulcrum of many a hurled insult ("Where'd you spend your summer vacation, *loser*, Willingdon Oakes?" "Everyone knows Conner's so crazy he belongs in Willingdon Oaks." "Haha, yeah. Only reason he's not there is his parents can't afford it."). But he didn't put up a fight. It took him only moments to decide he *wanted* to go: it would be a sort of ironic revenge, going to a mental hospital on purpose, and as a teenager John was predisposed to appreciate irony, an appreciation adults sadly outgrow.

His only concern had been what about his school work?

"Shoulda thought about that before you decided to become a faggot," his father said.

But John had lately been of the mind that school was, for the smartest people, a waste of time anyway. Something Jake had imparted on him. Sure, he needed a diploma, and in two weeks he'd return to his regular routine, but for now he could spend *more* time learning than he could in the beige classrooms of a noisy public high school. So his only request had been that on their way to Willingdon Oaks his parents allow him a stop at the library. They'd acquiesced and now in his new room he unpacked from his backpack a couple books on physics, a portable compendium of the works of James Joyce, *The Tao of Seneca*, *All the President's Men*, and Walter Isaacson's biography of the recently deceased Steve Jobs.

For the first several days in the institute—for that's what it was, an institute, not a "behavioral hospital" as the literature and website so proudly proclaimed—John barely touched the books. He started reading the Joyce compendium but couldn't make it past the dry introduction by some scholar from Brown or somewhere. Mostly he played games on his handheld system. That he'd been allowed to keep it must have been a fluke; surely such things were not permitted here. He met with a counselor twice a day. Each time the counselor was a different person. Never in those first few days did he see the same one twice. But that couldn't have been right. No way the place had so many counselors. Unless none of them *were* counselors, not in a licensed sense, probably just volunteers, posers, maybe even fellow patients (inmates?) like the male nurse who'd brought him to his room probably was . . . .

Or probably there were only one or two counselors and John just didn't care enough to remember the faces. Probably John just wasn't paying attention.

He didn't speak to his fellow patients, not after the first day. He tried the first day, at dinner, to make a friend. He sat at a chipped laminate-topped folding cafeteria table next to a kid who looked friendly enough. The kid was maybe a couple years younger than John and had fiery red hair. John said, "Hey neighbor!" and the kid didn't reply.

John took a bite from the bruised apple on his tray, a sip from the carton of chocolate milk. The kid was just staring at his own food, unspeaking, unbreathing.

"So, whatcha in for?" John asked cheerfully.

The kid looked up from his own tray. It seemed maybe he was going to say something pleasant, something neighborly. But then he snarled and hissed. Spittle flew from his mouth and onto John's t-shirt. Bits of chewed food, although the contents of the kid's tray looked remarkably untouched.

"Sorry," John said. "I guess I'll leave you alone."

Then the kid backhanded John's face and pushed him to the floor. Was on top of John, hitting him repeatedly with the back of his hands. The slaps were weak, pathetic. A security guard pulled the kid from John, lead him with the help of a nurse out of the cafeteria. Another nursed asked John whether he was okay. For several minutes John could hear the kid being dragged down a hallway, hissing, screaming, his laceless Converses screeching against linoleum.

John decided he wasn't going to try to talk to anyone again. He would just play his video games and in two weeks his parents would retrieve him and he would return to school and take it easy on all the rebelling, yes he would.

On the fourth day the battery in John's handheld gaming device died. The previous afternoon it had flashed a warning: BATTERY AT 20%. But it took five more hours of playtime to hit zero.

It was a miracle, really: a single charge was supposed to fuel only six hours of use. You could stretch that to eight or nine if you kept the screen brightness low. But in the four days he'd been here John must have racked up at least 20 hours of playtime, maybe more. He'd beaten one game, had moved on to another. It was as if Jesus himself had blessed the handheld gaming device: like loaves and fish the battery's charge had multiplied

But now, divine intervention aside, the thing was dead. John fished with a hand inside his backpack until he found the power cable. He inserted the male end into the handheld's female port and inserted the two-pronged plug into—

Fuck. This room didn't have any outlets.

But certainly it must. How else would they get power to the . . . ? The what? The only light in the room was overhead, controlled by a switch outside the door. The bathroom had only a sink and toilet—nobody was curling or blowdrying their hair in there.

John pulled the bed from the wall, but there was nothing behind it save for darker beige stripes where the paint hadn't faded. No outlets.

Fuckity fuck fuck.

Thus came, encroaching like a stormcloud and then a mass of stormclouds, John's first encounter with anxiety. The anxiety was a symptom of the sudden fear that he'd made a terrible mistake. Later encounters in his life with anxiety would be motivated by other fears: a fear that Beth did not love him, a fear that Beth loved a stranger in Berkeley more than him, a fear that Rebekah Fleckman did not love him and would abandon their friendship were she to become aware of his feelings for her, a fear that he deserved nothing of which he had. But this first anxiety was motivated by the fear that he'd made a terrible terrible mistake.

A *terrible* mistake. He had ten days left in this . . . asylum. How could he have thought the experience would be all sunshine and video games? Sunshine he hadn't seen in four days. The only people he'd spoken to had been a psychotic teen who'd bitchslapped him and a series of counselors all of whom smelled like they'd spent their lives rubbing cumin and chili powder into their pores in lieu of showering. His parents had not called him. His parents did not care about him. How could he have let himself so easily be dragged here? Dragged wasn't even the word —*dragged* implied resistance. He had not resisted, hadn't even entertained the notion. No, being here would be *fun*, he'd reasoned stupidly. It would be a *vacation*. Stupid John. Stupid stupid John. As if when they let him go he could expect to return to school like nothing had happened. As if he could get a job or go to college when he graduated. Certainly he couldn't, he realized now. Certainly there was some sort of permanent record affixed to him like a shadow, following him everywhere he would ever go, announcing:

JOHN HEMPEL: ONCE INSTITUTIONALIZED FOR INSOLENCE, FOR FAGGOTRY, FOR *TEEN*-NESS

Never in his life had it occurred to John that he was anything but the most intelligent. Never had he had his IQ tested but always he'd assumed it must be high: the upper limits of gifted, or even genius. But now . . . oh how stupid he was realizing he was.

There was nothing smart about irony. Nothing clever about thinking your parents would be impressed by your ironic actions —no sir.

A nurse came by to collect John for dinner. John said he wasn't feeling well, didn't think he could keep anything down. He had a feeling she wasn't supposed to but the nurse let him skip dinner. What he told her was true: in that moment he knew he couldn't stomach another tray of Willingdon Oaks food, whatever it might be. Probably stale macaroni and cheese, white bread with margarine, a carton of orange juice.

John lay on the bed. He was realizing now that *bed* was generous; *cot* was more accurate. He wondered whether he could sneak his power cable into the dining area, use one of the outlets there. One of the outlets into which they plugged the brown TVs on their TV carts and let the inmates watch movies on VHS sometimes. Or one of the outlets in the rec room, which also had TVs. They spent three to four hours a day in the rec room. Two in the morning and one or two in the afternoon. In the rec room John just put puzzles together (only to realize upon near completion a piece or two was cruelly missing—probably a drooling preteen had eaten it). There was workout equipment but he wasn't ever one for exercising and never would be. No one used the exercise equipment. Surely he could plug his handheld in when no one was looking. Let it charge all morning, retrieve it after lunch.

But that wasn't the point, was it? No longer did John care about his video games. He was caring about his future. He was caring about his future in a way he never had before. He was realizing his future was falling apart—there was no hope for seventeen-year-old John Hempel.

He fell asleep.

He woke and saw through the barred window it was still dark out. Never did he wake when it was still dark out. Always the sun woke him and then he used the bathroom and soon after a nurse took him to breakfast and then after breakfast to the showers, where he and the other kids were monitored. But this morning John knew the nurse wouldn't be coming for a while. There was no clock in the room (and since his handheld gaming system was dead he didn't have a timekeeper of his own), but he knew it would be hours.

He felt fresher than he had last night, less despairing, able more easily to focus on a single thought. He wanted to read but the moon didn't provide enough light, and since the switch was located outside the locked door he couldn't use the one in the room. He tried to return to sleep but he wasn't tired; he took that as a good sign.

So for a while he thought. And the thoughts did not overwhelm him. Instead they caressed him and pulled him close until they'd honed him in on one in particular. That word: *irony*.

He'd gotten it wrong.

Like Alanis Morisette he'd assumed that angst was enough for irony. He'd thought irony was when your parents sent you to a mental institution when you weren't crazy. But that wasn't ironic; that was just sad.

Irony was when your parents sent you to a mental institution even though you weren't crazy and while there you *became* crazy. Oh yes, that would be ironic. That irony would not be lost on anyone.

John hatched a plan. The plan had few steps. It's only real requirement was perfect, impactful timing.

For the next ten days John read the books he'd brought with him. At mealtimes he savored the unappetizing food. In the rec room he continued to do puzzles, but he chose more difficult ones. He started a 5000-piece puzzle, left it overnight, and when the next day he returned to find one of the other patients had destroyed it he was not dismayed. Still he did not talk to the other patients because he knew there was no time for making friends. He talked to the councilors, but only about pleasant things. One said, "Obviously you don't belong in here, but there's nothing I can do about that. But you'll be out in a few days."

John finished the books he'd brought. He enjoyed them all. He wanted to read more Joyce (the compendium had only selections of his longer works); he wanted to learn more about Apple and technology; he wanted to watch the film version of *All the President's Men*; he wanted to get his own iPhone someday, his own iPad. A pity he wouldn't get to do those things, he thought, but a necessary one if he were to make his point.

On the day of his release, an hour before his parents were scheduled to pick him up (and they *were* coming, he'd been assured; the administrative assistant had called to confirm), he packed his books, packed his handheld gaming device, packed his clothes, which hadn't been washed in two weeks. But he didn't pack the charging cable. Instead he pulled the bed to the center of the room, just below the light. He managed to remove the light's cover so that the bulb was exposed. He wrapped the AC end of the charging cable around the fixture, using the large adapter as an anchor. With the other end he tied a knot. He didn't know how to make a proper noose but he figured a regular knot would do: as long as the loop he made had time enough to press against his larynx. Satisfied everything would hold (teenage John, what one might call skinnyfat, weighed a soft 140 pounds), he moved the bed over just slightly. Then he stood on it again, put the loop around his neck, and stepped off.

As he hung there, he rationalized his actions: he was depressed. He hadn't been before but now he was, and thus he had every right to kill himself. Being in a mental hospital either creates a depression or draws to the surface a suicidal melancholia that's already present deep down in every human being. Like flipping an override switch, triggering primitive programming. It wasn't his fault.

John's mother was attending a Mary Kay party that afternoon, so his father said he would pick John up by himself. Wanting to get the damned thing over with, he arrived at Willingdon Oaks fifty minutes early. The administrative assistant said that wasn't a problem and sent a nurse to retrieve John. The nurse found John hanging from the light fixture, his face blue blue blue—but John was not yet dead. On a walkie talkie the nurse called for assistance as he supported John's body with his arm and shoulder.

When a counselor came to the foyer to tell Franklin Hempel that his son had just attempted suicide, Franklin said, "Wait—so does that mean I don't have to take him home today?"

So there they are: the three suicide attempts: in reverse chronological order: a heartsick self-conscious married man overdosing on painkillers, an unstable college student jumping from a bridge into icy waters, and an ironic despondent teenager hanging from a light fixture. It's worth noting that there would only ever be the three. John Hempel would never again make any attempt upon his own life. Thrice was enough.

Which made sense, three. Three, John would learn from one of Beth's books on esotera, is the first true number. The Pythagoreans believed three was the first true number. Zoroastrianism has three principles. Peter denied Christ three times. Wiccans worship the Triple Goddess. Genies grant three wishes. Octopuses have three hearts. When Beth fucked the guy in Berkeley on their honeymoon and John at the same time fucked Beth, in that room there were three people.

After he failed to hang himself from the light fixture of his room at Willingdon Oaks Behavioral Hospital, John was taken to the hospital for asphyxia. A wonder, the doctor said, he hadn't suffered brain damage. Upon release from the hospital his parents did indeed check him once again into Willingdon Oaks, where this time he was given a room even more secure. This one had no toilet or sink. The bed was bolted to the wall. When John had to take a piss or shit a nurse or security guard was required to accompany him to a communal bathroom. John was not allowed his gaming system this time, nor any other luxuries. Not even his own clothes.

One day while eating, which he always did alone now, he

was joined by the kid with the fiery red hair who had slapped him. "Hey," the kid said.

Reflexively John flinched.

"I remember you from before," the kid said. "Sorry, I went away for a while."

"Um—" John said.

"I know, I hit you. I remember. So sorry about that."

John said nothing.

"Oh, shit, wait. Did I *bite* you too? Sometimes I do that."

"No, you didn't bite me," John said.

"Okay, good. Good . . ." The kid seemed to stare past John for a long time, but when John turned to look in the direction of his gaze there was nothing there but a beige brick wall with a wordless diagram of the food pyramid.

"I'm going to sit over here," John said, and he moved to an adjacent table, which had other patients at it, but none of whom, mercifully, were interested in making conversation.

The red-haired kid said, to no one in particular, "If a tree gives a monologue in the forest, but it has nothing interesting to say, does it matter if anyone's around to hear it?" Then he left the cafeteria and John never saw him again.

After nearly a month, as he was finally being released from Willingdon Oaks, John found out his parents had moved to Florida. His dad called to tell him. "No offense kid. No hard feelings. Give us call sometimes if you want to talk." And he would call, a few times, but he'd speak only to his mother, and then eventually not even to her.

It was a simple matter for John to secure emancipation: his parents had effectively abandoned him, and he was weeks away from turning eighteen. He got his hands on a beat-up, barely running Dodge Dakota and lived in it while he finished high school, showering in the locker room, living off two meager school meals a day. It took some arguing, since he'd been away for over a month, but they let him finish high school. His GPA was good enough and he qualified for generous financial aid, so he applied to colleges, got accepted to the University of Montana, and he drove the Dakota cross country in one 29-hour stretch, at the tail-end of which it promptly broke down, and he left it where it died, on I-90 just outside of Gold Creek, hitchhiking the final 62 miles.

He never told Beth about his parents, his time in Willingdon Oaks. She knew things were strained but she didn't need to know how bad. It didn't seem fair to tell her. It's not like being a middle-class white male with parental estrangement made John *special*. Beth didn't even *have* parents. Her parents had *died*. Sometimes John wondered whether he'd married a queer woman as a further act of rebellion against his parents' homophobia. He couldn't have gay sex, because he wasn't gay, but he could have sex with someone who had gay sex.

Oh poor sweet Beth, he thought, how delicate, how ethereal —how he loved her. Oh how that love was the source of all the shame he was feeling and had ever felt.

3

"SO YOUR EARLY VIDEOS WERE about technology. Apple. Microsoft. Samsung. Phone reviews, stuff like that. But you've gotten away from those topics in recent months. Why do you think that is?"

John had expected the reporter to be older. He'd expected a weathered face sitting atop a cardigan sweater, a pencil behind the ear. A notepad pulled from a breast pocket. Dustin Hoffman. Robert Redford. Tell me, Mr. Hempel, who *are* you? What makes you you? I want to share your story with the world. I want to tell them what makes you tick.

Instead here he was sipping winter-flavored microbrews with a kid his own age, short hair that in the first few seconds of their meeting had been covered by a wool beanie, requisite balbo beard, taking notes on a tablet computer via bluetooth keyboard, iPhone laying at the varnished wood-cut-from-local-trees table's midpoint, recorder on. Probably not even a native Montanan. Probably from some town out east, or worse, from California, moved here to study writing, just out of school. Like—

—well like John, actually. Like John had been, briefly. A young, hopeful college-town "reporter", dreams of the *Washington Post* or the *New York Times*. Poor guy—probably he'd either spend his whole life here, writing for the *Bozeman Daily Chronicle*, or he'd end up submitting biased fluff pieces to the *Huffington Post* from his laptop at home in his slippers, having to write five such pieces a day, just to make a living. Maybe catch a break and become a columnist for the *Daily Beast*.

The reporter looked the way the guy who'd interviewed John over the phone for the *Buzzfeed* thing had sounded.

John was hardly nervous anymore, now that he knew he was talking to himself.

"I've always liked technology," John found himself spilling. "It started with video games, a long long time ago." He laughed. "Ha. I make it sound like I'm so old. I'm not old."

"You're . . . twenty-three?"

"Something like that. You know what? I *feel* old. Do you ever feel old, I mean like way older than you are? Fifty? Sixty?"

"Maybe not fifty, but sure—sometimes forty, thirty-five."

"It's this world, isn't it?" John said. "It's all this media. All these social networks. CNN. Twitter. Places like—"

"Interesting. If I may—CNN and Twitter, these are hardly the same."

"Aren't they, though? Okay okay, for a while there we were convinced they weren't, right? The big media folks were even kind of scared. Oh no—tweeters are breaking the news faster than us, what are we going to do? Anyone can say what they want there; there are no rules there; if people wanna swear they can swear. One hundred and forty characters of profanity. People like their media that way: unfiltered."

"Sure. Sure." The reporter was nodding.

"And so you know what they did? Places like CNN? They started *incorporating* the social media into the news. And I don't mean started their own accounts. I mean Twitter became the news, Facebook became the news, Instagram became the news. A Kardashian posts a picture of her bleached asshole and—wait, can I say bleached asshole?"

"The interview will be edited for clarity."

"Right. Good. Although you know on my YouTube channel I could totally say bleached asshole. I wouldn't, because that's not my style, but I could say it if I wanted to, which is kind of my point. So, anyway, a celebrity posts a picture and its *breaking news*. A controversial feminist rock star uses Facebook as a blogging platform, posts a long something about something something, and now we must report on it. Used to be just gossip sites did that. Tabloids. TMZ, right? But then Rachel Maddow's discussing Kanye's Instagram post. Anderson Cooper announces he's gay and CNN's talking about it as if it's some distant thing, as if he doesn't work for them, as if he's not probably right across the room."

"I think I'm starting to see your point," the reporter said.

"Are you, because I'm not sure I've figured out what it is myself yet."

The reporter laughed.

John seized the opportunity to take a sip of his beer before continuing. "But then what happened?"

The reporter made a slow half-shrug.

"Go on, you know it. What happened?"

"Um, Kim Kar—"

"Bingo," John said. "Donald Trump. Presidential candidate starts tweeting. Then he's the president elect. Then the president. Tweets some incendiary thing in the morning and while the news outlets spend the rest of the day debating whether he's finally gone too far he's off settling law suits or making war with Russia or prohibiting members of particular religious groups from entering the country. Here's a question: when everything is breaking news, and suddenly real news breaks, what term are we going to use?"

"So you're saying this is why you talk about the things you do on your channel."

"Yes. Right. Exactly. Because who else is going to? Who else is taking the time to *think* about what they have to say before they say it? Taking the time to consider whether something is even worth talking about in the first place."

The reporter was nodding again. "I see. I get it."

"Of course," John said, "I still talk about tech. I love tech. Last week I finally got the new iPhone"—he held the model up—"and I made a video about it."

"You like it?"

"It's fantastic. Flawed, of course, but fantastic. What isn't?"

The reporter made a few keystrokes. "I wanted to ask you about your background," he said. "You're married?"

John sipped his microbrew. "Mmmhmm. Seven months now, almost eight."

"But your wife never appears in any of your videos?"

"She's a private person. We're private. I think most people like me—content creators—are. We get to be selective in what we talk about, and that applies equilaterally to what we reveal about ourselves."

"Sure. But as a newlywed what's one piece of advice you'd give to other newlyweds?"

"That's a good one," John said. "Hmm—I'd have to think about that. I'm really not so wizened or anything—"

"We can come back to it."

"Yes, let's." John cracked a wry smile. "Maybe I'll come up with something."

"Hey," the reporter said, "*I'm* not even married. I had like three breakups just last year."

"Haha," John said.

"Speaking of which," the reporter said, in a segue that would prove to make no sense, "as a cisgendered white male, do you ever feel unqualified to be speaking out at all?"

John missed only the smallest of beats. "I'm not sure what you mean," he said. "Do *you* feel unqualified?"

"Well, I mean—I'm just a reporter."

"Okay, but I don't see the connection. I talk about world affairs, technology—sometimes I do informational videos on scientific of historical topics. I don't talk about—what do you call them?—trans issues, LGBT stuff, stuff like that. I guess in those respects I would be unqualified, as you put it, but I don't talk about those things."

The reporter nodded, took down some notes. "But so do you think you *should*?"

"Should what?"

"Spend more time talking about those issues?"

"I don't— But then I would feel unqualified . . ."

"But the stuff you *are* talking about . . . some people, many people, assert that when guys like you, guys like us, that is, talk about, well, anything, we're overshadowing the marginalized. We're not leaving them room to say their piece."

John squinted. "I'm not sure that's a valid argument," he said slowly. "There's infinite room on the internet. Everyone can have a voice. Granted, not everyone gets heard, but I think anyone can, if they want to be. And it's not just a matter of being the loudest person in a crowded room. Building an audience—"

"How *did* you build your audience? Any tips? Advice for people starting out?"

"Um . . ." John took a long sip of his beer. He'd ordered an apricot ale. It was a seasonal thing. You might think fruit and summer, but not apricot. Apricot was a winter beer. Apricot and cold were a regular pairing; you could find them at any brewery in town. John wondered why that was. Perhaps he could do a video on it. He set the glass down, held it with both hands, looked into the orange-amber liquid, unsure how he'd built his audience.

"Well," the reporter said. "Follow up question, then: Some content creators, as you call them, adopt alternate personas for their videos. Quirky personas. Humorously annoying personas. Et cetera. How do you think your decision to *not* adopt such a persona has affected your ability to build an audience?"

"Ah—*gimmicks*, I think, is the word you're looking for," John offered, happy to once again have something to criticize. "I guess I'm not an entertainer, per se. I'm a commentator. I offer serious commentary."

"But not always. Serious, I mean. I mean you *can* be pretty funny. And the cat thing . . ."

"That cat thing, yes. Well no one likes dull. I'm not saying I'm dull. But I attract a more serious audience, is all. People watch my videos because they want . . . perspective. Quirky characters are all fine and good. One YouTuber, really funny gal, pigtails in her videos, overalls, badly applied makeup, high-pitched voice, sort of thing—hilarious. I love her stuff. She even got a Netflix show, did you see that? Couple years ago? Before I even started. It wasn't that good, unfortunately, the Netflix show, but that's my point I guess. Better to retain control of your own creativity. Your own platform." Of course the truth was Bernard the Cat was the best thing that had ever happened to him. No one would be watching John's channel were it not for Bernard the Cat.

"Well," the reporter said, draining the last of his own beer, "I want to be respectful of your time. So just one last question. What's next for John Hempel?"

John pretended to take a moment to consider this. "More of the same," he said finally, "but better. I'm in the process of building a dedicated studio" (this was not true; the idea was a fresh one) "which should be done in . . . a few months. I'm hoping to start collaborating more with other creators. I'm going to open up a patron model, allow my viewers to start contributing to the financial success of the channel."

"So you can maintain that mythic control."

"Exactly."

"And if, say, you were offered a . . . I dunno, your own Netflix special—would you take the offer?"

"No," John said flatly. "Absolutely not."

The reporter nodded. Made a final note on his tablet.

"But you know what?" John said. "Can you, um, not print that last part. The 'absolutely not' part?"

The reporter laughed. "Of course." He tapped a few more times on the screen before putting the tablet away. "It's been a pleasure," he said, shaking John's hand. The two were standing now. "Look for the article in a week or so, maybe a couple weeks."

"Thanks." John watched the reporter leave. Exhausted, he sunk again into his chair. Pulling out his phone, he started scrolling social media. He ordered one more beer.

Buzzed, after taking a piss at the brewery, paying for his second pint (the first had been on the dime of the Bozeman *Daily Chronicle*), and flirting half-heartedly with the blonde probably-just-out-of-college flannel-wearing bartender who took his mobile payment, John sauntered over to Betty's Bakery Cafe.

The flirting, by the way, had been at Beth's suggestion. A few weeks ago, after she'd attended a feminist poetry reading at a bookstore downtown (hoping to read herself, but there were many hopefuls present and hardly enough time for all of them, so it had been lottery style, and Beth had not been chosen), and had met a . . . butch-ish thirty-something woman and consumed coffee with her, and then twice had slept with her before the woman left town, Beth expressed a concern. "I just feel like . . . like I'm taking *advantage* of this polyamory thing we have. Like because I'm enjoying the . . . fruits? . . . of it, and you're not, it's not so fair."

"It's fine," John had said. "Really it is. I'm just not very good at connecting with other people. You know that. Someday I will, I'm sure. You just keep doing you."

"Well," Beth had replied, embracing him, "have fun with it, is all. That's all I'm saying. I get that you're not comfortable hooking up with anyone else right now, but maybe you could try flirting a bit. Flirting is fun."

Flirting indeed *was* fun for most people, but it was also something John Hempel was abysmal at. How he'd piqued Beth's interest in their first online dating conversation he'd never know. Sensing his hesitation, Beth had led him through an exercise of sorts, she the encouraging prospect, dropping cues and hints about what he might want to say in response to the scenarios she conceived of, John the aggressor, responsible for taking offered lines and running with them, escalating. As a game, it had been fun, and they'd had scintillating role-play sex that night (although neither of them had come—not so unusual); in practice, with strangers, it was an anxiety trap.

As he walked to the bakery cafe, John shivered, wishing he'd brought a hat. He didn't like hats, detested the way they mussed his hair. Mussed hair just another source of social anxiety. He'd anticipated the reporter would want a photograph (he didn't), and he hadn't wanted mussed hair. But still, a hat for the walk after the interview would have been practical, an acquiescence to the Montana cold. A high of five Fahrenheit had been the day's prediction. Early afternoon and John's phone told him it had just reached two. The coldest on record, this winter would be, the experts said. That's what they were always saying now, every winter. The coldest on record. And every time they were right.

At least it wasn't snowing. Hadn't snowed all week. There was snow all around, sure, much of it still white, pure, untouched, but the roads were drivable, graveled, the sidewalks clear.

There was the new sign, the one that said "Betty's Bakery Cafe". The "Cafe" was new. Forever the place had just been Betty's Bakery, but now that they offered soups, sandwiches, and even, on Saturdays, homemade pizza . . . .

"Hey babe!" Beth said cheerfully as he entered. "How did it go?"

John pounded the bottoms of his boots against the welcome mat. "Fantastic," he said, unzipping his coat. "I think."

"I'm sure it was great. I'm sure *you* were great." She left her post behind the register and gave him a hug. A chaste peck on the lips. The place was mostly empty—two women at a corner table sharing soup. "Can I get you something to eat?" Beth asked.

John looked at the menu, half of which was a chalkboard of rotating daily specials. "I'd love a cup of the chili. And coffee."

"Pour-over?"

"French press is fine. Or, you know what, just give me drip, that way you can sit with me."

"I'd love to sit with you," Beth said.

A few minutes later she set two cups of coffee on the table. A minute after that, the bowl of chili. "It's not vegan," she said as she sat across from him. "It has meat in it."

"I think I'll manage," he replied.

John had gotten used to a relatively meat-free existence, now that Beth was ever more disciplined in her veganism. Occasionally she caved and ate some cheese, or an egg, but that was pretty much it. And since she did most of the cooking, John consumed meat only when eating out, which was more often than it used to be but still something of a rarity—it's not like his channel was raking in the ad-dollars, after all, and student loans, recording equipment, and a hi-res desktop computer (for editing) made for hefty debt. When he did eat meat, John couldn't shake the feeling that his wife was judging him. Beth was the least judgmental person he knew, and yet . . . .

If he were being honest, he'd noticed that Beth was putting on a little weight; it fluctuated, but as a rule, the stricter she was, the softer her face became, the less tight her belly, the more flaccid the ink of her many tattoos. No animal products meant more sugar, more margarine. Managing a bakery meant more pastries, more slices of vegan pizza. Of course, John would never vocalize this.

"Oh—remember," Beth said as John ate, "dinner tomorrow at our place, with Rebekah and her new boyfriend."

John had forgotten. "Is it on our—?" he took out his phone. "It's not on our shared calendar."

"Oh, I guess I forgot to add it."

"That's okay," he said, adding it himself, guessing at the time. "Her boyfriend. Arnie?"

"Aaron. You know that. He was in the military."

"Aaron. Right. Haiku kid." John hoped his jealousy was masked. And the shame that came with the jealousy. How, he wondered for the billionth time, could he not tell his wife he was in love with her best friend? He knew she wouldn't judge him, wouldn't express anger, might not even *feel* anger. With Beth there would be only love and understanding. Hell, practically every day she *encouraged* him to reveal his lusts, to chase after them like she did, but he *couldn't*. Didn't know why, but he couldn't.

Maybe it was because he had no lusts but one: Rebekah.

"Are you going to record when you go home?" Beth asked.

He shook his head, swallowed the beefy mouthful he'd been holding onto. "Probably not. Probably just read, or watch some other videos. You know how it is: something like this interview, feels like a whole day's work."

She smiled. "My husband," she said, understanding. Always understanding. And then, playfully: "But what are you going to do when you're famous? You'll have interviews *all* the time."

He laughed. It was a common refrain, always playful: what will you do when you're famous. "Oh, by the way," he said, wincing, "Jean-Luc knocked over one of your crystals. I think he may have chipped it."

"Which one?"

"The . . . sort of pinkish white one?"

"Oh, the calcite. I was using that this morning, left it out. It was already chipped. I got it cheaply because it was an imperfect specimen."

"Okay, good," John said.

"How's the soup?" Beth asked.

"Delicious. For someone who doesn't eat meat, you sure know how to cook it."

And then John was home again, the afternoon looming before him. He said hello to Jean-Luc, who was waiting for him at the door, having scurried to it from wherever he'd been making mischief as soon as he heard John's key in the lock. John kept his leg between the door and the doorframe as he entered so Jean-Luc would not escape. Since the cat had been a stray, John didn't see the harm in granting him access to the outdoors, but Beth disagreed. Wasn't it a little against Beth's essence, thought John, keeping an animal locked inside a small apartment? What about nature? What about *the wild*? What about the goddess who lived deep in the heart of the woods?

Beth would not be home for hours. Already it felt as if John hadn't seen her in days. That's how he felt every time he was not with her: like he hadn't seen her in days. He missed her. Pathetically, he missed her.

What to do for the next four hours, give or take?

There'd been a time, in college, when, faced with an afternoon of boredom, unable to muster within himself the motivation to do any sort of meaningful work, John would have just masturbated. Before meeting Beth, it wasn't unusual for him to masturbate three times per day. Ejaculate three times per day. Lay on his bed with his laptop on his chest, the screen too close to his face, his eyes going all dry from the pixelated light, tugging at his dick until it hurt. His roommates making fun of him even though they did it too, in their own rooms, because neither of them were getting any either. John had a little scar on his penis, at the midpoint of the shaft, a very little one, so small Beth hadn't even noticed until the third time she'd had her mouth on him. What was it, she'd asked. Embarrassed, he'd told her it was an . . . abrasion. Chafing that had scabbed and his self-control was so lacking that even with the scab he'd kept jerking off. Even though it hurt.

But it's passé, this topic. And frankly kind of boring: behold, a twenty-something with his dick in his hand, jerking it to porn!

Besides, John didn't do that anymore. He was married, could have all the sex he wanted (even if there was a vast difference between how regularly he orgasmed during masturbation versus actual sex). Hell, his wife was the horniest person in the world, so much that John's appetite alone could not satisfy her. And, more relevantly, now he had the *self-control*.

After the third and final suicide attempt, John decided he needed to cultivate control. Actually, he made the decision after the second attempt, after jumping off the Orange Street Bridge, into the frigid river—he just happened to have mostly failed in the cultivating that time, succeeding only enough to regain the confidence needed to call Beth, tell her he was sorry, tell her he was going to do better, try harder. But after the third attempt he found *all* the control. He found it in Beth's books.

One day, a week after he'd returned home from the hospital, Beth decided she finally felt comfortable leaving him alone again. Or rather, she felt it necessary, since she was the only one with a job, and she couldn't take more than a week off: citing a "family emergency" but refusing to give further detail would only get you so far.

"I'll be fine," John told her that morning, smiling. "I can keep myself occupied. I'm going to finally upload a video. Haha. Maybe lots of people will watch it. Maybe someday I'll be big. Haha." He was saying anything but *I won't try to kill myself again*, because he'd said that once before, and it had turned out to be a lie.

Beth smiled back at him, sweetly, sadly. "Okay, my love. But if you don't mind, I'm going to call you a couple times, just to make sure you're not lonely."

After she left he stayed in bed for another three hours. Fell asleep. This was pre-Bernard, so the sleep was not interrupted by a cat traipsing across his head. When finally he woke again he decided he was, indeed, going to make that video. But he needed help. He needed some assurance of success. He needed:

A spell!

Yes, it was a silly idea. John did not believe in magic, or magick, or however you wanted to spell it. He respected his wife's beliefs, loved her for them or in spite of them; and most important, he knew they made her happy. He knew her rituals, her meditations, her prayers to sacred stones and inhalations of musky-smelling incense, even the ways she sometimes folded or crossed her fingers, positioned her hands, drew them through the air, all gave her a sense of meaning. Most relevantly, they gave her *confidence*. Beth Hempel was the most confident person John knew.

So he spent that day reading her books. He read about divination. He read about crystals. He read about Chaldaean Oracles. He made note of a few spells he wanted to try—healing, love, wealth, *success*—but he couldn't wrap his head around which ingredients were which. The colored candles were easy enough. And anything that involved writing your desire on a piece of folded paper. But which stone was which? Was this a raven's feather, or a crow's? And besides, if he was reading this right, none of this would work because it wasn't the "most aligned" time of the month. It wasn't the right fucking phase of the moon.

Plus it was all bullshit anyway, spells and magicks. Even if part of him wanted to believe.

But then he'd come across a passage in one of the books. A guy named Aleister Crowley had written:

> *On each occasion that thou art betrayed into doing that thou art sworn to avoid, cut thyself sharply upon the wrist or forearm with a razor. . . . Thine arm then serveth thee both for a warning and for a record.*

This guy Crowley had something. *This*, John had realized, was how you maintained that illusive beast: self-control.

Which is why now, after his interview with the Bozeman *Daily Chronicle*, after lunch with his wife during which he couldn't stop thinking about her best friend, John is in the bathroom of their small apartment. And instead of masturbating he is taking a razor blade—a very sharp very thin razor blade, made in Japan, purchased via the miracle that is online shopping after telling his wife he wanted to start using a classic safety razor for his thrice-weekly shave because it was supposed to be better for your skin, more environmentally friendly, and ultimately cheaper than plastic disposables—and running it across the impureness of his right arm's white skin. He makes a line—two inches. He stares at the line. The line is invisible. Then the line turns red, glows red. Crimson. He dabs it after a few seconds with a wad of tissue. He breathes deeply through the pain. He puts a band-aid on. He'll remove the band-aid before Beth gets home. He ends up recording a new video even though he was sure he wasn't going to, a think piece on the American democratic process, the script of which he wrote a few days ago. Once a week or so he does this, the cutting. The key is just to slice the same small place every time, trace the same brachial line, open and reopen the same chasm in your skin. That way no one ever has to notice.

4

THE TIMER ON HER PHONE simulated a physical bell's ding-ding-ding and after turning it off, missing the first time because that little button on the screen was so hard to hit, she put on a mitt and then pulled the meal's final component from the oven and placed it on the table, where it, a pan of Brussels sprouts, cooked with bacon, pecans, and cranberries joined:

A separate pan of Brussels sprouts, cooked with just pecans and cranberries

A long fillet of salmon, baked in tin foil, the bone still in, cooked in canola spray

Potatoes, fried in coconut oil, sprinkled with salt

A bowl, the largest they owned, filled with raw kale, raspberry vinaigrette, almond slices, mandarin orange slices, and shreds of vegan parmesan cheese

Four white plates, the only four they owned, empty, waiting, patient

Four wine glasses, empty, waiting, patient

Assorted silverware, cloth napkins

A basket of warm rolls, from Betty's Bakery Cafe, topped with sesame seeds, peppered gingerly with currants

"Do you think we have enough food?" John asked, entering the kitchen from the living room, insomuch as it could be *called* entering when the two rooms aren't separated by any discernible vertical divider, no walls, no doorway, just the space where ugly brown carpet meets scratched linoleum.

He meant it as a joke, a bit of sarcasm, but Beth's eyes grew wide with concern. "I don't know. *Do* we? Should I have made something else? I can still make a dessert."

"Honey," John said. "There's more than enough food here. More than enough. Plus they're *bringing* dessert."

Beth surveyed the cornucopia. She adjusted the positioning of a three-pronged fork. Standing back, she said, "I suppose . . . . And there's always that vegan ice cream in the freezer. And I can make cookies—canned cookies, granted—in like twenty minutes."

John actually liked the vegan ice cream. He didn't like many things that were vegan for the sake of being vegan ("cheese", soy meats, etc.), but the ice cream was essentially frozen coconut milk with vanilla and sugar. It was even better, he might admit if you pressed him, than the real thing. He would not object to pulling the vegan ice cream out, scooping it atop warm chocolate chip cookies.

Or pie. Rebekah had texted they were bringing pie.

"They should be here any minute," Beth said, checking her phone. "At least I hope they are—everything's ready. Don't want it getting cold. Maybe I should have waited to pull things from the oven . . ."

"It'll be fine," John said absentmindedly, drifting back to the living room, where he'd been reading.

Or trying to read. Really he'd been staring at the screen of his tablet, focusing on his breathing, trying to calm the heart palpitations that grew more palpitationy each time his triune brain reminded his medulla oblongata that Rebekah was coming over, and she was bringing her new boyfriend. John had been watching a lot of British YouTubers lately, which led him to make the assumption that Rebekah's new boyfriend would be, if anything, a "wanker" if you wanted to apply the accent. He resumed the screen-staring. Bernard joined him on the sofa.

Bernard jumped ten miles high and fled the room via some mystical feline teleportation at the sound of the knock on the door.

"I'll get it!" Beth said, and John was grateful because answering doors always triggered his fight-or-flight response (he was discussing this with his therapist). Nevertheless, he put the tablet down, stood from the couch, and brushed as much cat hair as he could from his grey long-sleeved shirt and Goodwill-purchased Levi 505 jeans.

There were three hugs (between Aaron and Beth, Rebekah and John, and Rebekah and Beth) and one handshake (between Aaron and John). During the handshake John decided he didn't like Aaron, the overeager son of a bitch. Didn't like his tallness, his unanticipated lanky muscularity—John *had* expected the leanness, but in his imagination it had been a gawky, lumpish leanness, the leanness of a twenty-something who was still a teenager, who thought every date would lead to sex even though no date for him ever had, who wrote haiku in women's houses the morning after sleeping on their couch while the women vacuumed in the other room willing the guy to go away. Because that's what this Aaron was, as far a John had been led to believe. Seven months ago this Aaron had been nothing but a story, an anecdote told in an upscale Bozeman bar. A my-life-can't-get-any-worse story. A I'm-pretty-sure-I'm-done-dating-men story. A story that had given John hope that Rebekah might have that threesome with them after all, might find solace in Beth and John's collective arms now that, after all, some Berkeley stranger had. Of course, every tale of one of Rebekah's failed dates had been that kind of story; and it just so happened Aaron had been the last story they had heard. Still, John had expected acne, or a nervous limp.

And a limp there was, but it was the most confident limp John had ever seen. That gypsum cast—the obvious armor of an honorably wounded hero.

"John," said Beth, "why don't you take their coats."

Of course. Their coats. John mumbled something akin to "It's a pleasure to meet you", broke the handshake, and said, "Let me take those for you. I'll just put them on the bed. We haven't got a coat rack."

"Can't afford a proper one," Beth said. "Not yet, anyway. And haven't found one at Goodwill, or Craigslist. But I look sometimes."

Rebekah shrugged. "I don't have a coat rack either. I didn't realize a coatrack was something a person was supposed to have."

Beth laughed

John took the coats down the hallway. From the bedroom he could hear Aaron flattering his wife: "May I just say you're even more beautiful . . . more wispy . . . than Rebekah's made you out to be?"

John returned to the living room before Beth could finish giggling. "Isn't she the best?" he said, defensively, as if the other man had been insulting her. "I was in love with her the minute I saw her. Well, or her profile picture, more accurately."

"Online dating?" Aaron seemed to roll the words around his mouth.

"Yes—college students don't have much time, so why not use the internet to our advantage."

"I've never really used it. Signed up for one of them once—honestly don't remember which one—but I don't think there was a single girl in Ennis using it."

"Makes sense," John said. "Plus, I hear you didn't go to college."

"John!" said Beth.

Aaron shrugged. "What? He's right. I didn't."

This whole time Rebekah was just standing there, straddling the line between the kitchen and the living room. John looked at her, beckoned with his eyes as if to say *Why are you with this guy?*

Beth cleared her throat. John could probably count on one hand the times he'd heard Beth clear her throat. "Well, we want to hear all about it—about you—but why don't we do it at the dinner table? Just finished pulling things from the oven before you got here, so it's all still nice and hot."

"Of course," Aaron said. "And before I forget . . ." He handed John a bottle of red wine. One assumes he'd been holding it the entire time, but this was the first John had seen of it.

In one of Beth's books—a heavy tome on divination—John had read:

> *At least one early 19th century astrologer boldly stated that he did not believe that the planets influenced mankind directly but rather that they simply corresponded to the various conditions of men in the same way that the hands of his clock corresponded to his appetite for food.*

Like said astrologer, John did not believe in divination (or maybe the astrologer did, John couldn't really tell; truth be told all those books were poorly or overwritten, tending to obscure their meaning), but he did believe in appetite, in a periodic undeniable hunger for food. And boy tonight was he hungry!

Or at least he pretended to be, because Aaron it seemed most certainly was, and John would not be outeaten in his own home. So he piled his plate with fish, with salad, with potatoes, with a couple rolls. And he'd go back for seconds, yes he would. No matter that whatever Aaron was eating was being converted (instantly! just look at it!) into muscle fiber—John would do pushups tomorrow. He'd buy one of those pull-up bars you put in your doorframe. He'd start running. His therapist had been urging him to exercise, to establish a routine. "All that sitting you do only exacerbates your depression." And then it hit him (why hadn't he done this before?)—he'd sign up for the gym! The one Rebekah worked at! She'd see him working out there. She'd be impressed. Always when he'd bemoaned his own softness Beth had taken a small handful of his belly and said she thought it was cute, but when the softness began to melt, even she, he knew, would change her tune. Yes, a membership was costly, but with some rejiggering, they could afford it.

"Well, I quit the gym," Rebekah said.

Full stop. Record scratch. Pause with a mouth full of potato.

Beth had just asked Rebekah what was new. Said it had been so long since they'd really hung out, like Thanksgiving, we just don't get to see each other much anymore.

And Rebekah had replied with, "Well, I quit the gym."

And now John was attentive to the conversation, his fitness scheme forgotten (forever).

"Oh? Does that mean the hospital . . .?"

Rebekah nodded. "Yep. They gave me an actual position. It doesn't pay much, and so I have to work a lot of hours, and it's not really medical related, so I'm still volunteering to get that experience, plus of course there's school, so I'm, like, *really* busy, but that's what I need right now anyway. Focus, you know?"

"Totally," Beth said. "You always were more productive when you had a lot to do. Unlike me. Lazy lazy lazy."

"Oh please," said John. "I'm the lazy one. You practically run a bakery."

"Well, and I'm never going to finish the novel."

Aaron leaned in, speared a Brussels sprout with his fork, right from the serving tray. "You're a writer? That's right— Rebekah mentioned something about that."

Beth was blushing. "I mean, I'm trying. I have my degree in literature and creative writing, but I haven't done much with it. Obviously."

"What's your novel about?"

Beth blushed deeper. "It's kind of an urban fantasy story. Like dark magic, but modern times."

"I *love* urban fantasy. Have you read anything by Jacquiline Caine?"

"Goddess, *yes*! I have the entire *Windtalker* series on my bookshelf."

"No way! I've only read the first . . . two."

"Well, borrow the rest. They're all yours."

"Most kind." Aaron tipped an imaginary hat.

Most kind. Most kind. John looked at Rebekah. Wait—was that an eye roll? He rolled his in response. The corner of her mouth turned up—it would have been imperceptible had John not been looking for it.

There settled over the table that ungainly pall of silence that afflicts all but the luckiest of dinner parties at some point during the occasion. Unfortunate that it should visit this one so early. John ate his fish, his vegetables. Although there were still one and half of one on his plate, he helped himself to another roll and covered it generously with margarine. He ate from it. At his feet Jean-Luc Picat mewed, bumped violently his head into John's shin. Fish—the cat could smell it. The cat wanted it but would not reduce himself to outright begging.

Then Aaron said, "So . . . Beth . . . Rebekah told me you were a, um, vegan . . ."

"I am," Beth replied. And then she took his meaning. "Most of the time. I make exceptions for things like this. John insisted I couldn't make a tofurky or something like that—"

"Good call," said Rebekah. "I've had them. They're terrible."

"And I don't mind eating fish from time to time," Beth finished, giving her best friend's arm a little tap with her fist. "Especially for good friends."

Before the pall could resettle, Aaron swept it away for good. "And John, you make YouTube videos?"

John, mouth full (how well-timed), nodded.

"So *cool*."

"John just did a newspaper interview," Rebekah said. "Yesterday? Right?"

"Yes," said John.

"Nice," Aaron said. "Really cool, dude. And how did that go?"

"Yeah, how did it go?" echoed Rebekah.

"Spectacular!" Beth said for him. "Right, babe?"

"Oh, yes, spectacular."

Aaron looked at Rebekah. "So do they always do that?"

"Do what?" Beth asked, puzzled.

"Finish each other's sentences." Aaron continued to address Rebekah.

"Well, we don't really—" began John.

"Huh. I guess we do do that, don't we babe?"

"Maybe," said John. "Sometimes. I guess."

What sort of dinner party was this? Did John want to throw up right now? He suspected he did, only it wasn't manifesting as the corresponding physical sensation. Funny thing: time was long ago (so long ago) he would have given anything to be in the sort of relationship where the partners finished each other's sentences. Read each other's minds. And even though "spectacular" is not the word he would have used, reading his mind is what Beth did. Although she called it *intuition*. Did she intuit with the other people she was having sex with, he couldn't help but wonder. Did she *intuit* with the women? Did she *intuit* with the men?

Objectively he knew that "men" and "women" were not the correct words, in that Beth was not exactly promiscuous. She didn't have a million other partners, or even a dozen. There wasn't a harem at her beck and call. She just had this guy sometimes. Or that woman once a week. Never did she even sleep over. And occasionally she just met some new man, experienced just a few hours with him. John knew it was no big thing. There were not *men*. There were not *women*.

But still he was doubting her. Somewhere, deep inside.

He could hear the bathroom calling to him. Down the short hallway, across from the bedroom, there it was: the painkillers, or, better, the pain.

"Are you okay, babe?" Beth was asking him.

"Am I . . .?" '

"You look kind of sick. Is it the margarine? Sometimes John gets sick with the margarine. Maybe I should have used real butter—after all, I'm already eating the fish."

"No," John said. "I need to use the restroom." And he stood, fighting as he left the room the urge to check in with Rebekah, to know whether she looked at him, cared for him.

Some time passed. He applied a bandage and rolled down his sleeve. Two days in a row; never had he done it two days in a row. But now he had; it was not unlike masturbating.

When he returned to the table Beth was standing at the oven, and there had manifested in the air the scent of cookies.

"I forgot to bring dessert," Rebekah told John by way of explanation.

"Feeling better?" Beth asked.

"Oh, I'm fine," said John.

"Aaron was just telling us about the war. Or, well, I had just asked about it. He doesn't have to answer, if it's a sensitive subject."

John sat. How much food there was on his plate! Beth handed him a refilled glass of wine.

"Oh, not at all," Aaron said. "It's an important thing to talk about. I mean, was it difficult? Yes. I lost . . . a few things over there. A friend. A"—he gestured—"leg."

"Not a whole leg," Rebekah corrected.

Aaron laughed. "True, true. She's always reminding me: only part of the leg. Not even a visible part, just some nerves, a chunk of muscle."

John wondered what was funny about that. "So how did it —?"

"Shrapnel. It's just a bit of shrapnel in my leg. And they got it out, took a couple surgeries, repaired the damage best they could. Soon I'll be all healed and they'll take this cast off, which is only there to protect the wound. Wounds. Probably I won't even have the limp, once they take it off. They discharged me a few days ago."

"That's good news!" Beth said.

Aaron nodded. "Of course. Very good news. But you know, what's more interesting than the war—and we can talk more about the war if you want—is America, now that I've returned."

"How so?" John asked, taking a sip of his wine (that Aaron had provided), having no difficulty now (now that he'd reopened his Wound) settling into the role of interested host.

"Funny you should ask," Aaron said, even though it wasn't funny. It wasn't funny because Aaron's preceding statement had lain the path for just that question.

"How so?"

"Well, you're kind of what I mean. You're kind of the America I'm talking about?"

"Oh, yeah? That's fascinating. How so?"

"So we have this country now, right? This America? It kind of surprised us. It's not what we thought it was. Like for a long time we thought it was this one thing. I'm going to go back here, to the beginning, way back, if you'll indulge me. So what like five hundred years ago Washington and Hamilton and Benjamin Franklin are sitting in a room—"

"More like two-fifty," said Rebekah.

"What?"

"Two-hundred and fifty years ago. Not even."

"Yes, well,"—and John was pleased to see some piece of Aaron, something other than nerves or muscle tissue, fall away —"a long time ago these men are sitting in a room, signing a document. Like, I sign here, you sign there, and you sign there, right? And, boom, with those signatures we've created a new sort of country, a land of freedom and liberty. Yay for us. Right? So but what they didn't realize, these men, was that that liberty was a long time coming. It would be decades before they freed the slaves. Women didn't vote for like 300 more years. But then, granted, eventually these freedoms did occur. No more slavery. No more restrictions on women. Right? Good stuff. But then it started to skew the other way. Like fifty years ago. Feminism, right? Which is cool, but then, like, woah, too far, right? And then we realized maybe racism wasn't gone, which, not cool, sure, but then suddenly black people are so pissed off that maybe there's a *little* racism still left that they made anyone who wasn't black slaves. And then we're all slaves, right? All of us."

John looked at Beth, recognized understated horror on her face, as he knew he would. And on Rebekah's face . . . .

That's when John realized Rebekah had checked out. She was no longer with them, not in the present moment. And he understood: she'd checked out weeks ago, else how was she with this guy?

"And you're, in a way, part of this, right? Because you're part of the media. You're a media-maker, which is the word I'm using for it. I made it up, media-maker. I wrote a haiku if you want to hear it, about media-makers, warmongers, POTUS, it's in the style of . . ."

Aaron read three haiku there at the dinner table. They were handwritten on a sheet of paper, which he pulled from his pocket and read from. Beth suggested the party move to the living room, drink more wine. She forgot about the cookies. Burnt them. In the living room John read more haiku from a second sheet of paper. Very good, Beth told him, ever gracious. Rebekah didn't say much else all evening, accept to answer John when he said, "Wait a second, so, Aaron, you've been released from the hospital, but you're still in Bozeman, where are you staying here?"

And Rebekah answered, "We moved in together at the

beginning of the week."

Beth choked on her wine, coughed fitfully for several seconds.

In total they heard seven haiku that night.

As Rebekah and John walked across the lawn to Rebekah's car on the street, Beth said to her husband, "Oh, goddess, I don't think she's doing so well."

"No, not at all," John agreed, thinking, I want her, I want her.

"I mean I just don't think that guy's right for her."

"Well and I tried to tell you that," John said. "He's an arrogant prick, isn't he?"

Beth frowned. "That's the not the impression I got. I just think he's sad."

Whatever Haiku Kid had been tonight, John thought, it had not been sad. Nevertheless, Beth was probably right. She did have, after all, intuition.

Beth and John put the food away, cleaned the table. Then they went to their bedroom, where they fucked. Their fucking frightened the cats from the room, as it often did. At one point Beth screamed, "Hit me, you motherfucker! Choke me harder!" as she often did.

"But—" John said, for he never liked hitting her, even though she asked for it. He suspected the reason she asked was because he was otherwise bad at manifesting in her physical sensations during sex.

"Then use the whip. Or the flogger."

When the sex was over, and they lay there together, and the cats, no longer frightened, returned to the foot of the bed, Beth ran her finger over the pink bandage on John's arm. "What's this?"

"Oh," he said. "I burned myself earlier today. When I was putting the salmon in the oven. I thought I told you."

"No. Is it painful? Can I see it?"

"It's okay," John said, retracting his arm. "It just needs time to heal." He turned away from her and pulled the comforter over his shoulders. He started to drift off, aware his contact lenses were still in his eyes, not caring tonight that he'd regret this in the morning. He had no empathy for his future self. After a time he said, "Honey?"

"Yes babe?" Beth replied sleepily.

"Are you awake?"

"Yes," she said.

"Will you . . . do that thing?"

"Of course," she said. Turning onto her side, she scooted close to him, as if about to spoon him. And indeed she did spoon him, molding her legs to his, contouring her small soft breasts to the pathetic muscles of his middle back. Then she muttered a few words in an undertone, words he'd heard several times, words that had brought him comfort since the first time she said them, the night they agreed to get married, words he didn't understand, Sanskrit or Latin. Then she said, "Close your eyes. Breathe."

He did. He closed his eyes. He breathed. Like the distant tone of a cloister bell, growing closer, he began to feel her heart beat. Then his own. After a few seconds, the two beats were one beat, but stronger than one plus one should be.

Sometimes John had no choice but to believe in Beth's magic, or magick, or however you wanted to spell it.

"Thanks," he said. He was thinking about Rebekah Fleckman.

"Mmmhmm," Beth muttered, already asleep.

5

HE WAS RECORDING ANOTHER EDITION of John's Jaunts when he received the text message.

John's Jaunts were a special video format he recorded every so often, in which he sat in front of his camera, made continuous eye contact with the viewer, and in a mild-to-seething rage talked at length about a chosen topic. The topic was either one that had been on his mind for a while, something he couldn't stop thinking about and just *had* to discuss with you, dear viewer, or else something he pretended had been on his mind for a while now but really he'd picked it from a brainstormed list minutes before hitting *record*. "John's Jaunts" were not unlike rants. In fact, they were so not unlike rants that that's exactly what they were: rants. He was originally going to call them "John's Rants" but before uploading the first one he'd wondered whether maybe he shouldn't use some alliteration. It was a known fact that video titles with alliteration and/or rhymes got more clicks than those without. More clicks didn't necessarily convert to more total views, since views and thus payouts were counted only for videos that were watched by any one user for at least 30 seconds, and most people who clicked on a video had an attention span that kept them watching only the first 10 seconds before moving on to another video suggested in the sidebar—this too was a known fact. But still, more clicks sometimes did mean more views. Thus John decided "John's Rants" as a title could use improvement. After minimal deliberation he decided on "John's Jaunts". *Jaunts* sounded like *rants*. The two words had a similar punchy feel. You could write *rants* on your fist, one letter on each knuckle, and swing that fist at someone. You could almost do the same thing with *jaunts*, if you misspelled it or left off the *s*. *Jaunts* did not mean *rants*, but if John knew the sort of people who spent their days clicking YouTube videos, he knew most of them wouldn't know the difference. "John's Jaunts" sounded like something worth clicking on, listening to, at least if you were already a fan of John, if you cared what he had to say.

John tried to record at least one Jaunt a week. He liked recording Jaunts because they required minimal editing. For five to fifteen minutes he could just talk at the camera. In post he'd remove seconds or fractions of seconds here and there, between sentences, simulating fancy jump cuts. Everyone loved jump cuts. Sometimes John had to do research to prepare for a Jaunt, but he tried not to. People who tuned in to Jaunts, who wanted to hear jaunts (read: rants), didn't care about facts, only opinions. That was the nature of a jaunt, i.e. a rant. If John was doing an educational piece, a video meant to inform, to teach, a video requiring extensive research, knowledge, graphics, he did not publish it under John's Jaunts.

Worth noting was that John's Jaunts tended to get more views than any other kind of video John published. Whether that was attributable to the alliteration or to the fact that Jaunts took less energy to make than other videos and thus less energy to watch was not a known fact, although John did have a gut feeling.

Sometimes Jaunts were about politics. Or celebrities. Or Social Justice. Today's Jaunt was about modernity in literature.

(Like, but seriously. John had read three contemporary novels in the last six months, all released within the last two years: a detective story, gifted to him by Rebekah; the latest Nicholas Sparks romance, which Beth had loved despite herself and insisted John had to read, and John had to admit it was, indeed, endearing, something about the way their love of dachshunds brought the two characters together, despite their cultural—although each was still distinctly white American—differences; and that big one, like 700 pages, the everyone was talking about, you know, that one *everyone* was talking about, by that writer no one had heard from for, like, ten years, and it turned out she'd been off in Brussels or something, writing this epic modern novel, the one that well I'll be damned if it doesn't win the Pulitzer this year. And in those three novels, despite the bulk of each of them taking place during the late 2000s and the 2010s, and one of them even jumping ahead to the 2020s for a minute there, not a single character was glued to their smartphone. Of some 1900 pages, John could find fewer than ten where a character answered email or engaged with social media. In one every character read paper books and magazines, nary a mention of electronic books or tablets. The one that jumped into the near future *did* have everyone during that time period wearing Google Glasses, but even that . . . oh how wrong that was. It was like, John was trying to convey in this video, contemporary novelists had no regard for their characters; like they pretended to, sure, since that's all they focus on, but how can you say you care about your characters when you refuse to acknowledge the world they live in? The omission seemed particularly egregious in the detective novel, which took place in

San Francisco, and in which it was obvious a cursory examination of the victim's tweets's geotags would have revealed she wasn't even present at the location and time of the murder and had indeed faked her own death.)

John didn't expect this video to be one of his more popular —it was, after all, about books, and he suspected people who spent most of their time watching online videos couldn't give a flying fuck about books (something else contemporary literature seemed loath to acknowledge, for in contemporary literature everyone has a deep working knowledge of books despite thirty percent of people by their own admission not having read one— *one!*—in the last year). But it interested *him*, which was why he was filming it. You had to pepper your channel with topics you *wanted* to talk about, in addition to topics research revealed your audience wanted to hear, lest you go more deeply insane than you already were. Lest you feel compelled to kill yourself again, out of boredom.

John finished reciting a paragraph of his prepared script and began to cough on a drop of his own spittle. He paused the recording, took a sip of water. This was fine—he would just insert a jump cut there in post. He cleared his throat. He moved to resume recording. That's when he got the text message.

For a second annoyance was triggered by the buzzing of the phone. Annoyance at himself, and Beth, who was obviously the one texting him. At himself because you should always put your phone in airplane mode while recording videos, for this very reason. Annoyed at Beth because she knew not to text him during the day, unless he texted first; he had to *focus*, dear. But then he saw the text was not from Beth, but Rebekah, whom he also loved and who did not know not to text him during the working day. The text said:

Did you see this? Followed by a shortlink.

Of course he'd seen it, he thought upon clicking the link. It was the *Daily Chronicle* article, published last month. The underwhelming article. A mere 500 words tucked into a corner of the entertainment section. The article which had failed to capture any of the opinions that made John interesting. But then —wait a second—the opinions *were* there. This article was longer. Most of it was the same as before but it was longer. At least 200 words longer. This article was like 700 words. Then John saw the site's masthead; this was CNN.com. The byline read "Carl deMont, Bozeman, via the Associated Press".

The Associated Press! The AP had picked up the article. Also, Carl deMont—*that* was the reporter's name—what a great name.

John's phone buzzed again. He jumped back over to his messages. *The headline*, said Rebekah.

John jumped back over to the article. The headline. The headline! It said, "Popular YouTuber Bashes Traditional Media in the Harshest Way".

"Popular", "Bashes", "Harshest". These were great words. Sure, John wasn't exactly popular, not by exacting standards, but . . . but—

On a hunch, he jumped to his channel, which he hadn't checked today. He had new subscribers. Ten thousand new subscribers. Taking a series of meditative breaths his therapist had been teaching him, he paused. Then, after the breaths, he refreshed the page. Another 3000 subscribers.

This is great! he texted to Rebekah. *Thanks for sending it.*

Then he texted his wife: *Check this out! I'm already getting new subscribers from the publicity.*

Then he put his phone in airplane mode and tucked it out of sight. He resumed filming his Jaunt about modernity in literature. Because one must not get too excited, his therapist had told him. One must not get distracted, not by the bad things, and certainly not by the good. It's not the big events that make you who you are, but the little things you do each day. Focus.

The article would go mildly viral, like that winter flu that's always going around that everyone hears about but no one you know actually contracts. It would appear in Facebook's list of trending topics, near the bottom, depending on where you lived and who your friends were. CNN would hold a televised debate on the topic during one of its least-watched programs, just a five-minute segment, but they'd pipe John in via video chat and get his opinion. One of the talking heads would say, "Of course, you're far from the first person to make this argument, but you did it in a refreshing way." And even though he didn't think his way was particularly refreshing—indeed, he'd just been echoing sentiments he'd read in dozens of other places—John would record a Jaunt expounding on the topic. He'd record an informational video called "The Rise and Fall of Western Media". He'd experience a little rise in popularity, for a few weeks. By the time everyone forgot about the topic and the 24-hour news site and television channel returned to believing it was the end-all be-all of information, John's subscriber count would level out around 400,000. This wasn't a ton by most standards (the most popular content producers had subscriber counts in the tens of millions), but it was enough that he was able to start Skyping in a few B-grade guests. Which drove his subscriber count higher, a few hundred to a thousand a day, each day, one day at a time.

6

IN EARLY APRIL THE LAST of the Montana snow was melting, and Rebekah and Haiku Kid were still living together, crammed in a house with Rebekah's other roommates. And Rebekah was still attending her classes, and still working at the hospital. And Beth had made little headway on her novel, but sales at the bakery were up 50% from the same time last year, before she'd started working there. And John was sitting on his living room sofa, a cat curled into a ball on either side of him, one orange, one gray, his third cup of coffee on the table, steaming, too hot to drink yet, tablet in hand, reading an email he still couldn't believe had been sent to him, John Hempel:

> Mr. Hempel,
>
> I represent Carl Brownlee-Murphy Smith (hereby referred to as Mr. Brownlee-Murphy. Smith, he says, is so ordinary). You may know Mr. Brownlee-Murphy as the high-profile producer of such shows as *Italian Family Business*, *Cake Battles*, and *So Many Kids We've Lost Count* on TLC; *House Hitlers*, *Design Dreams & Disasters*, and *California Castles* on HGTV; as well as *Yesterday's News*, *Anderson Cooper Tells Jokes*, and *Politics!* on CNN.

It's those last three that should interest you, as Mr. Brownlee-Murphy is interested in discussing the creation of a new news/politics/lifestyle show with you as the star/host.

Are you available to come down to L.A. next week (the week of the 17th) to discuss potential options?

Mr. Brownlee-Murphy looks forward to your reply.

Sincerely,
Marta Millicent
Brownlee-Murphy Productions

John read the email a second time. Ten minutes later he'd read it for the twelfth. A gut reaction told him the email was a fake, a fraud, maybe spam. But his gut was often wrong. Trusting his gut often led him to make stupid decisions. So a quick Google search revealed that Carl Brownlee-Murphy Smith was in fact the producer of the aforementioned television programs. Some of them—namely, the TLC ones—he'd even exclusively created. He had the power, then, it followed, to create one more. Starring John.

But his gut still said: surely this is too good to be true, John. You don't get opportunities like this. You come from nowhere, have earned nothing.

A hoax, then. A prank. A gag. Perpetrated by one of John's friends. Except John had no friends, save for Rebekah Fleckman, and pranks weren't her style; neither was email. Beth too would never do this to him. His old roommates, then, from college? Or former coworkers from the paper? Members of a college study group? Had one of those former acquaintances read the AP article, seen John on CNN, gained wind of his newfound microfame? Unlikely: all those people were in Missoula, and everyone in Missoula was too stoned or high to watch CNN or political YouTube channels (unless said channel was devoted to Senator Bernie Sanders or was hosted by John Oliver, neither of which John's channel was).

Okay—so it probably wasn't a hoax, owing to lack of motive. Still wary, because even spam emails were known to contain factual information (that's how they get you), John glanced at the domain name of the sender address.

BrownleeMurphyProductions.tv. It was a real site. Links to the aforementioned shows. A photo of Mr. Brownlee-Murphy: fat, balding, clean. A generic contact form. Web2.0 design, not mobile responsive. It looked legitimate all right. It looked how John would expect the website of the creator of a show called *So Many Kids We've Lost Count* or *House Hitlers* to look. John typed a response.

He had neither seen nor heard of any of the referenced shows before reading this email, but in his reply he told Ms. Millicent that he was a big fan of . . . he picked one at random. He said of course he'd be interested in meeting with Mr. Brownlee-Murphy, how exciting. Next week worked great. When exactly? Here's my phone number.

Twenty minutes later he spoke to Ms. Milliecent on the phone. Next Thursday. Dinner. Catch, a popular seafood restaurant, do you like seafood? Normally people like Mr. Brownlee-Murphy don't do dinner meetings with people they haven't spoken to, only lunch or coffee, a very busy town, LA, but Mr. Brownlee-Murphy is especially excited about the possibilities, excited enough to do dinner, how's that sound?

It sounded great, John told her.

Wonderful. She'd email to confirm.

She hung up. John hung up. He realized there'd been no

mention of how he'd get there, to LA? Where was he staying? Did the producers pay for this sort of thing? Doubtful, else Ms. Millicent would have mentioned it. John checked flight and hotel rooms. The prices deflated his excitement.

Despite his increased subscriber count, John still wasn't rolling in dough. His income had grown to a few thousand dollars a month, before taxes. But taxes were substantial for the self-employed, the lonely content producer. Everything else went to aggressive student loan payments. Or new tech, because he was still sometimes reviewing tech, for fun, because he liked it. Beth made enough to cover rent and food and pet care. But they did have *some* money. Just nearly a thousand dollars, tucked away. Their one-year anniversary was in three months. They were going to take a trip. Nothing fancy. A cabin in Flathead Valley. A *nice* cabin. For two weeks, they were planning to stay there, reading, writing, swimming, having sex. Nothing fancy, but not exactly inexpensive.

But a TV deal! That's what was at stake here. And with a TV deal, John could afford to take Beth anywhere she wanted to go.

Morose, and annoyed at the perversity of this moroseness, at the unfairness of a world that made the conversation he was about to have an awkward one, John asked his phone's virtual assistant to call Betty's Bakery Cafe.

He should have known. Beth was the most generous woman in the world. Of course she didn't mind using the money for that. "This is wonderful news, my love. This is what you've always wanted. We can do something else for our anniversary. You just go to LA and focus on that meeting. I love you so much, babe. I'm so proud of you."

So John landed at LAX the afternoon of the 19th of April, a

Thursday. Just one carry-on bag. True to his minimalist philosophy. ("Hey, look," he'd said to Beth while packing. "One bag. Minimalism!" And she laughed, because she'd lately been teasing him about the subjectively unminimalist nature of his frequent consumer tech purchases.)

Strolling through the concourse, John checked the time on his smartwatch. It was 3:02. Dinner wasn't until eight. The glamorati always ate late, was the impression John had been given via online research. Odds were first there'd be cocktails, then dinner. Cocktails and then dinner with Carl Brownlee-Murphy Smith and his assistant, Marta Millicent. Vaguely John wondered what Marta Millicent looked like, how old she was; on the phone she'd had a seductive voice, if rushed. Then he chastised himself for thinking of her that way. Then he chastised himself for chastising himself, for just before he'd left the car as she and Rebekah dropped him off at the airport, Beth had said, "Hey, babe, have fun, okay? I mean it—you're going to a fun city, have fun." But of course he wouldn't. He would rather bemoan the fact that he was sleeping alone—so lonely—while Beth took advantage of the opportunity to have an alternate warm body beside her—which she would; her fellow feminist Bozeman coven member or someone, Emeline or someone, was keeping her company, in a lesbian way—than take advantage of the arrangement himself.

He sent Beth a text saying he'd arrived safely. He called for an Uber on his smartwatch. The car was eight minutes away. John had not had lunch. There had been no lunch served on the plane. John removed his wireless earbuds and approached an Auntie Anne's kiosk and bought a soft pretzel the size of his head, with cheese sauce. He ate the soft pretzel at the curb, while he waited. He could purchase things like the smartwatch and the wireless earbuds—both recent purchases, because they were business expenses and tax write-offs as long as he reviewed them. The pretzel, too, was a tax write-off. He had the receipt folded neatly in his pocket, so he could scan it for his records when he got to the hotel. The Uber approached the curb. John put the lid on the cup of cheese sauce, returned it and the three-quarters of a soft pretzel that were left to the paper bag they'd been given to him in. Greeted the driver. Told him which hotel he was going to.

Intuition told him he'd have plenty of time to get to the hotel, decompress (for John was feeling extremely compressed), and get to Catch in time for his appointment.

The drive to the hotel took nearly forty-five minutes. "Is nearly rush-hour," the driver said. "Is taking long time because every asshole trying to leave work early, see."

"Okay," John said. "So how long do you think it will take me to get from my hotel to Catch?"

"What is Catch?"

"Um—it's a restaurant. Downtown, I think."

"When you go to Catch?"

"Eight?"

"Ah. Hmmm. No, is no good. You must go downtown now, you don't want to be late for Catch. I'll take you now."

"But—" John's bag was small. This was just an overnight trip. But carrying it all evening, and into a fancy restaurant, and not checking into his hotel until so very late . . .

"There. Is rerouting," the driver said.

"But—" But it was already too late. The driver, with the hotel in view just hundreds of feet away, had made an illegal u-turn and was accelerating up the on-ramp for the . . . the 405? John knew nothing about Los Angeles, but the 405 was a thing, right? A big thing? And now the black sedan was storming down the highway ("Is everyone leaving work, see, so right now is no traffic to get downtown. Later will they go back downtown to party.") and the driver was telling John that everyone in this city partied too much. Everyone in America partied too much. Not like Cuba. In Cuba, nobody partied; they had good times, yes, enjoyed life, celebrated, but when a day was for working, and the next day was for working, you did not go out and get drunk and smoke cigars in the clubs. You did not go dancing. You got drunk and smoked cigars at home and you made love to your wife. The driver was from Cuba, see. He'd snuck out in the fall of 2016. Through Puerto Rico. Then through Mexico instead of Florida, up through New Orleans and then over to California. "I hear about Uber. *Everyone* making money driving for Uber! Is exciting! So I come over and learn English and am accepted to America and learn to drive." The key, the driver went on to explain, was getting out of Cuba ASAP "As soon as Donald Trump elected, I know I have just months to get to America. When he sworn in, who knew what was going to happen? They maybe not let me in, like Muslims." Fortunately, the driver had made it in time; he had an uncle who'd already made the trip, who had contacts, who helped him out and even gave him money when he first arrived. "And now . . . !" And now it was all self-driving car this, self-driving car that. Soon the driver would probably be out of a job. In Cuba, at least, he said, he'd had a job. And a wife. In Cuba he'd had a wife, and his wife had been fat, but she'd also been pretty and willing to make love to him.

It was five-thirty when the driver dropped him off in front of a downtown Starbucks. John was dismayed to receive the emailed receipt. Doubling back plus surge pricing did not for a low fare make. Then again, he'd saved a trip, kind of. He was standing in front of a Starbucks, bag in hand, unsure how to spend the next two-plus hours.

There *was* work to do. A new video he could upload, recorded yesterday. And maybe, if he was watching the channel, if Carl Brownlee-Murphy Smith saw that John had, on a *travel day*, committed to uploading a new video, he'd be impressed, for YouTube had no scheduling feature (what the fuck, YouTube?). John could use the Starbucks wifi. But also his legs were stiff and sore after hours on a plane, after over an hour in a cramped Uber; he needed to stretch them. A quick request to his smartwatch revealed another Starbucks on the other side of the block. And Catch was only three blocks away, a six-minute walk. John went to the second Starbucks.

The walk to the second Starbucks took forty-five seconds. On the way there, two homeless men, one in an expensive-looking tweed sportcoat, asked him for money; a black man with dreadlocks and gauged ears offered to sell him weed; a kid, maybe thirteen, asked whether John *had* any weed; a middle-aged man on a skateboard cut in front of him, nearly causing him to fall onto hard dirty cement; and Robert Downey Jr. walked out of a men's clothier, nearly caused the same, and said, "Pardon me."

In the Starbucks John pulled out his laptop and opened the messenger application and texted his wife: *You're never going to believe who I just saw on my way to Starbucks.*

She didn't respond right away. That's right: she was with her friend, and when she was with her friends she never checked her phone. "That's the key to a successful open relationship: you can be with multiple people, but when you're with someone, you must *be with them*." John had told his therapist he didn't like that arrangement; it seemed counterintuitive to him; wouldn't it be better if, when your partner was with someone else, you at least knew they were thinking about you, too? The therapist had just shrugged. The therapist always seemed uncomfortable when discussing John's open relationship (probably another sign he should see a different therapist).

A man approached John's table. Pierced eyebrow. Gauged ears. Slicked-back jet-black hair. Starbucks shirt. "If you wanna use the wifi, you're gonna hafta buy something. A coffee or something."

"Thanks," John said. "I was getting around to it." He glanced at his laptop screen. His new video was uploading. Very slowly on the over-trafficked wifi. Probably also they were still using old wireless tech. 802.11g probably; he hadn't even noticed a 5GHz signal. He would be here a while. His video was nearly 2.5 gigs. 1080p. Usually he shot in 4k (like any good content creator these days), but uploading 4k on a Starbucks connection was something only a masochist would do. A masochist who didn't have an important dinner meeting in a couple hours. But you had to at least do 1080p. Any content creator who uploaded videos at less than 1080p just wasn't valid, not in this decade. John disliked Starbucks coffee. He didn't hate it but he disliked it. But he also liked that consistency with which he disliked it: no matter where you went, no matter the city, Starbucks coffee was equally burnt, bitter, brewed with the same lack of care. So when he ordered the standard roast he knew what to expect, and he thanked the asshat with the gauged ears who gave it to him.

Hungry, he realized he'd left his soft pretzel and cheese sauce in the Uber. Too late to eat now anyway. Dinner was soon.

And there was the anxiety again: because would John even be able to keep his dinner down? Until now he hadn't felt nervous, but now he suddenly very nervous. He was having dinner—expensive dinner!—with a big shot producer. And the producer's assistant, who on the phone had sounded attractive. And if the dinner went well it could be the beginning of everything he'd ever wanted.

At the table where his video was uploading (33 percent) he tried those meditative breathing exercises his therapist had taught him. Interspersed with sips of caffeine. A counteractive combination. His therapist's voice in his head: "Don't forget to take walks. Exercise. *Change your state.*"

Suspending the upload (42 percent), John closed his laptop and stuffed it back into his bag. He left the coffee on the table. He left the Starbucks. He had to change his state.

Change your state. This admonishment came from a popular self-help guru. The guru had used the term in a series of best-selling audiocassettes in the late 1980s. In the late 1980s, everyone was changing their state. You could buy the cassettes for like ten bucks for the set of twelve at the time. In high school, after the first suicide attempt, John found the cassettes at a garage sale for a buck twenty-five. The set was missing two tapes, so he negotiated the price to seventy-five cents, which was all he had in his pocket at the time. He played the cassettes in the cassette deck of his Dodge Dakota, parked in the lot across the street from his high school, where he slept at night, on the nights he slept. On the first volume of the cassettes the self-help guru intoned in a raspy, Mariana Trench-deep voice, that, whenever you were feeling down, whenever you were lonely, or sad, or tired, or convinced that none of it was worth it, that everything was going down, all you had to do was *change your state. How* exactly to change your state he said he'd discuss later, on tape number seven, please don't skip ahead though because it's important that you take all this information in in the prescribed order, you want everything to turn out all right for you in the end, you want to be your best self, you want a successful, joyful life, you want to unleash your power. Ignoring this advice, John promptly removed tape number one with the intention of replacing it with tape number seven.

Tape number seven, it turned out, was one of the two missing cassettes, because of which John had saved fifty cents. Because of which he'd been capable of purchasing the cassettes in the first place. He never did find the missing cassette. He checked other garage sales. He visited his hometown's two used record stores. He went to the library and used a public computer to check the internet; on the internet he discovered the cassettes had been digitized in 2006, were available for purchase, updated and expanded, with a new introduction by the popular self-help guru and a new foreword by Leslie Nelson, who claimed the original edition of the tapes had, quote, "saved my life"; but the digital version cost $24.99; and there was no hope of searching for it on a torrent site, because on a public library computer or a school computer there were firewalls that blocked such sites, and John, despite his love of technology, was not a hacker, wasn't even knowledgable, could never hope to bypass such firewalls and not get caught. So he gave up on changing his state until a few months ago when his therapist said, "I think what you need to do, when you're feeling low, when you're feeling low and down, is change your state."

"*Wait*," John said. "What did you just say?"

"Change your state."

"Yes," John had exclaimed. "Yes! But what does that mean?"

All it meant, he was disappointed to learn, was move. Exercise. Do ten pushups, take a walk. Get your blood pumping.

Sprint a little. Get yourself breathing hard, is all you have to do. Change your physical state. If you're a liquid, become a solid for a while. If you're feeling rigid, stuck, allow yourself to fill the space around you, flow into your troubles. Change your state.

But John didn't like exercise. He walked, but he would not run. Pushups made his shoulders hurt. But of course he had another way of changing his physical state, of getting his blood pumping, or flowing.

He hadn't packed a razor, not for an overnight trip. His face's skin was smooth, would not produce even a simulacrum of stubble for days yet. And plus on planes they won't let you bring safety razors, not with the blades still in.

So from the Starbucks he marched to a Walgreens he'd seen across the street and up two blocks, its sign glowing red. When he'd entered the Starbucks the sky had been very blue, but now it was taking on a purple tinge. Purple and pink and orange. And also a smogishness, rays diffused through so many particulates.

Robert Downey Jr. was in the Walgreens, buying a pack of cigarettes. Only it wasn't RDJ, just a guy who looked like him. It *was* the guy John had seen exit the clothing store twenty minutes earlier, only that guy hadn't been RDJ either, just this guy, here, with a goatee and frazzled hair, little bits of gray, who looked like Robert Downey Jr. And this, this misidentification, made John sad.

John found the razor blades, but they were in a locked case, behind mesh doors. A sign: ASK FRONT DESK FOR ASSISTANCE. But he didn't want to ask front desk. So he bought a two-pack of yellow plastic Bic razors, which were not behind mesh doors, and returned to the Starbucks. On the way back to the Starbucks he reflected on the mesh doors: so much in that Walgreens had been behind mesh doors: razor blades, electric shavers, hairdryers, tobacco products, over-the-counter painkillers. Was this how they did things in LA? Was this how they had to do things?

The bathroom in the Starbucks required a key. The key was for customers only. When John asked for the key the barista with the gauged ears started to say, "You have to buy something first," but then he looked up, recognized John, sighed, and handed him a key attached to an unmisplacable ping pong paddle. "Bring it back," he said.

John tore up the skin on his fingertips prying the blade from one of the plastic Bic razors, but he got it loose. Wrapping it in toilet paper, he rolled a sleeve to his elbow and pressed the blade to his skin, seeking merciful release, changing his state.

"Well, helloooooo," said Carl Brownlee-Murphy Smith, standing fatly from behind the faux-bamboo-edged gloss-black-topped table. "It is indeed a pleasure." He stretched a hand forward, mumbling a sorrowful *whoops* when his forearm bumped and knocked over the glass pitcher of water that sat on the table, sending it tumbling to the floor, spilling the water onto the restaurant's marble floor and onto the lap of the thirty-something (forty-something? there was definite Botox there, around the mouth) who was sitting next to him. This woman was presumably Marta Millicent. Brownlee-Murphy winced at her. She smiled as if to assured him everything was okay. She indicated John with her head. Brownlee-Murphy looked back at John, stretched his arm a little further.

John, bagless, for the restaurant's hostess had offered to check it for him, took the hand. Brownlee-Murphy had a strong, if clammy, grip. John met its firmness. "Likewise," he said, even though *likewise* was not a regular piece of his vocabulary.

Marta Millicent convened with a passing waiter, who scuttled off to find a mop, and then John was introduced to her as well. "A pleasure," she said. "It's great to put a face to the voice."

Despite the obvious Botox, and maybe other plastic surgeries, John decided she was indeed as attractive as her voice on the phone had indicated. Brownlee-Murphy sat. Ms. Millicent sat. So John, too, sat. The waiter returned with a mop. Another waiter appeared with a fresh pitcher of water. He filled the four glasses on the table, and at first the quadratic number went unnoticed by John. "I'll return to take your drink order momentarily," the waiter said.

"No need," Brownlee-Murphy replied. "We'll take a large bottle of cold sake, not your finest bottle, something midrange, priced not outlandishly, please, but still good enough that we'll enjoy it cold."

"Of course."

"And four double Japanese scotches. And yes these I want to be your best. Spare no cost."

"Right away," the waiter said.

"Have you ever had Japanese scotch, Mr. Hempel?"

"I'm afraid I haven't," John said. "And please call me John. No one ever calls me Mr. Hempel. Like ever."

"Indeed. Indeed. No problem. The name, of course, is a misnomer."

"*My* name?"

"The *scotch*. Japanese scotch can be no such thing. But it's so good."

"Oh," John said. "Yeah—that makes sense."

"It's really just a single-malt whiskey," Ms. Millicent contributed. "And you can call *me* Marta."

"Marta," John said.

"And me you can call Carl, if you please. Well, then, Ms. King"—Carl looked at Marta—"Mr. King?"—Marta raised an eyebrow, shrugged—"Rene, I guess, then, is probably most appropriate" Carl said, "just went to the restroom. She—he?—shit—*they*—should be right back."

"Rene?" John asked, confused.

"Rene King," Marta said, as if repeating the first and last name clarified things. "She's the other YouTuber Carl is considering giving the content deal to."

"The other YouTuber . . ." There had been no mention in the email or on the phone of another YouTuber. "So it would be like a cohost thing."

Carl frowned. "'Fraid not. Two very different shows. What with you with the tech and politics and she with the social issues."

"I don't understand," John said. "I thought you were offering me a TV show."

"Well I am, aren't I? If you can convince me you're the one I should offer it to. I only have so much money for things like this, after all."

"I think, Carl," Marta said, "this should wait. Until Rene gets back. Or, better, until the main course has been served."

"Of course, of course," Carl said, laughing, his jowls moving not unjovially. "Always getting ahead of myself. This is what I pay Marta for. Thank you, Marta. It's an LA thing, John: never talk business until the main course has been served. Now in San Fran it's something different, let me tell you. In San Fran you talk business ASAP. You got a startup idea, you meet an investor, you lay it on 'em. You're standing next to Peter Thiel at a urinal and you give him your pitch even if it means he sees your big 'ol

289

dick. Better yet, you show him your dick if you think it'll sweeten the deal. You ever been there? San Francisco?"

"Yes," John said. "My honeymoon."

"Craziest place in the world. Now that you mention it—crazy place for a honeymoon."

"My wife and I had never been. We wanted to see it."

"Are we talking penises?" asked a new, feminine voice from behind John.

A figure seemed to glide into the seat next to him. "Rene King," it said, punching John intimately on the shoulder. "Proper pronouns they or she, I really don't give a shit. I got friends who call me they because that's what they think they should call me, other friends call me she because hello it makes far more grammatical-sounding sentence, and to my face most just call me Rene, the name I chose, nice and gender neutral."

The person John was looking at—for that's what she was, a person, and he knew enough to know that's all that matters, or at least that that's supposed to be all that matters, even if, despite your trying, it's just not, which is to say John was a little squicked out by androgyny (an aversion probably inherited from his father)—was small. She had short-cropped brown-red hair, parted on the left side, slicked back and sideways with hairspray. She had freckled cheeks, boney pale freckled cheeks. She wore purple eyeshadow and black lipstick. Her shirt was a black button-down, distinctly masculine, cut off at the shoulders, revealing pale freckled arms, thin but muscular. The shirt was form-fitting but not tight, and John couldn't tell whether the flatness of Rene King's chest was genuine or affected somehow. Black cargo pants. In a lot of ways, she looked like Beth, but both smaller and stronger, less soft, more masculine and more Irish, and, based only on what John could see, tattooless.

"Really like talking about them, penises," she said. "I find them fascinating on account of I don't have one."

Carl Brownlee-Murphy laughed raucously "She's just so *spunky*," he said to Marta.

Before John could introduce himself to Rene King or even get his bearings, the waiter reappeared, carrying four tumblers of deeply-golden liquid.

John had expected the whiskey to be white or clear. In his mind all alcoholic Japanese beverages were white or clear. Something to do with the rice.

"Now," Carl said, picking up his tumbler and motioning for everyone to refrain from sipping until he'd finished speaking, "you might think that, because it's Japanese, this would have to be made with rice. But that would be, in a way, racist—"

"Very racist," said Rene. She winked at John.

"—because this stuff, like Scotch whisky, is made from wheat, rye, or even malted barley. It is for all intensive purposes the same as Scotch, but made in Japan, so we can't call it Scotch, legally. Tell you the truth I've been drinking Scotch since my dad first gave me a sip when I was nine years old, and most of this Japanese stuff is better than what you'll ever get over there."

"Where?" John asked.

"Scotland. I'm saying this stuff is better than the real thing. Like a good cover band."

"Oh," John said.

"Well—try it. Both of you, *try* it. Marta's already had it."

They all sipped. John liked it. Peaty. But what he was wondering was how he could use his knowledge of Carl Murphy-Brownlee Smith's love of the stuff to his advantage. Like was there some way he could win this TV deal, a deal he hadn't known he'd be competing for, using the fact that the producer liked Japanese whiskey better than Scotch? Probably not, but anything was worth filing away for reference. And enthusiastic agreement with the man's likes couldn't be a bad place to start. So John said, "Fantastic! Really really delicious."

Rene smacked her blackly-painted lips. "It's 'for all *intents* and purposes,'" she said. "Not 'intensive.'"

"I don't know to what you are referring," Carl Brownlee-Murphy Smith replied.

The waiter returned. On his tray was a large ceramic carafe of saké and four small ceramic glasses. All the ceramics bore painted flowers. As the waiter placed the glasses on the table, then filled each one from the carafe, Carl informed everyone that saké, of course, *was* made from rice, in case you were now confused.

The waiter asked whether everyone was ready to order food. John realized he hadn't looked at a menu. In fact, there didn't appear to be a single menu on the table. Rene suggested that, since he'd proven so adept at ordering the drinks, they defer to Carl's judgement on food as well.

Which was a smooth thing to say, damn her. John could praise the producer's taste in liquor all night, but to suggest such taste was so good you trusted him to order your food—*that* was masterful flattery. *That* was how one got a television deal.

Carl rattled off, seemingly from memory, an assortment of sushis and sashimis. Also an American-sounding seafood soup. And lobster mac and cheese.

"Japanese is their specialty here," he said after the waiter had left, "but they do American seafood so well, too. And for dessert they have the best chocolate cake. I usually eat three slices."

"He does," Marta confirmed.

"I want you both to tell me about yourselves," Carl said,

finishing his whiskey with what John was fairly certain was only his second sip. "I've watched your videos, but, well, John, yours for example are light on personal content—"

"Except for the cat," Marta offered.

"Ha! Yes, the cat. That cat is *hilarious*. But what else can you tell me? About yourself?"

"Yes, what?" Rene King said, turning her chair and scooting it back, simultaneously making space and leaning in.

"Um—" John said. What was there to say? What about John Hempel might Carl find interesting? Even in the widely circulated *Daily Chronicle* article he'd declined to talk much about himself in a non-global way. "Well—I'm married," he said. "Going on like nine months now. Ten months. And I have . . . actually . . . *two* cats, not just the one. But the other one is camera shy I guess."

"Where were you born? That sort of thing," Carl said.

"The midwest."

"Everyone was born in the midwest," Marta said. "Where, specifically?"

"Your Wiki page is light on details," Rene King said.

"I have a Wiki page?"

"What drew you to political commentary?" Carl asked. "What motivated you to take on the responsibilities once carried by the media elite?"

"Masochism?" John offered, for how could he disclose that he felt no responsibility at all, that the quaint lines about the media in the *Daily Chronicle* interview had just been something he'd said, not felt, that he'd been reciting the diatribe of countless modern thinkers and tweeters?

For a moment Carl was silent. Then he laughed. "Ha! Ha. Indeed."

Then it occurred to John that, even if he was being asked to talk about himself, that was never the way to garner favor. So he asked, "What about you, Carl? How did you get into television?"

Carl beamed. John thought he saw Rene scowl before smiling. Marta was nodding. "Guess it's a long story," Carl said.

John leaned in. "I'd love hear it."

Rene definitely scowled.

John grinned.

Carl finished his little glass of sake, poured himself another, smacked his lips. "Might be we're gonna have to order another bottle of that. I was born in Alabama, forty-three years ago. Always wanted to be a storyteller, from the day I learned to read . . ."

"You barely have an accent," Rene observed.

"Got rid of it when I came out here. It still slips out sometimes, when I get excited or upset."

"I doubt it," Rene said. "You hide it so well. You sound like a native Californian."

Carl Brownlee-Murphy Smith beamed again, as if being a native Californian was his *real* dream.

Rene picked up the conversation then, like a needle she was weaving through a tapestry John had started, asking the right questions, applying the appropriate flattery. And John was hating her for it; if she kept this up, she'd walk away from this table with everything he ever wanted. He listened but hardly heard as Carl explained the story of his last names: something about an abusive father, then a step-father who adopted him, then a failed marriage upon moving out west, to a C-list actress, in which he tried to prove his hipness, his enlightenedness, by taking her last name, keeping it after the divorce, as a reminder or as a concession to his innate, indefatigable sense of nostalgia, he wasn't sure which. Talk of a drug overdose. A depression. Another overdose. Rehab. "Now I touch drugs never, never never, find my solace these days in alcohol, but only 'cause I like, mind, not because I need it."

"So brave," Rene said.

"Which part?"

"All of it. Your whole story is inspiring."

As Carl went on to explain the process by which he used the divorce money to produce his first television program a decade ago, an unseen thing for CourtTV, John excused himself to the restroom. "I'm so sorry. I'll only be a moment."

In a marble-lined stall he searched YouTube for Rene King. Her channel was the first result. She had—and this was devastatingly disheartening—over three million subscribers. That meant YouTube had sent her *two* of their coveted Creator Awards, aka Play Buttons, literally hand-sized-or-bigger metal rectangular trophies with a right-pointing arrow engraved in them. At three million subscribers she must have both silver and gold. John had neither; even at well over 100,000 subscribers he hadn't received his silver play button yet (lost in the mail, presumably?), and while he did not care about such things (like hell he didn't), to think of her, Rene, holding her two awards, caressing them, displaying them proudly in a recording studio, evoked jealousy. Plus at three million subscribers she already had a large audience, a group of devoted fans who would follow her to television—what network would choose John's lowly 400,000 guaranteed viewers instead of six times as many? Plus there was the theme of Rene King's channel, which John gleaned via the titles of her most recent uploads: gender politics, dysphoria, smashing the patriarchy, certain colored lives matter (perhaps more than others?), not only women have periods. These were the issues, John knew. This is what got clicks, and upvotes, and likes. John Hempel was just another white male, in a sea of white males, talking politics only just slightly left of center. He wasn't brave or special. Sitting in the too-lit stall at Catch, the hottest new seafood restaurant in LA, John realized he would not be getting this TV show.

But he *was* getting free food. And the opportunity to interact with someone who had or would be getting what he wanted—he could learn from her.

He put his phone back into his pocket. As he was washing his hands, his watch buzzed. There was a text from Beth: *Who?*

For the briefest of moments, he didn't understand the question. Then he remembered the context. He drew his response on the screen with his finger: *No one. I thought it was someone but it was no one.*

He rolled his sleeve to the elbow. The self-inflicted wound from earlier that evening was still fresh. He'd had no band-aids. He dabbed at the cut with a soapy paper towel until it was only a pink, bloodless line, then he rolled his sleeve down.

He returned to the table to find a milieu of laughter. Even Marta Millicent had tears running down one cheek. John affected an amused grin. "What'd I miss?"

Carl's jowls flapped. "You would have had to have been here. I said something about . . . about . . . and then Rene . . ." and any clues he might have offered disappeared into a huff of squeaky hysterical wheezing.

Rene King shrugged at John. "I'm really not that witty," she said. "I guess I just said the right thing at the right time."

"That would be the definition of wit," said John.

"And that, right there, would be exhibit A." She winked at him. He could not hate her.

The paroxysm had subsided by the time the food arrived. Carl ordered a second bottle of sake. John had consumed two of the small glasses. Rene two or three. Marta John hadn't been paying attention to. Carl, he was pretty certain, was drunk. Carl guided each diner in the proper method of consuming their food: sashimi with chopsticks, sushi with fingertips, seafood mac and cheese whatever way you please although a fork is customary. Once everyone had tried everything, and Carl was satisfied they were satisfied with his choices, he raised the topic of the evening.

"So," he said, wiping his hands on the cloth napkin he'd affixed to his collar, bib-like, "I would love—love love *love*—to offer a television show to both of you. Hell, there are a dozen other—" He looked at Marta.

"Content creators," she said.

"Content creators . . . who I would love to offer television shows to. So many smart people, am I right? But I just don't have the resources for that many right now, right? And, well, I'll be honest: this whole thing is a partnership with CNN, and nothing is a done deal, and it took a lot of communication, like many many calls to the right people, to even get the project considered. And it will take further convincing still."

"What, exactly, is the project," John asked.

"A talk show. A new kind of talk show. One where the host chooses the guest, sits down in a studio, one on one, talks social issues, politics. No entertainment talk. No fluff. Real issues."

"And that's a new kind of show? CNN—don't they have a dozen like it?"

"Well, yes, but not like this. We're looking for something young, something fresh, right? Like somebody who can be honest in a way the old media can't. Like what you talked about in that interview you did, John."

"Wait," Rene said. "So like you mean like what John is already doing on the internet. Or many other people are also doing on the internet."

Carl sighed, as if he'd expected this question. "Yes . . ." he said reluctantly. "Yes, but is that really sustainable? Wouldn't it be better if you could be *on TV*? Imagine the audience you could reach."

"But CNN only has like—"

"Two million viewers," John said. "At their highest." He'd made himself familiar with these numbers after the *Daily Chronicle* interview went viral.

"And I," Rene said—

"Have over three million subscribers," John said.

Rene raised an eyebrow. Which John found endearing in a victorious sort of way.

"I'm familiar with your work."

"Huh. I really didn't think you were."

"So my point," John said, addressing Carl again, "is why would Rene want to work with you, with CNN, when her own numbers are already higher?"

"So you're saying you *do*?" Rene asked John, the eyebrow going higher.

"I don't know," John said. "Maybe." Of course he did. Was it hypocritical? Sure. Did it mean more face time, more recognition, more opportunities? Probably. And what did John care about hypocrisy—he'd never been able to even define his own convictions. All he knew was he often felt so very lonely, so very alone, and broke, and he wanted to provide for his wife, and maybe someday they could have a family, they'd never discussed having a family, and also maybe if he was really truly famous, an authority, someone intelligent and intellectually strong, his wife would no longer want to have sex with other people, and maybe Rebekah Fleckman, too, would love him.

Marta Millicent shifted in her seat.

"Here's the thing," Carl Brownlee-Murphy Smith said, also shifting, bumping his gut into the table as he did so, rocking the contents of the second sake bottle. "CNN wants Rene."

Rene's eyes lit up. "They do?"

"They like your politics. And your . . . look."

"You mean the fact that I'm non-binary."

"Yes, that. No major network has a transgender anchor, see, and they like what it could do for their ratings."

"I'm not transgender. I'm non-binary."

"Right. Well, it's close, isn't it? And—"

"Not really. It can be but it's not."

"And but you have the looks."

"Because I'm, despite everything, kind of femme, is what you're saying."

"I guess that's the word for it. I don't really know about these things."

"That's the word," Marta said.

Rene said, "So—let me get this straight: the network wants me because I'm a mostly femme non-binary individual with a large established audience, and that's good for their ratings."

"Well, and your politics. They like your liberal politics. Like they could have gotten Katelyn Jenner or somebody, but she's a conservative."

"*I'm* liberal," John said.

"Not as much as she is," said Carl. "I've watched your videos. We've run projections. Rene's the better choice."

"So why have me come out here," John asked, "if you've already made your decision?"

"I hadn't, not finally. I needed to meet you both."

"But now you have?"

"I'll do it," Rene said.

"You *what?*" For John, like most people, was offended by hypocrisy if it was not his own.

"My audience is all like teenagers, early twenty-somethings. On CNN I could get the message out to an older demographic. The message is important."

"*Yes,*" Carl said, excited. "The *demographic.*" He looked at Marta. "See, I didn't even have to make that argument."

But Marta was staring somewhere in the vicinity of John's torso. "Hey, are you okay?" she asked John.

"What? I'm fine," John said.

"But your—"

"Jesus Christ!" said Carl. "Your *arm.*"

John looked down. He'd been clenching the table tightly in a grasp for stability. The flexion of his right forearm had triggered the tearing open of his fresh, unbandaged, self-inflicted wound. It was bleeding profusely. The blood was soaking through the long sleeve of his shirt, where all could see it. John reached for his napkin, which he hadn't done anything fancy with, hadn't tucked into his collar or laid neatly on his lap. He pulled his sleeve to his elbow and applied the napkin. The napkins in this place were black; the blood became invisible once it touched the napkin.

"Are you okay?" Rene asked.

John pulled the napkin from his skin. The wound hadn't been bleeding as profusely as it seemed: the redness of the blood had been deceptive. The wound was thin, light, but the skin around it was a deep pink: an ellipses of darkness from three inches above the wrist to three inches below the inside of the elbow. Never had the flesh around the cut been discolored before. "I'm fine," John said.

Carl reached for his arm, pulled it across the table, across a board laden with sashimi. "Is this self-inflicted? Did you do this?"

"No—" John yanked his arm away. The action agitated the cut; it began to bleed again. John reapplied the napkin. "It was an accident. I got it caught on a . . . on a—"

Again Carl grabbed his arm. "Marta—are you seeing this? Are you thinking what I'm think?"

"I think I am," Marta said.

John again yanked his arm from Carl's grasp. "Hey, what the fuck, man. Let go of me."

"A whole different program," Carl said. "A different network. TLC. Or maybe even Showtime. It would take a lot of honesty, the show, like you'd have to— you couldn't be afraid to be your real, true, self, you know? but people would love this. *Love* it. We'd need a catchy title. Like . . . hmmmm. *Cutting and Caring*. Or *Self-Harm/Self-Love*, with a slash between the two, like implying that they're two sides of the same coin."

"Or," Marta offered, "*My Depression*."

"No," Carl said. "Too sad. Not catchy. Sounds like a bad novel. Like a novel, am I right. But we'll get it. If those don't work, we'll figure out a name. Do you think we could schedule a meeting with TLC?"

"I'll get Adriano's assistant on the phone tonight. I'll get something on the calendar."

"Soon. This week."

"Wait a second," John said, finding a voice he'd briefly lost. "What the hell are you talking about?"

"Yeah," Rene said. "And what about my show on CNN?"

301

"John," Carl said. "Reality. I'm talking about a reality show. Kardashians. Real Housewives. But this one's YouTubers with self-harm problems . . ." He trailed off. Then he said, "Marta. Marta! YouTubers with mental problems. Like a whole series. We could get a bunch of them together, into a rehab center—"

"And their families," Marta said.

"Well of course their families. Friends. John, how would your family like to be on TV?"

"What? *No*. This isn't what I came here for. And I don't cut myself. This was an accident. I scraped my arm against a—"

"Ten thousand dollars per episode. Maybe twenty-five."

"We'll get Dr. Drew to do the rehab!" Marta exclaimed.

"Of course. Yes! Dr. Drew!"

"No. Absolutely not," John said.

"John," Carl said. "You don't understand. Depression is a gold mine. Everyone is depressed, but no one ever talks about it."

"It's true," said Marta, staring at her phone, her thumbs typing away. "I'm depressed."

"*I'm* depressed, too," Carl said. "You want your numbers to go up, you tell everyone how depressed you are. They'll love you for it. *Love* you."

John stood. "Fuck this." He threw the bloody napkin on the table. "You don't get to trade in this. You don't know what I've been through. My depression is not your depression. It's mine. It's *mine*." And he stormed out of the dinning room, past a confused hostess, and through the front door.

"Hey—"

It was only minutes later. John was standing next to the curb. He'd contemplated walking into traffic, but traffic was moving slowly—no car would hit him fast enough. Besides, he didn't want to die anymore, hadn't wanted to die for months. And as he stood there, watching the Porches, the yellow taxis, the Audis covered in their California dust, wondering what it would be like to be hit by one of them, but not wanting to be hit by one of them, it occurred to him that there was a difference between contemplating suicide and thinking about killing yourself.

He turned around. Rene King was there. "What do you want?" John asked.

"I just wanted to say sorry. For what happened in there. It wasn't cool."

John shrugged. "It wasn't your fault."

"Wasn't it?" She gestured at the street, at the buildings. "It's this town. This city. These people. And I am one of them."

"You seem decent enough to me." He meant it. He could not hate her.

"Listen—are you waiting for an Uber?"

"Yeah. It's"—he looked at his smartwatch—"three minutes away."

"Where are you going?"

"I have a hotel room. Across town."

"Across this town is . . . vague, but no matter what you mean it's a long way away."

John remembered he'd never checked in to the hotel. He wondered whether his room had been given away.

"My apartment is five blocks away," Rene said. "You can stay with me tonight."

John looked at her face. Her freckles seemed to sparkle at him. A wind blew; her pompadour did not sway. "I— Okay," John said. "Should we walk?"

"Oh no. We'll take your Uber. Shame to waste an Uber."

At her apartment she offered him a glass of whiskey. "It's not Japanese, I'm afraid. I'm a fan of cheap stuff, a little bit trashy stuff." She poured him a tumbler of Jack Daniels.

He'd taken one sip, she two, before their mouths found themselves intermingled with each other's. John did not know why he did it. Why now? He didn't love Rene King. He didn't even like her. But he didn't hate her. Until this point he'd slept with only one woman, one woman who didn't know she was his only one. One woman who'd slept herself with dozens . . . a dozen? . . . he didn't truly know. As Rene expertly worked the button of his pants John looked at his wedding ring.

Rene paused. "Second thoughts?" she asked. "We don't have to do this. You're married—I understand."

"No. It's okay. It really is. It isn't even cheating. We're in a . . . I was just thinking how funny it is . . . one of our rules is you have to keep the wedding ring on. It's supposed to be a form of honesty."

John grew nervous when the time came to remove Rene's clothes. What would he find under there? He unbuttoned her shirt as she'd unbuttoned his: there was no bra but breasts were there, small, but feminine, vaguely spherical—you could put your hands on them, the nipples were pink, round. Under her black jeans: mens boxer briefs, but under those: a vulva, smooth, wet.

They moved to Rene's bedroom and for some time John tried to enter her. More than once he found his way in, only to become anxious and slip out. Tumescence fought a battle of attrition with flaccidity.

"Everything okay?" Rene asked finally.

His erection surrendering, John settled against her headboard. "I'm sorry," he said. "This happens sometimes.

I'm . . . I get nervous. I've never been very good." Indeed, at home, where his dick was usually comfortable maintaining an engorged state, he still rarely made Beth come; he knew this. She didn't fake it—that wouldn't be honest—just told him once he'd come that she loved him, thanked him for the sex, and went to sleep spooning him or nuzzled in the crook of his arm.

"Oh—honey," Rene said. She sounded sad, but not piteous. "That's okay. Just—lay back."

He did. She crawled to the foot of the bed and, her body perpendicular to his, took his dick into her mouth. At first, nothing happened. "Relax," she told him. In time he grew and hardened. Never was he rock solid, but she kept him stiff enough that after ten minutes, with lots of saliva and handwork and attention to his scrotum, she was able to make him spurt into her mouth. She swallowed and smiled and laid next to him and said, "Now kiss me."

He kissed her. He could taste himself. He'd never tasted himself before. It was not unpleasant.

"Now, put your mouth on my tit."

While he worked his tongue, alternating each nipple, occasionally moving back to her mouth, she touched herself. He wanted to watch, to see how she did it, what direction she moved her fingers, where precisely she applied pressure—to learn; but he knew that wasn't what she wanted.

The next morning she traced a finger along his forearm, where the cut overnight had scabbed. "This looks like it could get infected," she said.

"I know. It's stupid."

"I've done it too," she told him.

He shifted so he could see her face better; she had her head on his bare chest and was looking up at him. "Really?" he asked

"Sure—when I was a teenager. For a few months there I did it a lot. And I'd punch things, too."

"Like pillows?"

"Like walls, doors, things that hurt."

"Oh."

"Have you ever talked about it?"

He shrugged. "I have a therapist. I think she kind of knows."

"But not, like, in public?"

He shook his head. "My wife doesn't even know. It's not usually so visible. I'm usually more careful."

"You should," she said. "Talk about it, I mean. You said yesterday that it was yours, that this was yours. It is. You should own it. You're allowed to hurt."

"I can't," he said.

"Why not? Are you afraid of the stigma?"

"Yes. And . . . well and it would just feel like whining. Like I'd just be whining."

"How so?"

"Like . . . I'm . . . privileged or whatever. What do I have to hurt myself about? I'm just a . . . how would you put it . . .?"

"A white cisgender male?"

"Exactly. A white cisgender male. And heterosexual," he added.

"Fuck that," she said. "You're no less valid than I am."

Twenty minutes later, as he was stepping out of her shower, he said, "Shit." He said it with some volume.

"What's up," she asked, poking her head into the bathroom.

"I left my bag at the restaurant."

"It's cool. I know the owner. I'll have them send it over."

"You know the owner?"

"Oh yeah. He used to be a YouTuber, too, before he opened

the restaurant. He never found an audience. Honestly? I hear the restaurant's not doing so well either."

A few hours later John sat in the terminal at LAX, his right sleeve rolled to the elbow, examining his wound. Meditating on it. From the corner of his vision he noticed a middle-aged woman three seats away, staring at it too. He looked at her. She turned away.

He fished inside his backpack and found those new wireless headphones he'd recently reviewed on the channel. He took out his phone and held it in front of his face, as far as his arm would reach. Then he adjusted, pulled his arm in closer, to a more comfortable position. After a moment, he reassigned the job of makeshift tripod to his left arm, so he would be free to record an image of his right. He activated the front facing video camera. "Hey guys," he said. "I know I don't really do daily vlogs, but I'm sitting here in the LAX airport and I have something important I want to say . . ."

He didn't post that video. His flight boarded, and airplane wifi, if you were willing to pay for it, sucked for uploading. But when he returned to the corner of his bedroom that functioned as his studio, he recorded and edited a better version, more professional, relating his own story and sharing researched statistics and figures and phone numbers for other sufferers to call, should they need help.

Two days later, the Huffington Post embedded his video in an article. They posted the article on their front page. For all intents and purposes, the video *was* the article. The headline read:

WATCH THIS VLOGGER START A DISCUSSION
ABOUT MENTAL ILLNESS IN THE BRAVEST WAY

The
Haiku
Kid

I KNOW I WASN'T OVER there very long: even if you count basic, at Fort Jackson, I was in The Army for like four months before the discharge. Honorable discharge, obviously. They don't discharge you any way but honorably when you've had your leg sliced open and it appears you'll lose the leg, even if upon return to home soil it becomes clear you *won't* lose the leg, won't even have trouble walking again, eventually. Or when you've seen your best friend cut in half.

I can't believe I'm in Rebekah Fleckman's bed right now. Every morning I can't believe I'm waking in Rebekah Fleckman's bed, and every night I can't believe I'm going to sleep in it. She calls it *our* bed, but it's hers. It's always been hers. I don't know who else has been in it but anyone who has it was never theirs. It isn't ours: I'm an outsider here. I live here but I don't *live* here. The day will come when Rebekah will realize she doesn't want to be with me, doesn't know why she invited me to move in. Why she even thinks I'm charming, which is what she tells me when I ask why she likes me: "You're cute, and charming."

It's not like I really ever see her, even though I share her bed. She's up so early now, has to get to class. Stays out so late working at the hospital. Comes home smelling like bedpans or formaldehyde or whatever chemicals they use in hospitals. Even if I wait up for her, talk to her for a few minutes when she gets home, I'm asleep before she's out of the shower. We only fuck on weekends. Quietly so as not to wake her roommates. Rebekah says she likes my body. Says I look good naked. I used to lift weights with my buddy Vance back in his basement in Ennis.

I can't believe I'm fucking Rebekah Fleckman.

Rebekah tells me I should get a job. I tell her I can't yet on account of the leg's still healing. Eventually I still won't have a job and she'll realize she doesn't want to be with me. Eventually she'll realize she doesn't like me, and she doesn't like school, and she doesn't have a fucking clue what she's going to do with her life.

I think she'll figure it out, though, even if right now she doesn't know. Her roommates don't know either—they've both graduated but they just work at coffee shops or something and complain to each other. Her friends don't know. The YouTuber and the vegan baker don't have any clue what they're going to do with their lives. The YouTuber thinks he knows, what with all the attention he's getting, but he doesn't know.

I tried reading those books Beth let me borrow. Couldn't get through them. I also tried reading some of Rebekah's mystery novels and I guess at least they were a little more entertaining. I don't like stories, only poetry. I only told Beth I liked those books because I saw them on her shelf, tilted my head to read the author's name when no one was looking. I wanted Rebekah's friends to like me. Before we went to their house for dinner that day Rebekah told me she thought her friends would like me.

It's like 11 PM and Rebekah won't be home for a couple hours. At least I'm in her bed, not on her couch.

Hungry. Want to grab something from the refrigerator, but I can hear the roommates out there. Don't want to see them. They don't like me. Vance would have called them cunts. "Don't let those bitches get to you you," he would have said. But he wouldn't have meant it. He was always letting bitches get to him.

I kept a journal during Basic and what counted for deployment, but I lost it in the explosion. Lost some good poems in the explosion.

I joined up when it became clear I didn't know what *I* wanted to do with my life. Too many days working with Vance at the construction company—he got me that job—followed by evenings playing video games in his basement.

"Go get us a couple more beers, will ya, babe?" he'd say to his girlfriend, who's name I don't remember (could be I lost some memories from the concussive force of the explosion, the doctors told me, could also be I didn't care) and who would oblige while we kept shooting at each other's avatars or trying to score a touchdown against each other's painstakingly recreated football teams.

"Maybe I should do this for real," I said one day after I got a headshot on some guy we were playing against online. I don't remember his username.

"Do what?" Vance said. "Play video games? Like in California?"

"No," I said. "Fight wars, battles. Like join the military."

He laughed. "Yeah right."

"No, I'm serious," I told him. "We could do it together. We could kill terrorists, save the world. We could be heroes."

He stopped playing for a moment and looked at me. Another player sniped him. "I don't think you're serious," he said.

The next day I enlisted. Kept trying to convince Vance to go with me, but he insisted he didn't want to. Liked his job. Owned a little house near the river. Took care of his mom. Had a girlfriend who blew him several times a week. Wouldn't give that up for the world.

A couple weeks before I shipped out to Basic I went on that first date with Rebekah. One last chance at a lay before The Army. I never wanted anything serious. I told Vance how I slept over and he assumed that meant we fucked and I never told him any different. Vance maybe would have liked Rebekah. I don't think she would have liked Vance, but she would have pretended to.

A week before Basic Vance's mom died—heart attack—and he found his girlfriend sleeping with the foreman from the construction company. We sold our trucks and a week later we were in South Carolina, breezing our way through BCT. It was the first time either of us had left Montana.

In Basic Training the rule is you never go anywhere alone. They call the concept *battle buddies*. Vance was mine. I was his. Other guys called us fags, called us *The* Battle Buddies—note the definite article. The drill sergeant told them to shut up and then added there was nothing wrong with fags in The Army anymore. And then he laughed. Muttered, "Thanks, Obama," and the other guys laughed too. The sergeant laughed harder. Then he told us all to straighten up. Called us a bunch of pussies.

After Basic Vance and I both decided on Infantry and they sent us together to Fort Benning.

A couple weeks before we would have finished Advanced

Infantry Training the situation in the Middle East escalated. Kind of went full tilt. Depending on who you ask it was either Trump's fault or some ambassador. All I know is the ambassador had ended up dead and they needed more men and shipped us and bunch of other guys out early. I've never paid specific attention to the details of politics.

Our A400M landed on the airstrip a couple hundred miles east of Baghdad and that's when they blew us up. A missile. Later they found out it had been fired by North Korea. Iraq had nothing to do with it and were just as pissed as the Americans. The missile hit the A400M and a wing flew off and splintered and from that wing a propeller blade came flying toward us. You ever see the wing of an A400M? They're huge. Vance pushed me down and the blade went through the softness of his gut from bellybutton all the way to the side and then stuck into my leg. Plus little pieces of shrapnel went into my leg also, sort of sunk into my flesh, imbedded themselves. I know it was only my leg but I thought I was dead until someone pulled Vance off me and shouted I needed to get in the truck.

I was back in Montana by the time the Christmas bombing happened in New York. Turned out ISIS took responsibility for that one, not the North Koreans.

Good news is the leg is almost better now and the cast is off and I can walk almost without the crutches and am only going to have a nasty scar.

I'm hungry but I'm not going to go get food because I really don't want to see Rebekah's roommates. Too bad she's not still roommates with my cousin Jenna. I wonder how Jenna's doing. Haven't talked to her since last summer.

Next month John and Beth are having an anniversary party

315

and Rebekah and I are going. Beth told Rebekah I have to be there. Rebekah said Beth was quite insistent for some reason, said it wouldn't work without me. They've been married for almost a year, John and Beth, which good for them, but I don't see it lasting.

I wrote this poem for Vance while I was in the hospital:

> *My battle buddy*
> *I think I may have loved you*
> *More than you loved me*

Our Depression

1

JOHN AND BETH HEMPEL WERE married in a civil ceremony in late July. Beth wore a sheer flowing dress, almost black but when the light hit it just right you could see it was only the darkest shade of shimmering gray, almost as if the gray was silver, real silver. This was Ebony. Beth in her own spiritual practice had never used a wand, but if she did, she'd have chosen one made of ebony wood. You can order ebony wands from various magick suppliers on the internet; far more difficult are they to make yourself. John, at the wedding, wore brown khakis, a dark blue shirt, a tie—silver, but not an ebony silver—that he found at Goodwill. He did not own a proper suit, and in the entirety of his life he never would; he wouldn't even buy one when, well into the future, he'd accept the first ever Producer award, an award that would in time become the online content producer equivalent of the Lifetime Achievement Oscar or literature's Nobel Prize. Fuck the Webby's—the Producer award would be where it was at.

The wedding ceremony was presided over by an elderly justice of the peace named Garrison McCarthy; he was small and wrinkled and wispy-haired and had spent his entire life in Montana; he'd been officiating civil ceremonies for fifty years.

The vows, modified, did not contain the words *till death do us part*, because you never know what's going to happen: you may die together, in a car crash like Beth's parents, say, and your spirits, if there are such things, may decide to remain forever and ever entwined, exploring the cosmos, the astral plane, the wherever, all the wherevers; or in life you might grow apart, get divorced, remain friends or never see each other again, whatever you think is best (maybe you'll decide you shouldn't see each other anymore, after the divorce, but then in the future that will change, and, while never marrying again, you'll find your ways back to each other, into each other's embrace and the comfort of each other's warm beds). The justice of the peace, who John and Beth and Rebekah all agreed was adorable, and who approved of the union over which he was presiding, and was doing the best he could, stumbled over the Latin phrase *omnia vincit amor*, which John requested be included because he thought Beth would appreciate the Latin because didn't they use Latin a lot in their spells and rituals? It isn't exactly true, the phrase, *omnia vincit amor*, when you think about it; you might as well just say *till death do us part*—the sentiment is the same. Rebekah was at the ceremony, in the little wood-panneled courtroom; she witnessed the signing of the certificate. Beth asked her college roommate Melanie to be a second witness, but Melanie didn't approve of the marriage, just as she hadn't approved of the courtship, and anyway she was traveling, so one of Rebekah's roommates, Jenna, came instead and left immediately after the ceremony, having no vested interest in the couple or their lives together.

Beth, John, and Rebekah went out for drinks. Beth and John had purchased an apartment in Bozeman, but they couldn't move in until just before the honeymoon, meaning there would be no time to unpack until after. For a week they stayed with Rebekah. Rebekah gave them her room—she insisted—and she slept on the couch.

Ten months before the wedding Beth had called John on his cell phone. He was in Missoula, homeless, had just been released from the hospital following his second suicide attempt, the same attempt that, until he came clean about his depression—and about his inclinations toward self-harm and self-withdrawal—on his YouTube channel, Beth had always believed was his first. She called him and he told her it was good to hear her voice, and she said it was good to hear his. He told her he was doing better. He told her this because he loved her, and he wanted to be with her forever, and while he didn't propose then and there, on the phone, he did say he wanted to see her again, and she agreed, and he came to Helena, hitched a ride with a stranger he found on Craigslist who was heading in that direction, and he told her he was homeless, and she told him she too was looking for a place to live, and so they found a little place there in Helena, together.

They lived for a while off the remainder of what Beth had made selling her grandmother's house. They lived nearly a year without jobs, their savings dwindling, John's student loans going unpaid. He hadn't finished classes. Hadn't received his degree. Neither had Beth. They spent their days in a squalid apartment, making love, the experience of making love never entirely satisfactory to either of them, not until Beth suggested they get some toys, experiment with being a little rougher. Most important was the experience of being together.

"I think we should get married," John said finally. "I know I've said it before but I'm in love with you."

Beth said you can't hurt me again. You can't hurt yourself again, because that would hurt me.

John said he wouldn't, not ever.

Beth said I don't know how to put this but I need to be able to see other people, too, if we're going to make this work.

That one took a while for John to understand. If he'd had the money to get a hotel room, or a friend with whom to stay, he might have left for a little while, to process things. As it was they just didn't talk for a few days. Beth gave John a book to read, about open relationships, about polyamory. He found a few websites. He joined an online forum. Finally he told her, okay, as long as he got to marry her, because he loved her.

She told him she loved him too. And she did.

Together they called Rebekah Fleckman, told her they were getting married, and guess what! they were moving to Bozeman, they'd be right there, with her. Wouldn't that be wonderful?

2

IN HINDSIGHT JOHN SHOULD HAVE discussed the video with Beth before he uploaded it. He should have discussed it with her before he *recorded* it.

"You should," his therapist said, "have discussed the fact that you were cutting yourself with her as soon as you started doing it, the cutting."

"I agree," Beth said.

They were on a couch together, John and Beth, in his therapist's office. They were holding hands. There was a great deal of tension in the room. Hurt and concern. But notable was the absence of anger.

"You should have told me, too," the therapist said. "You promised to be honest with me—that's the only way any sort of relationship can work."

"It is," Beth said, nodding.

"It just seemed like my own problem," John said. "And not even a problem, exactly. I didn't feel like I was doing anything wrong. It was just a private thing, like masturbating. Or fantasizing."

Beth squeezed his hand.

* * *

Beth was at the bakery when she first saw the video. She was in the back, where the ovens were and the stove and the dishwashing station. She was supervising the simmering of a large pot of tomato basil soup. The soup was a new recipe, and what she would never reveal was that its secret ingredients were chicken stock and beef bullion, rather than heavy cream. Heavy cream at least would have made the soup vegetarian, and if anyone who was aware of her vegan intentions had commented on that, she wouldn't have felt horrible admitting that, from time to time, she indulged in eggs, fish, and dairy—for the sake of her customers, of course: how could she serve for example a cheesy soufflé without tasting it? or a New England chowder without testing the freshness of the seafood she sourced? What she couldn't admit, for it would be too much, would embarrass her, would destroy her validity in the eyes of so many with whom she spent her time (the vegans, the feminists, the queers, the other Bozeman coven members), was that she also partook of things like the bakery's newly famous bacon cheddar scones, or that sometimes when making pastrami sandwiches she would pick off shreds of the brined meat for herself. It was just that it all tasted so good: the meat. And she'd be a fool to not admit to herself that when she avoided animal products her skin grew drier, her hair showed signs of brittleness, the flesh around her nine tattoos (for she'd gotten another one, just after Christmas, a gryphon, her favorite mythical creature) even sometimes itched. So for months now she'd been sneaking bites of animal flesh (or, yes, sometimes, when no one else was in the bakery, entire roast beef sandwiches) and adding meat-based broths to soups that were otherwise labeled vegetarian. So what that her stomach had these little rolls (rolls that Emeline said were adorable). The bakery's profits thanked her, and so did Karen, the owner and founder, who rumor had it was thinking of retiring within the next year, and who at one point had intended to sell the whole thing but now was thinking about maintaining a stake in it but withdrawing from daily operations, leaving control and most of the income to Beth, although she hadn't discussed any of this with Beth directly yet, only told her she was doing a wonderful job, keep it up, I'm very proud of what you're doing here. (Also, Emeline, just a few nights ago, while John was out of town, had, after going down on Beth, commented that Beth's come tasted better than ever, and Beth knew this could be the result only of her daily secret strips of bacon). Beth made penitence for her indulgence with extra long daily prayers and meditations. Once every 28 days she made a little sacrifice of her menstrual blood upon her altar.

She stirred the massive pot of soup with a long-handled ladle, tasted it, added a few teaspoons of salt, stirred, and tasted it again. She removed her rubber gloves and stepped into the back office, where her phone was. A new girl, Brie, like the cheese—the same cheese that the bakery had started featuring, baked with jam, as an optional pastry topping at only 50 cents a serving—was manning the front counter. Or womanning it, if you wanted to be politically correct; Beth strove to be politically correct. Personning it? Emeline would have said womynning it, and Beth, ever the English major, would have said she understood where Emeline was coming from but was *woman* really so bad, once you took into consideration the etymology, in particular the fact that for a very long time *man* really did just mean *human*, of any gender?

Beth was falling in love with Emeline. She had not told Emeline this, nor had she told John.

In February she had been manning the bakery's counter

during one of the new Wednesday-evening performance sessions the bakery had started hosting. Normally the bakery closed at 4pm, sometimes even earlier if all the day's goods had sold out, but on Wednesdays now they reopened at six, offering any leftover pastries at half price, but mostly selling just tea and coffee. In the intervening hours Beth rearranged the dinning area, moving the tables into the back and lining up the chairs theater style, several rows facing the left-hand wall, where she set up a microphone, a set of speakers. The nature of the performance varied from week to week. Sometimes the theme was open mic, music or poetry or short fiction reading. Occasionally during these nights Beth read some of her own work (when she did, John was sure to attend; when she didn't, he surrendered to his introversion, which she understood). Other nights a local musician would play an entire set, singer-songwriter, violinist, all acts low-key, quiet, relaxing. Once—and the booking of this performance had garnered particular praise from Karen, who herself rarely attended the Wednesday-night events–Beth had convinced John Mayer to play a handful of songs. Mayer lived in Paradise Valley, just thirty miles outside of town. "You're doing amazing things for Betty's Bakery Cafe," Karen had said.

The night Emeline walked in a local bluegrass duo was performing in the bakery. Thirty or so people were in attendance. Emeline approached the counter and bought an herbal tea. She didn't say anything else, just ordered the tea and then, after Beth presented it to her, winked. It was several minutes before Beth realized she hadn't charged for the drink.

By mid-March they were sleeping together once a week or so. At first they did not stay the night at each other's places— Beth never stayed the night with any partner but her husband, not Chad, not Vilma, but by design none of her other partnerships were long-lived. In time, however, Beth asked John whether he'd mind if she did stay with Emeline, just once a week or so, to keep her company, to give them more time to connect, to play, for while Emeline was comfortable with Beth's open lifestyle, she had no desire herself to be with more than one partner at a time. John said he understood, and Beth sensed he was telling the truth, even if nights alone were obviously hard for him. The cats were only so much company. Once, Beth suggested John and Emeline meet. John said no, that's okay, I don't really want to.

Emeline never even shared Beth's personal bed until John went to LA. This was the night Beth realized she was falling for Emeline. It wasn't exactly a conundrum, for the whole point of John and Beth's arrangement was that Beth might share the abundance of love she could picture within herself.

Beth Hempel loved everyone. Sometimes she felt as if she'd been cursed to love everyone. A curse she was able to mitigate by fucking women, fucking men, writing words, casting spells. She believed the curse found root the night her parents died, the night she realized she would never again love them as physical beings. But it had only grown painful, the curse, her junior year of college, just before she'd met John, perhaps, even, the very night she'd slept with Ric. Ric: rarely did she think of him as a physical presence, but often did she recall the grief in his eyes when he'd said: "I'm so sorry." As if he understood her curse, as if he'd been imparting its acceleration upon her himself with every aggressive thrust of his cock, and as if doing so was his *own* curse to bare.

Beth was in love with John. She was in love with Emeline. Rebekah. The girl Brie out front. Even Aaron, Haiku Kid. Each time she opened Tinder on her phone—she used Tinder now—she couldn't help but swipe right, no matter the face presented to her, and her heart hurt in such a lovely way each time she did so.

In the back office she picked up her phone from the desk, swiping through Tinder exactly what she was intending to do. Instead, she was presented with a notification: *John Hempel has uploaded a new video.*

Beth subscribed to two YouTube channels: 1) A popular makeup tutorialist and fashion vlogger, and 2.) her husband. Like anyone, she often found herself caught in the fount of the website's front page, the new videos, the Recommendeds and the For Yous, but only the new productions of these two people did she have a desire to be made immediately aware of. She enjoyed the tips about applying black lipsticks and eyeshadows, about creatively tying your black scarves and shawls. And while she didn't care strongly about politics—RIP Bernie—or technology, she couldn't not support her husband's work. Checking the clock on the office wall, a habit she had even though the very device she was holding was displaying the time in block white letters, she decided she could spare a few minutes to watch the video. John had only returned yesterday. He'd been sullen, distracted. She suspected the meeting had not gone well, which he'd confirmed, but she hadn't yet seen fit to press for details. So here she was surprised and delighted to see he was putting out creative work.

Beth swiped at the notification, taking her to the application, to the page of the relevant video. The thumbnail showed John smiling sadly, wearing a purple t-shirt, one arm held high but conspicuously pixelated in a tempting way, as if to say *click here to see what's underneath the blur effect*. Beth noted the attire—she hadn't seen her husband wear a t-shirt in some time. The video's title was "My Depression". The thumbnail was replaced with a black box and a white loading circle. The bakery had intentionally poor wifi, to discourage antisocial behavior. Beth moved to switch her phone over to a cellular signal.

"Excuse me. Beth?" said Brie, standing in the office doorway.

Beth looked up from her screen.

"I'm having trouble figuring out how to double the meat on a salad for this guy out here. Like how to charge him for it on the register."

"No problem," Beth said. "Let's go take a look."

Thence came the lunch rush, and Beth realizing, after a customer ordered it, that she still had to bring out the tomato basil soup. For two hours she and Brie alternated working the register, the espresso machine, the deli case, with Beth regularly stepping in to show the younger girl how to make a breve, ring up a side of balsamic dressing, slice a loaf of pumpernickel so when a customer got home he could proceed to butter it right away. It wasn't until Beth was walking home that she remembered to watch John's video.

As she watched it, half a block from their apartment, under the shadow of a ponderosa pine, she felt combinations of anger, sadness, and admiration. The feelings came in ebbs and flows, each welling in various degrees, receding, and then coming in again like the tide, over the course of the ten-minute video.

After several deep breaths, she resolved to show only empathy for her husband. Entering their apartment, calling out his name, receiving no response as she removed her shoes, rubbed out her sore feet, she briefly feared the worst. But then she found him in their bed, shirtless, face down, asleep. Carefully she took his arm, for the first time getting a real look at what he'd been doing to himself. How, she couldn't help but wonder guiltily, had she missed it all this time?

He stirred. He turned halfway over and his eyes blinked open.

"You've been crying?" Beth said, noticing the redness, the streaks of dried tears on his cheeks.

John raised a hand to his face. "I'm sorry," he said.

"Hey," she said, taking his hand. "It's okay. I love you."

"But the cat," he said, and he started sobbing again.

"The cat . . .? Which one?"

"Bernard. He just, he wouldn't stop shedding. He wouldn't stop. I had to make him stop." John was shaking now.

Beth began to panic. With a frantic turn of the head, she saw the the dark gray figure like a ghost walk into the room, meowing. Behind Bernard came Jean-Luc Picat. Both cats licked at her toes groggily, as if to say, *Hello Mom.*

John was still crying, but he was also, Beth realized, sleeping. Dreaming. Her poor husband, dreaming such horrible dreams.

"I don't know why I didn't tell you," John said under the therapist's watchful supervision. "I wanted to tell you, but I didn't want to hurt you. I guess I knew how much I had hurt you before, both those times . . ."

Beth almost corrected him, said *all three times,* but that wouldn't have been fair. The first suicide attempt had nothing to do with her. She hadn't been a part of his life then. "I understand," she said instead.

"But . . ." said the therapist.

"But what?" Beth asked.

"But did it still hurt you?"

"Well . . . yes."

"Then don't you think you should tell him that?"

Beth looked at John.

John held up a hand. "I got it. You don't have to *tell me* tell me. I hear you."

Beth suggested she continue to attend John's therapy sessions, maybe not all of them, but every couple weeks or so. John's therapist said she didn't think that was necessary. "I mean unless you want to, but I don't think couples' therapy is what you two need. Not at all. As a couple, you're doing fine. You're making your relationship work, open and otherwise. John, we just need honesty from you—that's all. With me, with Beth at home, and most importantly, with yourself."

That *with yourself* part struck John as trite, cliché; he couldn't help but mock it internally, even if he knew the therapist was right. But when *hadn't* he been honest with himself? That was the difficult detail to figure out: you can only correct a lie if you know what the lie is.

But he could start with full disclosure with respect to others. Beth and John walked home from the therapist's office in silence, but when they entered the apartment, he suggested they drink some coffee—there was that new roast they'd just purchased but hadn't yet tried, imported by a local shop from Ethiopia—and he could tell her everything that was on his mind. As they drank, each with a cat in their respective laps, he told her all about the trip to Los Angeles, starting with the soft pretzel, and ending, not a little reluctantly, with his overnight encounter with Rene King.

Coffee turned to wine and the ordering in of a large vegan pizza. John and Beth moved from the couch to the bedroom and talked as they'd never talked before. They talked the way most couples talk in the early months of their relationship: dreams, hopes, goals. What would they do now, the two of them? Would they have children? Would they stay here in Bozeman? In Montana? When John got famous—for surely he was going to be famous; any fool could see that—where would they go? Who would they know? What would they see? And Beth, her novel, the bakery. And their anniversary. They couldn't take a trip now, of course—they no longer had the money—but in the future surely they could. A second honeymoon. Back to San Francisco! Or Los Angeles (but then John nixed that idea, assured her LA wasn't, in his 24 hours of experience, that great). Or—wait—what about New York? Yes, New York City! Rebekah had liked it there. Soon, when John was famous, they would go to New York, together.

And in the meantime they'd have a party. Just friends. Just John and Beth Rebekah and Aaron. But it would be a *real* party. "I know just how to do it," Beth said.

"What do you mean? How?" John said.

But Beth just smiled. "Leave it to me, my love. It'll be a surprise. You're going to love it."

They watched a movie on John's laptop, there in bed. They put the pizza box, a few slices remaining in it, on the floor for the cats to inquire about and then plant themselves on. When the movie was over and the wine bottle was empty Beth kissed John's arm, told him she'd make it better. "With magick," she said.

As Beth slept next to him John remained awake, eyes closed. He tried to sleep, willed himself to be happy in this moment, content, but somewhere around midnight he realized that just wasn't who he was: a happy person. Happiness, as a constant, ever-present state was not something John Hempel was capable of attaining, and it was not, therefore, something he should waste his time aspiring to. Acknowledging this, he realized, was the meaning of being honest with oneself.

3

It's been said Montana has two seasons: Winter and August. While the sentiment is accurate, the statement isn't strictly true, for in April the last of the winter's snow had melted, and by May the temperature when Rebekah left in the mornings during her final week of classes was well above 50, even closing on 60, warming further as the day grew on.

Finals had been last week, and Rebekah knew already that she'd passed the few classes she was taking this semester. She would graduate with a 3.45, having achieved higher marks in the last two semesters than in the previous three years of college. After graduation—well, she wasn't sure . . . . Things were going well at the hospital; she'd just been offered a full-time job there, and it was a little better than what she doing now; less changing of bedpans and cleaning of sheets and more filing of insurance claims and admitting of patients. It wasn't life-saving work, but it was arguably more life-saving than what she'd been doing the last several months, first as a volunteer and then as a part-time employee.

And she was still enjoying all Bozeman had to offer when she remembered to take advantage of it. One could put down roots here. There was the food, even if food didn't particularly excite

Rebekah. There was the beer, which was more of a plus for her than the food. There were the people, Beth and John, who were her best friends, even if given their proximity she didn't see them nearly as much as you'd think she would, and even if when she stopped and asked herself what she felt for those people she had to admit wasn't more than warm affection; but warm affection was more than she seemed to feel for anybody else. And there was Aaron; Aaron was a warm body next to whom she could wake. Her other two roommates, whom she hated. Two independent bookstores, on the same block—what city could she afford to move to that could possibly offer two independent bookstores. Multiple solid coffee shops, although Rebekah didn't drink coffee. Mountains, far away but visible in all directions, still snow-peaked, white and blue and kind of black.

And also there was Reginald Martin. Rebekah was on her way to see him now. They had not slept together since before Christmas. He hadn't even raised the possibility, hadn't tried to seduce her again. She had not been to his apartment again. She saw him from time to time at the hospital, where he worked, one of the state's best cardiothoracic surgeons—who would have guessed? And also she'd seen him the last two weeks, in her Advanced Anatomy and Physiology course. The course was, like the Intermediate A&P course she'd taken last semester, supposed to be taught by Doctor Linda Epstein; and in fact it was, for all but the final few weeks. Linda Epstein, who during the Intermediate course had been on sabbatical, was the official report; but the official report had been false, a story, a way for Doctor Epstein to preserve a sense of human dignity she was afraid was being consumed from within. That's what all stories are, really, even the thrillers and the mysteries, the smut and the pornographies: a way of maintaining a sense that humans aren't losing their dignity. Doctor Linda Epstein had not been in Brussels last semester assisting with a field-defining research project; Doctor Linda Epstein had been dying of cancer. But then the cancer went away, and this semester she was well enough again to teach, and Rebekah took her class, and Rebekah dissected a pigeon, a fetal pig and an adult pig, and a fully grown tiger shark, not unlike the spiny dogfish from last semester, but way, way bigger—720p vs 4k resolution, was how Doctor Epstein had put it, using a metaphorical framework Rebekah would not otherwise have thought in the context of. Then two weeks ago Doctor Epstein's cancer had returned, and Doctor Reginald Martin had gracefully, if not morosely, for Linda was a close colleague and a good friend, taken over the class again. After finals he quietly informed everyone present that she had, in fact, passed away the previous evening, surrounded by her loved ones. Her death had been peaceful. Painless.

"I have a treat," Doctor Martin said now, after Rebekah and everyone else had entered the lab. "And judging by the number of you here today, some of your fellow classmates are going to be very disappointed, when they hear what they missed out on. This, students, is why you don't just check out after finals week, oh no, oh no."

He disappeared into a deep supply closet. Nonchalantly he returned, wheeling a dissection table, not unlike the standard dissection tables they were used to, except this one had a metal hood, in two pieces, enclosing the surface, like an outdoor meat smoker. Doctor Martin grinned. Then, with dramatic flourish, he opened the half of the hood nearest him. There were murmurs; none of the students could see what he'd revealed. Then, sans flourish this time, as if the sweepingness of the first gesture had been merely for his own satisfaction, he opened the other half. On the table was a body. A human body. White and pale and bloodless.

There were gasps. Some laughter, some of the laughter mirthful, some of it nervous. "I imagine," said Doctor Martin, "most of you have never seen a corpse. Well that's what this is, even if we in the medical community once it's reached this point so coldly refer to it as a cadaver. It's a dead human body, is what it is. Of course I know for a fact that a few of you," he added, looking at Rebekah, "have seen one."

Rebekah had, it was true. More than one now. Not like this, preserved for science, already sagittally cut and then sutured, post-autopsy, voluntarily donated to the pursuit of science, but freshly dead, whatever constituted the soul having just left it, genuinely corpse-like, person-like. She'd even been there once when a patient coded: she was adjusting a bouquet of white-and-yellow flowers someone had left for the patient, when suddenly the patient gasped, and choked, and a nurse came in, and then a doctor, and then the patient died. Rebekah never did ask exactly how it happened. Some irrational part of her wondered whether the fault was hers—if only she'd left the flowers as they were . . . or if only she'd rearranged them better, so that they were just so . . . . Doctor Martin was the doctor on that case. He came into the room minutes after time of death was recorded. She was still there. He looked at her and with a warmth he'd never exhibited before, not even in bed, told her it was obvious she cared, and that's how he knew she wasn't dead inside.

The following is how Rebekah Fleckman met John Hempel.

Spring Break, 2016. The plan had been for Rebekah to join her roommates in Cancun for just over a week. She'd purchased her ticket months before, and she'd had those months to apply for and secure a passport. And every day for those months she'd told herself she was going to do it—apply for the passport—she was going to get around to very soon, it was just so much trouble, though, going to the post office and filling out the thing and getting your picture taken, and plus you needed your birth certificate to apply, and her mom had hers back in Helena, and she just kept forgetting to ask her. Every time they spoke on the phone it would slip Rebekah's mind. And so eventually it was too late to apply for a passport, and she couldn't go to Cancun. Her roommates were upset, disappointed, what are you going to do about the money you spent? The tickets are nonrefundable. But it wasn't a big deal, Rebekah said, she rarely spent money, she could afford to lose a little. She told them she had applied for her passport, but there must have been a mix-up, because she never received it. Bureaucracy and all, you know? Government inefficiency and all that.

The truth being she didn't want to go to Cancun. When she purchased the ticket she had herself convinced she did, but while Rebekah was good at convincing herself of certain things, she was equally good at unconvincing herself.

So instead of flying to Cancun she drove to Missoula. It was lengthy drive—over 200 miles—but Rebekah passed it in silence. Enjoying first the flatness and then the mountains. She passed an undeveloped hot spring with three young people about her age, two guys and a girl, all topless, frolicking in the water, and she was grateful to be in Montana. Rebekah Fleckman was not immune to beauty.

When she pulled up to Beth's house, parking her car on the street, Beth rushed out to meet her. They hugged. Behind Beth uncertainly came the young man Rebekah had heard not so much about. When she'd discovered Beth was dating a man she was admittedly concerned, just a smidge, because the Beth Levitt she loved, the Beth Levitt she had gone to high school with, the Beth Levitt she'd met at a late-night garage party when she was fourteen, had never shown an interest in the opposite sex. Rebekah knew any man Beth had decided was worth dating must be either special or disastrous, and as the best friend it was her job to determine which.

John, Rebekah knew right away, was both. And isn't that the perfect mixture?

On the third and final night of that spring break trip Rebekah was sitting on Beth's couch. Beth was asleep on one couch, a knit blanket over her legs and torso, tucked up under her neck. Rebekah was on the other couch with John. Silently they passed a joint back and forth, inhaling, handing it off to the other. The television was on, but muted. Then they started talking. It was the first opportunity Rebekah had had to talk to John alone, to really gauge him. For a while they talked about school, work, hobbies. Then Rebekah did what a best friend has to do and looked over at Beth. "You're very luck to be with her," she told John. "Do you understand that."

"I do," John said. "I swear I do."

He gestured for the joint. Rebekah handed it to him.

John inhaled and then he said, "Can I be honest with you? Can I tell you something without you telling her?"

"I can't promise that. You know I can't promise that."

John nodded. "Yeah. Anyway, I guess tell her if you have to. What it is is I'm afraid I'm going to hurt her. I'm just like very seriously severely depressed—I always have been—and I'm afraid some day I'm going to hurt her or anyone else I end up with. I've hurt myself before. I don't know how long I can survive."

Rebekah, if she hadn't been high, and tired, and free for a week from the stresses of college classes, probably would have gotten upset, probably would have told John that well that was a pretty big piece of information, wasn't it? and what did he think he was doing, not telling Beth? information she maybe had a right to if she was going to be in a relationship with him? But instead she only nodded and said (and maybe it wasn't the right thing to say; maybe it was; she might never know), "I think we're all very seriously severely depressed. When you stop to look at the world it's obvious. So I just try not to stop to look at the world."

Then John put his hand on Rebekah's leg, and she put her hand on his hand, and for a while they sat like that, before Beth woke up and yawned and saw the time and told Rebekah let's get that air mattress set back up for you, yeah? and then we can all go to bed.

"Gather 'round," said Doctor Reginald Martin, excited. Everyone in the lab moved to encircle the dissection table. With finals over, their grades secure, half the class had not shown, so there was plenty of room.

Doctor Martin picked up a pair of stainless steel scissors and began to cut away the stitches perforating the cadaver's sternum. "Now of course this specimen, this body, has been dead a while. It's already undergone an autopsy. Everything inside will be nice and tidy for us."

"How did it—he—die?" A male student asked, raising his hand.

"A car accident, I believe, but all the damage was confined to the brain, so we're free today to take a look at . . . ah, yes, there they are. Look, students: lungs, trachea, and . . there . . . is the human heart."

Rebekah drove from campus down to Main Street, where she parked in a two-hour zone, fully intending to ignore the time limit. She didn't have to be at the hospital until 4pm, and it was now only 11. She could go home, but Aaron was there. She stopped inside Vargo's Jazz City & Books and bought a dusty used hardcover by Dorothy L. Sayers. "You'll like her," the glasses-and-sweater-wearing clerk said, "if you like mysteries. Here, try this, her first one, before you read one of the later ones." The book was called Who's Body? It cost four dollars.

Rebekah took the book a block away to Wild Joe's Coffee. At Wild Joe's she bought a bagel, a strip of beef jerky (grass-fed, Montana sourced, as most things in Bozeman were), and an extra-sweet chai latte. This was her first meal of the day, not counting the cheese stick she'd eaten early in the morning while applying her foundation.

Rebekah placed her new purchase on the table but did not at first dive into it. Instead she opened her messenger bag and took out a thick textbook, a pen, and a highlighter. She opened the textbook to a page marked by an orange sticky note. The textbook was riddled with sticky notes, but the one she opened to was the furthest one back, indicating the farthest page she'd read to. The other sticky notes had words on them, symbols, questions: here is something I need to revisit, here is something I can make an effort to use next time I'm at the hospital, here is something I don't understand. The book was called Rapid Interpretation of EKGs. Rebekah's was the sixth edition. There may or may not have been a more recent one, but she'd found this copy online for only twenty dollars, used. She read for twenty minutes about tachy-arrhythmias. Little stretches of focus, three minutes, four minutes. A sip of tea, a bite of bagel. Underline. Highlight. Finally she closed Rapid Interpretation, returned it to her bag along with the pen and highlighter, and moved from the table at which she was sitting to a comfier weathered brown leather armchair next to a fake fireplace whose fake fire was still burning despite the warm temperature outside. She started reading Who's Body? She closed the novel some time later when she discovered her cup of chai was empty. She considered ordering another one, unsure whether it would be wise to spend the money. Her bagel was mostly uneaten. The jerky had found its way, unopened, into a side pocket of her bag, where she might find it a few days later, finally ready for consumption. Rebekah pulled her phone from the same pocket. She checked Snapchat. While she was watching a snap shared by a young male nurse she worked with at the hospital (cute, dark skinned, into her), the phone rang.

"Hey," she said, placing it to her head.

"Hey, sis," Bret said.

Rebekah produced her headphones. She plugged them in, set the phone itself on her thigh. "What's up?" Bret never called her. They'd texted a few times since Christmas, and in that way you could tentatively say their relationship had grown stronger.

"I have a favor to ask."

Rebekah raised an eyebrow at no one in particular. "Yeah, sure, of course," she said. But what she could do for her brother, so many thousand miles away, she couldn't imagine.

"Great. Yeah—so, well." Bret coughed. He coughed for several seconds. He cleared his throat. "Sorry."

"You okay?"

"No, yeah—it's fine. I've had a cold the last couple weeks is all. I think I caught it from Darius."

"Ah. How is Darius?"

"He's . . . in jail."

"Oh?"

"Yeah. Just for the last few days."

"What did he—what happened?"

"It's no big deal. Just . . . a thing. Keeps asking me to bail him out, though. Keeps calling me."

"Oh. And are you going to?"

"I—I couldn't afford to if I wanted to," Bret said. "The analytics firm shut down a few months back. I moved out of Brooklyn."

"Oh."

"It's no big deal. I could get a similar job again if I . . . if I wanted, you know? Anyone would hire me."

"Sure. Yeah."

"So anyway . . . Darius can rot in jail as far as I care. Bastard."

"Okay," Rebekah said. She tried to sip from her chai, forgetting it was empty, her hands searching for something to do. She tucked the phone into her pocket and made for the counter to buy another drink. "So what do you need?" she asked. "Do you need"—she didn't want to say it—"money?"

"What? Oh, no. Of course not. Like I said, I could totally get another big job if I wanted. Money isn't a problem."

"Right, of course," Rebekah said. She held her cup to the barista, pointing to the letters on its side that indicated the nature of its former contents: chai, whole milk, double syrup. The barista nodded in affirmation that she understood Rebekah wanted another one. She held her hands a cup's height apart, mouthing, Same size? Rebekah nodded. Smiled in thanks, putting her eyes into the smile since she couldn't say the words.

"That said," Bret said, "I've decided to move back home, to Helena."

"Really?"

"Yeah. At least for a little while. For . . . for Dad's sake."

Rebekah nodded even though he couldn't see her. "Right— that makes sense."

"He just needs some help, now that Mom's taken off. Some help with the house. The business. Have you talked to him lately?"

"A bit," Rebekah said. Her father's calls to her had grown irregular. And when they did speak he called her Bek or Beks with decreased frequency, as if he hadn't the energy to express affection.

"Sis, I think he might be depressed."

"I wouldn't really know."

"Well I'm worried about him."

"Yeah."

The barista handed Rebekah her new drink. She took a sip, reveling in its hotness. She returned to the weathered chair.

"And maybe it's time I took over the pizza business anyway," Bret said.

"That makes sense."

"You know—we could share it. The company. I've been looking over Dad's papers. It's a good business. Well established. It makes money. Not amazing money but decent money by any middle-class family's standards. Mom relinquished all stake to it in the divorce, which was stupid, honestly, but she probably just didn't want the connection, you know? But we could share it."

"Bret—" Rebekah said.

"Hey, just think about it."

Rebekah was silent for a moment. Move back to Helena?

Spend her workdays doing paperwork, overseeing acned employees . . . ? The workdays would be short. Her parents had been working only part time for years.

"I was thinking—maybe even we could franchise," Bret added. "Really get some money."

"I'll think about it," Rebekah said.

"Okay. I'm not sure I could do it without a partner."

"I'll think about it," she repeated.

"Right, well. My favor— I'll be coming home in a few weeks. I'll be flying into Bozeman. I could've flown to Helena, but Bozeman was cheaper and I have a few things to take care of here before I leave. I was wondering if you could pick me up from the airport? And then drive me over to Helena?" He told her the date of his flight.

She checked her phone's calendar, which, aside from her work schedule and a few assorted dots marking random appointments, was empty. "I have my friends' anniversary party that night."

"I don't get in until 11:15. PM, that is."

"Then . . . sure. I could pick you up after the party."

"Thanks, sis. You're awesome. I owe you."

"It's no problem."

"You think about that pizza business, okay?"

She thought for a moment he was going to say I love you, but he hung up. Rebekah took another sip of her warm drink. She reopened the Dorothy L. Sayers book. By the time she had to leave for work, she'd read a hundred and fifty pages, drank three chai lattes, extra sweet, and finally finished her bagel. It was an everything bagel.

* * *

"So it's like some ritual thing?" Aaron asked, removing his t-shirt.

"Something like that. That's what she said," Rebekah replied. They were in her room. She looked at him. He was thin, thinner than before. She knew he did little besides sit in bed all day, occupying his mind somehow, and where the inactivity would have made a normal person put on weight, it caused Aaron to lose any muscle he once had. His back was vaguely scarred.

Aaron replaced the t-shirt with a light blue button-down. He fumbled with the buttons in a way that Rebekah couldn't help but find repulsive. He said, "But so like a pagan thing."

"Like a Wiccan thing, yeah."

"What does that even mean?"

"I think just like candles and stuff, incense."

"Am I going to have to pray?"

"I don't think so. I don't think Beth prays exactly."

"Good. Because neither do I."

"I pray," Rebekah said. "I pray all the time."

A pause on Aaron's side of the conversation. His shirt still half unbuttoned. Him unable to feed any button through a buttonhole on the first try. Rebekah wondered how he'd ever managed to put on a uniform. "You do?" he asked finally.

"No," Rebekah said. "That was a joke."

"Oh." He laughed. He finished buttoning his shirt. Rebekah was wearing slacks and an oversized but flowing dark blue knit sweater. She'd tried first to put on a dark blue dress, one stored long-forgotten in the back of her closet, but even though it fit she felt supremely uncomfortable in it. She'd changed to the skirt and sweater, her back to Aaron. Always when she changed in front of Aaron she found herself with her back to him. It was a subconscious action: she did not like him looking at her breasts. During sex she told him she didn't enjoy having her nipples played with—too sensitive, she said—but the reality was that him touching her there felt too intimate. Plenty of people had touched her breasts, but she did not want Aaron to. After several minutes Aaron said, "It's just weird, is all. The whole witch thing."

Rebekah shrugged. "It makes her happy. She's my friend and it makes her happy. If she needs my help to celebrate her anniversary in a way that she says will bless the next year of her marriage, then I'm going to give her my help."

"I get it," Aaron said, his shirt finally fully buttoned, tucked into his jeans. He combed his hair in front of Rebekah's vanity's mirror, making liberal use of a sticky neon green gel. "You're a good person, Rebekah."

"I—thanks," Rebekah said.

He turned to her, met her eyes across the bedroom. The room smelled of hairspray and cologne and unhung laundry. "That's why I—"

"John's in love with me," Rebekah said.

"I . . . what?"

"Oh, yeah—he's totally in love with me."

"Um, okay. That's—well that's awkward."

"Not really," Rebekah said, shrugging. "I've known as long as he has."

"Did he tell you this, that he's in love with you?"

Rebekah shook her head. "No, not at all. I'm just very good at deducing things." And, so that he could not speak, she told him as they left the house that she was, after all, a reader of mystery novels. Everyone who knew her knew she liked mysteries. But what they didn't know, she told him, because she liked to keep this a secret, was that she always guessed the ending. Even when the writing was shitty, Rebekah could tell the writing was shitty, and she factored this into her deductions; even with bad mysteries Rebekah always guessed the ending.

"That's impressive," Aaron said, as he slid into the passenger seat of her car. Then he said, "Fuck. I was going to wear a tie. I left my tie in the house. Hold on a minute while I run in and grab my tie."

As she waited, Rebekah wondered whether she'd have to help him tie it.

4

BUT THE THING ABOUT EPIPHANIES, especially midnight ones, is how easily you realize they cannot be eternally true. How quickly irrelevant they seem. How, if you ever again stop to reconsider them, wrong you suddenly know they were.

For this reason John Hempel would always strive for happiness. Sure, there would be many moments, uncountable moments, like that first one, where he, in some depressive state or after or during some comforting act (sleeping with his wife, sleeping with someone else, sleeping alone in a hotel bed, soft white sheets, pillows fluffier than anything he'd ever have at home), would realize he was never going to be happy, and he'd find solace in that realization, convinced it was really going to stick deep inside his brain this time; but in the morning he'd wake and want only to search for happiness again. When he was particularly lucky the comfort he'd find in unhappiness would last days, but still, it would last only days. John would always, forever, grow hungry again.

Hunger led to the creation of some truly beautiful work. Inspirational work. Work that changed lives.

On the day of the party that was to celebrate the one-year anniversary of his and Beth's marriage, John sat in his studio that was also his bedroom, at his desk in front of his 27-inch monitor, editing another edition of John's Jaunts. As his viewership grew, the "Jaunts" moniker was receiving more and more criticism— on last week's Jaunt, a quarter of the comments had been posted solely to notify him of the word's incorrect usage—but he knew he would always use it. It was too late to change it. It had become his thing, or one of his things, a central component of his brand. Today's Jaunt was on the topic of the difficulty of getting to the gym; it was a humorous video, its tone light, for John had recently started working out on a regular basis, and the only way he could maintain any sort of steady motivation was to poke fun of himself in a public way. In a few weeks he'd stop going.

He had 1,300,000 subscribers now. 1,323,114, to be precise, but that number often fluctuated from moment to moment—up or down, although the overall trend was up. He had received his YouTube Creator Award. Two of them, actually. One day he'd heard a knock on the door and there was a FedEx driver with a large package for him, signature required. Inside were the two trophies: silver, which we should have sent you a while ago, when you hit 100,000, sorry for the delay; and gold, commemorating the million-subscriber mark. The gold play button John had framed, and it was now on the wall above his monitor, where he could see it while he recorded. The silver he'd put back in the box, tucked it into a closet. The next day he'd received an email and then a phone call from one of YouTube's own representatives. How would you feel about a partnership? Now John was receiving a significant portion of the ad revenue each of his videos earned—in exchange for *suggestions* on the types of content folks at the video-hosting platform thought might be most effective.

As John edited today's Jaunt, he noted the video's lighting. It was a little washed out. It was time, he and Beth had decided during a recent discussion, for him to rent a studio outside the home, somewhere he could light properly, a permanent set. Doing so would mean losing the perpetual background presence of Bernard the Cat (have you ever tried moving a cat from one location to another?), but it was, after all, time John started taking this video production thing *seriously*? Don't you think? asked the representative from YouTube who consulted with him each week.

Also, said the representative, have you considered moving to LA? Or New York?

John fingered the scab running several inches down his right forearm. It was present, but clean. If he was lucky, and didn't pick at it, and continued to apply healing aloes, it might not even scar. He hadn't made another video about mental health, but he now wore short-sleeved shirts when recording.

He absently sucked on the pinprick at the tip of his left forefinger, from which a couple hours ago Beth had asked to draw a bit of his blood. "Just a drop. It's for a spell. It's important, I promise."

Never had she asked such a thing of him, but of course he'd obliged. She used a sterile sewing needle.

As John was uploading today's Jaunt his watched buzzed. At the same time, the message the buzzing was announcing slid into the top right corner of his monitor. *Sorry to bother you*, it said, *but Rebekah and Aaron just pulled up. You almost finished?*

This was a new rule: when Beth was home and John was working and Beth required his attention, she texted instead of knocking on or opening the bedroom door, in case he was recording or deep in concentration. That last part—deep in concentration—wasn't something John ever was, but it sounded good.

John stood. The video would finish uploading without him.

5

FOR BETH HEMPEL, FORMERLY BETH Levitt, sister of the Bozeman Chapter of the Montana Moonrise Coven (the meetings of which she attended only sporadically, like on special Wiccan holidays, for example Imbolc or Samhain or on solstices, because lately her practice was feeling more personal, more something she should be engaging in alone, more a communion between her body and her own personal spirit, than something meant to be shared with others—for didn't she do enough sharing already?), for this Beth Hempel the casting of spells was a literal, visual thing. When she made the lesser sign of the Pentagram—as she did now, invoking the goddess of protection—she could see the circle in the air before her. She could see the five-pointed star within the circle. It glowed. It was tangible. She had never tried to reach out to touch it, but she knew if she did it would be graspable. Sometimes it glowed blue; sometimes purple; today lavender.

The shape remained in space there as she turned her eyes down to the altar below it. It hung in her periphery. She took the piece of paper onto which she'd had her husband bleed and placed it in the altar's copper bowl. Then she took a needle, the same needle she'd used to prick her husband, freshly sterilized in the flame of a tobacco-and-rosehip-scented candle, and with it pricked her own finger, drew her own blood. She let the blood drop into the bowl. One two three drops. Then, sucking on her finger, she added a rose petal, a bit of her own perfume, and a tiny green scroll tied closed on which she'd written an incantation, a request for wealth, prosperity, and love in the second year of her marriage. She lit a match, dropped it into the bowl. The contents caught fire. As they burned, Beth imposed her will on the flame. The flame burned out. The circle and star above the altar changed from lavender to crimson, and then it disappeared.

This was part one of the ritual.

The ritual was of Beth's own design, culled from bits and piece of others' rituals, snippets she'd read in books, discussions she'd had in forums, results of her own experimentations.

Part two of the ritual occurred when Rebekah Fleckman and Haiku Kid arrived. One might wonder why Beth had chosen to involve Haiku Kid, all gangly and damaged and personality-less as he was, but Beth could see inside him. He was genuine. He was sincere. And he, like everyone else, she suspected, probably needed this.

John came from the bedroom, wearing a t-shirt and dark dark jeans. Rebekah and Aaron rang the doorbell. Beth handed everyone a glass of wine. Red wine: it had to be red wine. Rebekah, Beth knew, did not like red wine, but Beth told her it was important, and Rebekah took it.

John finished his first glass too quickly. Beth poured him another. Aaron downed his as they all sat in the living room, talking. How's life? Congratulations, on the anniversary, and on the subscriber count. Your channel's turning a year old soon, isn't it? Soon, yes, a few months. Well I suppose we'll have to have another celebration then. Oh yes, any excuse to drink good wine.

Dinner was light. Beth had made only a main course and a side this time. She poured John a third glass of wine, Aaron a second (and then, later, a third), and herself a second as well. Rebekah said she was still happy with the one, and Beth knew this was true. Beth had purchased two bottles. The friends could not be drunk, just comfortable, for if they were drunk the following events would have no meaning.

After dessert, the conversation turned toward sex, as conversations between young couples often do, never mind that Beth steered it there.

"You know," Beth said, her lips were stained lightly purple, "Rebekah and I made out with each other once."

"I did know this," John said, amused.

"No way!" said Aaron. He looked to Rebekah, as if for verification.

"It's true," Rebekah said, not unhappily.

"Damn," said Aaron. "That is hot."

To Rebekah Beth said, "Why don't we put on a show for them, my dear."

Rebekah considered. "Well, I mean—" She saw Aaron's eagerness and John's cool anticipation. "Yeah, why not? I've had enough to drink." Even though she had not. But Rebekah didn't need alcohol to lower her inhibitions. She could want to do something whether she wanted to or not, and right now she wanted to want it.

When, some minutes later, their lips parted, Beth turned to John and Aaron and said, "Now you two."

Rebekah laughed.

"*What?*" Aaron kind of choked.

"Yeah—what?" John said, less surprised.

"Just, you know—kiss," Beth said. "We did. Now you."

And after some reluctance, and some mocking encouragement from both women, they did.

Beth smiled at John. She smiled at Rebekah. She added to each glass a little more wine. As she poured into her husband's, she said "Happy anniversary, my love." She kissed him. Then she went back to kissing Rebekah.

6

Across the room John and Aaron were entwined in a way Rebekah never thought she'd see two men entwined. Even in porn she didn't think she'd see it, or at least would never go out of her way to. Watching them, though, as she herself was kissed by Beth—first her shoulder, then her neck, her cheeks, now her lips—Rebekah couldn't help but think how right it all looked, how right it all felt. This moment, this night, was where everything had been heading for the entire life of each and every person in this room. What would happen after, she didn't know.

Watching Aaron do what he was doing to John, she couldn't help but feel jealousy. Just a twinge, and for only a moment, but still, jealousy it was. Aaron, after all, had been interested in *her*. He'd come here with her. And while Rebekah at best was entirely disinterested in the man, and at worst found him unexplainably offensive, seeing him with someone else meant something. She hadn't expected it to mean something. But in an instant the meaning of that was gone, and she was back with Beth.

Beth was on Rebekah's neck again, intoxicated. Maybe even, if Rebekah wanted to admit it, intoxicating.

Rebekah inhaled. Exhaled. She could feel Beth's tongue on her collarbone. She did not giggle. She was not giggling. She was beyond that now. Nothing made Rebekah giggle anymore. When had she last giggled? Had it been that first time Beth kissed her, when they were high school seniors? Beth moved lower now. Lower. Lower. She lifted Rebekah's dark blue sweater, kissed her belly. Her bellybutton. She raised the sweater over Rebekah's head and Rebekah let her and the shirt dropped to the floor and for a long time Rebekah stood there, breathing, as Beth kissed her ribs, her bellybutton, her collarbone again.

Across the room John was moaning. On his face was a look of ecstasy, a brand of joy Rebekah herself would never feel and realized now she was okay with never feeling. He'd given himself, it seemed, entirely to what was happening. Rebekah too wanted to give herself, but also she didn't want to. Truly she didn't want to. She could stay here, could let this happen, could be a spectator or an active participant or a catalyst for every moment that might come after, a catalyst for everything destiny had planned. Destiny or Beth's gods and goddesses or the universe or science, logic, rationality, whatever those things were and whatever they had planned or didn't, Rebekah could be a part of it. She could *be* it. She wanted to want to be.

But she didn't want to be.

Beth pulled aside a cup of Rebekah's bra. Her black silky bra with decorative lace around its edges. Beth's mouth found Rebekah's nipple, and there was, indeed, pleasure there. And for just another moment—a second, half a second—Rebekah Fleckman let herself enjoy it.

Then she put one hand on each side of Beth's face. She bent her head. She kissed Beth's forehead tenderly. She pulled Beth from her breast and brought her up so their faces met. She leaned in and kissed Beth then, Rebekah's hands still on Beth's cheeks. Rebekah was doing the kissing. Then she pulled away, a strand of saliva hanging between the two sets of lips, stretching, stretching, breaking. "You are my best friend," Rebekah said.

Beth nodded.

Rebekah did not say that she was uncertain what *friend* meant; that every time she used it she was unsure.

Rebekah took Beth by the hand and led her to where John was. Where Beth's husband knelt between Aaron's legs and Aaron was running his fingernails through John's hair. Rebekah took John under an arm and brought him up, at the same time pushing gently Beth downward until the two were on an equal plane. With one more look at Beth, Rebekah kissed John. She kissed Aaron. Both of these light kisses, pecks. She pushed tenderly John and Beth together. When they were embracing, Rebekah moved her hands from both of them. When they brought Aaron in to join them, Rebekah backed away.

She adjusted her bra, pulled the cup back over herself. She found her oversized knit sweater on the floor and put it on, not quickly. Not slowly but not quickly. She found her purse on the coffee table and picked it up. Also on the table was the glass of wine she had not finished. She didn't finish it now. She left it there.

As she departed John and Beth's house she did not turn around and look at the threesome behind her on the sofa—to do so at this point seemed somehow invasive, an incursion. This was not her party. She took in the sounds the group was making, absorbed those sounds, let them become part of her, but she did not turn around or look back.

As she drove down the road, en route to Bozeman Yellowstone International Airport, her headlights illuminating only the world immediately in front of her—the asphalt, the guidelines, mailboxes and trees just at her periphery—Rebekah found herself thinking about her grad school applications. They were open on her computer at home, a dozen browser tabs. She didn't know where she was going to go, but she knew she was going to go somewhere. She was going to apply. She was going to go somewhere else. She didn't know where, not yet, but she knew wherever she applied she'd get in—and if she didn't . . . well, that's why she'd apply to everywhere. She'd go to Stanford. Harvard. Johns Hopkins. She'd leave the country and attend Oxford. Yale. Hell—she'd go to the University of Chicago. Or she'd go to Ann Arbor. Houston. She'd go to North Carolina, take out student loans, pay her tuition with stripper money if she had to. She'd sometimes thought she'd be a good stripper: detached and apathetic, but capable of emanating convincing passion . . . she was not dead inside.

She checked the clock. Her timing was perfect. Everything was perfect. Her brother's plane was landing. She would arrive just as he the reached pickup area.

Rebekah drove. She didn't know where she was going, but she knew she was ready to not stay here.

ABOUT THE AUTHOR

Shawn Mihalik is the author of five novels or novellas and the managing editor of *Paleo Magazine*. He's deeply interested in many things. Shawn lives in Central Oregon with his wife and two cats.